MRS. HENl

WITHIN THE MAZE

Volume 2

Elibron Classics
www.elibron.com

Elibron Classics series.

© 2005 Adamant Media Corporation.

ISBN 1-4021-9233-9 (paperback)
ISBN 1-4021-1773-6 (hardcover)

This Elibron Classics Replica Edition is an unabridged facsimile
of the edition published in 1872 by Bernhard Tauchnitz, Leipzig.

EACH VOLUME SOLD SEPARATELY.

COLLECTION

OF

BRITISH AUTHORS

TAUCHNITZ EDITION.

VOL. 1271.

WITHIN THE MAZE BY MRS. HENRY WOOD

IN TWO VOLUMES.

VOL. 2.

LEIPZIG: BERNHARD TAUCHNITZ.

PARIS: C. REINWALD & Cᶦᵉ, 15, RUE DES SAINTS PÈRES.

COLLECTION

OF

BRITISH AUTHORS

TAUCHNITZ EDITION.

VOL. 1271.

WITHIN THE MAZE BY MRS. HENRY WOOD.

IN TWO VOLUMES.

VOL. II.

WITHIN THE MAZE.

A NOVEL.

BY

MRS. HENRY WOOD,
AUTHOR OF "EAST LYNNE," ETC.

COPYRIGHT EDITION.

IN TWO VOLUMES.

VOL. II.

LEIPZIG

BERNHARD TAUCHNITZ

1872.

CONTENTS

OF VOLUME II.

―――

WITHIN THE MAZE.

CHAPTER I.

The Maze invaded.

The previous night's black cloud had culminated in a thunder-storm, and the morning air felt fresh and cool; but the blue sky was clear, the sun as bright as ever.

Lucy came down with sad eyes and a pale face. Her night had been one of mental pain. She was wondering how much longer she could keep up this mask of cheerfulness—which she would especially have to wear that day; and she knew that she could not have done it at all, then or at any other time, but for the very present help of God. Karl, waiting in the breakfast-room, turned to shake hands with her. But for their being alone, he would not have ventured on this eminently suggestive action.

"How are you to-day, Lucy?"

"Oh, quite well, thank you. Did you hear the storm?"

"Yes. It has cleared away some of the sultry heat. We shall have a lovely day."

The Lloyds were expected from Basham. When at the flower-show the previous day, Lucy had re-

marked that some of the hot-house plants were not as
fine as those at Foxwood: upon that, the General and
one of his daughters had simultaneously expressed a
wish to see those at Foxwood. Lucy at once gave
the invitation; and it was arranged that they should
spend the next day at the Court. She had told her
husband of this while Captain Lamprey was present;
but it had not been alluded to afterwards. She spoke
again now, while she and Karl were waiting breakfast
for Miss Blake, who was at Matins at St. Jerome's.

"I could not do less than ask them," she observed.
"I hope you are not vexed."

"You did quite right, Lucy," he cheerfully answered. "I shall be glad to see them."

"I don't know how many will come. Perhaps all;
except Mrs. Lloyd, who never goes out anywhere. I
hope Theresa will give up St. Jerome's for the rest of
the day, and stay at home to help me entertain them."

Karl smiled. "To make sure of that you should
invite Mr. Cattacomb."

"But you would not like that, would you?"

"No. I was only joking, Lucy. Here she is."

The Lloyds had said they would come early, and
Karl strolled out to meet the eleven o'clock train,
leaving his wife decorating her drawing-room with
flowers. Unhappy though Lucy was, she was proud
of her home, and pleased that it should find admiration in the eyes of the world.

As Karl was passing Clematis Cottage, he saw Mr.
Smith seated at the open window, leisurely enjoying
the freshened air, and smoking a cigar. Karl had
been wanting to take a close, observant view of him;
and he turned in on the spur of the moment. The

asking for something which he really required afforded
an excuse. Mr. Smith rose up to receive him gra-
ciously, and threw his half-smoked cigar out at the
window.

"I think you have the plan of the out-lying lands
of the estate, Mr. Smith, where the new cottages are
to be built? Will you spare it to me in the course of
the day? I will send Hewitt for it."

"Certainly, Sir Karl; it is at your service. Won't
you take a seat? The bit of a breeze at this open
window is quite refreshing."

Karl sat down. Mr. Smith's green glasses lay on
the table, and he could enjoy as clear a view of him
as he pleased. The agent talked away, all unconscious
no doubt that notes were being taken of his face and
form.

"It is his own hair," mentally spoke Karl. "'Very
dark brown,' they said; 'nearly black.' Just so. At
the time of the escape Salter had neither whiskers nor
beard nor moustache: the probability being, they
thought, that he had now a full crop of all. Just so,
again. Eyebrows: thick and arched, Grimley said:
these are not thick; nor, what I should call, arched:
perhaps there may be some way of manipulating eyebrows, and these have undergone the process. Eyes
brown: yes. Face fresh and pleasant: yes. Voice and
manners free and genial: yes. Age?—there I can't
make the two ends meet. I am sure this man's forty.
Is it Salter, or is it not?" finally summed up Karl. "I
don't know, I *think* it is: but I don't know."

"Truefit the farmer spoke to me yesterday, Sir
Karl," broke in Mr. Smith on his musings. "He was
asking whether you and Lady Andinnian viewed this

new farce on his grounds with approbation. That's
what he called it—farce. Meaning St. Jerome's."

"I suppose he does not like it," observed Karl.

"I fancy he does not really care about it himself,
one way or the other, Sir Karl; in fact, he signified as
much. But it seems his better-half, Mrs. Truefit, has
taken a prejudice against it: calling the ceremonies
'goings-on,' and 'rubbish,' and 'scandal,' and all sorts
of depreciating things. It is a pity Mr. Cattacomb
can't confine himself to tolerable common-sense. The
idea of their hanging that bell outside over the door,
and pulling it perpetually!"

"Yes," said Karl. "So much nonsense takes all
solemnity away."

"They are going to dress Tom Pepp in a white
garment now, while he rings it, with a red cross down
the back. It's that, I fancy, that has put up Mrs.
Truefit. I told the farmer that I believed Sir Karl
and Lady Andinnian did not favour the place: at least,
that I had never seen them attend it."

"And you never will," returned Karl, as he rose.

There was nothing to stay for; his observations
were taken, and he departed, having to walk quickly
to be in time at the station. Had he been free in
mind the matters connected with St. Jerome's might
have vexed him more than they did: but all annoyances were lost sight of in his one great care.

The train came in, and the party arrived by it; six
of them. Captain Lloyd, who was at home on leave;
two Miss Lloyds; a married sister and her husband,
Mr. and Mrs. Panton, at present staying on a visit;
and the General.

Karl had expressed pleasure at his wife's invitation; perhaps had felt it; but he could not foresee the unlucky contretemps that the visit was to bring forth. To his unbounded astonishment, his inward confusion, no sooner had his guests entered Foxwood Court, than they expressed a wish to see the place called the Maze, and requested Sir Karl to conduct them to it.

"I was telling Panton about the Maze last night—talking of the Court and its surroundings," observed the General. "Panton does not believe it possible that one could lose oneself in any maze whatever: so I promised him he should have a try at it. You will afford us the opportunity of seeing it, Sir Karl."

"I—I am not sure," stammered Karl, utterly taken aback, while his wife's face flushed a burning red. "I hardly think it is in my power, General. The lady who inhabits it desires to keep herself so very quiet, that I should not feel justified in intruding upon her. She is not in strong health, I believe."

"But we would not think of disturbing the lady," called out all the voices together. "We only wish to see the maze of trees, Sir Karl: not the dwelling-house. What's her name?"

"Grey."

"Well, we shall not hurt her. Does she live by herself?"

"While her husband is abroad. I am sure she will not choose to be intruded upon."

Sir Karl might as well have talked to the winds. All opposed him. Of course there was no suspicion that *he* had any personal objection; only that he wished to respect the scruples of his lady-tenant. At length, the General declared he would go over to Mrs. Grey, ask to see her, and personally prefer the request.

Poor Karl was at his wits' end. He saw that he should not be able to stem the storm—for he dared not be resolute in the denial, so fearful was he always of arousing any suspicion of there being a mystery in the place—and he was fain to yield. He would take them over, he said; but not before he had sent a note to say that they were coming. This he insisted on; it would be but common politeness, he urged; and they all agreed with him.

Hastily writing a few words to Mrs. Grey in his own room, he called Hewitt to take the note over, and gave him at the same time a private message to deliver to Ann Hopley. Of course Karl's object was to warn his brother to keep out of sight—and Mrs. Grey too. Hewitt looked more scared than his master.

"To think of their wanting to go over *there!*" he exclaimed in a low tone of covert fear.

"It can't be helped, Hewitt. Go."

A few minutes, and Hewitt came back with a message: which he delivered to his master in public. Mrs. Grey's compliments to Sir Karl Andinnian, and he was at liberty to bring his friends within her gates if he pleased. So they all started; Lucy with them.

Lucy with them!

The ladies had assumed it to be so much a matter of course that their hostess should accompany them, that Lucy, timid in her self-consciousness, saw not her way clear to any plea of excuse. And it might be that, down deep in her woman's frail heart, there was a hankering longing to see the inside of that place which contained her rival. In the midst of her indecision she glanced at Karl and hesitated. But he saw not the look or the hesitation: for all the sign he gave out, she was as welcome to go to the place as these guests were. It is true that Miss Blake fixed her eyes upon her, and Lucy coloured under it: but perhaps the very fact only served to speed her on the way.

The party started, passing out at the grand gates of Foxwood. Between that spot and the Maze, short though it was, they encountered Mr. Cattacomb. Miss Blake took upon herself to introduce him, and to ask him to accompany them, saying they were going to see that renowned show-place, the Maze.

"I did not know we had a show-place in the neighbourhood," drawled Mr. Cattacomb in his affectation.

"Neither have we," curtly rejoined Sir Karl, who would willingly have pitched Mr. Cattacomb over a mile elsewhere, but did not see an excuse for doing it. "The Maze was never constituted a show-place yet, Miss Blake. I feel anything but comfortable at intruding there to-day, I assure you. Between my wish to gratify my friends, and my fear that it may be objectionable to the occupant of the Maze, I am in a blissful state of uncertainty," he added in a laughing kind of way, for the general benefit, fearing he might have spoken too pointedly and shown that he was really ill at ease.

"Sir Karl is ultra-sensitive," remarked Miss Blake —and a keen observer might have fancied there was some sarcasm in her tone.

Karl rang the clanging bell—which might be heard far and wide; and Ann Hopley appeared, the key of the gate in her hand. She curtsied to the company as she admitted them.

"My mistress desires me to say, Sir Karl, that she hopes the gentle-people will see all they wish to see," cried the woman aloud, addressing the rest as much as she did Sir Karl. "Mrs. Grey begs they will pardon her not appearing to welcome them, but she is not well to-day, and has to keep her room."

"Mrs. Grey is very kind," returned Sir Karl. "We shall be cautious not to disturb her."

They filed of their own accord into the maze. The old trees had not been so beset with gay tongues and laughter for many a day. One ran here, another there; they were like school boys and girls out for a holiday. Ann Hopley was about to follow them in when the clanging bell at the gate once more sounded, and she turned back to open it. Karl, never at rest —as who could be, knowing what he knew—looked after her while he talked with the rest; and he saw that the visitor was a policeman.

His heart leaped into his mouth. Careless, in the moment's terror, of what might be thought of him, he broke off in the middle of a sentence to the General, and returned to the gate. His face was never very rosy, but every vestige of colour had forsaken it now. At a collected moment, he would have remembered that it was not in *that* way his brother would have been sought out—in the person of one solitary unarmed policeman—but fear scares probability away: as Rose had observed to him only the previous evening. Worse than all, the rest came flocking to the gate after him.

"Grey, ain't it?" the policeman was saying to Ann Hopley. He had a paper in his hand and a pencil.

"Mrs. Grey," replied the servant.

"Mrs. Grey. There ain't no husband, I think?"

"No."

"What's her Chris'en name?"

A warning glance shot from Sir Karl's eyes, cautioning Ann Hopley to be on her guard. In truth it was not needed: the woman was caution itself, and had her ready wits at hand always. Karl saw what it was—some parish paper about to be left—and was recovering his inward equanimity.

"My mistress's Christian name? Mary."

"Mrs. Mary Grey," repeated the policeman, writing down the name on the paper. "You'll please to give it her," he added, handing the paper in. "It have got to be attended to."

"All tax-papers for Mrs. Grey must come to Foxwood Court," interposed Sir Karl. "Mrs. Grey takes the house furnished, and has nothing to do with the taxes."

"Beg pardon, Sir Karl, but that there's a voting-paper for a poor-law guardian," said the man, touching his hat.

"Oh, a voting-paper. Let it go in then," concluded Sir Karl. Mrs. Grey had no more to do with voting than she had with taxes; but Sir Karl let it pass.

They were in the maze again; Ann Hopley having wound herself out of sight with the paper. Mr. Panton, the disbeliever, wound *himself* in and out of the trees and about the paths; but the voices always guided him back again.

"What a delightful place, Sir Karl!" cried Mrs. Panton. "Quite like a Fair Rosamond's Bower."

Sir Karl laughed in reply. And—as Miss Blake

noticed—there was not a trace of shame in his face. Lucy's colour, though, rose painfully.

"Let me see! it was a silken thread, was it not, that guided Queen Eleanor to her rival?" continued Mrs. Panton. "A cruel woman! I wonder whether she carried the bowl of poison in her hand?"

"I wonder if the woman who destroyed the Queen's happiness, had any forewarning in her dreams of the fate in store for her?" retorted Miss Blake, sharply— for she was thinking of another case, very near to her, that she judged to be analogous. "For her punishment, it is to be hoped she had."

"Oh, but you know she was so lovely, poor thing! One can but pity her; can we, Lady Andinnian?"

"I know nothing of it," spoke Lucy, in so chafed a tone that Karl turned to look at her.

"My opinion is, that the King should have taken half the bowl," said Miss Blake. "That would have been even justice, Mrs. Panton."

"Well, well, judge it as you will, Fair Rosamond was very beautiful; and her fate was shocking. Of course the Queen was incensed; naturally: and the crime of poisoning in those days was, I suppose, looked upon as no crime at all. I have always wished the Queen had been lost in the maze and the poison spilt."

"Suppose we get lost in this one!"

It was Miss Lloyd who spoke, hurriedly and somewhat anxiously. It brought most of them around her.

"There is no danger here, is there? Sir Karl, you know the way out, I suppose?"

Karl evaded the question. "If the worst come to the worst, we can set on and shout," he observed.

"But *don't* you know the clue? Is there not a clue? There must be!"

"I see nothing of the kind," returned Karl. "You forget that I am almost a stranger in the neighbourhood. We shall be all right. Don't fear."

How Lucy despised him for his deceit! She felt that he must have the clue: why else need he let himself within the gate with his key—at least, with any purpose of finding his way further in after it? Miss Blake caught her eye; and Lucy turned away, sick at heart, from the compassion Miss Blake's glance wore.

Sir Karl's "Don't fear" had been reassuring, and they dispersed about the Maze and lost themselves in it, very much as Miss Blake had once done. Mr. Cattacomb kept asking questions about the mistress of the Maze: why she lived there alone, where her husband was: for all of which Sir Karl could have struck him. He, Karl, would have contrived to keep them from the boundaries near the house: but they were as nine to one, and went whither they would: and, as had been Miss Blake's case, they got within view of it at last.

"What a pretty place!" was the involuntary exclamation from more than one.

It did look pretty: pretty and very cheerful. The windows of the house were open; the door of the porch was fastened back, as if to invite entrance. Not a sign or symptom existed of there being any cause for concealment.

So far good, and Karl felt satisfied. But, as his eyes went ranging far and wide in their longed-for

security, there was no doubt that he somewhere or
other caught sight of his imprudent brother; for his
face changed to an ashy paleness, and he groaned in
spirit.

"Adam is surely mad," was his mental cry.

Ann Hopley, who had probably been waiting about,
stepped up at this moment, and asked with much
civility if they would like to walk in-doors and rest.
Sir Karl, looking at his friends, as if for acquiescence
in his denial, declined. "We have *no right* to intrude," he whispered: and the General said so too.

"This might really do for a Rosamond's Bower!"
cried Mrs. Panton. "It is a sweetly pretty place."

The lawn was level as a bowling-green; the flowers
and shrubs surrounding it were well-kept, fragrant, and
blooming. Mounted on a ladder, nailing some branches
against a wall that probably belonged to a tool-house,
was the toothless old gardener, his knees swollen and
bent, his white smock frock rolled up around him.

"That's the gardener at his work, I suppose?" observed the General, whose eyes were dim.

"Yes, that's Hopley," said Karl.

"What d'ye call his name, Sir Karl?"

"Hopley. He is the woman's husband."

"I had a servant once of that name when I was
quartered at Malta. A good servant he was, too."

"That man yonder looks ill," remarked Mrs. Panton.

"I fancy he is subject to rheumatism," said Sir
Karl. "How is your husband?" he enquired of Ann
Hopley.

"Pretty middling, sir, thank you," she answered.
"He is getting in years you see, gentlefolks, and is
not as strong as he was."

"Will you be so good as precede us through the Maze and let us out," said Karl to her. "I think it is time we went," he added to the others: "we have seen all there is to see."

Ann Hopley, key in hand, went winding through the Maze, in and out of the numberless paths. It seemed to those following her that they only went round and round—just as it had seemed to Miss Blake that former day; and it took some time to get through it. The Reverend Mr. Cattacomb called it "a pilgrimage."

She was crafty, that faithful woman. Just as she had led Miss Blake a needlessly round-about way, so she led them now. Had she taken them direct through, who knew but they might have caught some inkling of the clue? While opening the gate, General Lloyd would have put half-a-crown into her hand. She would not take it.

"I'd rather not, sir; I've done nothing to merit it. Our mistress pays us both well. Thank you, sir, all the same."

"A good, respectable, honest servant, that," remarked the General, slipping the money into his pocket again.

Crossing the road from the Maze, the party came right in view of Clematis Cottage and Mr. Smith, who was leaning over the gate of it and staring with all his might. He raised his hat to the ladies generally, and then accosted Sir Karl, saying he had taken the plan, asked for, to the Court.

"Thank you," replied Karl.

"Who *is* that man?" cried Captain Lloyd with some energy as they went on. "I am sure I know him."

2 *

"His name's Smith," replied Karl. "He is a sort of agent on my estate."

"Smith—Smith! I don't recollect the name. His face is quite familiar to me, though. Where can I have seen it?"

Karl longed in his heart to ask whether the face had ever belonged to the name of Salter; but he did not dare. There had been a peculiar expression in Mr. Smith's eyes as he spoke to him just now, which Karl had read rightly—he was sure Smith wanted to speak to him privately. So, after the rest had entered the home gates, he turned back. The agent had not stirred from his place.

"What have those people been doing there, Sir Karl?" he asked, with a peremptory action of his hand towards the Maze.

Karl explained. He did not dare do otherwise. Explained in full.

"Curious fools!" cried the man angrily. "Well, no harm seems to have been done, sir. Seeing you all come out of the gate, I could not believe my eyes, or imagine what was up."

"I fancied you wished to speak to me, Mr. Smith."

"And so I do, Sir Karl. The letters were late this morning—did you know it? They've only just been delivered. Some accident, I suppose."

"I only know that none came to Foxwood Court this morning."

"Just so. Well, Sir Karl, I've had one; ten minutes ago. I wrote to make inquiries about that paragraph in the newspaper, and this letter was the answer to mine. It is as I thought. There's nothing known or suspected at all at headquarters; neither at Scotland

Yard nor Portland Island. It was the work of the penny-a-liner, hang him!——just an invention, and nothing else."

"To whom did you write?"

"Well, that's my business, and I 'cannot tell you. But you may rely upon what I say, Sir Karl, and set your mind at rest. I thought you'd like to know this, sir, as soon as possible."

"Thank you," replied Karl.

He went back to his guests, his brain busy. Was this true, that Smith said? Who then was Smith that he could get this information? Or, was it that Smith was saying it for a purpose?

CHAPTER II.

Recognised.

THE buff-coloured blinds were down before Mr. Burtenshaw's windows in the Euston Road, shutting out the glare of the afternoon sun, and throwing an unwholesome kind of tint over the rooms. In one of them, the front room on the first floor, sat the detective himself. It was indeed a kind of office as well as a sitting-room: papers strewed the table; pigeon holes and shelves, all filled, were ranged along the walls.

Mr. Burtenshaw had a complicated case in hand at that period. Some fresh information had just come in by a private letter, and he was giving the best attention of his clear mind to it: his head bent over the table; his hands resting on the papers immediately before him. Apparently he arrived at some conclusion: for he nodded twice and then began to fold the papers together.

The servant-maid, with the flaunty cap tilted on
her head, entered the room, and said to her master
that a gentleman had called and was requesting to
see him.

"Who is it?" asked Mr. Burtenshaw.

"He gave no name, sir. It's the same gentleman
who called twice or thrice in one day about a fort-
night ago: the last time late at night. He's very nice-
looking, sir; might be known for a gentleman a mile off."

The detective carried his thoughts back, and remembered. "You can show him up," he said. "Or
——stay, Harriet," he suddenly added, as the girl was
leaving the room. "Go down first of all and ask the
gentleman his name."

She went as desired; and came up again fixing her
absurd cap on its tottering pinnacle.

"The gentleman says, sir, that you don't know him
by name, but his solicitors are Messrs. Plunkett and
Plunkett."

"Ay. Show him up," said Mr. Burtenshaw. "He
has a motive for withholding his name," mentally added
the detective.

The reader need not be told that it was Karl Andinnian who entered. The object of his visit was to
get, if possible, some more information respecting
Philip Salter.

Day by day and week by week, as the days and
weeks went on, had served to show Karl Andinnian
that his brother's stay at the Maze was growing more
full of risk. Karl and Mrs. Grey, conversing on the
matter as opportunity occurred, had nearly set it down
as a certainty that Smith was no other than Salter.
She felt sure of it. Karl nearly so. And he was per-

suaded that, once Smith's influence could be removed,
Adam might get safely away.

The question ever agitating Karl's brain, in the
midnight watches, in the garish day, was—what could
he do in the matter?—how proceed in it at all with
perfect security? The first thing of course was to ascertain that the man was Salter; the next to make a
bargain with him: "You leave my brother free, and I
will leave you free." For it was by no means his intention to deliver Salter up to justice. Karl had realized too keenly the distress and horror that must be
the portion of a poor fugitive, hiding from the law, to
denounce the worst criminal living.

The difficulty lay entirely in the first step—the
identification of Smith with Salter. How could he ascertain it? He did not know. He could not see any
means by which it might be accomplished with safety.
Grimley knew Salter—as in fact did several of Grimley's brotherhood—but, if he once brought Grimley
within a bird's-eye view of Smith (Smith being Salter)
Grimley would at once lay his grasping hands upon
him. All would probably be over then: for the chances
were that Salter in revenge would point his finger to
the Maze, and say "There lives a greater criminal than
I; your supposed dead convict, Adam Andinnian."

The reader must see the difficulty and the danger.
Karl dared not bring Grimley or any other of the
police in contact with Smith; he dared not give them
a clue to where he might be found: and he had to
fall back upon the uncertain and unsatisfactory step
of endeavouring to track out the identity himself.

"If I could but get to know Burtenshaw's reason
for thinking Salter was in England," he exclaimed to

himself over and over again, "perhaps it might help me. Suppose I were to ask Burtenshaw again—and press it on him? Something might come of it. After all, he could but refuse to tell me."

Just as Karl, after much painful deliberation, had determined to do this, there arrived at Foxwood a summons for his wife. Colonel Cleeve was attacked with sudden illness. In the first shock of it, Mrs. Cleeve feared it might prove fatal, and she sent for Lucy. Karl took her to Winchester and left her, and at once took up his own abode for a few days in London. The Court had none too much attraction for him as matters stood, and he did not care to be left to entertain Miss Blake. So long as his wife stayed away, he meant to stay.

The following afternoon saw him at the detective's. Mr. Burtenshaw had thought his unknown visitor looking ill before: he looked worse now. "A delicate man with some great care upon him," summed up the officer to himself.

Karl, opening his business, led up to the question he had come to ask. Would Mr. Burtenshaw confide to him the reason for his supposing Philip Salter to be still in England? At first Mr. Burtenshaw said No; that it could not, he imagined, concern him or any one else to hear it. Karl pleaded, and pleaded earnestly.

"Whatever you say shall be kept strictly sacred," he urged. "It cannot do harm to any one. I have a powerful motive for asking it."

"And a painful one, too," thought the detective. Karl was leaning forward in his chair, his pale face slightly flushed with inward emotion, his beautiful grey eyes full of eager entreaty, and a strange sadness in their depths.

"Will you impart to me, sir, your motive for wishing to know this?"

"No, I cannot," said Karl. "I wish I could, but I cannot."

"I fancy that you m   know Salter's retreat, sir—
or think you know it: a   you want to be assured it
is he before you denour   him," spoke the detective,
hazarding a shrewd gue:

Karl raised his han   to enforce what he said,
speaking solemnly. "W   : I able to put my finger
this moment upon Salte: . would not denounce him.
Nothing would induce   e. You may believe me
when I say that, in aski   for this information, I intend no harm to him."

The detective saw h(true were the words. There
was something in Karl ɪ   linnian strangely attractive,
and he began to waver.

"It is not of much   onsequence whether I give
you the information or   ·hether I withhold it," he
acknowledged, giving wɛ   "The fact is this: one of
our men who knew Salt   thought he saw him some
three or four months ag   He, our man, was on the
Great Western line, goi   to Bath; in passing a station where they did not   op, he saw (or thought he
saw) Salter standing there. He is a cool-judging,
keen-sighted officer, and I do not myself think he
could have been mistaken. We followed up the scent
at once, but nothing has come of it."

Karl made no answer: he was considering. Three or four months ago? That was about the time, he fancied, that Smith took up his abode at Foxwood.

Previous to that, he might have been all over England, for aught Karl could tell.

"Just before that," resumed the detective, "another of the men struck up a cock-and-bull story that Salter was living in Aberdeen. I forget the precise reason he had for asserting it. We instituted inquiries: but, like the later tale, they resulted in nothing. As yet, we have no sure clue to Salter."

"That is all you know?" asked Karl.

"Every word. Has the information helped you?"

"Not in the least degree."

There was nothing else for Karl to wait for. His visit had been a fruitless one. "I should have liked to see Grimley once again," he said as he rose. "Is he in town?"

"Grimley is in the house now. At least, he ought to be. He is engaged in a case under me, and was to be here at three o'clock for instructions. Will you see him?"

"If you please."

It had occurred to Karl more than once that he should like to describe Smith accurately to Grimley, and ask whether the description tallied with Salter's. He could do it without affording any clue to Smith or his locality.

Mr. Burtenshaw rang, and told the maid to send up Grimley, if he had come. In obedience to this, Grimley, in his official clothes, appeared, and another officer with him.

"Oh, I don't want you just yet, Watts," said Mr. Burtenshaw. "Wait down stairs."

"Very well, sir," replied the man. "I may as well give you this, though," he added, crossing the room and placing a small box the size of a five-shilling-piece on the table. Mr. Burtenshaw looked at it curiously, and then slipped it into the drawer at his left hand.

"From Jacob, I suppose?"

"Yes, sir."

The man left the room. Karl, after a few preliminary words with Grimley, gave an elaborate and close description of Smith's figure and features. "Is it like Salter?" he asked.

"If it isn't him, sir, it's his twin brother," was Grimley's emphatic answer. "As to his looking forty, it is only to be expected. Nothing ages a man like living a life of fear."

Karl remembered how Adam had aged and was ageing, and silently acquiesced. He began to think he saw his way somewhat more clearly; that the man at Foxwood was certainly Salter. Handing over a gratuity to Grimley, and taking leave of Mr. Burtenshaw, he departed, leaving the other two talking of him.

"He has dropped upon Salter," remarked Grimley.

"Yes," said Mr. Burtenshaw. "But he does not intend to deliver him up."

"No!" cried the other in amazement. "Why not, sir?"

"I don't know," said Mr. Burtenshaw. "He said he had no intention of the kind—and I am sure he has not. It seemed to me to be rather the contrary —that he wants to screen him."

"Then he told you, sir, that he *had* found Salter?"

"No, he did not. We were speaking on supposition."

"Who is this gentleman, sir?"

"I don't know who he is. He keeps his name from me."

Mr. Grimley felt anything but satisfied with the present aspect of the affair. What right had this stranger, who wanted to know all about Salter, to refuse to denounce him? Once more he asked Mr. Burtenshaw if he did not know who he was, but the latter repeated his denial. During the discussion, the man Watts entered the room again, and heard what passed. He looked at Mr. Burtenshaw.

"Are you speaking of the gentleman just gone out, sir? I know him."

"Why, who is he?" asked Mr. Burtenshaw, who had taken out the little box again, and was opening it.

"Sir Karl Andinnian."

"Nonsense!" exclaimed the detective, aroused to interest. For Sir Karl Andinnian, brother to the criminal who had made so much stir in the world, was a noted name amongst the force.

"It is," said Watts. "I knew him the minute I came in. I was present at the trial in Northampton, sir, when his brother was condemned to death; this gentleman sat all day at the solicitors' table. I had gone down there on that business of Patteson's."

"No wonder he has a sad look," thought the detective. "Adam Andinnian's was a mournful case, and his death was mournful. But what interest can Sir Karl have in Salter?"

There was one, at least, who determined to ascertain, if possible, what that interest was—and that was Mr. Policeman Grimley. A shrewd man by nature, a very shrewd one by experience, he drew his own deductions—and they were anything but favourable to the future security of some of the inhabitants of Foxwood. Could Karl Andinnian have seen what his morning's work had done for him, he would have been ready to sit in sackcloth and ashes, after the manner of the mourners of old.

"Sir Karl's living at Foxwood Court with his young wife," ran Mr. Grimley's thoughts: "I know that much. Wherever this Salter is, it's not far from him, I'll lay. Hid in Foxwood, and no mistake! I'll get him unearthed if it costs me my place. Let's see; how shall I set about it?"

As a preliminary step, he gently sounded Mr. Burtenshaw; but found he could get no help from him: it was not the detective's custom to stir in any matter without orders. Mr. Grimley then slept a night upon it, and in the morning had resolved to strike a bold stroke. Obtaining a private interview with one who was high in the force at Scotland Yard, he denounced Salter, telling of Sir Karl Andinnian's visits to Burtenshaw, and their purport.

"Salter is in hiding at Foxwood, or somewhere in its neighbourhood, sir, as sure as that my name's Dick Grimley," he said. "I want him took. I don't care about the reward—and perhaps it would not be given to me in any case, seeing it was me that let the fellow go—but I want him took. He's a crafty fox, sir, mark you, though; and it will have to be gone about cautiously."

"If Salter be retaken through this declaration of

yours, Grimley, I daresay you'll get some of the reward," was the consoling answer. "Who knows the man? It will not do for you to go down."

"No, it wouldn't," acquiesced Grimley. "He knows me; and, once he caught sight of me, he'd make off like a rat sneaking out of a sinking ship. Besides, sir, I couldn't leave that other thing Mr. Burtenshaw has in hand."

"Well, who knows Salter, I ask?"

"Tatton does, sir; knows him as well as I do; but Salter does not know Tatton. Tatton would be the best man for it, too. Burtenshaw himself can't manage a case as Tatton does when it comes to personal acting."

There was a little more conversation, and then Grimley withdrew, and. Tatton was sent for. The grass could not be let grow under their feet in the attempt to re-take that coveted prize, Philip Salter.

This Tatton had begun life as an ordinary policeman: but his talents raised him. He was smart in appearance and manner, had received a fairly good education, conversed well on the topics of the day, could adapt himself to any society he might happen to be in, from that of a gentleman to a shoeblack, and was found to possess the rare prudence, the certain tact, necessary to undertake the conduct of delicate cases, and bring them to a successful conclusion. Grimley was correct, in judging that Tatton would be the right man to put on the track of Philip Salter.

CHAPTER III.

A New Lodger in Paradise Row.

THE sun was drawing towards the west, and the summer's afternoon was waning, for the days were not so long as they had been a month or two ago, when a gentleman, slight and rather short, with light eyes, fair curly hair, and about thirty years of age, alighted from the London train at Foxwood station. He had a black bag in his hand and a portmanteau in the van, and enquired of the porter the way to Foxwood.

"Do you mean Foxwood proper, sir; or Foxwood, Sir Karl Andinnian's place?" returned the porter.

"Foxwood proper, I suppose. It is a village, is it not?"

"Yes, sir. Go down the road to the left, sir, then take the first turning on your right, and it will bring you into Foxwood."

"Thank you," said the gentleman, and slipped a small silver coin into the porter's hand. He knew, nobody better, the value of a silver key: and the chances were that he might shortly get gossiping with this station porter about the neighbourhood and its politics.

Bag in hand, and leaving his portmanteau at the station, he speedily found himself in the heart of Foxwood. Casting about his eyes on this side and that, they settled on Paradise Row, on which the sun was shining, and on a white embossed card hanging in the first-floor window of the middle house, which card had on it, in large letters, "Apartments furnished."

At the open entrance-door of the same house stood a widow woman in a clean cap and smart black silk apron. Mrs. Jinks was en grande toilette that afternoon.

"It looks likely," said the stranger to himself. "Madame there will talk her tongue sore, I see, once prompted." And going up to the door, he politely took off his hat as he might to a duchess.

"You have apartments to let, I think, madam?"

"Good gracious!" cried the Widow Jinks, taken by surprise—for she was only looking out for the muffin-boy, and the slanting rays of the sun were dazzling her eyes, so that she had not observed the traveller. "I beg pardon, sir; apartments, did you say? Yes, sir, I've got my drawing-room just emptied."

It happened that an elderly lady from Basham and her grand-daughters had been lodging there for a month, the young ladies being ardent disciples of Mr. Cattacomb; but they had now left, and the drawing-room was ready to be let again. Mrs. Jinks went on to explain this, rather volubly.

"I will go up and look at it, if you please," said the stranger.

The widow ushered him along the passage towards the stairs, treading softly as she passed the parlour door.

"I've got a Reverend Gent lodging in there," she said, "minister of the new church, St. Jerome's. He has a meeting every Thursday evening, for Scripture reading, or something of that—exercises, I think they call it. This is Thursday, and they be all expected. But he wants his tea first, and that there dratted muffin-boy's not round yet. The Reverend Gent have dropped asleep on three chairs in his shirt sleeves, while he waits for it.——This is the drawing-room, sir."

The stranger liked the drawing-room very much; the sun made it cheerful, he said; and he liked the bed-room behind it. Mrs. Jinks rather hesitated at letting the two rooms alone. She generally let the bed-rooms at the top of the house with them.

"How long shall you be likely to stay, sir?" questioned she.

"I do not know. It may be a week, it may be a month, it may be more. I am seeking country air and rest to re-establish my health, ma'am, and want a quiet place to read in. I shall not give you much trouble."

Mrs. Jinks agreed to let him have the rooms at last, demanding a few shillings over the usual terms for the two: a bird in the hand, she thought, was worth two in the bush. Next she asked for references.

"I cannot refer you to any one here," he said, "for I don't know a soul in the place, and not a soul in it knows me. I will pay you every week in advance; and that I presume will do as well as references."

He laid down the sum agreed upon and a sovereign beside it. "You will be so good as to get in for me a few things to eat and drink, Mrs. Jinks. I should like to have some tea first of all, if convenient, and one of those muffins you spoke of. Well buttered, if you please."

"Yes, sir; certainly, sir. We get muffins at Foxwood all the year round, sir, on account of there being company in the place at summer time: in other towns, Basham, for instance, they are only made in winter. Buttered muffins and cress, sir, is uncommonly good together."

"Are they? I'll have some cress too."

Telling her, as well as he could remember, what articles he should want besides butter and muffins, and bidding her to add anything else that she thought he might require, he picked up his black bag to take it into the bed-room. Mrs. Jinks in her politeness begged him to let her take it, but he said certainly not.

"Is it all the luggage you've got, sir, this?"

"My portmanteau is at the station. I could not order it on until I knew where I should be; or, in fact, whether I should stay at Foxwood at all. Had I not found lodgings to my mind, ma'am, I might have gone on somewhere else."

"Foxwood's the loveliest, healthiest spot you can find, sir," cried the widow, eagerly. "Sweet walks about it, there is."

"So I was told by my medical man. One wants nice rural walks, Mrs. Jinks, after reading hard."

"So one does, sir. You are reading up for college, I suppose? I had a young gent here once from Oxford. He got plucked, too, afterwards. There's the muffin-boy!" added Mrs. Jinks, in delight, as the fierce ring of a bell and the muffin-call was heard beneath. "Oh, I beg pardon, sir, what name?"

The gentleman, who had his head and hands just then in his bag, merely responded that he was a stranger. Mrs. Jinks, in the hurry to be gone, and

confused with the ringing and the calling below, caught
up the answer as "Strange."

"A Mr. Strange," she said to herself, going down
with the money in her hand. "And one of the nicest
gents I've ever come across. 'Put plenty o' butter,'
says he. *He* ain't one as'll look sharp after every
crumb and odd and end, as too many of 'em does,
and say where's the rest of this, that it don't come up,
and where's the remainder of that."

Mrs. Jinks had a young help-mate when she was
what she considered in "full let;" a young damsel of
fourteen, who wore her hair in a pink net. Sending
the girl flying to the general shop for various things,
she set on to toast the muffins; and tea was speedily
served in both rooms. She took in the clergyman's
first. Mr. Cattacomb was asleep on the three chairs,
in his shirt sleeves. He was beginning to find his
work somewhat hard. What with the duties in the
church, the services, and sermons, and confessions,
and the duties out of church connected with little
boys and girls, and with those anxious Christians who
never left him alone, the young ladies, Mr. Cattacomb
was often considerably fatigued; and it was under
consideration whether his former coadjutor, the Reverend Damon Puff, should not be summoned to assist
him.

"Here's your tea, sir," said Mrs. Jinks, "and a
beautiful hot muffin. I couldn't get it up afore, for
the muffin-boy was late."

"My tea, is it, Mrs. Jinks?" replied Mr. Cattacomb,
slowly rising. "Thank you, I am dead tired."

And, perhaps in consequence of the fatigue, or
that Mrs. Jinks was not worth any display, it might

have been observed that the affectation, so characteristic of the reverend gentleman when in society, had entirely disappeared now. Indeed, it seemed at this undress moment that Mr. Cattacomb was a simple-mannered, pleasant man.

"I've been in luck this afternoon, sir, and have let my drawing-room floor," continued the widow, as she settled the tea-tray before him. "It's a Mr. Strange, sir, that's took it; a gent reading for Oxford, and out of health. His doctor have ordered him into the country for change, and told him he'd find quiet air and nice walks at Foxwood. You may hear his boots walking about overhead, sir. He seems to be as nice and liberal a gent as ever I had to do with."

"Glad to hear it," said Mr. Cattacomb, beginning upon his muffin vigorously. "We shall want more chairs here presently, you know, Mrs. Jinks."

The tea-tray had scarcely disappeared, and Mr. Cattacomb put on his coat and his fascinating company manners, before the company began to arrive. On these Thursday evenings Mr. Cattacomb gave at his own home a private lecture, descriptive of some of the places mentioned in holy Scripture. The lectures were attended by all his flock at St. Jerome's and by several young ladies from Basham. Of course it necessitated a great many seats; and the new lodger above was yet at his tea, when Mrs. Jinks appeared, her face redder than usual with running about, and begged the loan of "Mr. Strange's" chairs, explaining what they were wanted for.

"Oh, certainly: take them all, Mrs. Jinks," replied he, in the most accommodating manner possible. "I can sit upon the table."

Mrs. Jinks considerately left him one, however, and went down with the rest. He found out she had taken up the notion that his name was "Strange," and laughed a little.

"Some misunderstanding, I suppose, on her part when I said I was a stranger," thought he. "All right; I'll not contradict it."

While the bumping and thumping went on, caused by the progress of chairs down from the chambers and up from the kitchen, and the knocker and the bell kept up a perpetual duet, Mr. Strange (we will call him so at present ourselves) put on his hat to go round and order his portmanteau to be sent from the station. As he passed the parlour door it stood open; no one was looking his way; he had a good view of the interior, and took in the scene and the details with his observant eyes. A comfortable room, containing a dozen or two charming and chattering ladies, surrounded by a perfect epitome of tasty and luxurious objects that had been worked by fair fingers. Cushions, anti-macassars, slippers, scrolls, drawings enshrined in leather frames, ornamental mats by the dozen, cosies for tea-pots, lamp tops and stands, flowers in wax under shades, sweet flowers from hot-houses in water, and other things too numerous to mention.

"A man beset, that clergyman," thought Mr. Strange, with a silent laugh, as he bent his steps towards the railway. "He should get married and stop it. Perhaps he likes it, though: some of them do who have more vanity than brains."

So he ordered his portmanteau to No. 5, Paradise Row, contriving to leave the same impression at the

station that he had given Mrs. Jinks—a reading man
in search of quiet and health.

Mrs. Jinks presided at the arrival of the portmanteau, and saw some books taken out of it in the drawing-
room.   While her lodger's back was turned, she took
the liberty of peeping into one or two of them; and
finding their language was what she could not read,
supposed it to be Greek or Latin.   Before the night
was over, all Paradise Row, upwards and downwards,
had been regaled with the news of her new lodger,
and the particulars concerning his affairs.

"A scholar-gent, by name of Strange, who had
come down to read and get up his health, and had
brought his Greek and Latin books with him."

CHAPTER IV.

Nurse Chaffen on Duty.

HOW short a period of time may serve to bring
forth vital chances and changes!   Sir Karl and Lady
Andinnian were absent only a week, yet before they
returned a stranger had taken up his abode at Foxwood, indirectly brought to it by Karl himself; and
something had happened at the Maze.

Lucy was out amidst her plants and shrubs and
flowers the evening of her return, when the shadows
were lengthening on the grass.   Karl was writing
letters in-doors; Miss Blake had hurried up from dinner
to attend vespers.   In spite of the estrangement and
misery that pervaded the home atmosphere, Lucy felt
glad to be there again.   The meeting with her husband, after the week's entire separation, had caused
her pulses to quicken and her heart to bound with

something that was very like joy. Colonel Cleeve was out of all danger; was nearly well again. It had been a sharp but temporary attack of sickness. The Colonel and his wife had pressed Lucy to prolong her stay, had asked Sir Karl to come and join her; and they both considered it somewhat unaccountable that Lucy should have persisted in declining. Theresa was alone at Foxwood, was the chief plea of excuse she urged: the real impediment being that she and Karl could not stay at her mother's home together without risk of the terms on which they lived becoming known. So Karl, on the day appointed, went from London to Winchester, and brought Lucy home.

For the forbearance she had exercised, the patient silence she had maintained, Lucy had in a degree received the reward during this sojourn with her father and mother. More than ever was it brought home to her conviction then, that she would almost rather have died than betray it. It would have inflicted on them so much pain and shame. It would have lowered herself so in their sight, and in the sight of those old and young friends who had known her in her girlhood, and who whispered their sense of what her happiness must now be, and their admiration of her attractive husband. "Martyrdom rather than that!" said Lucy, clasping her hands with fixed resolution, as she paced the grass, thinking over her visit, on this, the evening of her return.

Karl came up to her with two letters in his hand. She was then sitting under the acacia tree. The sun had set, but in the west shone a flood of golden light. The weather in the daytime was still hot as in the middle of that hot summer, but the evenings and nights were cool. Lucy's shawl lay beside her.

"It is time to put it on," said Karl — and he wrapped it round her himself carefully. It caused her to see the address of the two letters in his hand. One was to Plunkett and Plunkett; the other to Mrs. Cleeve.

"You have been writing to mamma!" she exclaimed.

"She asked me to be sure and let her have one line to say you got home safely. I have given your love, Lucy."

"Thank you, Karl. And now you are going to the post."

"And now I am going to the post. And I must make haste, or I shall find the box shut."

He took his hand from her shoulder, where it had momentarily rested, and crossed the grass, Lucy looking after him.

"How thoughtful and kind he is!" she soliloquised. "It is just as though he loved me." And her imagination went off wandering at random, as imagination will. Once more she reverted to that former possibility—of condoning the past and becoming reconciled again. It was *very* good of him, and she felt it so, to have stayed that week in London. She fancied he had done it that she might know he did not spend his time at the Maze in her absence. And so, the evening shadows came on, and still Lucy sat there, lost in her dreams.

Miss Blake, it has been said, had hurried from dinner, to go to vespers. As she turned into the road from the Court, she saw a boy a little in advance of her on the other side, his basket on his arm. It was the doctor's boy, Cris Lumley, against whom Miss Blake had a grievance. She crossed over and caught him up just as he rang at the Maze gate.

"Now, Cris Lumley, what have you to say for yourself? For three days you have not appeared at class."

"'Tain't my fault," said Cris Lumley, who was just as impudent as he looked; a very different boy indeed from civil-natured Tom Pepp. "It be master's."

"How is it your master's?"

"What master says is this here: 'I be to attend to him and my place; or I be to give it up, if I wants to kick up my heels all day at school.'"

"I don't believe you," said Miss Blake. "I shall speak to Mr. Moore."

"Just do then," said the independent boy.

"The fact of the case is no doubt this, Cris Lumley—that you play truant for half the day sometimes, on the plea of being all that while at school."

"Master said another thing, he did," resumed the young gentleman, ignoring the last accusation. "He said as if Parson Sumnor warn't no longer good enough for me to learn religion from, he'd get another boy in my place, that he was good enough for. There! you may ask him whether he said it or not."

Declining to bandy further words with him until she should have seen the surgeon, Miss Blake was hastening on, when the fringe of her mantle caught against his medicine basket. It reminded her that some one must be ill. Battling for a moment with her curiosity, but not for long, she condescended to inquire who was ill at the Maze.

"It be the missis," replied Cris.

"The mistress! Do you mean Mrs. Grey?"

Mr. Lumley nodded.

"What is the matter with *her?*"

"Got a baby," said the boy shortly.

For the instant Miss Blake felt struck into herself, and was dumb. She did not believe it.

"He were born yesterday," added the boy. "This be some physic for him: and this be the missis's."

Throwing back the lid of one end of his basket, Miss Blake saw two bottles, done up in white paper. The larger one was addressed "Mrs. Grey," the small one "Mrs. Grey's infant."

She turned away without another word, feeling ready to sink with the weight of the world's iniquity. It pressed upon her most unpleasantly throughout the evening service at St. Jerome's, and for once Miss Blake was inattentive to the exhortations of the Rev. Guy. Looking at the matter as Miss Blake looked at it, it must be confessed that she had just cause for condemnation.

To return to Lucy. It grew dusk and more dusk; and she at length went in-doors. Karl came in, bringing Mr. Moore, whom he had overtaken near the gate: and almost close upon that, Miss Blake returned. The sight of the doctor, sitting there with Karl and Lucy, brought back all Miss Blake's vexation. It had been at boiling-point for the last hour, and now it bubbled over. The wisest course no doubt would have been to hold her tongue: but her indignation— a perfectly righteous and proper indignation, as she deemed it—forbade that. The ill-doing of the boy, respecting which she had been about to appeal to Mr.

Moore, was quite lost sight of in this ill-doing. There could be no fear of risking Jane Shore's sheet of penance in repeating what she had heard. It was her duty to speak: she fully believed that: her duty to open Lucy's obtuse eyes—and who knew but Sir Karl might be brought to his senses through the speaking? The surgeon and Lucy were sitting near the window in the sweet still twilight: Karl stood back by the mantel-piece: and they were deep in some discussion about flowers. Miss Blake sat in silence, gathering her mental forces for the combat, when the present topic should have died away.

"I—I have heard some curious news," she began then in a low, reluctant tone: and in good truth she was reluctant to enter on it. "I heard it from that boy of yours, Mr. Moore. He says there's a baby at the Maze."

"Yes," readily acquiesced Mr. Moore. "A baby-boy, born yesterday."

And Miss Blake, rising and standing at angles between the two, saw a motion of startled surprise on the part of Karl Andinnian. Lucy looked up, simply not understanding. After a pause, during which no one spoke, Miss Blake, in language softened to ambiguousness, took upon herself to intimate that, in her opinion, the Maze had no business with a baby.

Mr. Moore laughed pleasantly. "That, I imagine, is Mrs. Grey's concern," he said.

Lucy understood now; she felt startled almost to sickness. "Is it Mrs. Grey who has the baby?" was on the point of her tongue: but she did not speak it.

"Where is Mrs. Grey's husband?" demanded Miss Blake, in her most uncompromising tone.

"In London, I fancy, just now," said the doctor.

"*Has she one at all*, Mr. Moore?"

"Good gracious, yes," cried the hearty-natured surgeon, utterly unconscious that it could be of particular moment to anybody present whether she had or not. "I'd answer for it with my life, nearly. She's as nice a young lady as I'd ever wish to attend; and good too."

"For Lucy's sake, I'll go on; for his sake, standing there in his shame," thought Miss Blake, in her rectitude. "Better things may come of it: otherwise I'd drop the hateful subject for ever."

"Mr. Moore," she continued aloud, "Why do you say the husband is in London?"

"Because Mrs. Grey said something to that effect," he answered. "At least, I understood her words to imply as much; but she was very ill at the moment, and I did not question further. It was when I was first called in."

"It has hitherto been represented that Mr. Grey was travelling abroad," pursued Miss Blake, with a tone and a stress on the "Mr. Grey."

"I know it has. But he may have returned. I am sure she said she had been up to London two or three weeks ago—and I thought she meant to imply that she went to meet her husband. It may have been a false conclusion I drew; but I certainly thought it."

Sir Karl took a step forward. "I can answer for it that Mrs. Grey did go up," he said, "for I chanced to travel in the same carriage with her. Getting into the up-train at the station one day, I found Mrs. Grey seated there."

Lucy glanced towards him as he spoke. There

was no embarrassment in his countenance; his voice was easy and open as though he had spoken of a stranger. Her own face looked white as death.

"You did!" cried the doctor. "Did she tell you she was going up to meet Mr. Grey?"

"No, she did not. I put her into a cab at the terminus, and that's all I know about it. It was broiling hot, I remember."

"Well," resumed the doctor, "whether it was to meet her husband or whether not, to London she went for a day or two in the broiling heat—as Sir Karl aptly terms it—and she managed to fatigue herself so much that she has not been able to recover it, and has been very unwell ever since. This young gentleman, who chose to take upon himself to make his appearance in the world yesterday, was not due for a good couple of months to come."

Lucy rose and left the room, she and her white face. Karl followed her with his eyes: he had seen the whiteness.

"Is it a healthy child?" he asked.

"Quite so," replied the surgeon; "but very small. The worst of these little monkeys is, you can't send them back again with a whipping, when they make too much haste, and tell them to come again at proper time. Mrs. Grey's very ill."

"Is she?" cried Karl.

"Yes. And there's no nurse and no anything; matters are all at sixes and sevens."

"I hope she'll do well!" breathed Karl.

"So do I."

Miss Blake looked at the two speakers. The one seemed just as open as the other. She thought what a finished adept Karl Andinnian was getting to be in deception.

"I am going to the Maze now," said the doctor: "was on my way to it when you seduced me in here, Sir Karl. Good evening, Miss Blake."

He took his departure hastily as he spoke. He was, as he told them, on his way to the Maze then. Karl went with him to the outer gate, and then paced the lawn in the evening twilight.

"After all, it is well it's over," ran his thoughts. "This expected future illness was always putting itself in view when I was planning to get away Adam. Once Rose is well again, the ground will be, so far, clear. But good heavens! how it increases the risk! Here's Moore going in at any hour of the day or night, I suppose—and Adam so incautious! Well, I think he will take care of himself, and keep in seclusion for his own sake. And for myself—it brings more complication," he added with a sigh. "The child is the heir now instead of me: and the whole property must eventually come to him. Poor Lucy! I saw she felt it. Oh, she may well be vexed! Does she quite comprehend, I wonder, who this baby is, and what it will take from us?—Foxwood amidst the rest? I wish I had never married! I wish a merciful heaven had interposed to prevent it."

When Mr. Moore, some eight-and-forty hours previously, received a hurried visit from Mrs. Grey's servant, Ann Hopley, at the dusk of evening, and heard what she had to say about her mistress, he was excessively astonished, not having had the slightest idea that his services were likely to be wanted in any such way at the Maze. It is possible that some doubts of Mrs. Grey's position crossed his mind at the moment: but he was a good man, and he made it a rule never to think ill if he could by possibility think good; and when he came to see and converse with Mrs. Grey, he felt sure she was all she should be. The baby was born on the following morning. Since then the doctor, as Karl expressed it, had been going in at all hours: Ann Hopley invariably preceding him through the Maze, and conducting him out of it again at his departure. As he marched on to the Maze to-night after the above conversation at the Court, he wondered what Miss Blake had got in her head, and why she should betray so much anger over it.

Three or four days went on. The doctor passed in and out in the care of his patient, and never a notion entered his head that the Maze was tenanted by any save its ordinary inmates, or that one under a ban was lying there in concealment. Ann Hopley, letting her work go how it would, attended on her mistress and the baby; the old gardener was mostly busy in his garden as usual. On the fifth or sixth day from the commencement of the illness, Mr. Moore, upon paying his usual morning visit, found Mrs. Grey worse. There were rather dangerous symptoms of fever.

"Has she been exciting herself?" he privately asked of Ann Hopley.

"She did a little last night, sir," was the incautious admission.

"What about?"

"Well, sir—chiefly talking."

"Chiefly talking!" repeated the doctor. "But what were you about, to let her talk?" he demanded, sup-

posing Ann Hopley to be the only other inmate of
the house. "What possessed you to talk to her?"

Ann was silent. She could have said that it was
not with her Mrs. Grey had talked, but with her husband.

"I must send a nurse in," he resumed. "Not only
to see that she is kept quiet, but to attend to her
constantly. It is not possible that you can be with
her always with your housework to do."

But all of this Ann Hopley most strongly com-
bated. She could attend to her mistress, and would,
and did attend to her, she urged, and a nurse she
would not have in the house. From the first, this
question of a nurse had been a bone of contention:
the doctor wanting to send one in; Ann Hopley and
also Mrs. Grey strenuously objecting. So once more
the doctor yielded, and let the matter drop, inwardly
resolving that if his patient did not get better during
the day, he should take French leave to pursue his
own course.

Late in the afternoon he went in again. Mrs.
Grey was worse: flushed, restless, and slightly delirious.
The doctor said nothing; but when he got home, he
sent a summons for Mrs. Chaffen. A skilled nurse,
she; and first cousin to the Widow Jinks, both in respect to kin and to love of gossip.

That same evening, after dark, when Adam Andinnian was sitting in his wife's room, and Ann Hopley
was concocting something in a saucepan over the
kitchen fire, the gate bell clanged out. It had been
nothing unusual to hear it these last few days at any
hour; and the woman, putting the saucepan on the
hob for safety, went forth, key in hand.

No sooner had she unlocked the gate than Mr. Moore brushed past her, followed by a little thin woman with a bundle. Ann Hopley stared: but never a word said he.

"Keep close to me, and you won't lose yourself," cried he to the little woman; and went tearing off at a double-quick pace through the intricacies of the maze.

Ann Hopley stood like one bewildered. For one thing, she had not possessed the slightest notion that the surgeon knew his way through, for he had given no special indication of it, always having followed her. He could have told her that he had learnt the secret of the maze long before she came to Foxwood. It had been shown to him in old Mr. Throckton's time, whom he had attended for years. And, to see a second person pass in, startled her. All she could do was to lock the gate, and follow them.

On went the doctor; the little woman keeping close to his coat tails: and they were beyond the maze in no time. Mr. Moore had no private motive for this unusual haste, except that he had another patient waiting for him, and was in a hurry. In, at the open portico, passed he, and made direct for the stairs, the woman after him. Ann Hopley, miles behind, could only pray in agony that her master might escape their view.

But he did not. The doctor had nearly reached the top of the staircase, when a gentleman, tall, and in evening dress, suddenly presented himself in front, apparently looking who it might be, coming up. He drew back instantly, strode noiselessly along the corridor, and disappeared within a door at its extreme

end.　It all passed in a moment of time.　What with
the speed, and what with the obscurity of the stairs
and passages, any one, less practical than the doctor,
might have questioned whether or not it had happened
at all.

"That's Mr. Grey, come down," thought he.
"But he seems to wish not to be noticed.　Be it so."

Had he cared to make any remark upon it to
Mrs. Grey, he could not have done so, for she was
quite delirious that night.　And, as he saw no further
sign of the gentleman at any subsequent visit, he
merely supposed that Mr. Grey had come down for a
few hours and had gone again. And the matter passed
from his mind.

It did not so pass from the nurse's.　Mrs. Chaffen
had distinctly seen the gentleman in evening attire
looking down the stairs at her and the doctor; she
saw him whisk away, as she phrased it, and go into
the further room.　In the obscure light, Mrs. Chaffen
made him out to be a very fine-looking gentleman
with beautiful white teeth.　She had keen eyesight,
and she saw that much: she had also a weakness for
fine-looking men, and felt glad that one so fine as
this should be in the house.　It could not make much
difference to her; but she liked gentlemen to be in a
dwelling where she might be located: they made it
lively, were pleasant to talk to; and were generally to
be found more liberal in the offers of glasses of wine
and what not than the mistresses.　Like the doctor,
she supposed this was Mrs. Grey's husband, come down
at last.

She neither saw nor heard more of the gentleman
that night, though she sat up with her patient. Neither

did she on the following day—and then she began to
think it somewhat odd. At dusk, when Mrs. Grey
and the baby were both sleeping, she went down
stairs.

When Ann Hopley found the nurse installed there
and that she was powerless to prevent it, she had to
make the best of the unfortunate occurrence—and
most unfortunate it was destined to turn out in the
end. She gave the nurse certain directions. One of
them was, "Ring for everything you want, and I will
bring it up." The woman's meals also were brought
to her punctually: Ann's object of course being to
prevent her going about the house. But nurses are
but human. Mrs. Chaffen was longing for a word of
social gossip, and downstairs she went, this night, and
made her way to the kitchen. Ann Hopley was in it,
ironing at a table under the window.

"What do you want?" cried she, in a quick startled
tone, as the nurse appeared.

"I thought I'd get you to give me a sup o' beer,
Mrs. Hopley," was the answer. "I'm a'most faint,
stopping so long in that there room with its smell of
ether about."

"Why could you not have rung? I'll bring it up
to you."

In the very teeth of this plain intimation, Mrs.
Chaffen sat herself down on a chair by the ironing
board, and began fanning her face with a corner of
her white apron. "The missis is asleep," she said:
"she's a sight better to-night; and I shall stop here
while I drink the beer for a bit of relief and
change."

Ann took a small jug that was hanging on the

4*

dresser shelves, went down in the cellar, brought up the beer and poured it into a tumbler. Mrs. Chaffen took a good draught and smacked her lips.

"That ain't bad beer, is it, Mrs. Hopley?"

"Not at all," said Ann Hopley. "Drink it up."

She would not go on with her ironing, lest it might seem an excuse for the nurse to linger; she stood by the fire, waiting, and evidently wanting the nurse gone.

"Your husband's a-taking of it easy out there!"

Ann glanced from the window, and saw the gardener seated amongst a heap of drying weeds, his back against the tool house, and a pipe in his mouth.

"He has done his work, I suppose, for the day," she said.

"And he knows his missis's eyes can't be upon him just now," added the nurse, taking another draught. "He don't hardly look strong enough to do all this here big garden."

"You couldn't offend Hopley worse than by telling him that. His mistress says nothing about it now, it puts him up so. Last May, when he was laid up in bed with the rheumatis, she ordered a gardener in for two or three days to clear up some of the rough work. Hopley was not at all grateful: he only grumbled at it when he got about again."

"It's just like them good old-fashioned servants that takes pride in their work," said the nurse. "There's not many of the young uns like 'em. The less work they have to do the better it pleases *them*. Is that a hump now, or only a stoop of the shoulders?"

continued she, ignoring good manners in her sociability.

"It used to be only a stoop, Mrs. Chaffen. But those things, you know, always get worse with years."

Mrs. Chaffen nodded. "And gardening work, when one has a natural stoop, is the worst sort of work a man can take to."

"True," assented Ann. She had spoken absently all along, and kept glancing round and listening as though ill at ease. One might have fancied she feared a ghost was coming down the staircase.

"What be you a-harkening at?" asked Mrs. Chaffen.

"For fear the baby should cry."

"The baby's in a sweet sleep, he is. I wonder whether he'll get reared, that baby?—he's very little. Where's the gentleman?" abruptly inquired Mrs. Chaffen, after a pause.

"What gentleman?"

"Mrs. Grey's husband. Him we saw here last night."

If Ann Hopley had been apathetic before, she was fully aroused to interest now, and turned her eyes upon the nurse with a long stare.

"Why what is it that you are talking of?" she asked. "There has been no gentleman here. Mrs. Grey's husband is abroad."

"But I saw him," persisted the nurse. "He stood right at the head of the staircase when me and Dr. Moore was a-going up it. I saw him."

"I'm sure you didn't."

"I'm sure I did."

Then they went on, asserting and re-asserting.

Nurse Chaffen protesting, by all that was truthful, that
she did see the gentleman: Ann Hopley denying in
the most emphatic language that any gentleman had
been there, or could have been.   Poor woman! in her
faithful zeal for her master's safety; in her terrible inward fear lest this might bring danger upon him, she
went so far as to vow by heaven that no living soul
had been in the house or about it, save her mistress
and the infant, herself and Hopley.

The assertion had its effect.   Nurse Chaffen was
not an irreligious woman, though she did indulge in
unlimited gossip, and love a glass of beer when she
could get it; and she could not believe that a thing
so solemnly asserted was a lie.   She felt puzzled to
death: her eyes were good and had never played her
false yet.

"Have ye got a ghost in the house?" she asked at
length, edging a little nearer to the ironing board and
to Ann Hopley.

"I have never seen or heard of one."

"It's a rare old place this house.   Folks said all
kinds of queer things about it in Miser Throckton's
time."

"He left no ghost in it, that I know of," repeated
Ann.

"Well I never!   I can't make it out.   You might
a'most as soon tell me to believe there's no truth in
the Bible.   He stood atop o' the stairs, looking down
at me and the doctor.   It was dusk, I grant; a'most
dark; but I saw him as plain as plain could be.   He
had got white teeth and a suit of black on; and he
went off into that door that's at the fur end of the
passage."

A keen observer might have detected a sleeping terror in Ann Hopley's eyes; but she was habitually of calm manner and she showed perfect calmness now, knowing how much was at stake. A great deal had all along depended upon her ready presence of mind, her easy equanimity in warding off suspicion: it depended more than ever on her at this trying time, and she had her wits at hand.

"Your eyes and the dusk must have misled you, Mrs. Chaffen," she quietly rejoined. "Is it possible— I put it to yourself—that any gentleman could be in this house, and me and Hopley not know it? That night I had run down from my mistress's room, where she was lying off her head with the fever, and the baby asleep in its little bed by the fire, and was making a drop of gruel in the kitchen here, when the ring at the gate came. I had a great mind to send Hopley to open it: I heard him out yonder putting up his tools for the night: but I should have had to go close up to make him understand, for he's as deaf as a post; and his knees would have been a long while making their way through the maze. So I went myself: it seemed less trouble; and I let in you and the doctor. As to any soul's having been in the place, save me and Hopley and the missis and baby, it's a moral impossibility; and if necessary I could swear to it."

"Where do that there end door lead to?" questioned Mrs. Chaffen, only half-convinced and that half against her will.

"It leads to nowhere. It's a sitting-room. Mrs. Grey does not often use it."

"Well, this beats everything, this do. I'm sure I could have swore that a gentleman was there."

"It was quite a mistake. Hark! there *is* the baby."

Nurse Chaffen flew up the stairs. Ann Hopley went on with her ironing; her face, now that she was alone, allowing its terror scope.

"It is so foolish of my master to run risks just at this time, when the house is liable to be invaded by strangers!" she ejaculated wearily. "But who was to foresee the doctor would come bursting in like that? Pray Heaven master doesn't show himself again like that while the woman's here!"

Mrs. Chaffen sat in the sick-room, the awakened baby occupying her lap, and the problem her mind. Never in all her life had she felt to be in so entire a mist. Ann Hopley she could not and would not disbelieve: and yet, in her reasoning moments she was as fully persuaded that a gentleman had been there, and that she had seen him, as that the sun shone in the sky.

A day or two went on; and the subject was never out of the woman's mind. Now leaning to this side of the question, now wavering to that, she could not arrive at any positive conclusion. But, taking one thing with another, she thought the house was rather a strange house. Why did Ann Hopley want to keep her for ever in that one room?—as she evidently did want to—and prevent her from moving freely about the house? An unfortunate doubt took possession of her—was there a gentleman in the house after all; and, for some reason or other, keeping himself concealed? Unfortunate, because it was to bear unpleasant fruit.

"Be whipped if it is not the most likely solution o' the matter I've thought of yet!" cried she, striking her hand on the tall fender. "But how do he manage to hide himself from Ann Hopley?—and how do he get his victuals? Sure-*ly* she can't have been deceiving of me—and as good as taking oaths to an untruth! She'd not be so wicked."

From that time Mrs. Chaffen looked curiously about her, poking and peering around whenever she had the opportunity. One morning in particular, when Mrs. Grey was asleep, and she saw Ann go out to answer the bell, and Hopley was safe at the end of the garden, for she could hear him rolling the path there, Mrs. Chaffen made use of the occasion. She went along the passage to the door where the gentleman had disappeared, and found herself in a dull sitting-room wainscoted with mahogany, its wide, modern window looking to the maze. Keenly Mrs. Chaffen's eyes darted about the room: but there was no other outlet that she could see. The dark paneling went from the door to the window, and from the window round to the door again. After that, she made her way into the small angular passages that the house seemed to abound in: two of them were bedrooms with the beds made up, the others seemed to be out of use. None of them were locked; the doors of most of them stood open; but certainly in not one of them was there any trace of a hidden gentleman.

That same day when she had finished her dinner, brought up to her as usual, she hastily put the things together on the tray and darted off with it down stairs. Mrs. Grey feebly called to her; but the nurse, conveniently deaf, went on without hearing. The staircase was angular, the turnings were short, and Mrs. Chaffen, as she went through the last one, gave the tray an inadvertent knock against the wall. Its plates rattled, its glasses jingled, betraying their approach: and—if ever she had heard a bolt slipped in her life, she felt sure she heard one slipped inside the kitchen door.

"It's me, Mrs. Hopley, with the tray," she called out, going boldly on. "Open the door."

No answer. No signs of being heard. Everything seemed perfectly still. Mrs. Chaffen managed to lodge the tray against the door-post and hold it steady with one hand, while she tried the door with the other. But she could not open it.

"Mrs. Hopley, it's me with the tray. Please open."

It was opened then. Ann Hopley flung it wide and stood there staring, a saucepan in her hand. "What, have you brought the things down!" she exclaimed in a voice of surprise. "Why on earth couldn't you have let them be till I came up?"

The nurse carried her tray onwards, and put it on the board under the window. At the table, not having been polite enough to his wife to take off his flapping straw hat in her presence, sat the gardener, munching his dinner as toothless people best can, his back to the light.

"Why did you keep me waiting at the door?" asked the nurse, not pleased.

"Did you wait?" returned Ann Hopley. "I was in the back place there, washing out the saucepans. You might have come in without knocking."

"The door was bolted."

"The door bolted!—not it," disputed Ann. "The latch has got a nasty trick of catching, though."

"This is fine weather, Mr. Hopley!" said the nurse, leaving the point uncontested, and raising her voice.

He seemed to be, as Ann had formerly expressed it, as deaf as a post. Neither turning his head nor answering, but keeping on at his dinner. Ann bent her head to his ear.

"The nurse, Mrs. Chaffen, spoke to you, Hopley. She says what fine weather it is."

"Ay, ay, ma'am," said he; "fine and bright."

What more might have passed was stopped by the ringing of Mrs. Grey's bell; a loud, long, impatient peal. The nurse turned to run.

"For pity's sake don't leave her again, Mrs. Chaffen!" called out Ann Hopley with some irritation. "If you do, I shall complain to Mr. Moore. You'll cause the fever to return."

"I could be upon my oath that she slipped the bolt to keep me out," thought the nurse, hurrying along. "Drat the cross-grained woman! Does she fear I shall poison her kitchen?"

CHAPTER V.

Watching the House.

MRS. JINKS's new lodger, Mr. Strange, was making himself at home, not only at Mrs. Jinks's, but in the village generally, and gradually getting familiar with its stories and its politics. Talking with the men at the station one hour, chatting to the field labourers the next; stepping into the shops to buy tobacco, or paper, or lozenges, or what not, and staying a good twenty minutes before he came out again: Mr. Strange was ingratiating himself with the local world.

But, though he gossiped freely enough without doors and with Mrs. Jinks within, he did not appear anxious to cultivate intimacy with the social sphere; but rather avoided it. The Rev. Mr. Cattacomb, relying on the information that the new lodger was a gentleman reading for Oxford, had taken the initiative and made an advance to acquaintanceship. Mr. Strange, while receiving it with perfect civility, intimated that he was obliged to decline it. His health, he said, left him no alternative, and he had come to the country for entire quiet. As to his reading for Oxford, it was a mistake he hinted. He was reading; but not with a view of going to any college. After that, the gentlemen bowed when they chanced to meet in the passages or out of doors, exchanged perhaps a remark on the fine weather; and there it ended.

The reader has not failed to detect that this "Mr. Strange," the name caught up so erroneously by Mrs. Jinks, was in reality the shrewd detective officer sent down by Scotland Yard in search of Philip Salter. His instructions were, not to hurry matters to an abrupt conclusion and so miss his game, but to track out Salter patiently and prudently. A case on which he had been recently engaged *had* been hurried and lost. Circumstances connected with it had caused him to lose sight of his usual prudence: he thought he was justified in doing what he did, and acted for the best: but the result proved him to have been wrong. No fear, with this failure on his mind, and the caution of his masters in his ears, that he would be in over much hurry now. In point of fact he could not if he would, for there was nothing to make hurry over.

For some time not a trace of any kind could Mr. Strange find of Philip Salter. People with whom he gossiped talked to him without any reserve; he was sure of that; and he would artfully lead the conversation and twist it the way he pleased; but he could hear nothing of any one likely to be Salter. The man might as well never have been within a hundred miles of Foxwood; for the matter of that, he might as well never have had existence, for all the trace there was left of him. Scotland Yard, however, was sure that Salter was to be found not far off, and that was enough: Mr. Strange, individually, felt sure of it also.

Knowing what he had been told of the visits of Sir Karl Andinnian to Detective Burtenshaw, and their object, Mr. Strange's attention was especially directed to Foxwood Court. Before he had been three days in the place, he had won the heart of Giles the footman (much at liberty just then, through the temporary absence of his master and mistress) and treated him to five glasses of best ale at different times in different public-houses. Giles, knowing no reason for reticence, freely described all he knew about Foxwood Court: the number of inmates, their names, their duties, their persons, and all the rest of it. Not the least idea penetrated his brain that the gentleman had any motive for listening to the details, save the whiling away of some of the day's idle hours. There was certainly no one at the Court that could be at all identified with the missing man; and, so far, Mr. Strange had lost his time and his ale money. Of course he

put questions as to Sir Karl's movements—where he went
to in the day, what calls he made, and what he did.
But Giles could give no information that was avail-
able. Happily, he was ignorant of his master's visits
to the Maze.

In short—from what Mr. Strange could gather
from Giles and others, there was no one whatever
in or about Foxwood, then or in time past, that at all
answered to Philip Salter. He heard Mr. Smith spoken
of—"Smith the agent, an old friend of the Andinnian
family"—but it did not once occur to him to attempt
to identify him with the criminal. Smith the agent
(whom by the way Mr. Strange had not chanced yet
to see) was living openly in the place, going about
amid the tenants on the estate, appearing at church,
altogether transacting his business and pursuing his
course without concealment: that is not how Salter
would have dared to live, and the detective did not
give Smith a supicious thought. No: wherever Salter
might be he was evidently in strict concealment:
and it must be Mr. Strange's business to hunt him
out of it.

In the meantime, no speculation whatever had
been aroused in the village as to Mr. Strange himself.
He had taken care to account for his stay there at
the first onset, and people's minds were at rest. The
gentleman in delicate health was free to come and
go; his appearance in the street, or roads, or fields,
excited no more conjecture or observation than did
that of the oldest inhabitant. The Reverend Mr. Cattacomb was stared at whenever he appeared, in consequence of the proceedings of St. Jerome's: Mr.
Strange passed along in peace.

Still, he learnt nothing. Sir Karl and Lady Andinnian had returned home long and long ago; he
often saw them out (though he took care they should
not see him), together or separately as might be, Sir
Karl sometimes driving her in a beautiful little pony-
chaise: but he could learn no trace of the man he was
sent after. Sir Karl heard that some young student
was in the village, out of health and reading for Oxford; he somehow caught up the notion that it was
only a lad, and as he never chanced to see him,
thought no more of him. And whether Mr. Strange
might not have thrown up the game in a short time
for utter lack of scent, cannot be told. A clue—or
what he thought was a clue—arose at last.

It arose, too, out of a slight misfortune that happened to himself. Entering the house one evening at
dusk before the passage lamp was lighted, he chanced
to put his foot into a tray of wine-glasses, that the
young maid had incautiously placed on the floor outside the parlour-door. In trying to start back and
save the glasses, Mr. Strange slipped, went down with
his right hand upon the tray, broke a glass or two,
and cut his hand in three or four places. Miss Blake
was there at the time, helping to catechise some
young children: she felt really sorry for the mishap,
and kindly went upstairs to the drawing-room to see
its extent. The hand was in a bowl of warm water,
and Mrs. Jinks was searching for linen to bind it up.

"Why do you put it into warm water, Mr.
Strange?" she asked. "It will make it bleed all the
more."

"Some bits of glass may have got in," he replied.
"Will you have Mr. Moore?"

But he laughed at the notion of sending for a doctor to cut fingers, and he bound up the hand himself, saying it would be all right. The next day, in the afternoon, Miss Blake made her appearance in his room to inquire how the damage was progressing, and found Mrs. Jinks in the act of assisting him to dress it with some precious ointment that she vowed was better than gold, and would not fail to heal the cuts in a day or two.

Miss Blake had previously a speaking acquaintanceship with Mr. Strange, having often met him going in and out. She sat down; and the three were chatting amicably when they were pounced in upon by little Mrs. Chaffen. Happening to call in to see her cousin, and hearing from the maid downstairs what Mrs. Jinks was then engaged upon—dressing the gentleman's hand—the nurse ran up to offer her more experienced services.

She took the hand out of Mrs. Jinks's into her own, and dressed it and bound it up as well as Mr. Moore himself could have done. It was nearly over when, by a curious coincidence—curious, considering what was to come of it—the conversation turned upon *ghosts*. Upon ghosts, of all things in the world! Some noise had been heard in the house the previous night by all the inmates—which noise had not been in any way accounted for. It was like the falling down of a piece of heavy furniture. It had awoke Mr. Cattacomb; it had awoke Mrs. Jinks; it had startled Mr. Strange, who was not asleep. The history of this was being given to Miss Blake, Mr. Strange gravely asserting it could have been nothing but a ghost—and that set Mrs. Chaffen on. She proceeded to tell them with real gravity, not assumed, that she did believe a ghost, in the shape of a gentleman in dinner dress, haunted the Maze: or else that her eyes were taking to see visions.

It should be mentioned that after a week's attendance on Mrs. Grey, Nurse Chaffen had been discharged. The patient was then going on quite well: and, as Mr. Moore saw that it worried her to have the nurse there—for whom she seemed to have conceived an insurmountable dislike—he took her away. The summary dismissal did not please the nurse: and she revenged herself by reporting that the Maze had a ghost in it. As a rule, people laughed at her, and thought no more about it: this afternoon her tale was to bear different fruit.

She told it consecutively. How she had been quite flurried by being called out by Dr. Moore all on a sudden; how he had taken her straight off to the Maze without saying where it was she was going till she got to the gate; how she and the doctor had seen the gentleman at the top of the stairs (which she took it to be the sick lady's husband), and watched him vanish into an end room, and had never seen the least sign of him afterwards; how the servant, Mrs. Hopley, had vowed through thick and thin that no gentleman was, or had been, or could have been in the house, unbeknown to her and Hopley.

Nurse Chaffen talked away to her heart's content, enlarging upon points of her story. Not one of them interrupted her: not one but would have listened with interest had she run on until midnight. Mrs. Jinks from her love of marvellous tales; the detective be-

cause he believed this might be the clue he wanted
to Philip Salter; and Miss Blake in her resentful condemnation of Sir Karl Andinnian. For, that the "gentleman in dinner dress" was no other than Sir Karl,
who had stolen in on one of his secret visits, she
could have staked her life upon.

"A tall gentleman with dark hair, you say it looked
like?" questioned Mr. Strange indifferently.

"Tall for certain, sir. As to his hair, I don't
know; it might have been darkish. I see he had nice
white teeth."

"Salter had good teeth," was the mental comment
of the detective. "*I have found him.*"

"And in dinner dress?" added Miss Blake with a
cough.

"So it looked like, ma'am. The sort of coat that
gentlefolks wears in an evening."

"And you mean to say you never see him after;
never but that there one time?" tartly interposed the
Widow Jinks.

"Never at all. The rooms was all open to daylight while I was there, but he wasn't in never a one
of 'em."

"Then I tell you what, Betsey Chaffen; it was a
ghost, and you need not hesitate to stand to it."

"Well, you see he didn't look like a ghost, but
like an ordinary gentleman," confessed Mrs. Chaffen.
"What came over me, and what I can't make out,
was Ann Hopley's standing it out that neither ghost
nor gentleman was there: she said she'd take her
oath to it."

"Thank you, you've done my hand up beautifully,
Mrs. Chaffen," said the patient. "I should give my

credence to the spirit theory. Did Mr. Moore see the appearance of this ghostly gentleman?"

"Yes he did, sir. I'm sure he did. For he lifted his head like at the gentleman, and stood still when he got to the top of the stairs, staring at the room he had vanished into. I told him a day or two afterwards that Mrs. Hopley denied that any one had been there, and the doctor quietly said, 'Then we must have been mistaken.' I did not like to ask whether he thought it was a ghost."

"Oh I think you may depend upon the ghost," returned Mr. Strange, biting his lips to prevent a laugh.

"Well, sir, queer stories was told of that Maze house in the late tenant's time. My cousin Jinks here knows that well enough."

"It was haunted by more than one ghost then, if all folks told true," assented Mrs. Jinks. "Mr. Throckton's son—a wild young blade he was—hung hisself there. I was but a girl at the time."

"Ah, one of the old ghosts come back again; not been laid yet," solemnly remarked the detective, staring at Mrs. Chaffen. "Did the lady herself seem alarmed?"

"Well, sir, I can't say she did then, because she couldn't have seen it, and was too ill besides. But she had got a curious manner with her."

"Curious?" questioned Mr. Strange.

"Yes, sir, curious. As if she was always frightened. When everything was as still as still could be, she'd seem to be listening like, as though expecting to hear something. Now and then she'd start up in bed in a

5*

fright, and cry out What was that?—when there had been no noise at all."

"Feverish fancies," quietly remarked Mr. Strange, with a cough.

By and by, the party separated. As Nurse Chaffen was descending to the kit?hen, leaving Mrs. Jinks putting the room straight, | iss Blake, who had gone down first, put forth her | nd and drew the nurse into Mr. Cattacomb's parlou | :hat reverend man being absent on some of his past | l calls.

"I have been *so much* | erested in this that you have been telling us, nurse, | he breathed. "It seems quite to have taken hold oi | e. What was the gentle- man like? Did he resemb | any one you know—Sir Karl Andinnian, for instanc | "

"Why, ma'am, how cai | tell who he resembled? —I didn't get enough look | him for that," was the answer. "I saw his head | d the tails of his coat when he turned—and that | s all. Except his teeth: I did see them."

"And they were white ti | n—good teeth?"
"Oh, beauties. White a | even as a die."
"Sir Karl's teeth are · | te and even," nodded Miss Blake to herself. "H | Mrs. Grey any visitors while you were there, nurse

"Never a one. Never | soul came inside the gates, good or bad, but the doctor. I don't fancy the lady has made friends in the place at all, ma'am. She likes to keep herself to herself, Ann Hopley thinks, while Mr. Grey's away."

"Oh, naturally," said Miss Blake. And she dismissed the woman.

The Widow Jinks had a surprise that night. Mr.

Strange, hitherto so quiet and well conducted, asked for the latch-key! She could not forbear a caution as she gave it him: not to stay out too late on account of his health. He laughed pleasantly in answer; saying he expected a friend down by the last train from London, and might stay out late with him.

But he never went near the station, and he met no friend. Keeping as much in the shades of night as the very bright moon allowed him to do, Mr. Strange arrived by a roundabout way at the gate of the Maze, and let himself in with a master-key.

"The dolt I was, never to have suspected this shut-in place before!" he exclaimed. "Salter is lying here in concealment: there can be no doubt of it: and if his career's at an end he may thank his own folly in having allowed himself to be seen by the woman, Chaffen. Wonder who the sick lady is? Perhaps his wife: perhaps not. And now—how to get through this maze that they talk of? Knowing something of mazes, I daresay I shall accomplish it without trouble."

And he did. His keen intelligence, sharpened no doubt by experience, enabled him, if not to hit upon the clue, at least to get through the maze. A small compass was hanging to his watch-guard, and he lighted a match frequently to consult it. So he got through. He regarded the house from all points; he penetrated to the outer path or circle, and went round and round it: he made, so to say, the outer premises his own. Then he went through the maze to reconnoitre the house again.

It lay quiet, steeped in the moonlight. He stood at the back of the lawn, against the laurel trees that were beyond the flower beds, and gazed at it. In one of the rooms a night-light was burning faintly, and he fancied he could hear the continuous wail of an infant. To make sure whether it was so, or not—though in truth it mattered not to him, and was a very probable thing to happen—he stood forward a little on the lawn: but as that brought him into the moonlight, he retreated into the shade again. Most of the windows had blinds or curtains drawn before them; the only one that had none was the casement over the portico. Mr. Strange stood there as if rooted to the spot, making his silent observations.

"Yes; that's where my gentleman is lying concealed, safe enough! Safe enough as *he* thinks. There may be some difficulty in as safely unearthing him. He'd not dare to be here without facilities for guarding against surprise and for getting away on the first sound of the alarm bugle. This is a queer old house: there may be all kinds of hiding places in it. I must go to work cautiously, and it may be a long job. Suppose I look again to the door fastenings?"

The moon was beginning to wane when the detective officer with his false key got out again; and he thought he had his work tolerably well cut out to his hand.

The faint wailing had not been fancy. For the first week or two of the child's life it had seemed to thrive well, small though it was; but, after that, it began to be a little delicate, and would sometimes wail as though in pain. On this night the child—who slept with its mother—woke up and began its wail. Ann Hopley, whom the slightest noise awoke, hearing that her mistress did not seem to be able to soothe it, left her own bed to try and do so. Presently, in going to fetch some medicine-cordial for the child, she had to pass the casement window in the passage; the one that was uncurtained. The exceeding beauty of the night struck her, and she paused to look out upon it, the old black shawl she had thrown on being drawn closely round her. The grass shone in the moonlight; some of the leaves of the laurels flickered white in its rays. At that self-same moment, as the woman looked, some movement directed her attention to these very laurels: and to her utter horror she thought she saw a man standing there, apparently watching the house.

The sickness of intense fear seized upon her as she drew aside—but the black shawl and the small diamond panes of the casement window had prevented her from being observed. Yes: she was not mistaken. The man came forth for an instant into the moonlight, and then went back again. Ann Hopley's fear turned her heart to sickness. Her first impulse was to rush on through the passages and arouse Sir Adam Andinnian. Her second impulse was to wait and watch. She remembered her master's most dangerous fiery temperament, and the pistols he kept always loaded. This intruding man might be but some wretched night marauder, who had stolen in after the fruit. Watching there, she saw him presently go round in the direction of the fruit-trees, and concluded that her surmise was correct.

So she held her tongue to her master and mistress. The latter she would not alarm; the former she dared not, lest another night he should take up his stand at the window, pistol in hand. Two things puzzled her the next morning: the one was, how the man could have got in; the other, that neither fruit nor flowers seemed to have been taken.

That same day, upon going to the gate to answer a ring, she found herself confronted by a strange gentleman, who said he had called from hearing the house was to let, and he wished to look at it. Ann Hopley thought this rather strange. She assured him it was a mistake: that the house was not to let: that Mrs. Grey had no intention of leaving. When he pressed to go in and just look at the house, "in case it should be let later," she persisted in denying him admittance, urging her mistress's present sick state as a reason for keeping out all visitors.

"Is Mr. Grey still at home?" then asked the applicant.

"Mr. Grey has not been at home," replied Ann Hopley. "My mistress is alone."

"Oh, indeed! Not been here at all?"

"No, sir. I don't know how soon he may be coming. He is abroad on his travels."

"What gentleman is it, then, who has been staying here lately?"

Ann Hopley felt inwardly all of a twitter. Outwardly she was quietly self-possessed.

"No gentleman has been here at all, sir. You must be mistaking the house for some other one, I think. This is the Maze."

"A lady and gentleman and two servants, I understand, are living here."

"It is quite a mistake, sir. My mistress and us two servants live here—me and my husband—but that's all. Mr. Grey has not been here since we came to the place."

"Now that's a disappointment to me," cried the stranger. "I have lost sight of a friend of mine, named Grey, for the past year or two, and was hoping I might find him here. You are sure you don't know when Mr. Grey may be expected?"

"Quite sure, sir. My mistress does not know, herself."

The stranger stepped back from the gate to take his departure. In manner he was a very pleasant man, and his questions had been put with easy courtesy.

"And you are equally sure the house is not about to be vacated?"

"I feel sure of this, that if Mrs. Grey had thoughts of vacating it, she would have informed me. But in regard to any point connected with the house, sir, you had better apply to the landlord, Sir Karl Andinnian."

"Thank you; yes, that may be the best plan. Good morning," he added, taking off his hat with something of French civility.

"Don't think she is to be bribed," thought he as he walked away. "At least not easily. Perhaps I may in time work my way on to it."

Ann Hopley, locking the gate with double strength —at least, in imagination—pushed through the maze without well knowing whether she was on her head or her heels, so entirely had terror overtaken her. In the height and shape of this man, who had been thus questioning her, she fancied she traced a resemblance to the one who was watching the house in the night. What if they were the same?

"The end is coming!" she murmured, clasping her faithful hands. "As sure as my poor master is alive, the end is coming."

Not to her master or his wife, but to Karl Andinnian, did she impart all this. It happened that Karl went over to the Maze that evening. Ann Hopley followed him out when he departed, and told him of it amidst the trees.

It startled him in a more painful degree even than it had startled her: for, oh, what were her interests in the matter as compared with his?

"Inside the grounds!—watching the house at night!" he repeated with a gasp.

"Indeed, indeed he was, sir!"

"But who is it?"

"I don't know," said Ann; "I hoped it was only some thief who had come after the fruit: I thought he might have got over from the fields by means of a high ladder. That would have been nothing. But if the man who came to the gate to-day is the same man, it must mean mischief."

"You have not told my brother?"

"How could I dare to tell him, sir? He might watch for the man; and, if he came another night, shoot him. That would make things worse."

"With a vengeance," thought Karl. What was there to do? What could he do? Karl Andinnian went out, the question beating itself into his brain. Why, there seemed nothing for it but to wait and watch. He took off his hat and raised his bare head to the summer sky, in which some stars were twinkling, wishing he was there, in that blessed heaven above where no pain can come. What with one tribulation and another, earth was growing for him a hard rest-ing-place.

CHAPTER VI.

At Afternoon Service.

THE still quietness of the Sabbath morning shed its peace over Foxwood. Within the Court of that name—where the lawns were green and level, and the sweet flowers exhaled their perfume, and a tree here and there was already putting on its autumn tints—the aspect of peace seemed to be more especially ex-haled.

The windows of the rooms stood open. Inside one of them the breakfast was on the table yet, Miss Blake seated at it. Matins at St. Jerome's had been un-usually prolonged; and Sir Karl and Lady Andinnian had taken breakfast when she got home. The Reverend Damon Puff had now come to help Mr. Cattacomb; imparting to St. Jerome's an additional attraction.

While Miss Blake took her breakfast, Lucy went out amidst her flowers. The scent of the mignonette filled the air, the scarlet of the geraniums made the beds brilliant. Lucy wore one of her simple muslin dresses; it had sprigs of green upon it—for the weather was still that of summer, though the season was not, and the nightingales were no longer heard of an evening. Trinity church boasted a set of sweet-toned bells, and they were ringing on the air. When the Sacrament was administered—the first Sunday in each month—they generally did ring before service. This was the first Sunday in September. Lucy stooped to pick some mignonette as she listened to the bells. She was getting to look what she was—worn and unhappy. Nothing could be much less satisfactory than her life: it seemed to herself sometimes that she was like a poor flower withering for lack of sunshine. For the first time for several weeks she meant, that day, to stay for the after-service: her mind had really been in too great a chaos before: but this week she had been schooling herself in preparation for it, and praying and striving to feel tranquil.

Karl came round the terrace from his room and crossed the lawn. In his hand he held a most exquisite rose, and offered it to her. She thanked him as she took it. In manner they were always courteous to one another.

"What a lovely day it is!" she said. "So calm and still."

"And not quite so hot as it was a few weeks ago," he replied. "Those must be Mr. Sumnor's bells."

"Yes. I wish they rang every Sunday. I think—it may be all fancy, but I can't help thinking it—that people would go to church more heartily if the bells rang for them as they are ringing now, instead of calling them with the usual ding-dong."

"There is something melancholy in the ringing of bells," observed Karl, in abstraction.

"But, when the heart is in itself melancholy, the melancholy of the bells brings to it a feeling of soothing consolation," was Lucy's hasty answer. And the next moment she felt sorry that she had said it. Never, willingly, did she allude to aught that could touch on their estrangement.

"Talking of church, Lucy," resumed Karl, in a

different and almost confidential tone, "I am beginning to feel really annoyed about that place, St. Jerome's. They are going too far. I wish you would speak a word of caution to Theresa."

"I—I scarcely like to," answered Lucy, after a pause, her delicate cheek faintly flushing, for she was conscious that she had not dared to talk much on any score with Theresa lately, lest Theresa might allude to the subject of the Maze. Fearing that she avoided her when she could, so as to give no opportunity for private conversation. "She is so much older and wiser than I am—"

"Wiser?" interrupted Karl. "I think not. In all things, save one, you have ten times the good plain sense that she has. That one thing, Lucy, I shall never be able to understand, or account for, to my dying day,"

"And, moreover, I was going to add," continued Lucy, flushing deeper at the allusion, "I am quite sure that Theresa would not heed me, whatever I might say."

"Well, I don't know what is to be done. People are mocking at St. Jerome's and its frequenters' folly more than I care to hear, and blame me for allowing it to go on. I should not like to be written to by the Bishop of the Diocese."

"*You* written to!" cried Lucy in surprise.

"It is within the range of possibility. The place is on the Andinnian land."

"I think, were I you, I would speak to Mr. Cattacomb."

Karl made a wry face. He did not like the man. Moreover he fancied—as did Lucy in regard to Miss

Blake—that whatever he might say would make no impression. But for this he had spoken to him before. But, now that another was come and the folly was being doubled, it lay in his duty to remonstrate. The whole village gossiped and laughed; Sir Adam was furious. Ann Hopley carried the gossip home to her master—which of course lost nothing in the transit—and he abused Karl for not interfering.

They went to church together, Karl and his wife. It was a thinner congregation than ordinary. Being a grand field-day at St. Jerome's with procession and banners, some of them had gone off thither as to a show. Kneeling by her husband's side in their pew, Lucy felt the influence of the holy place, and peace seemed to steal down upon her. Margaret Sumnor was opposite, looking at her: and in Margaret's face there was a strange, pitying compassion, for she saw that that other face was becoming sadder day by day.

It was a plain, good sermon: Mr. Sumnor's sermons always were: its subject the blessings promised for the next world; its text, "And God shall wipe away all tears from their eyes." The tears rose to Lucy's eyes as she listened. Karl listened too, wrapt in the words. Just for the quarter of an hour it lasted—the sermons were always short the first Sunday in the month—both of them seemed to have passed beyond their cares into Heaven. It almost seemed to matter little what the trouble of this short span on earth might be, with that glorious fruition to come hereafter.

"I am going to stay," whispered Lucy, as the service ended. A hint to him that he might depart without her.

Karl nodded, but made no other answer. The

congregation filed out, and still he sat on. Lucy wondered. All in a moment it flashed upon her that he also must be going to stay. Her face turned crimson: the question, was he fit for it, involuntarily suggesting itself.

He did stay. They knelt side by side together and received the elements of Christ's holy Ordinance. After that, Karl was on his knees in his pew until the end, buried as it seemed in beseeching prayer. It was impossible for Lucy to believe that he could be living an ill life of any kind at that present time—whatever he might have done.

He held out his arm as they quitted the church, and she took it. It was not often that she did. Thus they walked home together, exchanging a sentence or two between whiles. Karl went at once to his room, saying he should not take anything to eat: he had a headache. Miss Blake had "snatched a morsel," and had gone out again to hear the children's catechism, Hewitt said. One thing must be conceded—that she was zealous in her duties.

And so Lucy was alone. She took a "morsel" too, and went to sit under the acacia tree. When an hour or so had passed, Karl came up, and surprised her with tears on her cheeks.

"Is it any new grief?" he asked.

"No," she answered, half lost in the sorrow her thoughts had been abandoned to, and neglecting her usual reticence. "I was but thinking that I am full young to have so much unhappiness."

"We both have enough of that, I expect. I know I have. But yours is partly of your own making, Lucy; mine is not."

"Not of his own making!" ran her thoughts. "Of his own planning, at any rate." But she would not say a word to mar the semi-peace which pervaded, or ought to pervade, their hearts that day.

"That was a nice sermon this morning," he resumed, sitting down by her on the bench.

"Very. I almost forgot that we were not close to Heaven: I forgot that we had, speaking according to earth's probabilities, years and years and years to live out here first."

"We shall have to live them out, Lucy, I suppose —by Heaven's will. The prospect of it looks anything but consolatory."

"I thought you seemed very sad," she remarked in a low tone. "I had no idea you were going to stay."

"*Sad!*" He laid his hand upon her knee, not in any particular affection, but to give emphasis to his word. "Sad is not the term for it, Lucy. Misery, rather; dread; despair—the worst word you will. I wished, with a yearning wish, that I was in Mr. Sumnor's heaven—the heaven he described—if only some others could go before me, so that I did not leave them here."

Lucy wondered of whom he spoke. She thought it must lie between herself and Mrs. Grey. Karl had been thinking of his poor proscribed brother, for whom the glad earth could never open her arms freely again.

"I think what Mr. Sumnor said must be true," resumed Lucy. "That the more sorrow we have to endure in this world, the brighter will be our entrance to the next. I am sure he has a great deal of sorrow himself: whenever he preaches of it he seems to feel it so deeply."

Karl appeared not to hear. He was gazing upwards, a look of patient pain on his pale face. There were moments—and this was one—when Lucy's arms and heart alike yearned to encircle him, and ask for his love to be hers again. She cared for him still—oh, how much!—and wished she could awake to find the Maze, and all the trouble connected with it, a hideous dream.

They sat on, saying nothing. The birds sang as in spring, the trees waved gently beneath the blue sky, and the green grass was grateful for the eye to rest upon. On the handsome house lay the glad sun: not a sound of every-day labour, in-doors or out, broke the stillness. All was essentially peace. Except—except within their own wearied breasts.

The bell of Trinity church rang out for service, arousing Lucy from her reverie. She said she should like to attend it.

"What! this afternoon?" exclaimed Karl. "You are not accustomed to go in the afternoon."

That was true. The heat of the summer weather had been almost unbearable, and Lucy had not ventured to church in it more than once a day.

"It is cooler now," she answered. "And I always like to go if I can when I have stayed for the communion."

But Karl held back from it: rather, Lucy thought, in an unaccountable manner, for he was ever ready to second any wish of hers. He did not seem inclined to go forth again, and said, as a plea of excuse, that he preferred to retain the impression of the morning's sermon on his mind, rather than let it give place to an inferior one. His head was aching badly.

"I do not ask you to come," said Lucy, gently. "I should like to go myself, but I can go quite well alone."

When she came down with her things on, however, she found him ready also; and they set off together.

It may be questioned, though, whether Lucy would have gone had she foreseen what was to happen. In the middle of the service, while the "Magnificat" was being sung, a respectable, staid woman entered the church with an infant in her arms. A beautifully dressed infant. Its long white robe elaborately embroidered, its delicate blue cloak of surpassing richness, its veil of lace dainty as a gossamer thread. The attire, not often seen at Foxwood, caught Lucy's eye, and she wondered who the infant was. It seemed to her that she had seen the nurse's face before, and began to ransack her memory. In an instant it flashed on her with a shock—it was the servant at the Maze.

She turned her eyes on her husband: not intentionally, but in an uncontrollable impulse. Karl was looking furtively at the woman and child—a red flush dyeing his face. Poor Lucy's benefit in the afternoon service was over.

The baby had come to be baptised. Ann Hopley sat down on a bench to which she was shown, just underneath the Andinnian pew. Towards the close of the second lesson, the clerk advanced to her, and entered on a whispered colloquy. Every word of which was distinct to Karl and Lucy.

"Have you brought this infant to be christened?"

"To be baptised," replied Ann Hopley. "Not christened."

The clerk paused. "It's not usual with us to baptise children unless they are so delicate as to render it necessary," said he. "We prefer to christen at once."

"But this child is delicate," she answered. "My mistress, who is herself still very ill, has got nervous about it and wishes it done. The christening must be left until she is better."

"It's the baby at the Maze, I think?"

"Yes. Mrs. Grey's."

The second lesson came to an end. Mr. Sumnor's voice ceased, and he stepped out of the reading desk to perform the baptism. Ann Hopley had drawn away the veil, and Lucy saw the child's face; a fair, sweet, delicate little face, calm and placid in its sleep.

The congregation, a very small one always in the afternoon, rose up, and stood on tiptoe to see and hear. Mr. Sumnor, standing at the font, took the child in his arms.

"Name this child."

"Charles," was the audible and distinct reply of Ann Hopley. And Lucy Andinnian turned red and white; she thought it was, so to say, named after her husband. As indeed was the case.

The child was brought back to the bench again; and the afternoon service went on to its close. There was no sermon. When Lucy rose from her knees, the woman and baby had gone. Karl offered her his arm as they quitted the church, but she would not take it. They walked home side by side, saying never a word to each other.

"*That* was the reason why he wanted to keep me away from church this afternoon!" was Lucy's indignant thought. "And to dress it up like that! How, how shall I go on, and bear?"

But Lucy was mistaken. Karl had known no more about it than she, and was struck with astonishment to see Ann Hopley come in. It arose exactly as the woman had stated. During the night the child had seemed so ill that its mother had become nervously uneasy because it was not baptised, and insisted upon its being brought to church that afternoon.

Meanwhile Ann Hopley had hurried homewards. Partly to get out before the rest and avoid observation, partly because she wanted to be back with her mistress. After passing the Court gates, in traversing the short space of road between them and the Maze, she encountered Miss Blake coming home from St. Jerome's. Miss Blake, seeing a baby sumptuously attired, and not at the moment recognizing Ann Hopley in her bonnet, crossed the road to inquire whose child it was. Then she saw it was the servant at the Maze: but she stopped all the same.

"I should like to take a peep at the baby, nurse."

"It's asleep, ma'am, and I am in a hurry," was the answer, given in all truthfulness, not in discourtesy; for it must be remembered than Ann Hopley had no grounds to suspect that this lady took any special interest in affairs at the Maze. "It slept all through its baptism."

"Oh it has been baptised, has it! At Mr. Sumnor's church?"

"Yes, at Mr. Sumnor's. There is no other church in the place but that," added the woman, totally ignoring St. Jerome's, but not thinking to give offence thereby.

Miss Blake put aside the lace and looked at the sleeping baby. "What is its name, nurse?"

"Charles."

"Oh," said Miss Blake, the same notion striking her, as to the name, that had struck Lucy. "It is Mr. Grey's name I suppose—or something like it."

"No, it is not Mr. Grey's name," replied the woman.

"Who is the baby considered like?" went on Miss Blake, still regarding it. "Its father or its mother?"

"It's not much like anybody, that I see, ma'am. The child's too young to show any likeness yet."

"I declare that I see a likeness to Sir Karl Andinnian!" cried Miss Blake, speaking partly upon impulse. For, in looking whether she could trace this likeness, her fancy seemed to show her that it was there. "What a strange thing, nurse!"

With one startled gaze into Miss Blake's eyes, Ann Hopley went off in a huff. The suggestion had not been palatable.

"If he's like Sir Karl, I must never bring him abroad again, lest by that means suspicion should come to my master," she thought, as she took the gate key from her pocket and let herself in. "But I don't believe it can be: for I'm sure there's not a bit of resemblance between the two brothers!"

"How plain it all is!" sighed Miss Blake, meekly regarding the cross upon her ivory prayer-book as she went over to the Court. "And that ridiculously simple Lucy does not see it! Bartimeus was blind, and so is she. He could see nothing until his eyes were opened: her eyes have been opened and yet she will not see!"

No, Miss Blake, neither could the self-righteous Pharisee see, when he went into the Temple to thank God that he was better than other men, and especially than the poor publican.

St. Jerome's was prospering. It had taken—as Tom Pepp the bell-ringer phrased it—a spurt. A rich maiden lady of uncertain age, fascinated by the Reverend Guy Cattacomb's oratory and spectacles, came over once a day in her brougham from Basham, and always put a substantial coin into the offertory-bag during the service.

The Reverend Damon Puff found favour too. He had a beautiful black moustache, which he was given to stroke lovingly at all kinds of unseasonable times, his hair was parted down the middle carefully, back and front, and he had an interesting lisp: otherwise he was a harmless kind of young man, devotedly attentive to the ladies, and not overburdened with brains. Mr. Puff had taken up his abode for the present at Basham, and came over in the omnibus. Two omnibus-loads of fair worshippers arrived now daily: there was frightful scuffling among them to get into the one that contained the parson.

But, flourishing though St. Jerome's was, people were talking about it in anything but a reverend manner. Sir Karl Andinnian was blamed for allowing it to go on unchecked—as he told his wife. Had Karl been a perfectly free man, unswayed by that inward and ever-present dread, he had certainly put a stop to it long ago, or obliged Farmer Truefit to do so; but as it was, he had done nothing. Not a single male person attended the services; and most of the ladies who did so were in their teens, or not much beyond them. Karl felt that this was not as it should be: but he had made no move to alter it. The sensitive fear of making enemies swayed him. Not fear for his own sake, but lest it should in some way draw observation on the Maze and on him whom it contained. When the mind is weighed down with an awful secret, danger seems to lie in everything, reasonable and unreasonable. But Karl found he must do something.

A comic incident happened one day. There came a lady to Foxwood Court, sending in her card as "Mrs. Brown" and asking to see Sir Karl Andinnian. Sir Karl found she was from Basham. She had come over to pray him, she said with tears in her eyes, that he would put a stop to the goings-on at St. Jerome's and shut up the place. She had two daughters who had been drawn into its vortex and she could not draw them out again. Twice and three times every day of their lives did they come over to Foxwood, by rail, omnibus, or on foot; their whole thoughts and days were absorbed by St. Jerome's: by the services, by cleaning the church, by Mr. Cattacomb's lectures at home, or in helping Mr. Puff teach the children. Sir Karl replied that he did not know what he could do in the matter, and intimated very courteously that the more effectual remedy in regard to the Miss Browns would be for Mrs. Brown to keep the young ladies at home. They would not be kept at home, Mrs. Brown said with a burst of sobs; they had learnt to set her at defiance: and—she begged to hint to Sir Karl—that in her opinion it was not quite the right thing for a young girl to be closeted with a young man, for half an hour at a time, under plea of confession, though the man did write himself priest. What on earth had they got to confess, Mrs. Brown wanted to know, becoming a little heated with the argument: if they'd confess how undutiful they were to her, their mother, perhaps some good might come of it.

Well, this occurred. Sir Karl got rid of Mrs. Brown; but he could not shut his ears to the public chatter; and he was conscious that something or other ought to be done, or attempted. He could not see why people should expect that it lay in his hands, and he certainly did not know whether he could effect anything, even with all the good will in the world. Mr. Cattacomb might civilly laugh at him. Not knowing whether any power lay with him, or not, he felt inclined to put the question to the only lawyer Foxwood contained—Mr. St. Henry.

But oh, what was this petty grievance to the great trouble ever lying upon him? As nothing. The communication made to him by Ann Hopley, of the night watches she had seen, of the stranger who afterwards presented himself at the Maze gate with his questions, was so much addition to his tormenting dread. Just about this time, too, it came to his knowledge through Hewitt, that inquiries were being made as to the Maze. Private, whispered inquiries, not apparently with any particular object; more in the way of idle gossip. Who was putting them? Karl could not learn. Hewitt did not know who, but was sure of the fact. The story told by Mrs. Chaffen, of the gentleman she had seen at the Maze the night she entered it, and "which it was at her wits' end to know whether he were a ghost, or not," was circulating round the village and reached

Karl's ears, to his intense annoyance and dismay. Added to all this, was the doubt that lay within himself, as to whether Smith the agent was Philip Salter, and what his course in the matter should be. In his own mind he felt persuaded that it was Salter, and no other; but the persuasion was scarcely sufficiently assured to induce him to act. He felt the danger of speaking a word of accusation to Smith wrongfully— the danger it might bring on his brother—and therefore he, in this, vacillated and hesitated, and did nothing.

Do not reproach Karl Andinnian with being an unstable or vacillating man. He was nothing of the kind. But he was living under exceptional circumstances, and there seemed to be risk to his unfortunate brother on the left hand and on the right. If discovery should chance to supervene through any rash step of his, Karl's, remorse would never cease from racking him to the end of his bitter life.

CHAPTER VII.

At Lawyer St. Henry's.

LAWYER ST. HENRY sat at his well-spread breakfast table. He was a little man with a bald head and good-natured face, who enjoyed his breakfast as well as all his other meals. Since his nieces had considered it necessary to their spiritual welfare to attend matins at St. Jerome's, the lawyer had been condemned to breakfast alone. The sun shone on the street, and Mr. St. Henry sat in a room that faced it. Through the wire blinds he could see all the passings and repassings of his neighbours; which he very well liked

to do; as well as the doings of Paradise Row opposite.

"Hallo!" he cried, catching sight of a face at Mrs.
Jinks's parlour window, "Cattacomb's not gone out this
morning! Puff must have come over early to officiate.
Thinks he'll take it easy, I suppose, now he's got an
underling: no blame to him, either. The girls will be
dished for once. Nobody goes down with 'em like
Cattacomb."

Laughing a little at the thought, he helped himself
to a portion of a tempting-looking cutlet surrounded
with mushrooms. This being nearly despatched, he
had leisure to look abroad again and make his mental
comments.

"There goes the doctor: he's out early this morning. Going to see old Etheredge, perhaps: wonder
how the old fellow is. And there's Mother Jinks
taking in a sweetbread. Must be for the parson's
breakfast. Sweetbreads are uncommonly good, too:
I'll have one myself to-morrow morning if it can be
got. Why, here comes Sir Karl Andinnian! *He* is
out early, too. That young man looks to me as
though he had some care upon him. It's a nice
countenance; very: and if—I declare he is coming
here! What on earth can he want?"

Sir Karl Andinnian was ringing the door-bell. It
has been already said that the lawyer's offices were in
Basham, for which place he generally started as soon
as breakfast was over. Therefore, if any client wished
to see him at Foxwood, it had to be early in the
morning or late in the evening. This was known and
understood.

Sir Karl was shown in, Mr. St. Henry glancing at

his breakfast-table and the three or four dirty plates upon it. He had finished now, and they sat down together at the window. Sir Karl, not to detain him unnecessarily, entered at once upon the question he had come to ask—Had he, or had he not, power to do anything with St. Jerome's? And the lawyer laughed a little; for St. Jerome's afforded him fun, rather than otherwise.

"Of course, Sir Karl, if Truefit choose to warn them off the land, he could do it," was the lawyer's reply. "Not without notice, though, I think: I don't know what the agreement was. As to yourself—well I am not clear whether you could do anything: I should like to see Truefit's lease before giving an opinion. But, if they were shut out of St. Jerome's to-day, they'd contrive to start another place to-morrow."

"That is quite likely," said Karl.

"My advice to you is this, Sir Karl: don't bother yourself about it," said the easy-going lawyer. "People expect you to interfere? Never mind that: let them expect. The thing will die away of itself when winter comes. Once the frost and snow set in, the girls, silly monkeys, won't be trapesing to St. Jerome's; neither will they come jinketing over by omnibusfuls from Basham. Wait and shut it up then. If you attempt to do it now, you will meet with wide opposition: by waiting, you may do it almost without any."

"You really think so!"

"I am nearly sure so," said the hearty lawyer. "There's nothing like bad weather for stopping expeditions of chivalry. But for having had the continuous sunshine the summer has given us, St. Jerome's would not have been the success it is."

"They have dressed Tom Pepp in a conical cap, and put a red cross all down his back outside," said Sir Karl.

The lawyer burst into a laugh. "*I* know," he said. "I hear of the vagaries from my nieces. It's fun for me. They go in for them wholesale, and come home with their heads full."

"But it is not religion, Mr. St. Henry."

"Bless me, no. Religion? The girls may give it that name; and perhaps one or two among them may be earnest enough in thinking it so; the rest are only after Cattacomb."

"There's another one now, I hear. One Puff."

"And a fine puff of wind *he* is. Got no more brains than a gander. I'll see Truefit and inquire what agreement it was he made with them, if you like, Sir Karl; but I should certainly recommend you to leave the matter alone a little longer."

Sir Karl thought he would accept the advice; and got up to leave. He often saw Truefit about the land, and could take an opportunity of questioning him himself. As he stood for a moment at the window, there passed down the middle of the street a stranger, walking slowly; that is, a stranger to Karl. It was Mr. Strange.

Now it happened that Karl had never yet seen this man—at least, he had never noticed him. For the detective, being warned by Grimley that Sir Karl had, or seemed to have, some reason for screening Salter—had kept out of Sir Karl's way. He thought it would not conduce at all to his success to let Sir

Karl know he was down there on the scent. There- fore, whenever he had observed Sir Karl coming along —and he had kept his eyes sharply open—he had popped into a shop, or drawn hehind a hedge, or got over a style into another field. And Karl, in his mind's abstraction—for it nearly always was abstracted, lost in its own fear and pain—had not thought of looking out gratuitously for strangers. But, standing up at the lawyer's window, the street close before him, he could not fail to observe those who passed up and down: and his attention was at once drawn to this man.

"Who is that?" he asked.

"That! oh, that's a Mr. Strange," said the lawyer, laughing again—and in his laugh this time there was something significant. "At least, that's his name *here*."

"And not elsewhere?"

"I fancy not."

"Is he staying at Foxwood? What is he doing here?"

"He is certainly staying at Foxwood. As to his business, I conclude it is something in the private detective line, Sir Karl."

Mr. Strange, whose attention in passing had been directed to some matter on the other side of the way and not to the lawyer's window, consequently he did not know that he was being watched, had halted a little lower down to speak to the landlord of the Red Lion. All in a moment, as Karl looked at him, the notion flashed into his mind that this man bore a strong resemblance to the description given by Ann Hopley of the man who had invaded the Maze. The

notion came to him in the self-same moment that the
words of the lawyer fell on his ears—"His business, I
conclude, is something in the private detective line."
What with the notion, and what with the words, Karl
Andinnian fell into a confused inward tumult, that
caused his heart's blood to stop, and then course
wildly on. Business at Foxwood, connected with detectives, must have reference to his brother, and to
him alone.

"A slight-made gentleman with a fair face and
light curly hair, looking about thirty," had been Ann
Hopley's description; it answered in every particular
to the man Karl was gazing at; gazing until he watched
him out of sight. Lawyer St. Henry, naturally observant, thought his guest stared after the man as though
he held some peculiar interest in him.

"Do you know who that man really is, Mr. St.
Henry?"

"Well, I'll tell you, Sir Karl. No reason why I
should not, for I have not been told to keep it a secret. Some little time back, my nieces grew full of
the new lodger at Mrs. Jinks's; they were talking of
him incessantly: A gentleman reading divinity——"

"Why, that's Mr. Cattacomb," interrupted Sir Karl.
"He lodges at Mrs. Jinks's."

"Not that ladies' idiot," cried the lawyer, rather
roughly. "I beg your pardon, Sir Karl, but the
Reverend Guy sometimes puts me out of patience.
This man has the upper rooms, Cattacomb the
lower——"

"But I—I thought that was a boy: a lad at his
studies," reiterated Karl, in some perplexity. "I assumed him to be a pupil of Cattacomb's."

"It is the man you have just watched down the street, Sir Karl. Well, to go on. My nieces were always talking of this new gentleman, a Mr. Strange, who had come to Foxwood to get up his health, and to read up for some divinity examination. That was *their* account. They said so much about him that I got curious myself: it was a new face, you see, Sir Karl, and girls go wild over that. One morning when I was starting for the office, the gig at the door, Jane ran out to me. 'Uncle,' she said, 'that's Mr. Strange coming down Mrs. Jinks's steps now: you can see him if you look.' I did look, Sir Karl, and saw the gentleman you have just seen pass. His face struck me at once as one that I was familiar with, though at the moment I could not tell where I had seen him. Remembrance came to me while I looked — and I knew him for an officer connected with the detective force at Scotland Yard."

Karl drew a long breath. He was listening greedily.

"About a year ago," resumed the lawyer, "my agent in London, Mr. Blair, had occasion to employ a detective upon some matter he was engaged in. I was in London for a few days at that time, and saw the man twice at Blair's—and knew him again now. It was this same Mr. Strange."

"And you say Strange is not his right name?"

"No, it's not."

"What is the right one?"

"Well, I can't tell you the right one, Sir Karl, for I cannot remember it. I am sure of one thing—that it was not Strange. It was a longer name, and I think rather a peculiar name; but I can't hit upon it.

He must be down here on some private business, and has no doubt his own reasons for keeping incog. I recollect Blair told me he was one of the astutest officers in the detective force."

"Has he recognised you?"

"He could not recognise me," said Mr. St. Henry, "I don't suppose he ever saw me to notice me. Each time that he called on Blair, it happened that I was in the front office with the clerks when he passed through it. He was not likely to have observed me."

"You have not spoken to him, then?"

"Not I."

"And—you don't know what his business here may be."

"Not at all. Can't guess at it. It concerns neither you nor me, Sir Karl, and therefore I have not scrupled to tell *you* so much. Of course you will not repeat it again. If he chooses to remain unknown here, and pass himself off for a student of divinity —doubtless for sufficient reasons—I should not be justified in proclaiming that he is a London detective, and so possibly ruin his game."

Sir Karl made a motion of acquiescence. His brain was whirling in no measured degree. He connected the presence of this detective at Foxwood with the paragraph that had appeared in the newspaper touching the escaped convict from Portland Island.

"Would there—would there be any possibility of getting to know his business?" he dreamily asked.

"Not the slightest, I should say, unless he chooses directly to disclose it. Why? You cannot have any interest in it, I presume, Sir Karl, whatever it may be."

"No, no; certainly not," replied Sir Karl, awaking

to the fact that he was on dangerous ground. "One is apt to get curious on hearing of business connected with detectives," he added, laughing; "as interested as one does in a good novel."

"Ay, true," said the lawyer, unsuspiciously.

"At Mrs. Jinks's he is lodging, is he?" absently remarked Karl, turning to depart; and inwardly marvelling how he could have caught up the notion that the person there was only a lad, a pupil of Cattacomb's.

"At Mrs. Jinks's, Sir Karl; got her drawing-room. Wonder how the Rev. Guy would feel if he knew the man over his head was a cute detective officer?"

"I suppose the officer cannot be looking after *him*," jested Sir Karl. "St. Jerome's is the least sound thing we know at Foxwood."

The lawyer laughed a hearty laugh as he attended Sir Karl to the door; at which Mr. St. Henry's gig was now waiting to take him into Basham.

It was not a hot morning, but Karl Andinnian took off his hat repeatedly on the way home to wipe his brow. The dreadful catastrophe he had been fearing for his unfortunate brother seemed to be drawing ominously near.

"But for that confounded Smith, Adam might have been away before," he groaned. "I know he might. Smith——"

And there Karl stopped; stopped as though his speech had been suddenly cut off. For a new idea had darted into his mind, and he stayed to ponder it.

Was this detective officer down here to look after Philip Salter?—and not after Adam at all?

A conviction, that it must be so, took possession

of him; and in the first flush of it the relief was inexpressibly great. But he remembered again the midnight watcher of the Maze and the morning visit following it; and his hopes fell back to zero. That this was the same man who had watched there could remain no doubt whatever.

Passing into his own room, Karl sat down and strove to think the matter out. He could arrive at no certain conclusion. One minute he felt sure the object was his brother; the next, that it was only Salter.

But, in any case, allowing that it was Salter, there must be danger to Adam. If this cunning London detective were to get into the Maze premises again and *see* the prisoner there, all would be over. The probability was, that he was personally acquainted with the noted criminal Adam Andinnian: and it might be, that he had gained a suspicion that Adam Andinnian was alive.

One thing Karl could not conceal from himself—and it brought to him a rush of remorse. If the detective had come down after Salter, he—he, Karl—must have been the means of bringing him there.

But for that unpleasant consciousness he would have gone straight off to Smith the agent, and told him of the trouble that was threatening Adam, and said, "What shall we do in it; how screen him?" But he did not dare. He did not dare to make a move or stir a step that might bring Smith and the detective in contact. He could not quite understand why, if Smith were really Salter, the detective had not already pounced upon him: but he thought it quite likely that Smith might be keeping himself out of sight. In short, the thoughts and surmises that crossed and re-crossed Karl's brain, some probable enough, others quite improbable, were legion. Not for the world, if he could help it, would he aid—further than he had perhaps unhappily aided—in denouncing Salter; and knowing what he had done, he could not face the man. He had never intended to harm him.

So there Karl was, overwhelmed with this new perplexity, and not able to stir in it. He saw not what he could do. To address the detective himself, and say whom are you after, would be worse than folly; of all people he, Karl Andinnian, must keep aloof from him. It might be that there was only a *suspicion* about Adam's being alive, that they were trying to find out whether it was so or not. For him, Karl, to interfere or show interest, would help it on.

But this suspense was well nigh intolerable. Karl could not live under it. Something he must do. If only he could set the question at rest, as to which of the two criminals the detective was after, it would be a good deal gained. And he could only do that by applying to Mr. Burtenshaw. It was not sure that he would, but there was a chance that he might.

Lady Andinnian was in her little sitting-room upstairs, when she heard Sir Karl's footstep. He entered without knocking: which was very unusual. For they had grown ceremonious one with another since the estrangement and knocked at doors and asked permission to enter, as strangers. Lucy was adding up her housekeeping bills.

"I am going to London, Lucy. Some business has arisen that I am very anxious about, and I must go up at once."

7*

"Business with Plunkett and Plunkett?" she asked, a slight sarcasm in her tone, though Karl detected it not, as she remembered the plea he had urged for the journey once before.

"No, not with Plunkett and Plunkett. The business, though, is the same that has been troubling my peace all the summer. I think I shall be home to-night, Lucy: but if I cannot see the person I am going up to see, I may have to wait in town until to-morrow. Should the last train not bring me down, you will know the reason."

"Of course your movements are your own, Sir Karl."

He sighed a little, and stood looking from the window. The first train he could catch would not go by for nearly an hour, so he had ample time to spare. Lucy spoke.

"I was going to ask you for some money. I have scarcely enough, I think, for these bills."

"Can you wait until I return, Lucy? I have not much more in the house than I shall want. Or shall I give you a cheque? Hewitt can go to the bank at Basham and cash it."

"Oh I can wait quite well. There's no hurry for a day or two."

"You shall have it to-morrow in any case. If I stay away as long as that I shall be sure to return during banking hours, and will get out at Basham and draw some money."

"Thank you."

"Good-bye, Lucy."

She held out her hand in answer to his, and

wished him good-bye in return. He kept it for a minute in his, stooped and kissed her cheek.

It brought a rush of colour to her face, but she said nothing. Only drew away her hand, bent over her figures again, and began adding them up steadily. He passed round to his chamber, putting a few things in a hand-bag in case he had to stay away the night.

Then he went down to his room and penned a few lines to Adam, entreating him to be unusually cautious. The note was enclosed in an outer envelope, addressed to Mrs. Grey. He rang the bell for Hewitt, and proceeded to lock his desk.

"I want you to go over to the Maze, Hewitt," he said in a low tone—and had got so far when, happening to raise his eyes, he saw it was Giles and not Hewitt who had entered. Karl had his wits about him, and Hewitt came in at the moment.

"Hewitt, I want you to step over to the Maze and inquire whether the plumbers have been there yet. There's something wrong with a drain. Ask the servants at the same time how their mistress is getting on. And——"

Giles had stood gaping and listening. Karl broke off to bid him look for his umbrella.

"No message, Hewitt, and no answer," breathed his master, as he handed him the note. "Put it in your pocket."

"All right, sir," nodded Hewitt, and was away before Giles came back with the umbrella. And Karl got off at last.

Perhaps Mr. Burtenshaw was astonished, perhaps not, to see Sir Karl Andinnian enter that same afternoon. He, the detective, was poring over his papers, as usual, but he turned from them to salute his visitor.

"Will you take a seat, Sir Karl, for two minutes. After that, I am at your service."

"You know me, then, Mr. Burtenshaw!" exclaimed Karl.

"The man who happened to come into the room with Grimley, the last time you were here, sir, said you were Sir Karl Andinnian," replied the officer without scruple. "Take a seat, sir, pray."

Mr. Burtenshaw placed four or five letters, already written, within their envelopes, directed, and stamped them. Then he quitted the room, probably to send them to the post, came in again, and drew a chair in front of Karl. "He is looking worse than ever," was the mental summary of the detective—"but what a nice face it is!"

Ay, it was. The pale, beautiful features, their refined expression, the thoughtfulness in the sweet grey eyes, and the strange sadness that pervaded every lineament, made a picture that was singularly attractive. Karl had one glove off; and the diamond and opal ring he always wore in remembrance of his father flashed in the sunlight. For the buff blinds were not down to-day. He had wished to give the ring back to his brother, when he found he had no right to it himself, but Adam had insisted upon his keeping it and wearing it, lest "the world might inquire where the ring was gone." Another little deceit, as it always seemed to Karl.

"I have called here, Mr. Burtenshaw, to ask you to answer me a question honestly. Have you — stay though," he broke off. "As you know me, I presume you know where I live?"

"Quite well, Sir Karl. I was at the Court once in Sir Joseph Andinnian's time."

"Ay, of course you would know it. Now for my question. Have you sent a detective officer down to Foxwood after Philip Salter?"

"I have not," replied Mr. Burtenshaw, with, Karl thought, a stress upon the "I."

"But you know that one is there?"

"Why do you ask me this?" cried Mr. Burtenshaw, making no immediate reply.

"Because I have reason to believe, in fact to know, that a detective officer is at Foxwood, and I wish to ascertain what he is there for. I presume it can only be to search after Philip Salter."

"And what if it were?" asked Mr. Burtenshaw.

"Nothing. Nothing that could in any way affect you. I want to ascertain it, yes or no, for my own private and individual satisfaction."

"Well, you are right, Sir Karl. One of our men has gone down there with that object."

Karl paused. "I suppose *I* have led to it," he said. "That is, that it has been done in consequence of the inquiries I made of you."

"Of those you made of Grimley, sir, not of me. I had nothing to do with sending Tatton down——"

Karl caught at the name. "Tatton, do you call him?" he interrupted. And Mr. Burtenshaw nodded.

"He calls himself 'Strange' down there."

"Oh, does he? He knows what he is about, Sir Karl, rely upon it."

"Who did send him down?"

"Scotland Yard. It appears that Grimley, taking up the notion through you that he had found a clue to the retreat of Salter, went to Scotland Yard, announced that Salter was in hiding somewhere in the neighbourhood of Foxwood, and asked that a search should be set on foot for him."

Karl sat thinking. If the man Tatton went down after Philip Salter, what brought him within the grounds of the Maze, watching the house at night? Whence also that endeavour to get in by day, and his questions to Ann Hopley? Was it Tatton who did this?—or were there two men, Strange and Tatton?

"What sort of a man is Tatton?" he asked aloud. "Slight and fair?"

"Slight and fair; about thirty years of age, Sir Karl. Curly hair."

"They must be the same," mentally decided Karl. "I presume," he said, lifting his head, "that Tatton must have started on this expedition soon after I was here last?"

"The following day, I think."

"Then he has been at Foxwood over long. More than long enough to have found Salter if Salter's there, Mr. Burtenshaw."

"That depends upon circumstances, Sir Karl," replied the detective, with a wary smile. "I could tell you of a case where an escaped man was being looked after for twelve months before he was unearthed—and he had been close at hand all the while. They have as many ruses as a fox, these fugitives."

"Nevertheless, as Tatton has not yet found Salter, I should consider it a tolerably sure proof that Salter is not at Foxwood."

Mr. Burtenshaw threw a penetrating gaze at his visitor. "Will you undertake to give me your word, Sir Karl, that you do not *know* Philip Salter to be at Foxwood?"

"On my word and honour I do not know him to be there," said Karl, decisively. "I should think he is not there."

He spoke but in accordance with his opinion. The conviction had been gaining upon him the last few minutes that he must have been in error in suspecting Smith to be the man. How else was it, if he was the man, that Tatton had not found him?

"Salter *is* there," said the detective—and Karl pricked up his ears to hear the decisive assertion. "We have positive information from Tatton that he is on his trail:—I am not sure but he has seen him. For the first week or two of Tatton's sojourn there, he could discover no trace whatever of the man or his hiding-place; but accident gave him a clue, and he has found both: found his hiding-place and found him."

"Then why does he not lay his hands upon him?" returned Karl, veering round again to the impression that it must be Smith.

"It is only a question of time, Sir Karl. No doubt he has good reasons for his delay. To *know* where a man is hiding may be one thing; to capture him quite another. Too much haste sometimes mars the game."

"Tatton is going to remain at Foxwood, then?"

"Until the capture is accomplished, certainly."

Karl's heart sunk within him at the answer. While Tatton was delaying his capture of Smith, he might be getting a clue to another escaped fugitive down there—Adam Andinnian. Nay, had he not already the clue? Might not this very delay be caused by some crafty scheme to take both criminals at once— to kill two birds with one stone? He asked one more question.

"Mr. Burtenshaw, how was it that suspicion was directed at all to Foxwood?"

"Grimley took up the notion after your second visit here, Sir Karl, that you had a suspicion of Salter yourself. I thought you understood this. Grimley fancied you were in the habit of seeing some one whom you believed, but did not feel quite sure, might be Salter. And he judged that the individual, whether it was Salter or not, must be in hiding near your dwelling-place—Foxwood."

Ay; Karl saw how it was. *He* had done this. He and no other, had brought this additional danger upon his ill-fated brother, whom he would willingly have given his own life to shield.

There was nothing more to be asked of Mr. Burtenshaw: he had learnt all he came to hear. And Sir Karl with his load of care returned to Foxwood by the evening train.

CHAPTER VIII.

Another Kettle-Drum.

COMMOTION at Mrs. Jinks's. Another afternoon kettle-drum on a grand scale. The two pastors, and more guests than could squeeze into the parlour. All the Foxwood ladies and an omnibus load or two from Basham.

Mr. Strange sat in his drawing-room on a three-legged stool; the one that supported Mrs. Jinks's tub on washing days. His chairs had been borrowed. He had good-naturedly given up every one: so Mrs. Jinks introduced the wooden stool. These crowded meetings below had amused him at first; but he was getting a little tired with the bustle and the noise. Every time the street door was knocked at, it shook his room; the talking below could be heard nearly as plainly as though he were taking part in it. Still it made a little diversion in Mr. Strange's solitary existence, if only to watch the arrival of the articles needed for the feast, and to smell the aroma of the coffee, made in the kitchen in a huge kettle. The supplies did not concern Mr. Cattacomb; his gentle flock took that on themselves, cost and all. There was no lack of good things, but rather a super-abundance: since the Rev. Mr. Puff had come to augment the clerical force, the contributions had been too profuse. So that every one connected with the entertainment was in the seventh heaven of enjoyment and good humour; except Mrs. Jinks.

Perched on the hard stool, Mr. Strange, for lack of other employment, had noted the dainties as they came in. The wisest of us must unbend sometimes. A basket of muffins full to the brim; eleven sorts of jam—since it was discovered that the Reverend Guy loved preserves to satiety, the assortments had never failed; thirteen kinds of biscuits, trays of cake, glass pots of marmalade and honey, ripe rich fruits of all tempting colours, chocolate creams, candied oranges, lovely flowers.

Mr. Strange grew tired of looking; his head ached

with the noise, his eyes with the splendour of the ladies' dresses. For the company was arriving now, thick and threefold.

There had arisen a slight, a very slight, modicum of displeasure at Mr. Cattacomb. That zealous divine had been met four or five times walking with Mr. Moore's third daughter, Jemima: at the last lecture he had distinctly been seen manœuvring to get the young lady next to him. It gave offence. While he belonged to them all, all adored him; but let him once single out one of them for favour more than the rest, and woe betide his popularity. "And that little idiot of a Jemima Moore, too, who had not two ideas in her vain head!" as Jane St. Henry confidentially remarked. However, the Reverend Guy, upon receiving a hint from Miss Blake that he was giving umbrage, vowed and protested that it was all accident and imagination—that he hardly knew Miss Jemima from her sisters. So peace was restored, and the kettle-drum grew out of it.

"I must have my chop all the same, Mrs. Jinks," said Mr. Strange to the widow; who had come up-stairs to ask the loan of his sugar tongs, and looked very red and excited over it.

"In course, sir, you shall have it. It might be ten minutes later, sir, than ord'nary, but I do hope you'll excuse it, sir, if it is. You see how I'm drove with 'em."

"I see that there seems to be a large company arriving."

"Company!" returned Mrs. Jinks, the word causing her temper to explode; "I don't know how they'll ever get inside the room. I shall have to borrow a form from the school next door but one, and put it in the passage for some of 'em; and, when that and the chairs is filled, the rest must stand. Never as long as I live, will I take in a unmarried parson-gent again, if he's one of this here new sort that gets the ladies about him all day in church and gives drums out of it. Hark at the laughing! Them two parsons be in their glory."

"The ladies must be fond of drums, I should think, by their getting them up so frequently," remarked Mr. Strange.

"Drat the huzzies!—they'd be fond of fifes too if it brought 'em round Cattakin," was the widow's uncomplimentary rejoinder. "Better for 'em if they'd let the man alone to drink his tea in quiet and write his sermons—which I don't believe ever does get writ, seeing he never has a minute to himself. Hark at that blessed door!" she continued; and indeed the knocking was keeping up a perpetual chorus. "If they'd only turn the handle they could come in of theirselves. I said so to the Miss St. Henrys one cleaning day that I had been called to it six times while scrubbing down the kitchen stairs, and the young ladies answered me that they'd not come in to Mr. Cattakin's without knocking, for the world."

"I suppose not," said Mr. Strange, slightly laughing.

"Hang that knocker again. There it goes! And me with all the drum on my shoulders. You should see the muffins we've got to toast and butter downstairs, sir; your conscience 'ud fail you. Betsey Chaffin has come in to help me, and she and the girl is at it like steam. I'm afeared that there stool's terrible hard for you, Mr. Strange, sir!" broke off the widow, in condolence.

"It's not as soft as velvet," was the reply. "But I'm glad to oblige: and I am going out presently. Get my chop and tea up when you can."

Mrs. Jinks disappeared; the hum continued. Whether the two parsons, as Mrs. Jinks surmised, felt "in their glory," cannot be told: the ladies were certainly in theirs. These kettle-drums at Mr. Cattacomb's were charmingly attractive.

When Mr. Strange did not return home for his chop at mid-day, he took it with his tea. His tray was yet before him when the kettle-drum trooped out to attend vespers. At least, the company who had formed the drum. The two reverend gentlemen hastened on together a little in advance; Miss Blake led the van behind; and curious Foxwood ran to its windows to see.

Mr. Strange, who had nothing particular on his hands or mind that evening, looked after them. Example is infectious. He felt an inclination to follow in their wake—for it had not been his good fortune yet to make one of the worshippers at St. Jerome's; he had never indulged himself with as much as a peep inside the place. Accordingly, Mr. Strange started, after some short delay, and gained the edifice.

The first object his eyes rested on, struck him as being as ludicrous as an imp at the play. It was Tom Pepp in a conical hat tipped with red, and a red cross extending down his white garmented back. Tom Pepp stood near the bell, ready to tinkle it at parts of the service. It may as well be stated—lest earnest

disciples of new movements should feel or take offence
—that the form and make of the services at St. Jerome's were entirely Mr. Cattacomb's own; invented
by himself exclusively, and not copied from any other
standard, orthodox or unorthodox. The description
of it is taken from facts. Mr. Strange, standing at
the back near to Tom Pepp, enjoyed full view of all:
the ladies prostrate on the floor, *actually prostrate*,
some of them, the Reverend Guy facing them with the
whites of his eyes turned up; Damon Puff on his
knees, presenting his back to the room and giving
every now and then a surreptitious stroke to his
moustache. The detective had never seen so complete a farce in his life, as connected with religion.
He thought the two reverend gentlemen might be
shut up for a short term as mutinous lunatics, by way
of receiving a little wholesome correction: he knew
that if he had a daughter, he would shut *her* up as
one, rather than she should make a spectacle of herself as these other girls were doing.

The services over, Tom Pepp set on at the bell to
ring them out with all his might—for that was the
custom. Most of them filed out; as did Mr. Damon
Puff; and they went on their way. A few of them
stopped in, for confession to Mr. Cattacomb.

It was growing dusk then. A train was just in,
and had deposited some passengers at the station.
One of them came along, walking quickly, as if in
haste to get home. Happening to turn his head towards St. Jerome's as he passed it, attracted by the
bell, he saw there, rather to his surprise, standing just
outside the door, Mr. Moore's strong-minded sister.
She peered at him in the twilight; she was no longer

so quick of sight as she had been; and recognized Sir
Karl Andinnian.

"What, is it you, Miss Diana!" he cried, stopping
to hold out his hand. "Have you gone over to St.
Jerome's?"

"I'd rather go over to Rome, Sir Karl," was the
candid answer. "I may lapse to St. Jerome's when I
get childish perhaps, if it lasts so long. There's no
answering for any of us when the mind fails."

Sir Karl laughed slightly. He saw before him the
receding crowd turning down towards Foxwood village,
and knew that vespers must be just over. The ringing
of Tom Pepp's bell would have told him that. It was
clanging away just above Miss Diana's head.

"You have been to vespers, then," remarked Sir
Karl again, almost at a loss what to say, and unable
to get away until Miss Diana chose to release his
hand.

"Yes, I have been to what they call vespers," she
rejoined tartly; "more shame for a woman of my sober
years to say it, as connected with this place. Look
at them, trooping on there, that Puff in the midst,
who is softer than any apple-puff ever made yet!"
continued Miss Diana, pointing her hand in the direction of the vanishing congregation. "*They* have gone;
but there are five staying in for confession. Hark!
Hark, Sir Karl! the folly is going to begin."

A sweet, silvery-toned bell rang gently within the
room, and the clanging bell of Mr. Pepp stopped at
the signal. The Reverend Guy had gone into the
confessional box, and all other sounds must cease.

"I should think they can hardly see to confess at
this hour," said Sir Karl jestingly.

"They light a tallow candle, I believe, and stick it in the vestry," said Miss Diana. "Five of them are staying to-night, as I told you: I always count. They go in one at a time and the others wait their turn outside the vestry. Do you think I am going to let my nieces stay here alone to play at that fun, Sir Karl? No: and so I drag myself here every confessional night. One of them, Jemima, is always staying. She is a little fool."

"It does not seem right," mused Sir Karl.

"Right!" ejaculated Miss Diana in an angry tone, as if she could have boxed his ears for the mild word. "It is wrong, Sir Karl, and doubly wrong. I do not care to draw the curb-rein too tightly; they are not my own children, and might rebel; but as sure as they are living, if this folly of stopping behind to confess is to go on, I shall tell the doctor of it. I think, Sir Karl—and you must excuse me for saying so to your face—that you might have done something before now, to put down the pantomime of this St. Jerome's."

"Only this very morning I was with St. Henry, asking him what I could do," was the reply. "His opinion is, that it will cease of itself when the cold weather comes on."

" *Will* it!" was the sarcastically emphatic retort. "Not if Cattacomb and the girls can help it. It's neither cold nor heat that will stop them!"

"Well, I am not sure about the law, Miss Diana. I don't know that St. Henry is, either."

"Look here, Sir Karl. If the law is not strong enough to put down these places, there's another remedy. Let all the clergy who officiate at them be

upwards of fifty years old and *married*. It would
soon be proved whether, or not, the girls go for the
benefit of their souls."

Sir Karl burst into a laugh.

"It is these off-shoots of semi-religious places,
started up here and there by men of vanity, some of
whom, I venture to say it, are not licensed clergymen,
that bring the shame and the scandal upon the true
church," concluded Miss Diana. "There: don't let us
talk of it further. Have you come from the train?"

"Yes. I had to run up to London for an hour or
two to-day."

"Then I daresay you are tired. Give my love to
your wife," added Miss Diana, as she wished Sir Karl
good evening and turned into St. Jerome's again to
watch over her niece Jemima.

Sir Karl strode onwards. He had just come home
from his interview with Mr. Burtenshaw. Miss Diana
Moore and her sentiments had served to divert his
mind for a moment from his own troubles, but they
were soon all too present again. The hum of the
voices and sound of the footsteps came back to him
from the crowd, pursuing its busy way to the village:
he was glad to keep on his own solitary course and
lose its echo.

Some one else, who had come out of St. Jerome's
but who could not be said properly to pertain to the
crowd, had kept on the solitary road—and that was
Mr. Strange. He knew the others would take the
direct way to the village and Mrs. Jinks's, and perhaps
that was the reason why he did not. But there was
no accounting for what Mr. Strange did: and one thing
was certain—he had been in the habit lately of loiter-

ing in that solitary road a good deal after dusk had fallen, smoking his cigar there between whiles.

Sir Karl went on. He had nearly reached the Maze, though he was on the opposite side, when at a bend of the road there suddenly turned upon him a man with a cigar in his mouth, the end of it glowing like an ember. The smoker would have turned his head away again, and passed on, but Sir Karl stopped. He had recognized him: and his mind had been made up on the way from London, to speak to this man.

"I beg your pardon. Mr. Tatton, I think."

Mr. Tatton might possibly have been slightly taken to at hearing himself addressed by his own name: but there was no symptom of it in his voice or manner.

"The same, sir," he readily answered, taking the cigar from his mouth.

"I wish to say a few words to you," pursued Sir Karl. "As well perhaps say them now as later."

"Better, sir. No time like the present: it's all we can make sure of."

"Perhaps you know me, Mr. Tatton?"

"Sir Karl Andinnian—unless I am mistaken," replied the detective, throwing away his cigar.

Sir Karl nodded, but made no assent in words. He would have given a portion of his remaining life to discern whether this man of law, whom he so dreaded, knew, or suspected, that he had not a right to the title.

"I have just come from London," pursued Sir Karl. "I saw Mr. Burtenshaw there to-day. Finding that you were down here, I wished to ascertain whether or not you had come here in search of one Philip Salter. And I hear that it is so."

S *

The officer made no remark to this. It might be, that he was uncertain how far he might trust Sir Karl. The latter observed the reticence: guessed at the doubt.

"We may speak together in perfect confidence, Mr. Tatton. But for me, you would not have been sent here at all. It was in consequence of a communication I made myself, that the suspicion as to Salter reached Scotland Yard."

"I know all about that, Sir Karl," was the reply. "To tell you the truth, I should have made my presence here at Foxwood known to you at once, and asked you to aid me in my search; but I was warned at Scotland Yard that you might possibly obstruct my work instead of aiding it, for that you wished to screen Salter."

"Scotland Yard warned you of that!" exclaimed Sir Karl.

"Yes. They had it from Grimley."

"The case is this," said Sir Karl, wishing with his whole heart he could undo what he had done. "Some short while back, I had a reason for making some enquiries respecting Philip Salter, and I went to my solicitors, Plunkett and Plunkett. They could not give me any information, and referred me to Mr. Burtenshaw. Burtenshaw introduced Grimley to me, and I saw them both twice. But I most certainly never intended to imply that Salter was in this neighbourhood, or to afford just grounds for sending down to institute a search after him."

"But I presume that you do know Salter is here, Sir Karl."

"Indeed I do not."

The officer was silent. He thought Sir Karl was intending to deceive him.

"I can tell you that he is here, Sir Karl—to the best of my belief. I could put out my hand at this minute and almost touch the dwelling that contains him."

They were nearly opposite the Maze gates, close upon the gate of Clematis Cottage. Karl wondered, with an anxiety, amounting to agony, *which* of the two dwellings was meant. It would be almost as bad for this man to take Salter as to take Adam Andinnian, since the capture of the former might lead to that of the latter.

"You say to the best of your belief, Mr. Tatton. You are not sure, then?"

"I am as sure as I can be, Sir Karl, short of actual sight."

"Good night, Sir Karl."

The interruption came from Mr. Smith, who was leaning over his gate, smoking a pipe. Karl returned the salutation and passed on.

"He seems to have a jolly kind of easy life of it, that agent of yours, Sir Karl?" remarked the officer.

"Do you know him?" questioned Karl.

"Only by sight. I have seen Mr. Smith about on the land; and I took the liberty this afternoon, meeting him by chance near the Brook field, of asking him what the time was. The spring of my watch broke last night as I was winding it."

Karl's heart was beating. Had he been mistaken in supposing Philip Smith to be Philip Salter? Had he been nursing a foolish chimera, and running his head—or, rather, his poor brother's head—into a noose for nothing? God help him, then!

"You seem to know my agent well by sight," he breathed, in a tone kept low, lest its agitation should be heard.

"Quite well," assented the officer.

"Is he—does he bear any resemblance to Salter?"

"Not the slightest."

Karl paused. "You are sure of that?"

Tatton took a look at Sir Karl in the evening dusk, as if not able to understand him. "He is about the height of Salter, and in complexion is somewhat similar, if you can call that a resemblance," said he. "There is no other."

Karl spoke not for a few moments: the way before him was darkening. "You knew Salter's person well, I conclude?" he said presently.

"As well as I know my own brother's."

Another pause; and then Karl laid his hand upon the officer's arm, bespeaking his best attention.

"I am sorry for all this," he said; "I am vexed to have been the cause of so much trouble. Your mission here may terminate as soon as you will, Mr. Tatton, for it is Smith that I was suspecting of being Salter!"

"No!" cried Tatton in surprised disbelief.

"On my solemn word, I assert it. I suspected my agent, Smith, to be Salter."

"Why, Sir Karl, I can hardly understand that. You surely could not suppose it to be within the bounds of probability that Philip Salter, the fugitive criminal, would go about in the light of day in England as your agent goes—no matter how secluded the spot might be! And five hundred pounds on his head!"

How a word of ridicule, of reason even, will serve to change our cherished notions! Put as the cool and experienced police officer put it, Karl seemed to see how poor and foundationless his judgment had been.

"The whole cause of the affair was this," he said, hoping by a candid explanation to disarm the suspicions he had raised. "A circumstance—I own it was but a slight one—put it into my head that Philip Smith, of whom I had known nothing until he came here a few months ago as my agent, might be the escaped prisoner Philip Salter. The idea grew with me, and I became anxious—naturally you will say—to ascertain whether there were any real grounds for the suspicion. With this view I went up to see if Plunkett's people could give me any information about Salter or describe his person; and they referred me to Mr. Burtenshaw."

"Well, sir?" interposed Tatton, who was listening attentively.

"I am bound to say that I obtained no corroboration of my suspicions, except in regard to the resemblance," continued Sir Karl. "Burtenshaw did not know him; but he summoned the man who had let him escape, Grimley. As Grimley described Salter, it seemed to me that it was the precise description of Smith."

"There is a kind of general resemblance, I admit, Sir Karl, and the description of one might perhaps sound like that of the other. But if you knew the two, you would see how unlike they are."

"Grimley's description seemed to me to be that of

Smith," went on Karl. "I came back here, strengthened in my opinion: but not fully confirmed. It was not a satisfactory state of things, and the matter continued to worry me. I longed to set it at rest, one way or the other; and I went up again to town and saw Grimley and Mr. Burtenshaw. When I came back once more, I felt nearly as sure as a man can feel that it was Salter."

"And yet you did not denounce him, Sir Karl. You would never have done it, I suppose?"

"I should not," admitted Karl. "My intention was to tax Smith with it privately, and—and send him about his business. Very wrong and illegal of me, no doubt: but I have suffered too severely in my own family by the criminal law of the land, to give up another man gratuitously to it."

At this reference to Sir Adam Andinnian, Mr. Tatton remained silent from motives of delicacy. He could understand the objection; especially as coming from a refined, sensitive, and merciful natured man, as Sir Karl appeared to be.

"Well, sir, I can only say for myself that I wish your agent had been Salter," he resumed: "my hands would have been upon him before to-night. But is it true that you have no other suspicion, Sir Karl?"

"What suspicion?"

"That the real Salter is in hiding at Foxwood."

Karl's heart beat a shade faster. "So far from having any suspicion of that kind, I am perfectly certain, now that you have proved to me Smith is not Salter, that he is not at Foxwood. I know every soul in the place and around it."

"Were you acquainted with the real Salter, Sir Karl?"

"No."

"You take no interest in him, I presume?"

"None whatever."

During the conversation they had been slowly pacing onwards, had passed the Court gates, and were now fairly on the road to Foxwood. It seemed as if Sir Karl had a mind to escort Mr. Tatton to his home.

"By the way," he said, "why did you call yourself Strange down here?"

"I never did," answered Tatton, laughing slightly. "The widow Jinks gave me that name: I never gave it myself. I said to her I was a stranger, and she must have misunderstood me; for I found afterwards that she was calling me Mr. Strange. It was rather convenient than otherwise, and I did not set it right."

Karl strolled on in silence, wondering how all this would end and whether this dangerous man—dangerous to him and his interests—was satisfied, and would betake himself to town again. A question interrupted him.

"Do you know much of a place here called the Maze, Sir Karl?"

"The Maze is my property. Why?"

"Yes, I am aware of that. What I meant to ask was, whether you knew much of its inmates."

"It is let to a lady named Grey. Her husband is abroad."

"That's what she tells you, is it? Her husband is there, Sir Karl, if he be her husband. *That* is where we must look for Philip Salter."

Something born of emotion, of sudden fear, seemed to flash across Karl's eyes and momentarily blind him. A wild prayer went up for guidance, for help to confront this evil.

"Why do you say this?" he asked, his voice controlled to a calm indifference.

"I have information that some gentleman is living at the Maze in concealment, and I make no doubt it is Salter. The description of his person, so far as I have it, answers to him. Until to-night, Sir Karl, I have believed that it was to the Maze your own suspicions of Salter were directed."

"Certainly not—on my word of honour as a gentleman," was the reply. "I feel sure you are mistaken; I know you are. Mrs. Grey lives alone at the Maze, save for her servants: two old people who are man and wife."

"I am aware the general belief is that she lives alone. It's not true, though, for all that, Sir Karl."

"Indeed it is true," returned Karl, calmly as before, for he did not dare to show too much zeal in Mrs. Grey's cause. "I have been over there pretty often on one matter or another—the house is an old one, and no end of repairs seem to be wanted to it—and I am absolutely sure that no inmate whatever is there, save the three I have mentioned: the lady, and the man and woman. I do not count the infant."

"Ay; there; the infant. What does that prove?"

"Nothing—as to your argument. Mrs. Grey only came to the place some five or six months ago. Not yet six, I think."

"Rely upon it, Sir Karl, the lady has contrived to blind you, in spite of your visits, just as she has blinded the outside world. Some one is there, concealed; and I shall be very much surprised if it does not turn out to be Salter. As to the two old servants, they are bound to her interests; are of course as much in the plot as she is."

"I know you are mistaken. I could stake my life that no one else is there. Surely you are not going to act in any way on this idea!"

"I don't know," replied Mr. Tatton, with inward craft. "Time enough. Perhaps I may get some other information before long. Should I require a search-warrant to examine the house, I shall apply to you, Sir Karl. You are in the commission of peace, I believe."

Sir Karl nodded. "If you must have one, I shall be happy to afford it," he said, remembering that if it came to this pass, his being able to avert the Maze privately beforehand, would be a boon. And with that they separated: the detective continuing to pace onwards towards Paradise Row, Sir Karl turning back to his own house.

But the events of the evening, as concerning the Maze interests, were not altogether at an end. Miss Blake was the last to come out of the confessional, for the rest had taken their turn before her. It was tolerably late then; quite dark; and both Aunt Diana and Tom Pepp were rampant at being kept so long. They all turned out of St. Jerome's together, including Mr. Cattacomb; and all, save Miss Blake and the boy, went in the direction of the village. Tom Pepp, having locked up and doffed his bell-ringing garments, proceeded the other way, accompanied by Miss Blake.

She was going to visit a sick woman who lived next door to Tom's mother. Miss Blake had her good points, though she was harsh of judgment. This poor woman, Dame Bell, was dying of consumption; the end was drawing near, and Miss Blake often went to sit by and read to her. The boy had told her at vespers that night that it was thought she could hardly live till morning: hence the late visit. She found her very ill, and stayed to do what she could.

It was striking ten when Miss Blake quitted the cottage: she heard the quarters and the strokes told out from the distant church at Foxwood. The night was a still one. Tom Pepp, waiting outside, gallantly offered to attend her home. She accepted the escort readily, not caring to go alone, as it was so late.

"But I fear it will be keeping your mother up, Tom," she said, in hesitation. "I know you go to bed early."

"That's nothing, um," said Tom. "Mother have got her clothes from the wash to fold to-night. She telled me I was not to let you go back alone. It have been a rare good day for drying."

So they set off together, talking all the way, for Tom was an intelligent companion, and often had items of news to regale the public with. When they came within view of the Maze gates and Clematis Cottage, the loneliness of the way was over, and Miss Blake sent the lad back again, giving him a three-penny-bit.

She was on the Maze side of the way, not having crossed since leaving Mrs. Bell's cottage. And she had all but reached the gates, when the sound of advancing footsteps grew upon her ear. Drawing back

amidst the trees—not to watch for Sir Karl Andinnian as she had watched at other times, for she believed him to be in London, but simply to shield herself from observation, as the hour was so late—Miss
Blake waited until the footsteps should have gone by.

The footsteps did not go by. They halted at the
gate: and she, peeping through the leaves, saw it was
Sir Karl. He took the key from his pocket as usual,
opened the gate, locked it after him, and plunged
into the maze. Miss Blake heaved a sigh at man's
inventions, and kept still until there was no fear that
her rustling away would be heard. Then she moved.

She had never been in all her life so near screaming. Taking one step forward to depart, she found
herself right in the arms of somebody who had coat
sleeves on; another watcher like herself.

"I beg your pardon, ma'am."

"Good gracious, Mr. Strange, how you frightened
me!" she whispered. "Whatever are you doing here?"

"Nay, I may ask what you were doing," was the
smiling retort. "On your way home, I take it. As
for me, I was smoking my cigar, and it has gone out.
That was our friend, Sir Karl Andinnian, I fancy,
who let himself in there."

"Oh yes, it was Sir Karl," was the contemptuous
answer, given as they walked on together. "It is not
the first night by a good many he has been seen
stealing in at those gates."

"Paying his court to Mrs. Grey!" returned Mr.
Strange, really speaking without any sinister motive,
and his mind full of Salter.

Miss Blake, in the honest indignation of her heart,
and lately come from the upright exhortations of the

Reverend Guy, allowed her sentiments their play. Mr. Strange's remark, made in all innocence, had seemed to show her that he too knew of the scandal.

"It is shameful!" she said. "Doubly shameful in Sir Karl, a married man."

Mr. Strange pricked up his ears. He caught her meaning instantly.

"Nonsense!" said he.

"I wish it was nonsense," said Miss Blake. "When the woman, Betsy Chaffen, was telling the tale in your rooms that day, of the gentleman she saw, and whom she could never see afterwards, I could hardly contain myself, dear sir, knowing it was Sir Karl."

"And—and—do you mean—do you think that there's no Mr. Grey there—no gentleman inmate, I would say?" cried the detective, surprised for once.

"Mr. Grey!" she repeated, scoffingly. "The only 'Mr. Grey' that exists is Sir Karl Andinnian; I have known it a long while. One or two others here know it also. It is a scandal."

She wished him good night with the last words, crossed the road, and let herself into the grounds of the Court by one of the small gates, leaving Mr. Strange looking after her like a man in a dream, as he tried to solve the problems set a-working in his brain.

CHAPTER IX.

Only a Night Owl.

THE wide window of the upper sitting-room at the Maze was thrown open to the night air. Gazing forth from it, stood Sir Adam Andinnian and his wife. He was in his usual evening dress, that he so obstinately continued to persist in assuming in the teeth of remonstrance: she wore a loose white robe and a blue cashmere shawl over it. She looked delicately fragile, very weak and ill still; and this was the first day that she had left her chamber for any length of time. There was no light in the sombre room: before light was allowed to come in, the window would be closed and the shutters shut for the night.

Not a word was being spoken between them. She had not long come into the room. A great terror lay on both their hearts. At least, it did on hers: and Sir Adam had grown to feel anything but easy. The suspicions, that appeared to be attaching themselves to the Maze outside the walls, were producing their effects on the comfort of the inmates within: and perhaps these suspicions were feared all the more because they did not as yet take any tangible or distinct form. That a detective officer was in the neighbourhood looking about, Adam had heard from his brother; and that it was the same man who had been seen by Ann Hopley watching the house in the moonlight and who had boldly presented himself at the gate the next day demanding permission to enter, Sir Adam had no doubt whatever of. Karl, too, was taking to write him notes of caution.

Brave though he was, he could not feel safe. There was not a moment of the day or night but he might see the officers of justice coming in to look for him. His own opinion was, that he should be able to evade them if they did come; to baffle their scrutiny; but he could not feel quite as easy as though he were on a bed of rose-leaves. In consequence of this apprehension, the ears of himself and his wife were ever on the alert, their eyes rarely went off the watch, their conscious hearts never lost the quick beat of fear. It was enough to wear them both out.

Can the reader really realize, I wonder, what the situation was? Can he only imagine one single hour of its terrors, or picture its never-ceasing, prolonged doubt and agony? I think not. It cannot be adequately told of. Behind and before there was the awful vista of that dreadful Portland Island: look which way they would, nothing else presented itself.

A gentle breeze suddenly arose, stirring the trees outside. Never an unexpected sound, however faint, was heard, but it stirred their beating hearts; stirred them to a fast, fluttering, ugly throbbing. It was but the wind; they knew it was only that: and yet the emotion did not subside quickly. Rose had another great anxiety, separate and apart: perhaps he had it also in a degree, but he did not admit it. It was on the score of her husband's health. There could be no doubt that something or other was amiss, for he had occasional attacks of pain that seemed to arise without any explainable cause. Ann Hopley, who considered herself wise in ailments, declared that he ought to see a doctor. She had said it to her master ineffectually; she now began to say it to her mistress. Sir Adam laughed when his wife was present, and ridiculed her advice with mocking words of pleasantry; but Ann Hopley gave nothing but grave looks in return.

The fact was, she knew more than Rose did: more than Sir Adam intended or would allow his wife to know. One day, going to a part of the grounds where she knew she should find her master, she dis-covered him on the ground amidst the trees in a fainting-fit, his face of a bluish-white. Some acute pain, or spasm, sharper than he had ever felt before, had caused him to lose consciousness, he said, when he recovered; and he threatened the woman with un-heard of pains and penalties if she breathed a word to her mistress. Ann Hopley held her tongue accord-ingly: but when Rose was about again she could see that Adam was not well. And the very impossibility of calling in a medical man to him, without arousing curiosity and comments that might lead to danger, was tormenting her with its own anxiety.

"The baby sleeps well to-night, Rose."

"He has slept better and has been altogether easier since he was baptised," was her answer. "It is just as though he knew he had been made a little Christian, and so feels at rest."

"Goose!" smiled Sir Adam. "Don't you think you are sitting up too late, you young mamma?"

"I am not tired, Adam. I slept well this after-noon."

"It is later than perhaps you are aware of, Rose. Hard upon ten."

"Would you like to have lights?" she asked.

"No. I'd rather be without them."

She also would rather be without them. In this extended cause for fear that was growing up, it seemed safer to be at the open window looking out, than to be shut up in the closed room where the approaches of danger could neither be seen nor heard. Perhaps the same kind of feeling was swaying Sir Adam.

"You are sure you are well wrapped up, Rose?"

"Certain. And I could not take cold in this weather. It is like summer still."

All around was quiet as death. The stars shone in the sky: the gentle breeze, that had ruffled the trees just before, seemed to have died away. Breaking just then upon the stillness, came the sound of the church clock at Foxwood, telling its four quarters and the ten strokes of the hour after it. The same quarters, the same strokes that Miss Blake also heard, emerging from Dame Bell's cottage. The husband and wife, poor banned people, stood on again side by side, they hardly knew how long, hushing the trouble that was making a havoc of their lives, and from which they knew there could be no certain or complete escape so long as time for him should last. Presently he spoke again.

"Rose, if you stay here longer I shall close the window. This night air, calm and warm though it is, cannot be good for you——"

She laid her warning hand upon his arm. The ears of both were quick, but he was speaking at the moment, and so she caught the sound first. A pause of intense silence, their hearts beating almost to be heard; and then the advance of footsteps, whether stealthy ones or not, might be distinctly traced, coming through the maze.

"Go, Adam," she whispered.

But, before Sir Adam could quit the room, the whistle of a popular melody broke out upon the air, and they knew the intruder was Karl. It was his usual advance signal. Ann Hopley heard it below and opened the heavily barred door to him.

"You are late to-night, sir."

"True. I could not come earlier, Ann: it was not safe."

Poor Karl Andinnian! Had he but known that it was not safe that night, later as well as earlier! That is, that he had not come in unwatched. For, you have understood that it was the night mentioned at the close of the last chapter, when his interview with Mr. Strange had taken place on his return from London, and the detective and Miss Blake had subsequently watched him in.

"Now then, Karl," began Sir Adam, when the room was at length closed and lighted, and Ann Hopley had gone down again, "what was the precise meaning of the cautionary note you sent me to-day?"

"The meaning was to enjoin extra caution upon you," replied Karl, after a moment's hesitation, and an involuntary glance at Rose.

"If you have anything to say and are hesitating because my wife is present you may speak out freely," cried the very *un*-reticent Sir Adam. Rose seconded the words.

"Speak, Karl, speak," she said, leaning towards him with a painful anxiety in her tone. "It will be a relief to me. Nothing that you or any one else can say can be as bad as my own fears."

"Well, I have found out that that man is a London detective," said Karl, deeming it best to tell the whole truth. "He is down here looking after an escaped fugitive. Not *you*, Adam: one Salter."

"One Salter?" echoed Sir Adam, testily, while Rose started slightly. "Who's he? What Salter? Is there any Salter at Foxwood?"

"It seems that the police in London have been

9*

suspecting that he was here and they sent this detective, who calls himself Strange, to look after him. Salter, however, cannot be found; there's no doubt that the suspicion was altogether a mistake; but, unfortunately, Strange has had his thoughts directed to the Maze, and is looking after it."

"After me?" cried Adam.

"No. I do not believe there exists the smallest suspicion that you are not in the family vault in Foxwood churchyard. He fancies some one is concealed here, and thinks it must be Salter."

"But why on earth should his suspicions be directed to the Maze at all?" demanded Sir Adam, with a touch of his native heat.

"Ah, why! We have to thank Moore for that, and your own incaution, Adam, when you allowed yourself to be seen the night he brought Nurse Chaffen in. It seems the woman has talked of it outside; telling people, and Strange amid the rest, that it was either a real gentleman in dinner attire, or a ghost in the semblance of one. Some have taken unhesitatingly to the ghost theory, believing it to be a remanent of the Throcton times; but detectives are wiser men."

"And so this man is looking after the Maze!"

"Just so. He is after Salter, not after you."

Sir Adam made no immediate observation. Rose, listening eagerly, was gazing at Karl.

"Is it *sure* that Salter is not in the place?" she asked in a low tone. "That he has not been here?"

"Quite sure, Rose. The idea was a misapprehension entirely," replied Karl, returning her meaning glance. "Therefore, you see," he added, by way of giving what reassurance he could, "the man you have so dreaded is not on the track of Adam at all; but on the imaginary one of Salter."

"One scent leads to another," broke forth Sir Adam. "While the fellow is tracking out Salter, he may track out me. Who's to know that he has not a photograph of Adam Andinnian in his pocket, or my face in his memory?"

"I should like to ask him the question, whether he knew Sir Adam Andinnian personally; but I fear I dare not," remarked Karl. "A suspicion once awakened would not end. Your greatest security lies in their not knowing you are alive."

"My only security," corrected Sir Adam. "Well, Karl, if that man has his eyes directed to the Maze, it puts an end to all hope of my trying to get away. Little doubt, I suppose, but he is watching the outer walls night and day; perhaps with a dozen comrades to help him."

"For the present, you can only stay where you are," acknowledged Karl. "I have told you all this, Adam, to make you doubly careful. But for your reckless incaution I would have spared you the additional uneasiness it must bring."

"Even though the man does know me, the chances are that he would not find me if he came in," mused Sir Adam aloud. "With my precautions, the task would be somewhat difficult. You know it, Karl."

"Yes, but you are not always using your precautions," returned Karl. "Witness you here, sitting amidst us openly this evening in full dress! *Don't* do in so future, Adam! conceal yourself as you best can —I beseech it of you for the love of Heaven. When this present active trouble shall have subsided—if in

God's mercy it does so subside—why then you may resume old habits again. At least, there will not be so much risk: but I have always considered them hazardous."

"I'll see," assented Sir Adam. Which was a concession from *him*.

"Be on your guard day and night. Let not one moment of either season find you off it, or unready for any surprise or emergency. Strange talked about applying for a search-warrant to examine the house. Should he do so, I will warn you of it, if possible. But your safer course is to be looking for the enemy with every ring that the bell gives, every breath that stirs the trees in the labyrinth, every sound that vibrates on the air."

"A pretty state of things!" growled Adam. "I'm sure I wish I never had come here!"

"Oh that you had not!" returned Karl.

"It's my proper place, though. It is. My dear little son, heir to all, ought to be brought up on his own property. Karlo, old fellow, that remark must have a cruel ring on your ear: but I cannot put the child out of his birthright."

"I should never wish you to do it, Adam."

"Some arrangement shall be made for the far-off future; rest assured of that, and tell your wife so. In any case, Foxwood will be yours for one-and-twenty years to come, and the income you now enjoy, to keep it up with. After the boy shall be of age ——"

"Let us leave those considerations for the present," interrupted Karl. "All of us may be dead and buried before then. As for me, I seem not to see a single step before me, let alone a series of years."

"Right, Karl. These dreams lay hold of me sometimes, but it is worse than silly to speak of them. Are you going?"

"Yes. It is late. I should not have come in to night, but for wishing to warn you. You will try and take care of yourself, Adam?" he affectionately added, holding out his hand.

"I'll take care of myself; never fear," was Sir Adam's light answer as he grasped it. "Look here, brother mine," he resumed, after a slight pause, and his voice took a deeper tone. "God knows that I have suffered too heavily for what I did; He knows that my whole life, from the rising up of the sun to its going down, from the first falling shade of night's dark curtain to its lifting, is one long, unbroken penance: and I believe in my heart that He will in His compassion shield me from further danger. There! take that to comfort you, and go in peace. In your care for me, you have needed comfort throughout more than I, Karl."

Retaining his brother's hand in his while Karl said good night to Rose, Adam went down stairs with him, and beyond the door after Ann Hopley had unbarred it. It was only since the advent of the new fears that these extra precautions of barring up at sunset had been taken.

"Don't come out," urged Karl.

"Just a step or two."

Karl submitted: he felt secure enough against active danger to-night. But it was in these trifles that Adam's natural incaution betrayed itself.

"Karl, did you tell all you knew?" he began as

they plunged into the maze. "Was there more behind that you would not speak before the wife?"

"I told you all, Adam. It is bad enough."

"It might be worse. Suppose they were looking after me, for instance, instead of this fellow Salter! I shall baffle them; I don't fear."

"Adam, you shall *not* come farther. If the man got in one night, he may get in another. Good-bye."

"Good-bye, dear old anxious fellow!"

"Go in, and get the door barred."

"All right. A last good night to you!"

Karl walked on, through the intracacies of the maze. Adam stood listening for a moment, and then turned to retrace his steps. As he did so, the sharp dart of pain he was growing accustomed to went through him, turning him sick and faint. He seized hold of a tree for support, and leaned against it.

"What on earth can be the matter with me?" ran his thoughts after it had subsided, and he was getting out his handkerchief to wipe from his brow the cold drops of agony that had gathered there. "As Ann Hopley says, I ought to see a doctor: but it is not to be thought of; and less than ever now, with this new bother hanging over the house. Hark! Oh, it's only the wind rustling the leaves again."

He stayed listening to it. Listening in a dreamy kind of way, his thoughts still on his malady.

"I wonder what it is? If the pain were in a different direction I might think it was the heart. But it is not *that*. When my father was first taken ill of his fatal illness, he spoke of some such queer attacks of agony. I am over young for his complaint,

though. Does disease ever grow out of anxiety, I
wonder? If so——"

A whirl and a rustle just over his head, and Sir
Adam started as though a blow had struck him. It
was but a night owl, flying away from the tree above
with her dreary note and beating the air with her
wings; but it had served to startle him to terror, and
he felt as sick and faint again as he did just before
from the physical pain. What nerves he possessed
were on the extreme tension to-night. That Adam
Andinnian, the cool-natured equable man, who was
the very opposite of his sensitive brother Karl, and
who had been unable to understand what nerves were,
and to laugh at those who had them—that he could
be thus shaken by merely the noise of a night bird,
will serve to show the reader what his later life had
been, and how it had told upon him. He did not let
this appear, even to those about him; he kept up his
old rôle of cool carelessness—and in a degree he was
careless still, and in ordinary moments most incautious
from sheer want of thought—but there could be no
doubt that he was experiencing to the full all the bitter
mockery, the never ceasing dread and hazard of his
position. In the early days, when the attempted escape
from Portland Island was only in contemplation, Karl
had foreseen what the life must be if he did escape.
An existence of miserable concealment; of playing at
hide and seek with the law; a world-wide apprehension, lying on him always, of being retaken. In short,
a hunted man who must not dare to approach the
haunts of his fellow-men, and of whom every other
man must be the necessary enemy. Even so had it
turned out: Adam Andinnian was realizing it to the

full. A great horror lay upon him of being recaptured: but it may be questioned whether, had the choice been given him, he would not rather have remained a prisoner than have escaped to this. Even as he stood there now, in the damp still night, with all the nameless, weird surroundings of fancy that night sometimes brings when the spirit is in tune for it, he was realizing it unto his soul.

The glitter of the stars, twinkling in their dusky canopy, shone down upon him through the interstices of the trees, already somewhat thinning their leaves with the approach of autumn; and he remained on, amid the gloom, lost in reflection.

"I should be better off *there*," he murmured, gazing upwards in thought at the Heaven that was beyond; "and it may be that Thou, O my God, knowest that, in Thy pitiful mercy. As Thou wilt. Life has become but a weary one here, full of pains and penalties."

"Master!" came to him in a hushed, doubtful voice at this juncture. "Master, are you within hearing? My mistress is feeling anxious, and wants the door bolted."

"Ay, bolt and bar it well, Ann," he said, going forward. "But barred doors will not keep out all the foes of man."

Meanwhile Karl had got through the maze; and cautiously, after listening, let himself out at the gate. No human being, that he could discern, was within sight or hearing; and he crossed the road at once. Then, but not before, he became aware that his agent, Mr. Smith, was in that favourite spot and attitude of his, leaning his arms on the little garden gate, his green glasses discarded—as they generally were after sunset.

"Good-night," said Karl in passing. But some words of the agent's served to arrest his progress.

"Would you mind stepping in for one moment, Sir Karl? I wanted to say just a word to you, and have been watching for you to come out."

"Is it anything particular?" asked Karl, turning in at the gate at once, which Mr. Smith held open.

"I'll get a light, sir, if you will wait an instant."

Karl heard the striking of a match in-doors, and Mr. Smith reappeared in the passage with a candle. He ushered Karl into the room on the left-hand; the best room, that was rarely used.

"This one has got its shutters closed," was the explanatory remark. "I generally keep the others open until I go to bed."

"Tell me at once what it is you want," said Karl. "It is late, and I shall have my household wondering where I am."

"Well, Sir Karl, first of all, I wish to ask if you are aware that you were watched into the Maze to-night?" He spoke in the lowest whisper; scarcely above his breath. The agent's one servant had been in bed at the top of the house long before: but he was a cautious man.

"No. Who watched me?"

"Two people, sir. One was Miss Blake, the lady staying with you at the Court; the other was a confounded fellow who is at Foxwood for no good, I guess, and is pushing his prying nose on the sly into everything."

"Do you mean Mr. Strange?"

"That's the name: a lodger at Mother Jinks's. He and the lady watched you in, Sir Karl; they stood close by the gate among the trees; and then they walked off down the road together."

Karl's pulses beat a shade more quickly. "Why should they have been watching me? What could be their motive?"

"Miss Blake did not intend to watch—as I take it. I saw her coming along with a sharpish step from the direction of that blessed St. Jerome's, late as it was—Cattacomb may have been treating his flock to a nocturnal service. When she was close upon the Maze she must have heard your footsteps, for she drew suddenly behind the trees to hide herself. After you were in, she came out of her shelter, and another with her—the man Strange. So he must have been hidden there beforehand, Sir Karl: and, I should say, to watch."

Karl was silent. He did not like to hear this. It seemed to menace further danger.

"I went in to warn Sir Adam against this man," he observed; "to tell him never to be off his guard, day or night. He is a London detective!"

"What—Strange is?" exclaimed the agent, with as much astonishment as his low tones allowed him to express. "A London detective, Sir Karl?"

"Yes, he is."

Mr. Smith's face fell considerably. "But—what is he doing down here?" he inquired. "Who's he after? *Surely* not Sir Adam?"

"No, not Sir Adam. He is after some criminal who—who does not exist in the place at all," added Karl, not choosing to be more explicit, considering

that it was the man before him whom he had suspected
of being the said criminal, and feeling ashamed of his
suspicions now that they were dispelled, and he had
to speak of it with him face to face. "The danger is,
that in looking after one man the police may come
upon the track of another."

The agent nodded his head. "But surely they do
not suspect the Maze?"

"They do suspect the Maze," replied Karl. "Owing
to the tattling of the woman Mr. Moore took there—
Nurse Chaffen—they suspect it."

Mr. Smith allowed a very unorthodox word to issue
through his closed teeth, applied not only to the lady
in question, but to ladies in general.

"The man Strange has been down here looking
after some one whom he can't find; who no doubt is
not in the neighbourhood at all, and never has been,"
resumed Karl. "Strange's opinion, however, was—and
is—that the man is here, concealed. When he heard
Chaffen's tale of the gentleman she saw in evening
dress at the Maze, but whom she never saw again and
therefore concluded he was hidden somewhere about
the house not to show himself to her, he caught up
the notion that it was the man he was after. Hence
his suspicions of the Maze, and his watchings."

"It's a very unfortunate thing!" breathed the agent.

"You see now, Mr. Smith, how much better it
would have been if Sir Adam had never come here.
Or, being here, if he had been allowed to go away
again."

"He can't attempt it now," was the quiet retort of
the agent. "With a detective's eyes about, it would
be only to walk straight into the lion's mouth."

"Just so. We all know that."

"I wish to heaven I *could* get him away!" spoke
the agent impulsively, and it was evident that his heart
was in his words. "Until now I believed he was as
safe here as he could be elsewhere—or safer. What
the devil brings a confounded detective in this quiet
place? The malignant fiend, or some implacable fate
must have sent him. Sir Karl, the danger is great.
We must not shut our eyes to it."

Alas, Karl Andinnian felt that, in a more cruel
degree than the agent could. It was *his* work; it was
he who had brought this hornet's nest about his unfortunate brother's head. The consciousness of it lay
heavily upon him in that moment; throat and tongue
and lips were alike parched with the fever of remorse.

"May I ask you for a glass of water, Mr. Smith?"
broke next from the said dry lips.

"I'll get it for you in a moment, sir," said the agent,
rising with alacrity.

Karl heard another match struck outside, and then
the steps of the agent retreating in the direction of
the pump. In his restlessness of mind he could not
sit still, but rose to pace the room. A small set of ornamental book-shelves, hanging against the wall, caught
his attention: he halted before it and took down a
volume, mechanically, rather than with any motive.

"Philip Salter. From his loving mother."

The words met Karl's eyes as he opened the book.
Just for a moment he questioned whether his sight
was deceiving him. But no. There they were, in a
lady's hand, the ink dry and faded with time. It was
Bunyan's "Pilgrim's Progress."

"*Is* it Salter, after all?" mentally breathed Karl.

Mr. Smith came in again with the glass of water as the doubt was running through Karl's mind. Thanking his agent for the water, he drank it at a draught, and sat down with the book in his hand.

"I have been amongst your books, you see, Mr. Smith. A sound old volume, this."

"So it is, Sir Karl. I dip into it myself now and then."

"Did you know this—this Mr. Philip Salter?"— holding the book open at the words.

For answer the agent threw his eyes straight into Karl's face, and paused. "Did *you* know him, Sir Karl?"

"I never knew him. I have heard somewhat about him."

"Ay, few persons but have, I expect," returned the agent, with a kind of groan. "He was my cousin, sir."

"Your cousin!" echoed Karl.

"My own cousin: we were sisters' sons. He was Philip Salter; I am Philip Smith."

Karl's eyes were opened. In more senses than one.

"The fool that Philip Salter showed himself!" ejaculated Philip Smith—and it was evident by the bitter tone that the subject was a sore one. "I was in his office, Sir Karl, a clerk under him; but he was some years younger than I. He might have done so well: none of us had the smallest idea but what he was doing well. It was all through private and illegitimate speculation. He got into a hole where the mire was deep, and he used dangerous means when at his wits' end to get himself out of it. It did for him what you know, and it ruined me; for, being his cousin, men thought I must have known of it, and my place was taken from me."

"Where is he now?" asked Karl.

"I don't know. Sometimes we think he is dead. After his escape, we had reason to believe that he got off to Canada, but we were never made certain of it, and have never heard from him in any way. He may be in some of the backwoods there, afraid to write."

"And this was his book?"

"Yes. Most of his small belongings came into my hands. The affair killed his mother: broke her heart. He was all she had, save one daughter. Sir Karl, do you know what I'd do if I had the power?" fiercely continued Smith. "I would put down by penal laws all these cursed speculators who, men of straw themselves, issue their plausible schemes only to deceive and defraud a confiding, credulous public; all these betting and gambling rogues who lay hold of honest natures to lure them to their destruction. But for them, Philip Salter had been holding up his untarnished head yet."

"Ay," assented Karl. "But that will never be, so long as the greed of gold shall last. It is a state of affairs that can belong only to a Utopian world; not to this."

He put out his hand to Philip Smith when he left —a thing he had never done voluntarily before—in his sensitive regret for having wronged the man in his heart: and went home with his increased burden of perplexity and pain.

CHAPTER X.

One Day in her Life.

LIFE was to the last degree dreary for Lucy Andinnian.   But for the excitement imparted to her
mind from that mysterious building, the Maze, and
the trouble connected with it, she could scarcely have
continued to go on, and bear.   It was not a healthy
excitement: no emotion can be that, which has either
jealousy or anger for its origin.   Let us take one day
of her existence, and see what it was: the day following the one last told of.

A mellow, bright morning.   The pleasant sun, so
prolific of his bounties that year, was making the
earth glad with his renewed light, and many a heart
with it.   Not so Lucy's: it seemed to her that never a
gleam of gladness could illumine hers again.   She sat
in her room, partly dressed, after a night of much
sleeplessness.   What sleep she had was disturbed, as
usual, by dreams tinged with the unpleasantness of
her waking thoughts.   A white wrapper enfolded her,
and Aglaé was doing her hair.   The woman saw how
weary and spiritless her mistress was becoming; but
not a suspicion of the true cause suggested itself, for
Lucy and her husband took care to keep up appearances, and guarded their secret well.   Aglaé attempted
to say a word now and again, but received no en-
couragement: Lucy was buried in a reverie.

"We are growing more estranged day by day," ran
her thoughts.   "He went to London yesterday, and
never said why; never gave me the least explanation.
After he came home at night, and had taken some-

thing to eat, he went out again. To the Maze, of course."

"Will my lady please to have her hair in rolls or in plats this morning?"

"As you please, Aglaé." And, the weary answer given, her thoughts ran on again.

"I fancy Theresa had seen him go there. I can't help fancying it. She had all her severe manner on when she came in last night, but was so pityingly kind to me. And I could bear all so much better if she would not be pitiful. It was past ten. That poor Mrs. Bell is likely to die, and Theresa had been to read to her. I kept hoping she would go to bed, and she did not. Is it wrong of *me* to sit up, I wonder, to see what time he comes in?—would Margaret say it was? She got her silks and her work about, and I had mine. He has hardly ever been so late as last night. It was half-past eleven. What right has she to keep him, or he to stay? He said, in a light, indifferent kind of tone, by way of excuse, that he had been talking with Smith, and the time slipped by unheeded. Theresa drew in her lips till she seemed to have none at all, and gave him just one scornful glance. Yes: she had certainly seen him go in elsewhere, and she knew that the excuse was not true. I took my candle, and came up here—and have had one of my most wretched nights again—and neither I nor Aglaé could find that book that comforts me. It was very cruel of Karl to marry me: and yet—and yet—would I be unmarried if I could? Would I break even from this distressing life, if it involved a separation for ever? I fear not. The not seeing him day by day would be a worse fate even than this is."

"Did my lady think to ask Sir Karl whether he had put away that book that is missing?" interposed Aglaé, quite unconscious that her lady had not seen Sir Karl since the book was missed, any more than she herself had: and moreover that he was not likely to see it.

"I have not asked him yet. Perhaps I took it downstairs yesterday."

"Which robe, my lady?"

"The Swiss muslin."

Aglaé left her when she was ready, and Lucy took her Bible for a few minutes, and said her prayers. Never did prayers ascend from a more wrung or troubled heart. The book she had mislaid was one of those little gems of consolation that can only be estimated in *need*. It had been given to Lucy by Miss Sumnor.

She stood a few minutes at the open window, gazing at the sunny morning. The variegated leaves of the changing trees—getting, alas! bare as Lucy's heart felt—the smooth lawn, which Maclean was rolling, the still bright flowers, the sunlight glittering on the lodge. All these fair things were hers; and yet, she could enjoy them not.

She went down: putting away all the sadness from her face that she could put, and looking in her pretty dress as fair as the sunshine. Hewitt came in with the coffee, and Lucy took her place at table. They never waited for Miss Blake. St. Jerome's was exacting, and Mr. Cattacomb somewhat uncertain as to the precise time at which he let out his flock. Hewitt went across the lawn to tell his master, who was talking to Maclean, that the breakfast was ready.

10*

Karl came in through the open doors of the window. She glanced up and hid her eyes again: the more attractive he looked—and he always did look attractive—the greater her sense of pain. The fresh air was sweet and pleasant, and a good fire burnt in the grate.

"Good morning, Lucy."

She put down the sugar-tongs to give him her hand, and wished him good morning in a tone that no eavesdropper could have found fault with. They were quite civil to each other; nay, courteous; their intercourse much like that of true friends, or a brother and sister. After playing so long at this for the sake of keeping up appearances to their household and the world, it had become quite easy—a thing of habit.

"What shall I give you?" he asked.

"An egg, please."

"Maclean thinks that fir-tree is dying."

"Which fir-tree?"

"The large one by the ferns. He wants to root it up and make a bed there. What do you think?"

"I don't mind how it it. Is your coffee sweet enough?"

"Yes."

Hewitt appeared with the letters. Two for Miss Blake, one for Lady Andinnian, none for Sir Karl. Lucy read hers; glad of the help it afforded to occupation: for she did but toy with her breakfast, having little appetite now.

"It is from mamma," said Lucy. "She is going to stay with my aunt in London. I suppose you did not call on Lady Southal yesterday?"

"I? No."

"You have promised to do so for some time past."

"But I have not been able. When the mind is harassed with worry and business, social calls get put aside. Is Mrs. Cleeve well?"

"Yes, and papa better. He is going to stay at home himself. They desire to be remembered to you."

Karl bent his head in acknowledgment. And thus, talking indifferently of this and that, the meal came to an end. Karl asked his wife if she would go out to look at the fir-tree, and hear what Maclean said—he was always scrupulous in consulting her wishes as the Court's mistress. She brought her parasol at once.

Karl held out his arm, and she took it. As they went down the steps, Miss Blake appeared. They waited to greet her, and to shake hands.

"You must want your breakfast, Theresa. There are two letters for you on the table. Oh, and I have heard from mamma. She is going to stay with Aunt Southal in London."

Lucy took Karl's arm again, and they went off with the gardener. Miss Blake probably did want her breakfast; but she spared a minute or two to look after them.

"I wonder if anyone was ever so great a hypocrite?" ran her comment. "And to think that I once believed him to be the most noble and best of men. He dared to speak disparagingly of that pure saint, Mr. Cattacomb, the other day. Good patience! what contrasts there are in the world! And the same Heaven made them both, and permits both! One cannot understand it here. As to Lucy—but I wash my hands of *her*."

Lucy was soon back again. Miss Blake had but read her letters, and begun her breakfast. Karl had passed into his own room.

The morning wore on. Theresa went out again; Karl was shut up and then he went out; Lucy was left in the house alone. It was usually so. She had given her orders, and no earthly thing else remained to do—save let her heart prey upon itself. When she had gone pretty nearly out of her mind, she put her bonnet on, and betook herself to Mrs. Whittle, the widow of the man who had died suddenly at the station in the summer. Passing out at the extreme gate of the Court, Lucy had but to skirt the wood, and in three minutes was at the cottage: one of a row.

She had taken to come here when she was very particularly miserable—as she felt this day. For the lesson it read to her was most salutary, acting as a kind of tonic. That this poor woman was slowly dying, there could not be much doubt of. She had been in ill health before her husband's death, and the blow struck too severely on the weakened frame. But for Karl and his wife the family must have taken refuge in the workhouse. Lucy went in and sat down on a low wooden stool. Mrs. Whittle, about to-day, was in the easy-chair, sent to her from the Court, her three little girls around her, the eldest eight years of age. Two younger children, boys, played on the floor.

"I am teaching them to sew, ma'am," she said to

Lucy. "Bessy has got her hand pretty well into it; but the other two haven't. When I lie awake at nights, my lady, and think how little it is they know of any sort of labour yet, and how soon I may be taken from them, and be able to teach no more, my heart fails me. I can only set on to cry, and to pray God to forgive me all my short-comings."

The tears had come into her eyes, and were falling down her hectic cheeks. She had been very pretty once, but the face was wasted now. Lucy's eyelashes were wet.

"But I think you look better, Mrs. Whittle. And as to short-comings—we all might own to those."

"It seems to me that I could have brought them on better if I'd known what was coming, ma'am. Until that night when my husband was carried home on a shutter, I had not had a thought of death, as being likely to concern any of us at home here. And now the time seems to be coming to an end, and I'm leaving them, and they know nothing."

"I hope you will get better yet," said Lucy.

"I don't think so, ma'am. I should like to if I could. The very distress that is upon me about my children seems as if it kept me back. Nobody can know what it is to leave a family of young children to the world, till they come to it themselves. There's a dreadful yearning upon me always, my lady, an aching like, at the thought of it. Mr. Sumnor, he is very good and kind, and he comes here, and tells me about heaven, and how free from care I shall be, once I get to it. But oh, ma'am, when I must leave these little ones here, with nobody to say a word to keep them from the world's bad ways, how do I know that *they* will ever get to heaven?"

The woman had never spoken out as she was speaking to-day. Generally she had seemed calm and resigned—to get well, or to die. Lucy was intensely sorry for her. She would take herself to task for being so miserable with this real distress close at hand, and for at least the rest of the day allow it to read her a salutary lesson.

Passing in at the small gate again, she made her way to the acacia tree and sat down under it, letting her parasol fall to the ground. Karl, who was at home again, could see her from his window, but he did not attempt to go to her. And so she idled away the morning in weariness.

Theresa appeared at luncheon; but Sir Karl did not. Lucy remembered that a parcel she was expecting from London ought to be at the station (only an autumn mantle) and thought she would go in the pony-chaise for it. Anything for a change — for a break in her monotonous life. So the chaise was ordered, and the groom to drive it. It came round, and she was getting in when Karl approached.

"Are you going to drive yourself, Lucy?"

"Oh no. Robert is coming."

"I will go, then. We shall not want you, Robert."

"But I was only going to the station," she said.

"To the station?"

"I think my new mantle may be there."

He drove off, turning towards the station. The mantle was not there: and Karl continued his drive as far as Basham. They said very little to one another. Just a remark on the scenery, or on any object passing: nothing more. Karl pulled up at the saddler's shop, to give some direction about a set of harness they were making for him. Just as he got into the chaise again, somebody passed and took off his hat, with a "Good afternoon, Sir Karl."

It was Mr. Tatton. Karl wondered what he was doing in Basham. Of course, the detective might be there for fifty things, totally unconnected with his profession: but nevertheless the sight of him awoke uneasiness in Karl's mind. When a heavy dread lies upon us, the most trifling event will serve to stir up suspicion and augment fear.

Karl drove home again, and Lucy went up to her little sitting-room. She was owing a letter to Mrs. Cleeve, but held back from writing it. Great though her affection was for her mother, she hated now to write. It was so impossible to fill up a letter—as it seemed to Lucy—and yet guard her secret. She could not say "Karl and I are doing this;" or "Karl and I are doing the other:" and yet if she did not say something of this kind of their home life, or mention his name, her fancy suggested that it would look strange, and might arouse doubt. Conscience makes us cowards. She might have sent a letter that day, saying, "I have just got home from a drive with Karl;" and "Karl and I decided this morning to have that old fir-tree by the rocks dug up;" and it would be quite true: but Lucy in her strict integrity so disliked the deceit the words would imply, that she shrank from writing them.

Footsteps on the gravel below: *his* footsteps: and she went to the window to glance out. Yes, he was going straight down the gravel walk, and through the large gates. Going where? Her heart beat a little quicker as the question crept in. To the Maze? The query was always suggesting itself now.

He turned that way—and that was all she could tell, for the trees hid the road from her view. He might be going to his agent's; he might be going to some part or other of his estate; but to Lucy's jealous mind the probability seemed perfectly clear that his destination was that shut-in house, which she had already begun to hate so much. And yet—she believed that he did not go in by day-time. Lucy wondered whether Fair Rosamund, who had disturbed the peace of her queen, was half as fair as this Rosamund, now turning her own poor heart to sickness.

More footsteps on the gravel: merry tongues, light laughter. Lucy looked out again. Some of the young ladies from the village had called for Theresa, and they were now going on to St. Jerome's. For laughter such as that, for the real lightness of heart that must be its inevitable accompaniment, Lucy thought she would have bartered a portion of her remaining life.

Aglaé came in, her hands and arms full of clouds of tulle and blue ribbon.

"Look here, my lady—these English modistes have no taste at all. They can't judge. They send this heavy satin ribbon, saying it is the fashion, and they put it in every part of the beautiful light robe, so that you cannot tell which is robe, the tulle, or the ribbon. My lady is not going to wear that, say I; an English modiste might wear it, but my young lady never. So I take the ribbons off."

Lucy looked round listlessly. What did all these adornments matter to her? Karl never seemed to see now what she was dressed in: and if he had seen, he would not have cared.

"But what is it you are asking me, Aglaé?"

"I would ask my lady to let me put just a quarter of as much ribbon on: and silk ribbon, not satin. I have some silk in the house, and this satin will come in for a heavier robe."

"Do whatever you like, Aglaé."

"That's well," said Aglaé. "But I wish my lady would not show herself quite so indifferent," added the woman to herself as she withdrew. "She could not care less if she were the old grandmother."

The afternoon passed to its close, Lucy reading a bit and working a bit to beguile the time. Whether the book or the work lay before her, her mind was alike far away, brooding over the trouble that could never leave it. Then she went down to dinner in her evening dress of silk. No stranger was present: only herself, Karl, and Theresa. It was generally thus: neither she nor he had spirits to bring guests about them often. Theresa told them of a slight accident that had happened at the station that afternoon, and it served for a topic of conversation. Dinner was barely over when Miss Diana Moore called in. She was not given to time her visits ceremoniously; but she was always welcome, for Karl and Lucy both liked her. Miss Diana generally gave them the news of the place, and she began now. In some inexplicable manner the conversation turned on the Maze. At least, something was said that caused the place to be incidentally mentioned, and it served to draw Miss Diana's thoughts to what they might otherwise not have reverted to.

"The senseless geese that people are!" she cried.

"Did you hear of that ghost story that arose about the Maze?"

Karl bit his lip. Lucy looked at Miss Diana: she had heard nothing.

"Mother Jinks told me to my face the other day that there could not be a doubt it was Mr. Throcton's son haunting it. My brother—Mr. Moore—had seen it, she said, as well as Nurse Chaffen: a gentleman in evening dress, who appeared to them and vanished away again. She believed it, too."

"I fancy it has been rather more materially accounted for," put in Miss Blake, not at all sorry of the opportunity to give a side fling at Sir Karl.

"Well, what I hear people have found out now is, that the ghost was only Sir Karl Andinnian, who had called in there after or before his dinner," said Miss Diana, laughing. "What do you say to it, Sir Karl?"

Sir Karl did not know what to say. On the one hand it was most essential to do away, if possible, with the impression that any strange gentleman had been at the Maze; on the other, he did not care to admit that he paid evening visits there. Of the two evils, however, the last was the least.

"It may have been myself, Miss Diana. I cannot say, I'm sure. I remember I went over one evening, and stayed a few minutes."

"But it was while Mrs. Grey was ill with fever."

"Just so. I went to enquire after her."

"Well, I suppose it was you, then. I asked William about it, but he is as close as wax when he likes, and professed not to know what I was talking of. One thing is clear, that he could not have recognised you, Sir Karl. It was nearly dark, I believe. That little baby at the Maze is very delicate."

"By the way, Miss Diana, talking of such people, what does Mr. Moore think of poor Whittle's widow?" asked Sir Karl. "My wife says she is very ill."

The conversation was turned — Sir Karl's object in speaking. Miss Diana talked of Mrs. Whittle, and then went on to other subjects.

But it will be readily seen how cruelly these and similar incidents tried Lucy Andinnian. Had an angel come down from heaven to assure her the gentleman in evening attire was *not* Sir Karl, she would have refused to believe it. Nay, he had, so to say, confessed it—in her presence.

Miss Diana departed. Karl went out with her, and did not come in again. Lucy knew he had gone to the Maze. She went up to her room, and stood there in the dark watching for his return. It was nearly ten when he appeared: he had been spending all that time with her rival!

Even so. Sir Karl had spent it at the Maze. As the autumn evenings grew darker, he could go over earlier and come away earlier. Lucy wondered whether this state of things was to last for ever, and how much longer she could continue to bear and make no sign.

To her weary bed again went she. To the anguish of her outraged heart; to her miserable, sleepless hours, and her still more miserable dreams. Jealousy as utterly mistaken and foundationless has too often inflicted torment lively as this.

It is a "green-eyed monster, which doth make the food it feeds on."

CHAPTER XI.
Mrs. Chaffen disturbed.

WE have now to return to Mr. Strange. That eminent detective was, to tell the truth, somewhat puzzled by his interview with Sir Karl Andinnian, held in the road; thrown, so to say, slightly on his beam ends. The earnest assurances of Sir Karl—that the individual he had been suspecting was the agent Smith, and that there was not, and could not be, any gentleman residing at the Maze—had made their due impression, for he saw that Sir Karl was a man whose word might be trusted. At the same time he detected, or thought he detected, an undue eagerness on Sir Karl's part to impress this upon him; an eagerness which the matter itself did not justify, unless Sir Karl had a private and personal motive for it. Musing on this, Mr. Strange had continued to walk about that evening instead of going on to his lodgings; and when Miss Blake surprised him underneath the trees at the Maze gate—or, rather, surprised herself by finding him there—he had not sought the spot to watch the gate, but as a shelter of seclusion while he thought. The stealthy entrance of Sir Karl Andinnian with a key taken from his pocket, and the whispered communication from Miss Blake, threw altogether another light upon the matter, and served to show what Sir Karl's personal motive might be. According to that lady's hints, Sir Karl was in the habit of stealing into the Maze, and that it was no one but Sir Karl himself who had been seen by Nurse Chaffen.

Mr. Detective Strange could not conceal from his acute brain that, if this were true, his own case was almost as good as disposed of, and he might prepare to go back to town. Salter, the prey he was patiently searching out, was at the Maze or nowhere—for Mr. Strange had turned the rest of the locality inside out, and knew that it contained no trace of him. If the gentleman in the evening dress, seen by Nurse Chaffen, was Sir Karl Andinnian, it could not have been Philip Salter: and, as his sole motive for suspecting the Maze was that worthy woman's account of him she had seen, why the grounds of suspicion seemed slipping from under him.

He thought it out well that night. Well and thoroughly. The tale was certainly likely and plausible. Sir Karl Andinnian did not appear to be one who would embark on this kind of private expedition; but, as the detective said to himself, one could not answer for one's own brother. Put it down as being Sir Karl that the woman saw, why then the mystery of her not having seen him again was at an end: for while she was there Sir Karl would not be likely to go to the Maze and show himself a second time.

The more Mr. Strange thought it out, the further reason he found for suspecting that this must be the true state of the case. It did not please him. Clear the Maze of all suspicion as to Salter, and it would become evident that they had been misled, and that so much valuable time had been wasted. He should have to go back to Scotland Yard and report the failure. Considering that he had latterly been furnishing reports of the prey being found and as good as in his hands, the prospect was mortifying. This would be the second consecutive case in which he had signally failed.

But it was by no means Mr. Strange's intention to take the failure for granted. He was too wary a detective to do that without seeking for proof, and he had not done with Foxwood yet. The first person he must see was Mrs. Chaffen.

Somewhat weary with his night reflections and not feeling quite so refreshed as he ought, for the thing had kept him awake till morning, Mr. Strange sat down to his breakfast languidly. Watchful Mrs. Jinks, who patronized her easy lodger and was allowed to visit his tea, and sugar, and butter, and cheese with impunity, observed this as she whipped off the cover from a dish of mushrooms that looked as though it might tempt an anchorite.

"You've got a headache this morning, Mr. Strange, sir. Is it bad?"

"Oh, very bad," said Mr. Strange, who did not forget to keep up his rôle of delicate health as occasion afforded opportunity.

"What things them headaches are!" deplored Mrs. Jinks. "Nobody knows whence they come nor how to drive 'em away. Betsey Chaffen was nursing a patient in the spring, who'd had bilious fever and rheumatis combined; and to hear what she said about that poor dear old gentleman's head——"

"By the way, how is Mrs. Chaffen?" interrupted Mr. Strange, with scant ceremony, and no regard to the old gentleman's head. "I have not seen her lately."

"She was here a day or two ago, sir; down in my kitchen. As to how she is, she's as strong as need be: which it's thanks to you for inquiring. *She* never has nothing the matter with her."

"Is she out nursing?"

"Not now. She expects to be called out soon, and is waiting at home for it."

"Where is her home?"

"Down Foxglove Lane, sir, turning off by Mr. Sumnor's church. Bull, the stonemason, lives in the end house there, and she have lodged with 'em for years. Bull tells her in joke sometimes that some of 'em ought to be took ill, with such a nurse as her in the house. Which they never are, for it's as healthy a spot as any in Foxwood."

Mr. Strange had a knack of politely putting an end to his landlady's gossip when he pleased, and of sending her away. He did so now: and the widow transferred herself and her attentions to Mr. Cattacomb's parlour.

People must hold spring and autumn cleanings, or where would their carpets and curtains be? Mrs. Chaffen, though occupying but one humble room (with a choice piece of furniture in it that was called a "bureau" by day, and was a bed by night) was not exempt from the general sanitary obligations. Mrs. Bull considered that she instituted these periodical bouts of scrubbing oftener than there was occasion for: but Betsey Chaffen liked to take care of her furniture—which was her own—and was moreover a cleanly woman.

On this self-same morning she was in the thick of it: her gown turned up about her waist, her hands and arms bare to the elbow, plunged into a bucket of soapsuds, herself on her knees, and the furniture all heaped together on the top of the shut-up bureau in the corner, when one of the young Bulls came in with

the astounding news that a gentleman was asking for
her.

"Goodness bless me!" cried the poor woman,
turning cold all over, "it can't be that I'm fetched
out, can it, Sam?—and me just in the middle of all
this mess!"

"He said, was Mrs. Chaffen at home, and could
he see her," replied Sam. "He's a waiting outside."

Mrs. Chaffen sat back on her heels, one hand
resting on the bucket, the other grasping the wet
scrubbing-brush, and her face the very picture of con-
sternation as she stared at the boy. She had believed
herself free for a full week to come.

"Is it Mr. Henley himself, Sam?"

"It ain't Mr. Henley at all," said Sam. "It's the
gentleman what's staying at Mrs. Jinks's."

"What the plague brings him here this morning
of all others, when I've got the floor in a sop and
not a chair to ask him to set down upon!" cried the
woman, relieved of her great fear, but vexed nevertheless to be interrupted in her work, and believing
the intruder to be Mr. Cattacomb, come on one of his
pastoral visits: for that excellent divine made no scruple,
in his zeal, of looking in occasionally on Mr. Sumnor's
flock as well as his own. "Parsons be frightful bothers
sometimes!"

"'Tain't the parson; it's the t'other one," said Sam
Bull.

Mrs. Chaffen rose from her knees, stepped gingerly
across the wet floor, and took a peep through the
window. There she saw Mr. Strange in the centre of
a tribe of young Bulls, dividing among them a piece

of lettered gingerbread. Sam, afraid of not coming in for his share of the letters, bolted out of the room.

"Ask the gentleman if he'll be pleased to step in, Sam, and to excuse the litter," she called after the boy. "I don't mind *him*," she mentally added, seizing upon a mop to mop the wet off the floor, and then letting down her gown, "and he must want something particular of me; but I'd not have cared to stand Cattakin's preaching this busy morning."

Mr. Strange came in in his pleasant way, admiring everything, from the room to the bucket, and assuring her he rather preferred wet floors to dry ones. While she was reaching him a chair and dusting it with her damp apron, he held out his hand, pointing to where the cuts had been.

"Look here, Mrs. Chaffen. I have been thinking of coming to you this day or two past, but fancied I might see you in Paradise Row, for I'd rather have your opinion than a doctor's at any time. The hand has healed, you see."

"Yes, sir; it looks beautiful."

"But I am not sure that it has healed properly, though it may look 'beautiful,'" he rejoined. "Feel this middle cut. Here; just on the seam."

Mrs. Chaffen rubbed her fingers on the same check apron, and then passed them gently over the place he spoke of. "What do you feel?" he asked.

"Well, sir, it feels a little hard, and there seems to be a kind of knot," she said, still examining the place.

"Precisely so. There's a stiffness about it that I don't altogether like, and now and then it has a kind

11*

of a prickly sensation. What I have been fancying is, that a bit of glass may possibly be in it still."

But Mrs. Chaffen did not think so. In her professional capacity she talked nearly as learnedly as a doctor could have talked, though not using quite the same words. Her opinion was that if glass had remained in the hand it would not have healed: she believed that Mr. Strange had only to let it alone and have a little patience, and the symptoms he spoke of would go away.

It is not at all improbable that this opinion was Mr. Strange's own; but he thanked her and said he would abide by her advice, and gave her a little more gentle flattery. Then he sat down in the chair she had dusted, as if he meant to remain for the day, in spite of the disorder of affairs and the damp floor, and entered on a course of indiscriminate gossip. Mrs. Chaffen liked to get on quickly with her work, but she liked gossip better; no matter how busy she might be, a dish of *that* never came amiss; and she put her back against another chair and folded her bare arms in her apron, and gossiped back again.

In a smooth and natural manner, apparently without intent, the conversation presently turned upon the gentleman (or ghost) Mrs. Chaffen had seen at the Maze. It was a theme she had not tired of yet.

"Now you come to talk of that," cried the detective, "do you know what idea has occurred to me upon the point, Mrs. Chaffen? I think the gentleman you saw may have been Sir Karl Andinnian."

Nurse Chaffen, contrary to her usual habit, did not immediately reply, but seemed to fall into thought.

"Was it Sir Karl?"

"Well now that's a odd thing!" she broke forth at last. "Miss Blake asked me the very same question, sir—was it Sir Karl Andinnian?"

"Oh, did she. When?"

"When we had been talking of the thing in your rooms, sir—that time that I had been a dressing of your hand. In going down stairs, somebody pulled me, all mysterious like, into the Reverend Cattakin's parlour: I found it was Miss Blake, and she began asking me what the gentleman looked like and whether it was not Sir Karl."

"And was it Sir Karl?"

"Being took by surprise in that way," went on Mrs. Chaffen, disregarding the question, "I answered Miss Blake that I had not had enough time to notice the gentleman and could not say whether he was like Sir Karl or not. Not having reflected upon it then, I spoke promiscuous, you see sir, on the spur of the moment."

"And was it Sir Karl?" repeated Mr. Strange. "Now that you have had time to reflect upon it, is that the conclusion you come to?"

"No, sir; just the opposite. A minute or two afterwards, if I'd only waited, I could have told Miss Blake that it was not Sir Karl. I couldn't say who it was, but 'twas not him."

This assertion was so contrary to the theory Mr. Strange had been privately establishing that it took him somewhat by surprise.

"Why are you enabled to say surely it was not Sir Karl?" he questioned, laughing lightly, as if the matter amused him.

"Because, sir, the gentleman was taller than Sir

Karl. And, when I came to think of it, I distinctly saw that he had short hair, either lightish or grayish: Sir Karl's hair is a beautiful wavy brown, and he wears it rather long."

"Twilight is very deceptive," remarked Mr. Strange.

"No doubt of that, sir: but there was enough light coming in through the passage windows for me to see what I have said. I am quite positive it was not Sir Karl Andinnian."

"Would you swear it was not?"

"No, sir, I'd not swear it: swearing's a ticklish thing: but I am none the less sure. Mr. Strange, it was not Sir Karl *for certain*," she added impressively. "The gentleman was taller than Sir Karl and had a bigger kind of figure, broader shoulders like, and it rather struck me at the time that he limped in his walk. That I couldn't hold to, however."

"Just the description of what Salter would most likely be now," mused the detective, his doubts veering about uncomfortably. "He would have a limp, or something worse, after that escapade out of the railway carriage."

"Well, if you are so sure about it, Mrs. Chaffen, I suppose it could not have been Sir Karl."

"I can trust my sight, sir, and I *am* sure. What ever could have give rise to the thought that it was Sir Karl?" continued she, after a moment's pause.

"Why, you must know, Mrs. Chaffen, that Sir Karl Andinnian is the only man in Foxwood who is likely to put on evening dress as a rule. And being a neighbour of Mrs. Grey's and her landlord also, it was not so very improbable he should have called in, don't you see?"

Thus enlightened, Mrs. Chaffen no longer wondered how the surmise had arisen. She reiterated her assertion that it was not Sir Karl; and Mr. Strange, gliding into the important question of soda for cleaning boards, versus soap, presently took an affable leave.

There he was, walking back again, his thoughts almost as uncertain as the wind. Was Miss Blake's theory right, or was this woman's? If the latter, and the man was in truth such as she described him, taller and broader than Sir Karl, why then he could, after all, have staked his life upon the Maze being Salter's place of concealment. What if both were right? It might be. Sir Karl might be paying these stealthy visits to Mrs. Grey, and yet be totally ignorant that any such person as Salter was at the Maze. They would hardly dare to tell him; and Salter would take care to conceal himself when Sir Karl was there. At any rate, he—Mr. Strange—must try and put the matter to rest with all speed, one way or the other. Perhaps, however, that resolution was more easy to make than to carry out. As a preliminary step he took a walk to the police station at Basham, and was seen in the street there by Sir Karl Andinnian.

CHAPTER XII.

Baffled.

THE Maze, in all its ordinary quietness, was lying at rest under the midday sun. That is, as regards outward and visible rest: of inward rest, the rest that diffuses peace in the heart, there was but little. It was the day following the expedition of Mr. Strange to the house of Bull the stonemason.

Mrs. Grey's baby was lying in its cot. Mrs. Grey, who had been hushing it to sleep, prepared to change her morning wrapper for the gown she would wear during the day. A bouquet of fresh-cut flowers lay on the dressing-table, and the chamber window stood open to the free, fresh air. Ann Hopley was in the scullery below, peeling the potatoes for dinner, and the old man servant was out somewhere over his work. As the woman threw the last potato into the pan, there came a gentle ring at the gate bell. She turned round and looked at the clock in the kitchen.

"Who's that, I wonder? It's too early for the bread. Any way, you'll wait till I've got my potatoes on, who- ever you may be," concluded she, addressing the un- known intruder.

The saucepan on, she went forth. At the gate stood an inoffensive-looking young man with a large letter or folded parchment in his hand.

"What do you want?" asked Ann Hopley.

"Is this the Maze?"

"Yes."

"Does a lady named Grey live here?"

"Yes."

"Then I've got to leave this for her, please."

Taking the key from her pocket, Ann Hopley un- suspiciously opened the gate, and held forth her hand to take the parchment. Instead of giving it to her, the man pushed past, inside; and, to Ann Hopley's horror, Mr. Strange and a policeman suddenly ap- peared, and followed him. She would have closed the gate upon them; and she made a kind of frantic effort to do so: but one woman cannot effect much against three determined men.

"You can shut it now," said Mr. Strange, when they were inside. "Don't be alarmed, my good woman: we have no wish to harm you."

"What do you want?—and why do you force yourselves in, in this way?" she inquired, frightened nearly to death.

"I am a detective officer belonging to the London police force," said Mr. Strange, introducing himself in his true character. "I bring with me a warrant to search the house called the Maze and its out-door premises"—taking the folded paper from the man's hand. "Would you like me to read it to you before I go on?"

"Search them for what?" asked Ann Hopley, feeling angry with herself for her white face. "I don't want to hear anything read. Do you think we have got stolen goods here?—I'm sure you are enough to scare a body's senses away, bursting in like this!"

Mr. Strange slightly laughed. "We are not looking for stolen goods," he said.

"What for then?" resumed the woman, striving to be calm.

"For some one whom I believe is concealed here."

"Some one concealed here! Is it me?—or my mistress?—or my old husband?"

"No."

"Then you won't find anybody else," she returned with an air of relief. "There's no soul in the place but us three, and that I'll vow: except Mrs. Grey's baby. And we had good characters, sir, I can tell you, both me and my husband, before Mrs. Grey engaged us. Would we harbour loose characters here, do you suppose?"

It was so much waste of words. Mr. Strange went without further parley into the intricacies of the Maze, calling to the policeman to follow him, and bidding the other—who was a local policeman also in plain clothes: both of them from Basham—remain near the gate and guard it against anybody's attempted egress. All this while the gate had been open. Ann Hopley locked it with trembling fingers, and then followed the men through the maze, shrieking out words of remonstrance at the top of her voice. Had there been ten felons concealed within, she made enough noise to warn them all.

"For goodness sake, woman, don't make that uproar!" cried the detective. "We are not going to murder you."

The terrified face of Mrs. Grey appeared at her chamber window. Old Hopley was gazing through the chink of the door of the tool-house, which he was about to clean out. The detective heeded nothing. He went straight to the house door and entered it.

"Wait here at the open door, and keep a sharp look round inside and out," were his orders to the policeman. "If I want you, I'll call."

But Ann Hopley darted before Mr. Strange to impede his progress—she was greatly agitated—and seized hold of his arm.

"Don't go in," she cried imploringly; "don't go in, for the love of heaven! My poor mistress is but just out of her confinement and the fever that followed it, and the fright will be enough to kill her. I declare to you that what I have said is true. There's nobody on these premises but those I've named: my mistress and us two servants, me and Hopley. It *can't* be one of us you want!"

"My good woman, I have said that it is not. But, if it be as you say—that there's no one else, no one concealed here—why object to my searching?"

"For her sake," reiterated the agitated woman; "for the poor lady's sake."

"I must search: understand that," said Mr. Strange. "Better let me do it quietly."

As if becoming impressed with this fact, and that it was useless to contend further, Ann Hopley suddenly took her hands off the detective, leaving him at liberty to go where he would. Passing through the kitchen, she began to attend to her saucepan of potatoes.

Armed with his full power, both of law and of will, Mr. Strange began his search. The warrant had not been obtained from Sir Karl Andinnian, but from a magistrate at Basham: it might be that he did not feel sufficiently assured of Sir Karl's good faith: therefore the Maze was not averted beforehand.

It was not a large house; the rooms were soon looked into, and nothing suspicious was to be seen. Three beds were made up in three different chambers: the one in Mrs. Grey's room and two others. Was one of these occupied by Salter? The detective could not answer the doubt. They were plain beds in plain rooms, and it might be that the two servants did not sleep together. Knocking at the door, he entered Mrs. Grey's chamber: the baby slept in its cot: she stood at the glass in her dressing-gown, her golden hair falling about her.

"I beg your pardon; madam; I beg your pardon a thousand times," said the detective, with deprecation, as he removed his hat. "The law sometimes obliges us to do disagreeable things; and we, servants of it, cannot help ourselves."

"At least tell me the meaning of all this," she said with ashy face and trembling lips. And he explained that he was searching the house with the authority of a search-warrant.

"But what is it you want? *Who* is it?"

Again he explained to her that they were looking after an escaped fugitive, who, it was suspected, might have taken refuge in the Maze.

"I assure you, sir," she said, her gentle manner earnest, her words apparently truthful, "that no person whatever, man or woman, has been in the Maze since I have inhabited it, save myself and my two servants."

"Nevertheless, madam, we have information that some one else has been seen here."

"Then it has been concealed from me," she rejoined. "Will you not at least inform me who it is you are searching for? In confidence if you prefer: I promise to respect it."

"It is an escaped criminal named Salter," replied the officer, knowing that she would hear it from Sir Karl Andinnian, and wishing to be as civil to her as he could.

"Salter!" returned Mrs. Grey, showing the surprise that perhaps she did not feel. "Salter! Why Salter —at least if it is Salter—is the man who lives opposite these outer gates, and goes by the name of Smith. Salter has never been concealed here."

The very assertion made by Sir Karl Andinnian. Mr. Strange took a moment to satisfy his keen sight that there was no other ingress to this room, save by the door, and no piece of furniture large enough to conceal a man in, and was then about to bow himself out. But she spoke again.

"On my sacred word of honour, sir, I tell you truth. Sir Karl Andinnian—my landlord—has been suspecting that his agent, Smith, might turn out to be Salter: I suspected the same."

"But that man is not Salter, madam. Does not bear any resemblance to him. It was a misapprehension of Sir Karl's."

"And—do I understand that you are still looking for him here?—in the Maze? I do *not* understand."

"Not looking for that man Smith, madam, but for the real Salter. We have reason to think he is concealed here."

"Then, sir, allow me to affirm to you in all solemnity, that Salter is not, and never has been concealed here," she said with dignity. "Such a thing would be impossible without my knowledge."

He did not care to prolong the conversation. He had his work to do, and no words from her or anyone else would deter him from it. As he was quitting the room, he suddenly turned to ask a question.

"I beg your pardon, madam. Have you any objection to tell me whether your two servants, Hopley and his wife, occupy the same room and bed?"

For a moment or two she gazed at him in silence, possibly in surprise at the question, and then gave her answer almost indifferently.

"Not in general, I believe. Hopley's cough is apt to be troublesome at night, and it disturbs his wife. But I really do not know much about their arrangements: they make them without troubling me."

The detective proceeded on his mission. He soon discovered the concealed door in the evening sitting-room, and passed into the passage beyond it. Ah, if Salter, or any other criminal, were in hiding within its dark recesses, there would be little chance for him now! The passage, very close and narrow, had no egress on either side; it ended in a flight of nearly perpendicular stairs. Groping his way down, he found himself in a vault, or underground room. Mr. Strange was provided with matches, and lighted one. It was a bare place, the brick walls dripping moisture, the floor paved with stone. Here he discovered another narrow passage that led straight along, it was hard to say how far, and he had need to strike more than one match before he had traversed it. It ended in a flight of stairs: which he ascended, and—found himself in a summer-house at the extreme boundary of the garden.

So far the search had not realized his expectations. On the contrary, it was so unsatisfactory as to be puzzling to his experienced mind. There had been no tracks or traces of Philip Salter; no indication that the passages were ever used; and the doors had opened at his touch, unsecured by bolt or bar.

Taking a look round him while he strove to solve more than one problem, the detective slowly advanced along the garden. All the garden ground surrounding the house, it must be understood, whether useful or ornamental, was *within* the circle of the maze of trees,

Turning a corner, after passing the fruit trees and vegetables, he came in view of the lawn and of the green-house; also of Ann Hopley, who was plucking some thyme from the herb bed.

"Have you found what you were looking for, sir?" she asked, every appearance of animosity gone, as she raised her head to put the question when he came near.

"Not yet."

"Well, sir, I hope you are satisfied. You may take my word for it that you never will."

"Think not?" he carelessly said, looking about him.

"Any way, I am not sorry that you have been through them subterranean places underground," she resumed. "My mistress and I have never ventured to look what was in them, and she has not much liked the thought of their being there. We got Hopley to go down one day, but his shoulders stuck in a narrow part, and he had to force 'em back and come up again."

The detective stepped into the green-house, and stood a moment admiring the choice flowers and some purple grapes ripening above. Ann Hopley had gathered her herbs when he came out, and stood with them in her hand.

"If you'd like to take a few flowers, sir, I'm sure Mrs. Grey would not wish to object. Or a bunch of grapes. There's some ripe."

"Thank you, not now."

He pulled open the tool-house door, only partly closed, and looked in on Hopley. The old man was cleaning it out. Sweeping the floor with a besom and raising a cloud of dust enough to choke a dozen throats, he was hissing and fizzing over his work.

Hopley looked very decrepid to-day: his swollen knees were bent and tottering: his humped back was all conspicuous as he stood; while his throat was enveloped in some folds of an old scarlet comforter.

"Mr. Hopley, I think," said the detective, politely. "Will you please tell me the name of the gentleman that's staying here?"

But Hopley, bent nearly double over his work, took no notice whatever. His back was towards the detective; and he kept on his hissing and fizzing, and scattering his clouds of dust.

"He does not hear you, sir," said Ann Hopley, advancing. "He's as deaf as a post, and can make out no voice but mine: especially when he has one of his sore throats upon him, as he has to-day. For my part, I think these bad throats have to do with the deafness. He is always getting them."

Stepping into the midst of the dust, she shook her husband by the arm somewhat roughly, and he raised his head with a start.

"Here, Hopley, just listen a minute," she screamed at the top of her voice. "This gentleman is asking you to tell him the name of the gentleman who is staying here — that's it, is it not, sir?" — and Mr. Strange nodded acquiescence. "The name, Hopley, the name."

"I've never see'd no lady here but the missis," said old Hopley at length, in his imperfect articulation, caused by the loss of his teeth, as he touched his broad-brimmed hat respectfully to the stranger, and looked up, leaning on the besom.

"Not a lady, Hopley; a gentleman," bawled Ann.

"I've see'd no gentleman here at all."

"He is rather stupid as to intellect, is he not?" cried the detective to the wife.

She resented the imputation. "Not at all, sir; no more than deaf people always seem to be."

"What gentleman be it?" asked Hopley. "Smith the agent comes for the rent at quarter-day, and Sir Karl Andinnian came over one morning about the well."

"Neither of those," roared out Mr. Strange. "The gentleman that's hiding here."

"Not them, Hopley," called Ann in his ear. "The gentleman that's hiding here, he says."

"Hiding where?" asked Hopley. "In them underground places? I never know'd as anybody was hiding in 'em."

"Ask him if he'll swear that no man whatever is in hiding here, Mrs. Hopley."

"The gentleman says will you swear that no man is in hiding here at the Maze?" repeated Ann, somewhat improving upon the question.

"I'll swear that there's neither man nor woman in the place, sir, to my knowledge, hiding or not hiding, but us two and the missis," was the answer, given directly to Mr. Strange, and as emphatically as his utterly toothless mouth allowed. "I swear it to my God."

"And you may trust him, sir," said Ann quietly. "I don't believe he ever told a lie in his life: much less took an oath to one. Hopley's honest and straightforward as the day, though he is a martyr to rheumatism."

Mr. Strange nodded his head to the man and left him to his sweeping. The work and the hissing began again before he was clear of the door. In both the tool-house and the green-house no possible chance was afforded of concealment—to ascertain which had doubtless been the chief motive for the detective's invasion of them.

"I don't believe the old man knows about it," ran his thoughts; "but the woman *does*."

Ann Hopley carried her herbs in-doors, and began picking them. Mr. Strange, calling the policeman to his aid, made as thorough a search out of doors as the nature of the premises and the puzzling maze of trees allowed. There was a closed-in passage of communication through the labyrinth, between the back of the house and the outer circle: but it was built solely with a view to convenience—such as the bringing in of coals or beer to the Maze; or, as Ann Hopley expressed it, the carrying of a coffin out of it. The detective had its doors unbolted and unbarred, and satisfied himself that it afforded no facility for concealment. Borrowing a candle of her, he went again to the secret passages underground, both policemen with him, to institute a more minute and thorough examination.

There ensued no result. And Mr. Detective Strange withdrew his men and finally departed himself; one mortifying word beating its unsatisfactory refrain on his brain:

"Baffled."

———

CHAPTER XIII.

At Scotland Yard.

ONCE more on his weary way to London went Karl Andinnian, on the same weary business that he had gone before; but this time he was proceeding direct to the place he had hitherto shunned—Scotland Yard.

The extreme step, taken by the detective Tatton, in searching the Maze, had alarmed Karl beyond measure. True, the unfortunate fugitive, hiding there, had managed to elude detection: but who could say that he would be able to do so another time, or how often these men of the law might choose to go in? The very fact of their not being actually in search of Sir Adam, but of a totally different individual, made it seem all the more unbearably cruel.

In Mrs. Grey's dire distress and perplexity, she had sent that same night for Karl—after the search—and he heard the whole that had taken place. Adam confessed he did not know what was to be done, or how avert the fate—recapture—that seemed closely impending; and Rose almost fell on her knees before Karl, imploring him with tears to try and save her husband from the danger. Karl took his remorse home with him: remorse arising from the knowledge that *he* had brought all this about, he, himself, in his insane inquiries after Salter: and, after much anxious consideration, he resolved to go on the morrow to Scotland Yard.

It was past noon when he reached his destination. After he had stated confidentially the nature of his

12*

business—that it was connected with the search after
Philip Salter, then being carried on at Foxwood by
Detective Tatton—he was told that it was Mr. Superintendent Game who must see him upon the point:
but that at present the superintendent was engaged.
Karl had to wait: and was kept waiting a considerable
time.

Could Karl's eyes have penetrated through two
walls and an intervening room, he might have been
greatly astonished to see the person with whom the
superintendent was occupied. It was no other than
Tatton himself. For the detective, taking a night
after the search to think over matters, just as Karl had
done, had come to the determination of placing the
history of his doings at Foxwood before his superiors,
and to leave with them the decision whether he should
go on with his search, or abandon it. Accordingly,
he also had proceeded to London that morning, but
by an earlier train; and he was now closeted with
Mr. Superintendent Game—who had given him his
original instructions, and had, specially, the Salter
affair in hand—and was laying before him a succinct
narration of facts, together with his various suspicions
and his bafflings. Before the interview was over, the
superintendent was as well acquainted with the Maze,
its rumours and its mysteries and with sundry other
items of Foxwood gossip, as Tatton himself could be.

"A gentleman waiting—had been waiting some
time—to see Mr. Game on the Foxwood business,"
was the interruption that was first brought to them:
and both Mr. Game and Tatton felt somewhat surprised thereby. What gentleman could be engaged
on the Foxwood business, except themselves?

"Who is it?" asked the superintendent. And a card was handed in.

"Sir Karl Andinnian."

A moment's pause to revolve matters, and then the superintendent issued his fiat.

"See him in five minutes."

The five minutes were occupied with Tatton; but he was safely away ere they had expired, carrying with him his orders to wait; and Sir Karl Andinnian was shown in. The superintendent and the visitor met for the first time, and glanced at each other with some curiosity. The officer saw, in the brother of the noted and unfortunate criminal, a pale, refined, and essentially gentlemanly man, with a sad but attractive face that seemed to tell of sorrow; the other saw a spare man of middle height, who in age might have been his father, and whose speech and manners betokened a cultivation as good as his own.

Taking the seat offered him, Karl entered at once upon his business. Explaining shortly and truthfully the unfortunate suspicion on his own part, that had led to his inquiries about Salter of Mr. Burtenshaw, and to the subsequent dispatch of Tatton to Foxwood. He concealed nothing; not even the slight foundation for those suspicions—merely the having seen the name of Philip Salter in a pocket-book that was in the possession of Philip Smith; and related his recent explanation with Smith; when he learnt that he and Salter were cousins. Karl told it all: and the officer saw, and believed, that he was telling it truly. Karl then went on to relate how he had himself sought an interview with Tatton on his last return from London —whither he had gone to try and convince Mr.

Burtenshaw that it was *not* Salter; that he had learnt
from Tatton then that his suspicions were directed to
a house called the Maze, as the place of Salter's concealment, and that he, Sir Karl, had assured Tatton
on his word of honour as a gentleman that it was altogether a mistaken assumption, for that Salter was
not at the Maze, and never had been there. He had
believed that Tatton was convinced by what he said:
instead of which, he had taken the extreme and, under
the circumstances, most unjustifiable step of proceeding to the house with a search warrant and two policemen, to the terror of the lady inhabiting it, Mrs. Grey,
and her two old servants. It was to report this to
Tatton's superiors at head-quarters that he had now
come up from Foxwood, Sir Karl added; not, he emphatically said, to complain of Mr. Tatton or to get
him reprimanded, for no doubt the man, in doing
what he had done, had believed it was but his duty:
but to request that instructions might be given him
to leave Mrs. Grey in tranquillity for the future. She,
feeling much outraged and insulted by the suspicion
that she could have a common criminal like Philip
Salter concealed in her home, had sent for him,
Sir Karl, as her landlord, to beg him to protect her
if in his power, and to secure her from further moles-
tation.

Mr. Superintendent Game listened to Sir Karl's
narrative as attentively and with as much apparent
interest as though it comprised information that he
had never in all his life heard of: whereas, in point
of fact, Tatton had just been going over the same
facts with him, or nearly the same. He admitted to
Sir Karl that it no doubt did seem to Mrs. Grey an

unjustifiable step, an unaccountable intrusion; if indeed Salter were not concealed there and she knew nothing of him.

"I assure you, as I assured Tatton, that she does not," spoke Karl, with almost painful earnestness. "There is not an iota of foundation for supposing Salter ever was at Foxwood; certainly he was never at the Maze."

"Tatton is an experienced officer, Sir Karl. You may depend upon it that he had good reasons for what he did."

"That he fancied he had: I admit that. But they were utterly groundless. I should have thought that had any one lady, above another, been exempt from suspicion of any kind, it was Mrs. Grey. She lives a perfectly retired life at the Maze during her husband's absence, giving offence to none. To suppose she would allow the fugitive Salter, a man whom she never knew or saw, to be concealed within her domains is worse than preposterous."

"It is hazardous to answer so far for any one, Sir Karl," was the rejoinder—and Karl thought he detected a faint smile on the speaker's lips. "Especially for a woman. The best of them have their tricks and turns."

"I can answer for Mrs. Grey."

Mr. Superintendent Game, whose elbow as he faced Sir Karl was leaning on a desk-table, took it off and fell to pushing together some papers, as though in abstraction. He was no doubt taking time mentally to fit in some portions of Karl's narrative with the information possessed by himself. Karl waited a minute and then went on.

"I am sure that this lady would be willing to make a solemn affidavit that she knows nothing of Salter; and that he is not, and never has been, concealed there; if by so doing it would secure her exemption from intrusion for the future."

"Yes, no doubt," said the officer somewhat absently. "Sir Karl Andinnian," he added, turning briskly to face him again after another pause, "I assume that your own part in this business was confined to the sole fact of your entering on the misapprehension of taking your agent Smith to be Salter."

"That's all. But do you not see how I feel myself to be compromised: since it was my unfortunate endeavour to set the doubt at rest, by applying to Burtenshaw, that has originated all the mischief and brought the insult on Mrs. Grey?"

"Of course. But for that step of yours we should have heard nothing of Salter in connection with Foxwood."

Karl maintained a calm exterior: but he could have ground his teeth as he listened. It was too true.

"Then, with that one exception, Sir Karl, I am right in assuming that you personally hold no other part or interest in this affair, as regards Salter?"

"As regards Salter? None whatever."

"Well now," resumed the superintendent, in a confidential kind of tone, "we can talk at our ease for a minute. Does it not strike you, Sir Karl, as an impartial and impassioned looker-on, that there is something rather curious in the affair, taking one thing with another?"

"I fail to catch your meaning, sir," replied Karl,

gazing at the superintendent. "I confess no such idea has occurred to me. Curious in what way?"

"We shall come to that. Philip Smith has been your agent about six months, I believe."

"About that."

"Whence did you have him? Where did he live before?"

"I really do not know. My mother, the late Mrs. Andinnian, who was occupying Foxwood Court during my absence abroad, engaged him. She became ill herself, was unable to attend to anything, and deemed it well to employ some one to look after my interests."

"Report runs in Foxwood—all kinds of gossip have come up to me from the place." The superintendent broke off to add—"that Smith is only your honorary agent, Sir Karl; that he gives it out he is an old friend of the Andinnian family."

"I can assure you that Smith is my paid agent. He has a house to live in, and takes his salary quarterly."

"The house is exactly opposite the Maze gates?"

"Yes," said Karl, beginning to feel somewhat uncomfortable at the drift the conversation appeared to be taking.

"Is there any truth in the statement that your family knew him in earlier days? You will see in a minute, Sir Karl, why I ask you all this. I conclude there is not."

"I understood my mother to imply in her last illness that she had known something of him: but I was not sure that I caught her meaning correctly, and she was too ill for me to press the question. I had never heard of any Smith myself, and the chances were that I misunderstood her. He makes himself useful about the estate, and that is all I have to look to."

"Report says also—pardon me for recurring to it, Sir Karl—that he makes himself a very easy kind of agent; seems to do as he likes, work or play, and spends most of his time smoking in his front garden, exchanging salutations with the passers-by and watching his neighbour's opposite gate."

Had it been to save his life, Karl Andinnian could not have helped the change that passed over his countenance. What was coming? He strove to be cool and careless, poor fellow, and smiled frankly.

"I fancy he is rather idle—and given to smoke too much. But he does well what he has to do for me, for all that. Mine is not a large estate, as you may be aware, and Sir Joseph left it in first-rate condition. There is very little work for an agent."

"Well, now, I will ask you a last question, Sir Karl. Do you think Smith's residence at Foxwood is in any way connected with the Maze?"

"Connected with the Maze!" echoed Sir Karl, his face never betraying the uneasiness that his beating and terrified heart was beginning to feel all too keenly.

"That is, connected with its tenants."

"In what way would it be possible?"

"Look here. Philip Smith presents himself at Foxwood Court about six months ago, soliciting the agency of your estates from Mrs. Andinnian—as there is little doubt he did so present himself to her, and solicit. Now it was a very singular thing for him to do, considering that his previous life (as I happen to know) had in no way whatever qualified him for the situation,

He knew no more of land or the duties of a land-agent than does this inkstand on my table. Why did he attempt to take such a place?"

"For the want of something else to do, probably," replied Karl. "He told me himself the other day, that his cousin's fall ruined him also, by causing him to be turned from his situation. As to the duties he has to perform for me, a child might be at home in them in a week."

"Granted. Let us go on. Mr. Smith's installation at your place as agent was closely followed by the occupancy of the Maze, Mrs. Grey and her servants arriving as its tenants. Was it not so, Sir Karl?"

"I—think it was," assented Karl, appearing to be recalling the past to his memory, and feeling himself in a bath of horror as he saw that the all-powerful man before him, powerful to know, to rule, and to act, was quite at home behind the scenes.

"Well, I cannot help thinking that the one may have been connected with the other; that Smith's appearance at your place, and the immediately-following occupancy of the Maze, may have been, so to say, connecting links in the same chain," continued the superintendent. "A doubt of it was floating in my mind before I had the honour of seeing you, Sir Karl: but I failed to detect any adequate cause; there was none on the surface. You have now supplied that, by telling me who Smith is—Salter's relative."

"Indeed I cannot understand you," said Karl, turning nevertheless from hot to cold.

"The Maze is a place—what with its surrounding labyrinth of trees and its secret passages and outlets —unusually favourable for concealment. A proscribed man might hide himself there for years and years, and never be discovered unless suspicion were accidentally drawn on him. I think the chances are that Salter is there; and that his cousin, Smith, is keeping guard over him for his protection, while ostensibly fulfilling only the duties of your agency. They may have discovered in some way the desirable properties of the Maze and laid their plans to come to it accordingly."

It was so faithful a picture of what Smith was really doing at Foxwood—though the one he was watching over was a very different man from Salter—that Karl Andinnian almost thought some treacherous necromancy must have been at work. All he could do was, to speak forcibly against the view, and to declare that there could not be any foundation for it.

"That is only your opinion against mine, Sir Karl," observed the superintendent courteously. "You may rely upon it, I think, that the fact of Salter's being there would be kept from you, of all people."

"Do you forget the slur you would cast on Mrs. Grey?"

"As to that, Salter may be some relative of hers. Even her husband—even her brother. I remember it was said, at the time his case fell, that he had one sister. In either case, of course Mrs. Grey—the name she goes under—would not allow the fact of his concealment there to transpire to you."

How could Karl meet this? Sitting there, in his perplexity and pain, he could not see a step before him.

"You have forgotten that Tatton has searched the Maze from roof to basement, Mr. Superintendent."

"Not at all. It tells nothing. There are no doubt

other hidden places that he did not penetrate to in that first search. At best, it was but a superficial one."

That "first" search. Was all security slipping from Karl's feet, inch by inch?

"Believe me, you are wrong," he said; "your notion is an utterly mistaken one. I assure you on my word of honour, as truly and solemnly as I shall ever testify to any fact in this world, that Salter is not within the Maze, that he never has been. Mind you, sir, I *know* this. I go over occasionally to see poor Mrs. Grey in her loneliness, and am in a position to speak positively."

An unmistakable smile sat on the officer's face now. "Ay," he said, "I have heard of your occasional nocturnal visits to her, Sir Karl. The young lady is said to be very attractive."

At the first moment, Sir Karl did not detect the covert meaning. It came to him with a rush of indignation. The superintendent had rarely seen so haughty a face.

"No offence, Sir Karl. 'Twas but a joke."

"A joke I do not like, sir. I am a married man."

"Est-ce que cela empêche"—the other was beginning: for the conclusion he had drawn, on the score of Sir Karl's evening visits, was a very decided one; but Karl put a peremptory stop to the subject. He deemed the superintendent most offensively familiar and unwarrantably foolish; and he resented in his angry heart the implied aspersion on his brother's wife, the true Lady Andinnian, than whom a more modest and innocent-natured woman did not exist. And it never entered into the brain of Karl Andinnian to suspect that the same objectionable joke might have been taken up by people nearer home, even by his own wife.

The interview came to an end. Karl went away, uncertain whether he had made sufficient impression, or not, to ensure the Maze against intrusion for the future. The superintendent did not say anything decisive, one way or the other, except that the matter must be left for his consideration. It might all have been well yet, all been well, but for this new complication, this suspicion rather, touching Smith and Salter jointly! He, Karl, had given the greatest rise to this, he and no other, by stating that day that the men were cousins. He asked himself whether Heaven could be angry with him, for whatever step he took for good only seemed to lead to mischief and make affairs worse. One assurance he did carry away with him: that the young lady at the Maze might rest content: her peace personally should not be molested. But that was not saying that the house should not be.

After Sir Karl's departure, the superintendent's bell rang and Tatton was recalled. A long conversation ensued. Matters known were weighed; matters suspected were looked at: and Mr. Tatton was finally bidden back to Foxwood.

Karl had gone direct from Scotland Yard to take the train. A fast one, which speedily conveyed him home. He walked from the station, and was entering his own gates when Hewitt—who seemed to have been gossiping at the lodge with the gardener's wife, but who had probably been lingering about in the hope of meeting his master—accosted him; and they went up the walk together.

"I am afraid something is amiss at the Maze, sir," began the man, looking cautiously around and speaking in a low tone.

"Something amiss at the Maze!" echoed Karl, seized with a terror that he did not attempt to conceal.

"Not *that*, sir; not the worst, thank Heaven! Sir Adam has been taken ill."

"Hush, Hewitt. No names. Ill in what way? How do you know it?"

"I had been to carry a note for my lady to old Miss Patchett, Sir Karl. Coming back, Ann Hopley overtook me; she was walking from the station at a fine rate. Her master had been taken most alarmingly ill, she said; and at any risk a doctor must be had to him. They did not dare to call in Mr. Moore, lest he might talk to the neighbours, and she had been to the station then to telegraph for a stranger."

"Telegraph where?"

"To Basham, sir. For Dr. Cavendish."

Karl drew a deep breath. It seemed to be perplexity on perplexity: and he saw at once how much danger this step must involve.

"What is the matter with him, Hewitt? Do you know?"

"It was one of those dreadful fainting-fits, sir. But they could not get him out of it, and for some time thought he was really dead. Mrs. Grey was nearly beside herself, Ann said, and insisted on having a doctor. He is better now, sir," added Hewitt, "and I think there's no need for you to go over unless you particularly wish. I went strolling about the road, thinking I might hear or see something more, and when Ann Hopley came to the gate to answer a ring, she told me he was quite himself again but still in bed. It was the pain made him faint."

"I cannot think what the pain is," murmured Karl. "Has the doctor been?"

"I don't think he has yet, Sir Karl."

Karl lifted his hat to rub his aching brow. He saw his wife sitting under one of the trees, and went forward to join her. The wan, weary look on her face, growing more wan, more weary, day by day, struck on him particularly in the waning light of the afternoon.

"Do you do well to sit here, Lucy?" he asked, as he flung himself beside her, in utter weariness.

"Why should I not sit here?"

"I fancy the dew must be already rising."

"It will not hurt me. And if it did—what would it matter?"

The half reproaching, half indifferent accent in which it was uttered, served to try him. He knew what the words implied—that existence had, through him, become a burden to her. His nerves were strung already to their utmost tension; the trouble at his heart was pressing him sore.

"Don't *you*, by your reproaches, make matters worse for me, Lucy, to-day. God knows that I have well-nigh more than I can bear."

The strangely-painful tone, so full of unmistakable anguish, aroused her kindly nature. She turned to him with a sigh.

"I wish I could make things better for both of us, Karl."

"At least, you need not make them worse. What with one thing and another—"

"Well?" she said, her voice softened, as he paused.

"Nothing lies around me, Lucy, but perplexity and dread and pain. Look where I will, abroad or at home, there's not as much as a single ray of light to cheer my spirit, or the faintest reflection of it. You cannot wonder that I am sometimes tempted to wish I could leave the world behind me."

"Have you had a pleasant day in town?" she asked, after a little while.

"No, I have had an unsatisfactory and trying day in all ways. And I have come home to find more to try me: more dissatisfaction *here*, more dread abroad. 'Man is born to trouble as the sparks fly upwards.' Some of us are destined to realise the truth in ourselves all too surely."

He looked at his watch, got up, and walked indoors without another word. Lucy gazed after him with yearning eyes; eyes that seemed to have some of the perplexity he spoke of in their depths. There were moments when she failed to understand her husband's moods. This was one.

CHAPTER XIV.

Ill-omened Chances.

KARL ANDINNIAN was tempted bitterly to ask of his own heart whether he could have fallen under the displeasure of Heaven, so persistently did every fresh movement of his, intended for good, turn into an increased bank of danger. Poor Sir Adam had more need to question it than he; for nothing but ill-omened chances seemed to pursue him.

It is quite probable that when Ann Hopley and her flurried mistress decided to telegraph for Dr. Cavendish of Basham, they had thought, and hoped, that the doctor would come back by train, pass quietly on foot into the Maze, so pass out again, and the public be none the wiser. Dr. Cavendish, however, who was out when the telegram arrived, drove over later in his gig; and the gig, with the groom in it, paced before the Maze gate while the doctor was inside, engaged with his patient.

Just then there occurred one of those unhappy chances. Mr. Moore, the surgeon, happened to walk by with his daughter, Jemima, and saw the gig—which he knew well—waiting about. It took him by surprise, as he had not heard that anyone was ill in the vicinity. The groom touched his hat, and Mr. Moore went up to him.

"Waiting for your master, James? Who is he with? Who is ill?"

"It's somebody down yonder, sir," replied the man, pointing back over his shoulder to indicate the Maze; but which action was not intelligible to the surgeon.

"Down where? At the Court?"

"No, sir. At the Maze."

"At the Maze! Why, who can be ill there?" cried Mr. Moore.

"I don't know, sir. Master had a telegram, telling him to come."

At that moment Dr. Cavendish was seen to leave the gate and come towards his gig. Mr. Moore walked quickly forward to meet him, and the gig turned.

"I suppose you have been called to Mrs. Grey, doctor," observed the surgeon, as he shook hands. "Has she had a relapse? I wonder she did not send for me. I have but just given up attending her."

"Mrs. Grey?" returned the Doctor. "Oh, no. It is a gentleman I have been called to see."

"What gentleman?" asked the surgeon in surprise. "There's no gentleman at the Maze."

"One is there now. I don't know who it is. Some friend or relative of the lady's, probably. Ah, Miss Jemima! blooming as ever, I perceive," he broke off, as the young lady came slowly up. "Could you not give some of us pale, over-worked people a receipt for those roses on your cheeks?"

"What is it that's the matter with him?" interposed the surgeon, leaving his daughter to burst into her giggle.

Dr. Cavendish put his arm within his friend's, led him beyond the hearing of Miss Jemima, and said a few words in a low tone.

"Why, the case must be a grave one!" exclaimed Mr. Moore aloud.

"*I* think so. I don't like the symptoms at all. From some cause or other, too, it seems he has not had advice till now, which makes it all the more dangerous."

"By the way, doctor, as you are here, I wish you would spare five minutes to see a poor woman with me," said Mr. Moore, passing from the other subject. "It won't hinder you much longer than that."

"All right, Moore. Who is it?"

"It's the widow of that poor fellow who died from

sun-stroke in the summer, Whittle. The woman has
been ailing ever since, and very grave disease has
now set in. I don't believe I shall save her; only
yesterday it crossed my mind to wish you could see
her. She lives just down below there; in one of the
cottages beyond Foxwood Court."

They got into the gig, the physician taking the
reins, and telling his groom to follow on foot. Miss
Jemima was left to make her own way home. She
was rather a pretty girl, with a high colour, and a
quantity of light brown curls, and her manners were
straightforward and decisive. When the follies and
vanities of youth should have been chased away by
sound experience, allowing her naturally good sense
to come to the surface, she would, in all probability,
be as strong-minded as her Aunt Diana, whom she
already resembled in many ways.

The autumn evening was drawing on: twilight had
set in. Miss Jemima stood a moment, deliberating
which road she should take; whether follow the gig,
and go home round by the Court, or the other way.
Of the two, the latter was the nearer, and the least
lonely; and she might—yes, she might—encounter Mr.
Cattacomb on his way to or from St. Jerome's. Clearly
it was the one to choose. Turning briskly round when
the decision was made, she nearly ran against Mr.
Strange. That gentleman had just got back from
London, sent down again by the authorities at Scotland Yard, and was on his way from the station. The
Maze had become an object of so much interest to
him as to induce him to choose the long way round
that would cause him to pass its gates, rather than
take the direct road to the village. And here was

another of those unfortunate accidents apparently springing out of chance; for the detective had seen the gig waiting, and halted in a bend of the hedge to watch the colloquy of the doctors.

"Good gracious, is it you, Mr. Strange?" cried the young lady, beginning to giggle again. "Why, Mother Jinks declared this afternoon you had gone out for the day!"

"Did she? Well, when I stroll out I never know when I may get back: the country is more tempting in autumn than at any other season. That was a doctor's gig, was it not, Miss Jemima?"

"Dr. Cavendish's of Basham," replied Miss Jemima, who enjoyed the honour of a tolerable intimacy with Mrs. Jinks's lodger—as did most of the other young ladies frequenting the parson's rooms.

"He must have come over to see some one. I wonder who is ill?"

"Papa wondered, too, when he first saw the gig. It is somebody at the Maze."

"Do you know who?"

"Well, they seemed to talk as if it were a gentleman. I did not much notice."

"A gentleman?"

"I think so. I am sure they said 'he' and 'him.' Perhaps Mrs. Grey's husband has arrived. Whoever it is he must be very ill, for I heard papa say the case must be 'grave,' and the doctor called it 'dangerous.' They have gone on together now to see poor Hannah Whittle."

Not since he had had the affair in hand had the detective's ears been regaled with so palatable a dish. That Philip Salter had been taken ill with some malady or another sufficiently serious to necessitate the summoning of a doctor, he fully believed. Miss Jemima resumed.

"I must say, considering that papa is the medical attendant there, Mrs. Grey might have had the good manners to consult him first."

"It may be the old gardener that's ill," observed the detective slowly, who had been turning his thoughts about.

"So it may," acquiesced Miss Jemima. "He's but a poor, creaky old thing by all accounts. But no—they would hardly go to the expense of telegraphing for a physician for him with papa at hand."

"Oh, they telegraphed, did they?"

"So the groom said."

"The girl is right," thought the detective. "They'd not telegraph for Hopley. It is Salter. And they have called in a stranger from a distance in preference to Mr. Moore close by. The latter might have talked to the neighbourhood. You have done me a wonderful service, young lady, if you did but know it."

Mr. Strange did not offer to attend her home, but suffered her to depart alone.

Miss Jemima, who was rather fond of a little general flirtation, though she did perhaps favour one swain above all others, resented the slight in her heart. She consoled herself after the manner of the fox when he could not reach the grapes.

"He's nothing but a bear," said she, tossing her little vain head as she tripped away in the deepening gloom of the evening. "It is all for the best. We might have chanced to meet Mr. Cattacomb, and then he would have looked daggers at me. Or—my goodness me!—perhaps Aunt Diana."

Mr. Strange strolled on, revolving the aspect of affairs in his official mind. His next object must be to get to speak to Dr. Cavendish and learn who it really was that he had been to see. Of course it was not absolutely beyond the cards of possibility that the sick man was Hopley. It was not impossible that Mrs. Grey might have some private and personal objection to the calling in again of Mr. Moore; or that the old man had been seized with some illness so alarming as to necessitate the services of a clever physician in preference to those of a general practitioner. He did not think any of this likely, but it *might* be; and only Dr. Cavendish could set it at rest.

Perhaps some slight hope animated him that he might obtain an immediate interview with Dr. Cavendish on the spot, as he returned from Mrs. Whittle's cottage. If so, he found it defeated. The gig came back with the two gentlemen in it, and it drove off direct to the village, not passing Foxwood Court at all, or the detective; but the latter was near enough to see it travel along. Mr. Moore was dropped at his own house, and the groom—who had been sent on there—taken up; and then the gig went on to Basham.

"I must see him somehow," decided the detective —"and the less time lost over it, the better. Of course a man in the dangerously sick state this one is represented to be, cannot make himself scarce as quickly as one in health could; but Salter has not played at hide-and-seek so long to expose himself unnecessarily. He would make superhuman efforts to elude us, and rather get away dying than wait to be taken. Better strike while the iron is hot. I must see the doctor to-night."

He turned back to the station; and was just in time to watch the train for Basham go puffing out.

"That train has gone on before its time!" he cried in anger.

After reference to clocks and watches, it was found that it had gone on before its time by more than a minute. The station-master apologised: said the train was up three or four minutes too early; and, as no passengers were waiting to go on by it, he had given the signal to start rather too soon. Mr. Strange gave the master in return a bit of his mind; but he could not recall the train, and had to wait for the next.

The consequence of this was, that he did not reach Basham until past nine o'clock. Enquiring for the residence of Dr. Cavendish, he was directed to a substantial-looking house near the market-place. A boy in buttons, who came to the door, said the Doctor was not at home.

"I particularly wish to see him," said Mr. Strange. "Will he be long?"

"Well, I don't know," replied the boy, indifferently; who, like the rest of his tribe, had no objection to indulge in semi-insolence when it might be done with safety. "Master don't never hardly see patients at this hour. None of 'em cares to come at night-time."

"I am not a patient. My business with Dr. Cavendish is private and urgent. I will wait until he comes in."

The boy, not daring to make objection to this, ushered the visitor into a small room that he called the study. It had one gaslight burning; just enough to illumine the book-shelves and a white bust or two that stood in the corners on pedestals. Here Mr. Strange was left to his reflections.

He had plenty of food for them. That Salter was at the Maze, he felt as sure of as though he had already seen him. Superintendent Game had informed him who Smith the agent had acknowledged himself to be—Salter's cousin—and stated his own views of the motives that induced his residence at Foxwood. This was an additional thread in the web of belief Mr. Strange was weaving; a confirmatory link that seemed all but conclusive. In the short period that elapsed between his interview with Nurse Chaffen, chez elle, and his run up to London, he had seen his friend Giles, the footman, and by dint of helping that gentleman to trace days back and recall events, had arrived at a fact that could neither be disputed nor controverted—namely, that it could not have been Sir Karl Andinnian who was seen at the Maze by her and the surgeon. On that evening, Sir Karl, his wife, and Miss Blake had gone to a dinner party at a few miles distance. At the self-same minute of time that the event at the Maze took place, they were seated with the rest of the company at the dinner table, Mr. Giles himself standing behind in waiting. This was a fact: and had Miss Blake taken a little trouble to ascertain from Nurse Chaffen *which* evening it was the mysterious gentleman had presented himself to view, and then recalled the day of the dinner, she would have discovered the fallacy of her belief in supposing him to have been Sir Karl.

Mr. Strange had, however, discovered it, and that

was unfortunately more to the purpose. Whatever might be the object of Sir Karl's private visits to the Maze—and upon that point Mr. Strange's opinion did not change, and he had laughed quietly over it with the superintendent—it was not Sir Karl who was seen that night. It was a great point to have ascertained: and the detective thought he had rarely held stronger cards at any game of chance than were in his hands now. That Mrs. Grey would prove to be Salter's sister, he entertained no doubt of.

But the waiting was somewhat weary. Ten o'clock. Unless Dr. Cavendish made his appearance shortly, Mr. Strange would lose the last train, and have the pleasure of walking all the way from Basham. He was standing before one of the busts—the late Sir Robert Peel's—when the door opened, and there entered a quiet lady-like woman, with cordial manners and a homely face. It was Mrs. Cavendish.

"I am so sorry you should have to wait so long for my husband," she said. "If I knew where he was gone, I would send to him: but he did not happen to tell me before he went out. Your business with him is of importance, I hear."

"Yes, madam: of importance to myself. Perhaps he will not be much longer now."

"I should think not. Will you allow me to send you in a glass of wine?"

He thanked her, but declined it; and she went away again. A short while, and a latch-key was heard in the house door, denoting the return of its master. Some few words were exchanged in the hall between Dr. Cavendish and his wife—and the former entered: a short, quick-speaking man, with grey whiskers.

As a matter so much of course that it hardly needs mentioning, the detective had to be no less crafty in conducting this interview than he was in some other matters. To have said to Dr. Cavendish, "I want from you a description of the patient you were called to see to-day, that I may ascertain whether it be indeed an escaped criminal of whom I am in search," would have been to close the doctor's mouth. It was true that he might open his cards entirely and say, "I am Detective Tatton from Scotland Yard, and I require you in the name of the law to give me all the information you can about the patient;" and, in that case it was possible that the doctor might deem himself obliged to give it. But he preferred to keep that master-stroke in hand, and try another way.

He possessed pleasant manners, and had a winning way with him—it has been already said; he spoke as a gentleman. Sitting down close to the doctor, he began enquiring in an earnest tone after the new patient at the Maze, and spoke so feelingly about patients in general, that he half gained the physician's heart.

"You are some close friend of the gentleman's?" observed Dr. Cavendish. And the word "gentleman" set the one great doubt at rest.

"I am most deeply interested in him," said the detective: and the unsuspicious doctor never noticed the really sophistical nature of the answer.

"Well, I am sorry to tell you that I think him very ill. I don't know what they can have been about not to call in advice before." And in a few short words he stated what disease the symptoms seemed to threaten.

It startled the detective. He was sufficiently acquainted with surgery to know that it was one of difficulty and danger.

"Surely, Dr. Cavendish, he is not threatened with *that?*"

"I fear he is."

"Why, it will kill him! It is not curable, is it?"

"Rarely, if ever, when once it has certainly set-in."

"And it kills soon."

"Generally."

Mr. Strange looked very blank. To hear that his prize might escape him by death—or might die close upon his capture, was eminently unsatisfactory. It would be a termination to the great affair he had never thought of; would tarnish all the laurels in a business point of view: and he was, besides, not a hard-hearted man.

"He is very young for that kind of thing, is he not, doctor?"

"Yes. Rather so."

"What brings it on, sir, in general?"

"Oh, various causes."

"Will trouble induce it?—I mean *great* trouble; anxiety; care?"

"Sometimes. Especially if there should be any hereditary tendency to it in the system."

"Well, I did not expect to hear this."

"Are you his brother?" asked the Doctor, seeing how cut-up the visitor looked. "Not that I detect any likeness."

"No, I am not his brother; or any other relative. Do you consider it a hopeless case, Dr. Cavendish?"

"I have not said that. I should not be justified in saying it. In fact, I have not yet formed a positive opinion on the case, and cannot do so until I shall have examined further into it. All I say at present is, that I do not like the symptoms."

"And—if the symptoms turn out to be what you fear; to threaten the malady you speak of—what then?"

"Why then there will be very little hope for him."

"You are going over to him again, then?"

"Of course. To-morrow. He is not in a state to be left without medical attendance."

"How long do you think it has been coming on, doctor?"

"I cannot tell you that. Not less than a twelve-month, if it be what I fear."

Mr. Strange played with his watch-chain. He wanted the description of the man yet—though, in fact he felt so sure as hardly to need it, only that detectives do not leave anything to chance.

"Would you mind telling me what you think of his looks, Dr. Cavendish?"

"Oh, as to his looks, they are the best part about him. His face is somewhat worn and pallid, but it is a very handsome face. I never saw a nicer set of teeth. His hair and short beard seem to have gone grey prematurely, for I should scarcely give him forty years."

"He is only five-and-thirty," spoke the detective, thinking of Salter. And that, as the reader may recall, was also about the age of Sir Adam.

"Only that? Then in looks he has prematurely aged."

"In his prime, say two or three years ago, he was

as good-looking a man as one would wish to see," observed the detective, preparing to give a gratuitous description of Salter. "A fine, tall, upright figure, strongly-built withal; and a pleasant, handsome, frank face, with fine dark eyes and hair, and a colour fresh as a rose."

"Ay," acquiesced the physician: "I only saw him in bed, and he is now much changed, but I should judge that would be just the description that once applied to him. You seem to hint at some great trouble or sorrow that he has gone through: he gives me just that idea. Of what nature was it?—if I may ask."

"It was trouble that was brought on by himself—and *that* is always the most trying to bear. As to its nature—you must pardon me for declining to particularise it, Dr. Cavendish, but I am really not at liberty to do so. Do not put the refusal down to discourtesy. It is not yet over: and the chances are that you will certainly hear all about it in a day or two."

Dr. Cavendish nodded. He assumed the words to imply that the patient himself would enlighten him. As to the detective, his mission was over; and well over. He had learnt all he wanted: what he had suspected was confirmed.

"That beautiful young woman, living alone at the Maze—what relative is she of his?" asked the doctor, as his visitor rose and took up his hat.

"His sister," was the rather hazardous answer.

"Oh, his sister. Mr. Moore could not make out who the patient was. He thought it might be the husband who had returned. When I asked his name, to write a prescription for the chemist, Mrs. Grey said I might put it in hers—Grey."

"I thank you greatly for your courtesy, Dr. Cavendish."

"You are welcome," said the doctor. "Mind, I have not expressed any certain opinion as to his non-recovery. Don't go and alarm him. What I have said to you was said in confidence."

"You may depend upon me. Good night."

Mr. Detective Strange had to walk from Basham, for the last train was gone and his return half-ticket useless. Basham police station was nearly opposite the doctor's, and he stepped in there to leave a message on his way. In the satisfaction his visit had afforded him, he did not at all mind the night-walk: on the morrow, the long-sought-for Salter, who had dodged them so vexatiously, would be in their hands, the prey would have fallen. A satisfaction, however, that was not without alloy, in the damping circumstances that encompassed the man's state of health. And for that he could but feel compassion.

Midnight was chiming from the clock at Foxwood as he reached the Maze—for he preferred to take that round-about way. Halting at the gate, he looked about and listened for a minute or two. Then he let himself in with his master-key, and went through the labyrinth.

The house lay in silence. All seemed still as the grave. There was no light, no sound, no token of illness inside; no, nor even of inmates. He gently put the said key in the entrance-door to see if it would yield. No: the door was not only locked but bolted and barred. He went to the summer-house, leading up from the underground places, and found the trap-door there also bolted and barred within. All was as secure as wary hands could make it.

"And it is welcome to remain so until to-morrow," breathed the detective as he turned to thread his silent steps back through the maze; "but then, Mr. Philip Salter, you are mine. Neither bolts nor bars can save you then."

And he finally let himself out again at the gate with that ingenious instrument, the key. To be polite, we will apply a French name to it, and call it a passe-partout.

But Dr. Cavendish, reflecting afterwards upon the interview, rather wondered who the stranger was, and whence he had come; and remembered then that he had totally omitted to ask his name.

CHAPTER XV.

Ann Hopley startled.

THE morning sun was chasing the dew from the grass: and the lawn at the Maze, glittering so brightly in the welcome rays, told no tales of the strange feet that had, unbidden and unsuspected, trodden it in the night. Mrs. Grey, looking wondrously pretty and delicate in her white morning gown, with her golden hair as bright as the sunshine, sat at breakfast in a little room whose window was beside the entrance porch. Her baby, wide awake, but quiet and good, lay covered up on the sofa in its night-dress. She was talking to it as she eat her breakfast, and the wide-open little eyes were turned to her as if it understood.

"Good little darling! Sweet, gentle baby! It does

not scream and fight as other babies do: no never. It is mamma's own precious treasure—and mamma is going to dress it presently and put on its pretty worked robe. Oh, baby, baby!" she broke off, her mood changing, and the distress at her heart rising to the surface, above the momentary make-believe dalliance, "if we could but be at rest as others are! We should be happier than the day has hours in it."

The accession of illness, attacking Sir Adam on the previous day, the great risk they ran in calling in a doctor to him, had shaken poor Rose's equanimity to the centre. She strove to be brave always, for his sake; she had been in the habit of keeping-in as well as she could the signs of the dread that ever lay upon her, and she had done so in a degree yesterday. But in the evening when the doctor had safely gone, and the day and its troubles were over, she had yielded to a sudden fit of hysterical weeping. Her husband came into the room in the midst of it. He partly soothed, partly scolded her: where was the use of fretting, he asked; better take matters as they came. With almost convulsive efforts she swallowed her sobs and dried her eyes; and turned the tables on him by gently reproaching him with getting up, when Dr. Cavendish had peremptorily enjoined him to stay in bed. Sir Adam laughed at that: saying he felt none the worse for his fainting fit, or whatever it was, and was not going to lie a-bed for all the doctors in Christendom.

The cheery morning sun is a great restorer—a gladdening comforter: and Rose felt its influence. During her sleepless night, nothing could be more disheartening, nothing more gloomy than the view pervading her mind: but this morning, with that glorious light from heaven shining on all things, she and the earth alike revived under it. One great thing she felt incessant thankfulness for; it was a real mercy—that that miserable visitation of the detective and his policemen had not been delayed to the day of Sir Adam's illness. Had they caught him in bed, no earthly power, she thought, could have saved him. Karl, stealing over for a few minutes at night, to see for himself what this alarm of increased illness of his brother's could mean, had warned them both to be prepared, for he had reason to fancy the search might be repeated.

"This spot is getting more dangerous day by day," murmured Rose to herself, pouring out another cup of tea. "Oh, if we could but get away from it! London itself seems as though it would be safer than this."

She proceeded with her meal very slowly, her thoughts buried in schemes for their departure. Of late she had been ever weaving a web of possibility for it, a cunning plan of action: and she thought she had formed one. If necessary *she* would stay on at the Maze with her baby—oh, for months—for years even —so that Adam could but get away. Until this man the detective—more feared by her, more dreadful to contemplate than any man born into the world yet— should take his departure from the place, nothing might be attempted: they could only remain still and quiet; taking what precautions they could against surprise and recapture, and she praying always that her husband might be spared this last crowning calamity: beyond which, if it took place, there would never more be anything in this world but blank despair.

Ann Hopley was upstairs, making the beds, and attending to matters there generally. Until her room was ready, and the fire had burnt up well to dress the baby by, Mrs. Grey would stay where she was: consequently she was at full liberty to linger over her breakfast. There was something in the extreme quietness of the little child, and in its passive face, that to a more experienced eye might have suggested doubts of its well-being: a perfectly healthy infant is apt to be as troublesome as it can be. Mrs. Grey suspected nothing. It had improved much since its baptism, and she supposed it to be getting strong and healthy. A soft sweet plaintive note escaped the child's lips.

"Yes, my baby. Mamma has not forgotten you. The room will soon be warm, and baby shall be dressed. And then mamma will wrap it up well and wrap herself up, and sit out of doors in the sunshine. And papa——"

The words broke off in a low wail of horror; her heart seemed to die away in the faintness of sick despair. Something like a dark cloud had passed the window, shutting out for a moment the glad sunshine on the grass. It was Mr. Detective Strange: and, following closely on his heels, were the two same policemen, both of them this time in official clothes. They had come through the maze without warning, no doubt by the help of the passe-partout, and were making swiftly for the entrance-door—that lay open to the morning air. Her supposition was that they had fathomed Adam's system of concealment.

"God help us! God save and protect us!" breathed the poor wife, clasping her hands, and every drop of blood going out of her ashy face.

Mr. Strange, who had seen her through the window, was in the room without a moment's delay. He was courteous as before; he meant to be as considerate as the nature of his mission allowed him to be: and even before he had spoken a word, the keen, practised eye took in the visible signs. The small parlour affording no possibility for the concealment of Salter; the baby on the sofa; the breakfast, laid for one only, of which Mrs. Grey was partaking.

He was very sorry to be obliged to intrude upon her again: but he had orders once more to search the Maze, and could but obey them. And he begged her to believe that she herself, individually, should be subjected to no annoyance or restraint.

She made no answer: she could collect neither thoughts nor words to do so in her terrible fear. Mr. Strange retreated with a bow and closed the door again, making a mental comment upon her evident distress, her ghastly looks.

"There's no mistake, I think, that he is ready to our hands this time: her face alone would betray it. The curious thing is—where was he before?"

Ann Hopley had finished the rooms, and was kneeling before the fire in her mistress's chamber, coaxing an obstinate piece of coal to burn, and blowing at it with her lips with all her might, when a slight noise caused her to turn. There stood Mr. Strange, a policeman at his elbow. She had not heard the entrance. Up she got, and stood staring; unable to believe her eyes, and startled almost into screaming. But she knew how much lay upon her—almost life or death.

"Goodness bless me!" cried she, speaking freely,

as she strove to brave it out, and shaking inwardly.
"Whatever brings you folks here again?"

"We have to go through the house once more."

"How did you get in?"

"Quite legally," replied Mr. Strange. "I have to
do my duty."

So entirely was she unprepared for this, and perhaps fearing that in her state of dismayed perplexity
she might let fall some dangerous word of admission,
feeling also that she could do no good to her master
by staying, but might do harm, Ann Hopley withdrew,
after giving the fire a gentle lift with the poker, and
went down to the kitchen with a cool air, as if resolved
not to let the affair interrupt her routine of work.
Taking up a small basket of what she would have
termed "fine things," recently washed, consisting of
caps and bits of lace, and such like articles pertain-
ing to the baby, she carried it out of doors beyond
the end of the lawn, and began putting the things on
gooseberry bushes to dry. Old Hopley was pottering
about there, doing something to the celery bed. The
policeman left on guard below, and standing so that his
sight could command all things, surveyed her movements
with a critical eye. She did not go out of his sight,
but came back with the basket at once. While spread-
ing the things, she had noted him watching her.

"I daresay I'm a kind of genteel prisoner," ran
her thoughts. "If I attempted to go where those ugly
eyes of his couldn't follow me, he might be for order-
ing me back, for fear I should be giving warning to
the master that they are here. Well, we can do nothing; it is in Heaven's hands: better they came in to-
day than yesterday!"

Mr. Detective Strange had rarely felt surer of anything than he was that he should find Philip Salter in bed, and capture him without the slightest difficulty in his sick state. It was not so to be. Very much to his amazement, there appeared to be no sign whatever of a sick man in the place. The rooms were all put in order for the day, the beds made; nothing was different from what it had been at the time of his previous entrance. Seek as he would, his practised eye could find no trace—nay, no possibility—of any hidden chamber. In fact, there was none.

"Where the deuce can the fellow be?" mused Mr. Strange, gazing about him with a thoughtful air.

The underground places were visited with as little success, though the search he made was minute and careful. He could not understand it. That Salter had not been allowed time to escape out of doors, so rapid was their first approach, he knew; but, nevertheless, the trees and grounds were well examined. Hopley lifted his poor bent back from his work in the celery-bed—from which, as the watching policeman could have testified, he had not stirred at all—to touch his straw hat when the detective passed. Mr. Strange answered by a nod, but did not accost him. To question the deaf old man would be only waste of time.

There was some mystery about all this; a mystery he—even he—could not at present fathom. Just one possibility crossed his mind and was exceedingly unwelcome—that Salter, alarmed by the stir that was being made, had in truth got away. Got away, in spite of the precautions that he, Strange, in conjunc-

tion with the police of Basham, had been for the past
day or two taking, secretly and unobserved.

He did not believe it. He did not wish to believe it. And, in truth, it seemed to him not to be
possible, for more reasons than one. A man in the
condition of health hinted at by Dr. Cavendish would
be in no state for travelling. But still—with the Maze
turned, as he honestly believed, inside out, and showing no signs or trace of Salter, where was he?

This took up some time. Ann Hopley had got
her preparations for dinner forward, had answered the
butcher's bell and taken in the meat: and by and by
went across the garden again to cut two cauliflowers.
She was coming back with them in her apron, when
Mr. Strange met her, and spoke.

"I have a question or two to put to you, Mrs.
Hopley, which I must desire of you to answer—and
to answer correctly. Otherwise I shall be obliged to
summon you before the magistrates and compel your
answers on your oath. If you are wise you will avoid
giving me and yourself that trouble."

"As far as answering you goes, sir, I'd as soon answer as be silent," she returned, in a temperate but
nevertheless injured tone. "But I must say that it
puts my temper up to see an innocent and inoffensive
young lady insulted as my poor mistress is. What
has she done to be signalled out for such treatment?
If she were not entirely unprotected here, a lone woman, you'd not dare to do it. You told her the other
day you were in search of one Salter: and you know
that you looked in every hole and corner our house
has got, and must have satisfied yourself that no Salter
was here. And yet, here you come in, searching again!"

"It was not Salter, I suppose, who was ill yesterday; for whom Dr. Cavendish was telegraphed?" rejoined Mr. Strange, significantly, having allowed her speech to run on to its end. "Perhaps you will tell me that?"

"Salter! That I'll take my oath it was not, sir."

"Who was it, then?"

"Well, sir, it was no one that you could have any concern with."

"I am the best judge of that. Who was it? Remember, I ask you in the name of the law, and you must answer me."

"That gentleman came down on a short visit to my mistress, and was taken ill while he stayed. It frightened us out of our senses; it was a fainting-fit, or something of that sort, but he looked for all the world like a man dead; and I ran off and telegraphed for a doctor."

The detective's eyes were searching Ann Hopley through and through. She did not flinch: and looked innocent as the day.

"What has become of him?"

"He went away again last night, sir."

"Went away, did he!"—in a mocking tone of incredulity.

"He did, sir. After the doctor left he got up and dressed and came down, saying he was better. He didn't seem to think much of his illness; he had been as bad, he said, before. I confess I was surprised, myself, to hear he was going away, for I thought him not well enough to travel. But I believe he was obliged to go."

"What was his name?"

"I did not hear it, sir. He was here but a few hours in all."

"Look here, Mrs. Hopley: if you will tell me where that gentleman came from, and what his name is, I will give you five sovereigns."

Her eyes opened, apparently with the magnitude of the offer.

"I wish I could, sir. I'm sure I should be glad to earn all that, if it were in my power; for I don't believe Hopley will be able to work over-much longer, and we are laying up what little we can. I think he came from London, but I am not sure: and I think he's going off to some foreign country, for he and my mistress were talking of the sea. She wished him a good voyage and a safe landing. I heard her."

The detective paused. Was this true or false? "What was his name? Come, Mrs. Hopley?"

"Sir, I have said that I did not hear his name. He came without our expecting him, or I might have heard beforehand. My mistress called him Edward: but of course that must be his Christian name. I understood him to be some relation of hers."

"I wonder what Hopley could tell me of this?" cried the detective, looking at her.

"Hopley could tell you nothing—but of course you are welcome to ask him if you please. Hopley never saw him at all, as far as I know; and I did not say anything to the old man about it. If you question Hopley, sir, I must help you—you'd be a month making him hear, yourself."

"How is it that you keep your husband in ignorance of things?—as you seem to do."

"Of what things, sir?" rejoined the woman. "I'm

sure I don't keep things from him: I have no things to keep. It's true I didn't tell him of this. I was uncommonly tired last night, for it had been a trying day, and full of work besides; and it takes no little exertion, I can testify, to make Hopley understand. One can't gossip with him, as one can with people who have got their hearing."

This was no doubt true. The detective was frightfully at fault, and did not conceal from himself that he was. The woman seemed so honest, so open, so truthful; and yet he could have staked his professional fame that there lay mystery somewhere, and that the sick man had *not* gone away. Instinct, prevision— call it what you will—told him that the man was lying close to his hand—if he could only put that hand out in the right direction and lay it on him. Bending his head, he took a few steps about the grass: and Ann Hopley, hoping she was done with, went into the kitchen with her cauliflowers.

Letting them fall on to the dresser out of her apron, she gave a sharp look around, in-doors and out. The detective was then conversing with his two policemen, whom he had called up. Now was her time. Slipping off her shoes—though it was not likely her footsteps could be heard out on the lawn—she went across the passage, and opened the door of the little room: from which Mrs. Grey, in her fear and distress, had not dared to stir.

"Mistress," she whispered, "I must give you the clue of what I have been saying, lest they come and ask you questions too. It would never do for us to have two tales, you one and me another. Do you mind me, ma'am?"

"Go on, Ann. Yes."

"The sick gentleman came unexpectedly yesterday, and was taken sick here. You and me got frightened, and sent telegraphing off for a doctor. He got up after doctor left—said he was better—didn't seem to think much of his illness, said he had been as bad before. Went away again at night; *had* to go; was going off to sea, I thought, as I heard you wish him a good voyage and safe landing. I didn't know his name, I said; only heard you call him Edward: thought it was some near relation of yours.—Can you remember all this, ma'am?"

"Oh yes. You had better go back, Ann. If they see you talking to me—oh, go back! Ann, I—I feel as though I should die."

"Nay, but you must keep up," returned the woman in a kind tone. "I'll bring you in a beat-up egg with a drop of wine in it. And, ma'am, you might say he was your brother if they come to close questioning: or brother-in-law. Don't fear. I'd lay all I'm worth they won't light upon the master. Twice they went within a yard or two of him, but——"

There was some noise. Ann Hopley broke off, closed the door softly, stole back again, and slipped her feet into her shoes. In less than a minute, when one of the men sauntered up, throwing his eyes through all the windows, she was in the scullery pumping water over her cauliflowers with as much noise as she could make.

Ann Hopley had judged correctly. Mr. Strange went to the little room, knocking for permission to enter, and there held an audience of its mistress. The baby lay on her lap now, fast asleep. His questions were tended to get a confirmation—or contradiction—of the servant's ready tale. Mrs. Grey, though in evident tremor, and looking only fit for a ghost, had caught the thread of her lesson well, and answered correctly. Some particulars she had to improvise; for his questions were more minute than they had been to Ann Hopley.

His name?—Grey. What relation?—Brother-in-law. What did he come down for?—To say good-bye before embarking for Australia. Where would he take ship?—She did not know; forgot: oh, now she remembered, it was Gravesend. Was she in the habit of seeing him?—Not often. He was never long together in one place, always travelling about. But was he in a fit state to travel? She did not know. She had thought he looked very ill and begged him to remain at least until to-day, but he said he could not as he might lose his ship. Did he come down to Foxwood by train?—Oh yes, by train: there was no other way. And go up by train?—To be sure. *Which* train?—One of the evening trains: thought it was past eight when he left the Maze.

"It's the time for my mistress to take her egg," interposed Ann Hopley at this juncture, entering the room with the said egg in a tumbler. "I suppose she's at liberty to do it."

To this last little fling Mr. Strange answered nothing. Ann Hopley put the tumbler on the table and withdrew. Poor Mrs. Grey looked too weak and ill to lift it to her lips, and let it stay where it was.

"Can it possibly be true that you are still in search of Philip Salter?— here?" she asked, raising her troubled eyes to the detective's.

"It is quite true," he replied.

"And that you really believe him to be concealed here?"

"Madam, I could stake my life upon it."

She shook her head in feeble impotence, feeling how weak she was to combat this fixed belief. It was the old story over again. Nevertheless she made one more effort. Mr. Strange was watching her.

"Sir, I do not know what to say more than I said before. But I declare to you once again, as solemnly as I can ever speak anything in this life, as solemnly as I shall one day have to answer before my Maker, that I know nothing of Philip Salter. He never was here at all to my knowledge, later or earlier. Why will you not leave me in peace?"

Mr. Detective Strange began to think that he should have to leave her in peace. Twice had he carried this fortress by storm to search at will its every nook and corner: and searched in vain. Armed with great power though he was, the law would not justify these repeated forcible entries, and he might be called to account for exceeding his duty. But the man was there—as surely as that the sun was in the heavens: and yet he could not unearth him. He began to think there must be caves underground impenetrable to the eye of man, with some invisible subtle entrance to them through the earth itself—and perhaps a subterranean passage communicating with Mr. Smith's abode opposite.

And so, the second search ended as the first had done—in signal failure. Once more there was nothing left for the detective but to withdraw his men and himself, and to acknowledge that he was for the time defeated.

CHAPTER XVI.

Up the Spouts and down the Drains.

TURNING his face towards the railway station after quitting the Maze, with the view of making some enquiries, as to what passengers had alighted there the previous day and had gone back again—not that he believed one syllable of the tale told him—Mr. Strange encountered the gig of Dr. Cavendish bowling down. The physician recognised him and pulled up.

"What's this I hear, sir, about my patient's having gone off again?" cried the doctor in a sharp tone.

"I have heard the same," replied Mr. Strange. "But I don't believe it."

"Oh then—you are not privy to it? You did not send him?"

"Not I, Dr. Cavendish. I went to the Maze betimes this morning to—to pay him a visit; and I was met with a tale that the bird had flown."

"I can tell you, sir, that he was in a *most unfit* state to travel," said the doctor with angry emphasis. "I don't know what the consequences will be."

"Ay, if he had gone. But it's all moonshine."

"What do you mean by 'moonshine?' Has he gone, or has he not?"

"They say at the Maze he has; but I am sure he has not," was the answer. "There was a motive for his being denied to me, Dr. Cavendish; and so—and so—when I went in this morning they concocted an impromptu tale of his departure. That's what I think."

"They must have concocted it last night then,"

said the doctor. "The letter, informing me of the circumstance, was posted last night at Foxwood—and therefore must have been written last night."

"Did they write to tell you he had gone?" asked the detective, after a slight pause.

"Mrs. Grey wrote. I got it by the post this morning. She would not trouble me to come over again, she said, as my patient had found himself obliged to leave last night. But I *have* troubled myself to come," added the doctor, wrathfully, "and to see about it; for, of all mad acts, that man's getting up from his bed yesterday, and starting off by a shaking railway train was the maddest. Drive on, James."

The groom touched the horse at the short command, and the animal sprang forward. Mr. Strange thought he would let the station alone for a bit, and loiter about where he was. This letter, written last night, to tell of the departure, somewhat complicated matters.

A very short while, and the doctor came out again. Mr. Strange accosted him as he was about to step into his gig.

"Well, Dr. Cavendish, have you seen your patient?"

"No, I have not seen him," was the reply. "It is quite true that he is gone. I find he is embarking on a sea voyage, going off somewhere to the other end of the world, and he had to go up, or forfeit his passage-money."

"They told you, then, what they told me. As, of course, they *would*," he added inwardly.

"But there's something in it I don't altogether understand," resumed the doctor. "Not a syllable was spoken by the patient yesterday to denote that he was on the move, or that he had been on the move, even only to journey down from London. On the contrary, I gathered, or fancied I gathered, from the tenor of his remarks that he had been for some time stationary, and would be stationary for an indefinite period to come. It was when I spoke to him about the necessity of keeping himself quiet and free from exertion. What I don't understand is why he should not candidly have told me that he had this voyage before him."

Mr. Strange did not answer. Various doubts were crowding upon him. *Had* the man got away? in disguise, say? But no, he did not think it.

"By the way, you did not tell me your name," said the doctor, as he took his seat in the gig.

"My name! oh, did I not? My name is Tatton."

Dr. Cavendish bent down his head and spoke in a low tone. His groom was adjusting the apron.

"You hinted last night at some great trouble that this gentleman was in, Mr. Tatton. I have been wondering whether that has to do with this sudden departure —whether he had reasons for being afraid to stay?"

"Just the question that has occurred to me, Dr. Cavendish," confessed the detective. "If he has gone away, it is fear that has driven him."

The gig bowled onwards. Mr. Strange stood still as he looked after it: and had the pleasure of seeing Mr. Philip Smith smoking his long pipe at his own window, and regarding the landscape with equanimity. He went on the other way.

"Good morning, Mr. Tatton."

Mr. Tatton turned on his heel and saluted Sir Karl Andinnian, who had followed him up. There was a degree of suppressed indignation in Karl's face rarely seen.

"Is this true that I have just heard, Mr. Tatton," he began, calling the man by his true name—"that you have been again searching the Maze? My butler informs me that he saw you and two policemen quit it but now."

"It is true enough, Sir Karl. Salter is there. At least, he was there yesterday. There cannot be the slightest doubt that the sick man to whom Dr. Cavendish was called was Salter. I obtained a description of him from the doctor, and should have recognized it anywhere."

What was Karl to say? He could not attempt to deny that a sick man had been there. It was an unfortunate circumstance that Sir Adam, in regard to height and colour of hair, somewhat answered to the description of Philip Salter.

"Sir Karl, you must yourself see that there's a mystery somewhere," resumed the detective, who (having taken his clue from Superintendent Game) honestly believed that the baronet of Foxwood Court cared not a rap for Salter, and had no covert interest in the matter, beyond that of protecting his tenant at the Maze. "Some one, who is never seen by the public, is living at the Maze, that's certain; or, at any rate, dodging us there. Remember the gentleman in evening attire seen by the surgeon and nurse; and now there's this gentleman sick abed yesterday. These men could not be myths, Sir Karl. Who, then, are they?"

From sheer inability to advance any theory upon the point, lest he should do mischief, Karl was silent. These repeated trials, these shocks of renewed dread, were getting more than he knew how to bear. Had they come upon Adam this morning? He did not dare to ask.

"As to the tale told me by the woman servant and Mrs. Grey—that the sick gentleman was a relative who had come down by train and left again, it will not hold water," contemptuously resumed the detective. "Men don't go out for a day's journey when they are as ill as he is—no, nor take long sea voyages. Why, if what Dr. Cavendish fears is correct, there cannot be many weeks of life left in the man he saw yesterday; neither, if it be so, can the man himself be unconscious of it."

Karl's heart stood still with its shock of pain.

"Did Dr. Cavendish tell you that, Mr. Tatton?"

"Yes. Well, now, Sir Karl, that man is at the Maze still—I am convinced of it; and that man is Salter."

"What did you find this morning?"

"Nothing. Nothing more than I found before. When I spoke of the sick man, and asked where he was, this cock-and-bull tale was told me, which, of course, they had got up among themselves."

"As I said before, Mr. Tatton, I feel certain—I am certain—that you will never find Salter at the Maze; from the simple fact that he is not there to find—I am sure of it. I must most earnestly protest against these repeated annoyances to my tenant, Mrs. Grey; and if you do not leave her alone for the future, I shall see whether the law will not compel you. I do not—pray understand—I do not speak this in enmity to you, but simply to protect her."

"Of course I understand that, Sir Karl," was the

ready answer. "There's no offence meant, and none taken. But if you could put yourself in my place, you'd see my difficulty. Upon my word, I never was so mystified before. *There Salter is.* Other people can see him, and have seen him; and yet, when I search I find no traces of him. A thought actually crossed my mind just now, whether there could be a subterranean passage from the Maze to Clematis Cottage, and that Salter makes his escape there to his cousin on occasion. I should like to search it."

"Come and do so at once," said Karl, half laughing. "Nothing convinces like ocular demonstration. I give you full permission, as owner of the cottage; I doubt not Smith will, as its tenant. Come and ask him."

The detective was in earnest, and they crossed over. Seeing them making for the gate, Mr. Smith came out of his house, pipe in hand. It was one of those long churchwardens. Karl spoke a few words of explanation. Mr. Detective Tatton suspected there might be secret rooms, or doors, or fugitives hidden in Clematis Cottage, and would like to search it. After the first momentary look of surprise, the agent remained unruffled.

"Pass on, sir," said he, extending the thin end of his pipe to indicate the way. "You are welcome. Go where you please: search into every nook and corner; up the spouts and down the drains. If you surprise old Betty, tell her you're the plumber."

Mr. Strange took him at his word. Karl and the agent waited in the sitting-room together.

"Is it after Sir Adam, sir?" breathed the agent.

"No. No suspicion of him. It's after the other I told you of. Hush! Better be silent."

The agent put his pipe away. Karl stood at the open window. Old Betty, the ancient servant, came in with a scared face. She was a little deaf, but not with a deafness like Hopley's over the way.

"It's all right, Betty," called out her master. "Only looking to the drains and spouts."

Satisfied in one sense of the word—for in truth it was readily seen by the most unprofessional eye that there were no means afforded for concealment in the shallow-built cottage—the officer soon joined them again. He had not had really a suspicion of the cottage, he said by way of apology: it was merely a thought that crossed him. Mr. Smith, however, did not seem inclined to take the matter quite indifferently now, and accosted him.

"Now that you are satisfied, sir, perhaps you will have no objection to tell me who the individual may be, that you have fancied I would harbour in my house. I heard before from Sir Karl that you were after some one."

From the tone he spoke in, a very civil tone, tinged with mockery, the detective caught up the notion that Smith already knew; that Sir Karl must have told him: therefore he saw no occasion for observing any reticence.

"When you know that we are looking for Philip Salter, you need not be so much surprised that we have cast a thought to this house as Salter's possible occasional refuge, Mr. Smith."

The very genuine astonishment that seized hold of Smith, pervading his every look, and word, and gesture, was enough to convince those who saw it that he was unprepared for the news.

"Philip Salter!" he exclaimed, gazing from one to the other, as if unable to believe. "*Philip Salter!* Why, is he here? Have you news that he is back in England?"

"We have news that he *is* here," said the detective blandly. "We suspect that he is concealed at the Maze. Did you not know it, Mr. Smith?"

Mr. Smith sat down in the chair that was behind him as if sitting came easier than standing, in his veritable astonishment.

"As Heaven is my judge, it is a mistake," he declared. "Salter is not at the Maze; never has been. We have never heard that he is back in England."

"Did you know that he left England?"

"Yes. At least, we had good reason to believe that he got away shortly after that dangerous escape of his. It's true it was never confirmed; but the confirmation to his family lies in the fact that we have never since heard of him, or from him."

"Never?"

"Never. Were he in England we should have been sure to have had some communication from him, had it only been an application for aid—for he could not live upon air; and outlets of earning are here closed to him. One thing you and ourselves may alike rest assured of, Mr. Detective—that, once he got safely away from the country he would not venture into it again."

What with one disappointment and another, the detective almost questioned whether it were not as Smith said; and that Salter, so far as Foxwood was

concerned, would turn out to be indeed a myth. But
then—who was this mysterious man at the Maze? He
was passing out with a good day when Mr. Smith resumed.

"Have you any objection to tell me what gave
rise to your suspicion that Salter was at Foxwood?
Or in England at all?"

But the officer had tact; plenty of it; or he would
not have done for his post; and he turned the question off without any definite answer. For the true
originator of the report, he who had caused it to reach
the ears of Great Scotland Yard, was Sir Karl Andinnian.

Very conscious of the fact was Karl himself. He
raised his hat from his brow as he went home, to
wipe away the fever-damp gathered there. He remembered to have read somewhere of one of the tor-
tures devised by inquisitionists in the barbarous days
gone by. An unhappy prisoner would be shut in a
spacious room; and, day by day, watched the walls
contracting by some mysterious agency, and closing
around him. It seemed to Karl that the walls of the
world were closing around him now. Or, rather,
round one who had become dearer to him in his
dread position than himself—his most ill-fated brother.

At home or abroad there was not a single ray of
light to illumine or cheer the gloom. Abroad lay apprehension; at home only unhappiness, an atmosphere
of estrangement that seemed to have nothing home-
like or true in it. Karl went in, expecting to see the
pony-chaise waiting. He had been about to drive his
wife out; but, alarmed by the report whispered to him
by Hewitt, and unable to rest in tranquillity, he had

gone forth to see about what it meant. But the chaise was not there. Maclean was at work on the lawn.

"Has Lady Andinnian gone?" he enquired, rather surprised—for Lucy had not learned to drive yet.

"My leddy is somewhere about the garden I think, Sir Karl," was the gardener's answer. "She sent the chay away again."

He found his wife sitting in a retired walk, a book in her hand, apparently reading it. Lucy was fading. Her face, worn and thin, had that indescribable air of pitiful sadness in it that tells of some deep-seated, ever-present sorrow. Karl was all too conscious of it. He blamed her for her course of conduct; but he did not attempt to conceal from himself that the trouble had originated with him.

"I am very sorry to have kept you waiting, Lucy," he began. "I had to go to Smith's on a little matter of business. You have sent the chaise away."

"I sent it away. The pony was tired of waiting. I don't care to go out at all to-day."

She spoke in an indifferent, almost a contemptuous tone. We must not blame her. Her naturally-sweet temper was being sorely tried: day by day her husband seemed to act so as to afford less promise of any reconciliation.

"I could not help it," was all he answered.

She glanced up at the weary accent. If ever a voice spoke of unresisted despair, his did then. Her resentment vanished: her sympathy was aroused.

"You look unusually ill," she said.

"I am ill," he replied. "So ill that I should be almost glad to die."

Lucy paused. Somehow she never liked these

semi-explanations. They invariably imbued her with a sense of self-reproach, an idea that she was acting harshly.

"Do you mean ill because of our estrangement?"

"Yes, for one thing. That makes all other trouble so much worse for me that at times I find it rather difficult to put up with."

Lucy played with her book. She wished she knew where her true duty lay. Oh how gladly, but for that dreadful wrong ever being enacted upon herself, would she fall upon his arm and whisper out her beseeching prayer: "Take me to you again, Karl!"

"Should the estranged terms we are living on, end in a total and visible separation, you will have the satisfaction of remembering in your after life, Lucy, that you have behaved cruelly to me. I repeat it: cruelly."

"I do not wish to separate," murmured Lucy.

"The time may soon come when you will be called upon to decide, one way or the other; when there will be nothing left to wait for; when all will be known to the world as it is known to us."

"I cannot understand you," said Lucy.

"Let it pass," he answered, declining as usual to speak openly upon the dreaded subject; for, to him, every word, so spoken, seemed fraught with danger. "You can guess what I mean, I daresay: and the less said the better."

"You seem always to blame me, Karl," she rejoined, her voice softening almost to tears.

"Your own heart should tell you that I have cause."

"It has been very hard for me to bear."

"Yes; no doubt. It has hurt your pride."

"And something besides my pride," rejoined Lucy, with a faint flush of resentment.

"What has the bearing and the pain for you been, in comparison with what I have had to bear and suffer?" he asked with emotion. "I, at least, have not tried to make it worse for you, Lucy, though you have for me. In my judgment, we ought to have *shared* the burden; and so made it lighter, if possible, for one another."

Ay, sometimes she had thought that herself. But then her womanly sense of insult, her justifiable resentment, would step in and scatter the thought to the winds. It was too bad of Karl to reflect on her "pride."

"Is it to last for ever?" she asked, after a pause.

"Heaven knows!" he answered. "Heaven knows that I have striven to do my best. I have committed no sin against you, Lucy, save that of having married you when—when I ought not. I have most bitterly expiated it."

He spoke like one from whom all hope in life has gone; his haggard and utterly spiritless face was bent downwards. Lucy, her love all in force, her conscience aroused, touched his hand.

"If I have been more harshly judging than I ought, Karl, I pray you and heaven alike to forgive me."

He gave no answer: but he turned his hand upwards so that hers lay in it. Thus they sat for some time, saying nothing. A singing bird was perched on a tree in front of them; a light cloud passed over the face of the blue sky.

"But—you know, Karl," she began again in a half whisper, "it has not been right, or well, for—for those to have been at the Maze who have been there."

"I do know it. I have repeatedly told you I knew it. I would almost have given my life to get them out. It will not be long now; I fear, one way or the other, the climax I have been dreading seems to be approaching."

"What climax?"

"Discovery. Bringing with it disgrace and pain and shame. It is when I fear that, Lucy, that I feel most bitterly how wrong it was of me to marry. But I did not know all the complication; I never anticipated the evils that would ensue. You must forgive me, for I did it three-parts in ignorance."

He clasped her hand as he spoke. Her tears were gathering fast. Karl rose to depart, but she kept his fingers in hers, her tears dropping as she looked up at him.

"I ask, Karl, if we are to live this kind of life for ever?"

"As you shall will, Lucy. The life is of your choosing, not of mine."

One long look of doubt, of compassion, of love, into each other's eyes; and then the hand-clasp that so thrilled through each of them was loosed; the fingers fell apart. Karl went off to the house, and Lucy burst into a storm of sobs so violent as to startle the little bird, and stop its song.

CHAPTER XVII.

Taken from the Evil to come.

DREADFUL commotion at Mrs. Jinks's. Young ladies coming in, all in excitement; the widow nearly off her head. Their pastor was ill.

On a sofa before his parlour fire, he lay extended, the Reverend Guy; his head on a soft pillow, his feet (in embroidered slippers) on an embroidered cushion. The room was quite an epitome of sacred decorations, crosses lay embedded amid ferns; illuminated scrolls adorned the walls. Something was wrong with the reverend gentleman's throat: his hands and brow were feverish. Whether it was merely a relaxed throat, or a common soreness, or a quinsy threatening him could not be decided in the general dismay. Some thought one way, some another; all agreed in one thing—that it must be treated promptly. The dear man was passive as any lamb in their ministering hands, and submitted accordingly. What rendered the case more distressing and its need of recovering treatment all-urgent, was the fact that the morrow would be some great day in the calendar, necessitating high services at St. Jerome's. How were they to be held when the chief priest was disabled? Damon Puff was all very well; but he was not the Reverend Guy Cattacomb.

The Widow Jinks, assuming most experience by reason of years, and also in possessing a cousin who was a nurse of renown, as good as any doctor on an emergency, had recommended the application of "plant" leaves. The ladies seized upon it eagerly: anything to allay the beloved patient's sufferings and stop the progress of the disorder. The leaves had been procured without loss of time; Lawyer St. Henry's kitchen garden over the way having had the honour of supplying them; and they were now in process of preparation in the ladies' fair hands. Two were picking, three boiling and bruising, four sewing, all inwardly intending to apply them. The Widow

Jinks had her hands full below: gruel, broth, jelly, ar-
row-root, beef-tea, custard puddings, and other things
being alike in the course of preparation over the
kitchen fire: the superabundant amount of sick dainties arising from the fact that each lady had ordered
that which seemed to her best.   What with the care
of so many saucepans at once, and the being called
off perpetually to answer the knocks at the front door,
the widow felt rather wild; and sincerely wished all
sore throats at Jericho.   For the distressing news had
spread; and St. Jerome's fair worshippers were coming
up to the house in uninterrupted succession.

It fell to Miss Blake to apply the cataplasm.   As
many assisting, by dint of gingerly touching the tip of
the reverend gentleman's ears or holding back his shirt
collar as could get their fingers in.   Miss Blake, her
heart attuned to sympathy, felt stirred by no common
compassion.   She was sure the patient's eyes sought
hers: and, forgetting the few years' difference in their
ages, all kinds of flattering ideas and sweet hopes
floated into her mind—for it was by no means incum-
bent on her to waste her charms in wearing the wil-
lows for that false renegade—false in more ways than
one—Karl Andinnian.   Looking on passively, but not
tendering her own help amid so many volunteers, sat
Jemima Moore in a distant chair, her face betokening
anything but pleasurable ease.   There were times when
she felt jealous of Miss Blake.

The leaves applied, the throat bound up, and some
nourishment administered in the shape of a dish of
broth, nothing remained to be essayed, save that the
patient should endeavour to get some sleep. To enable
him to do this, it was obvious, even to the anxious

nurses themselves, that he should be left alone. Miss Blake suggested that they should all make a pilgrimage to St. Jerome's to pray for him. Eagerly was it seized upon, and bonnets were tied on. A thought crossed each mind almost in unison—that one at least might have been left behind to watch the slumbers: but as nobody would help another to the office, and did not like very well to propose herself, it remained unspoken.

"You'll come back again!" cried the reverend sufferer, retaining Miss Blake's hand in his, as she was wishing him good-bye.

"*Rely* upon me, dear Mr. Cattacomb," was the response—and Miss Blake regarded the promise as sacred, and would not have broken it for untold gold.

So they trooped out: and Mr. Cattacomb, left to himself and to quiet, speedily fell into the desired sleep. He was really feeling ill and feverish.

The time was drawing on for the late afternoon service, and Tom Pepp stood tinkling the bell as the pilgrims approached. Simultaneously with their arrival, there drove up an omnibus, closely packed with devotees from Basham, under the convoy of Mr. Puff. That reverend junior, his parted hair and moustache and assumed lisp in perfect order, conducted the service to the best of his ability; and the foreheads of some of his fair hearers touched the ground in humility when they put up their prayers for the sick pastor.

The autumn days were short now; the service had been somewhat long, and when St. Jerome turned out its flock, evening had set in. You could hardly see your hand before you. Some went one way, some another. The omnibus started back with its freight: Mr. Puff, however (to the utter mental collapse of those inside it) joined the pilgrims on their return to Mr. Cattacomb's. Miss Blake went straight on to Foxwood Court: for, mindful of her promise to the patient, she wished to tell Lady Andinnian that she should not be in to dinner.

Margaret Sumnor was staying with Lucy: her invalid sofa and herself having been transported to the Court. The rector and his wife had been invited to an informal dinner that evening; also Mr. Moore and his sister: so Miss Blake thought it better to give notice that she should be absent, that they might not wait for her. Jemima Moore, a very good-natured girl on the whole, offered to accompany her, seeing that nobody else did; for they all trooped off in the clerical wake of Mr. Puff. As the two ladies left the Court again, they became aware that some kind of commotion was taking place before the Maze gate. It was too dark to see so far, but there was much howling and groaning.

"Do let us go and see what it is!" cried Miss Jemima. And she ran off without further parley. The irruption into the Maze of Mr. Detective Tatton—who was by this time known in his real name and character—had excited much astonishment and speculation in Foxwood; the more especially as no two opinions agreed as to what there was within the Maze that he could be after. The prevailing belief amid the juvenile population was, that a menagerie of wild beasts had taken up its illegitimate abode inside. They collected at hours in choice groups around the gate, pressing their noses against the iron work in the hope.

of getting a peep at the animals, or at least of hearing them roar. On this evening a dozen or two had come down as usual: Tom Pepp, having cut short the ringing out, in his ardour to make one, had omitted to put off the conical cap.

But these proceedings did not please Sir Karl Andinnian's agent at Clematis Cottage. That gentleman, after having warned them sundry times to keep away, and enlarged on the perils that indiscriminate curiosity generally brought to its indulgers, had crossed the road to-night armed with a long gig-whip, which he began to lay about him kindly. The small fry, yelling and shrieking, dispersed immediately.

"Little simpletons!" cried Miss Jemima Moore, as the agent walked back with his whip, after explaining to her. "Papa says the police only went in to take the boundaries of the parish. And—oh! There's Tom Pepp in his sacred cap! Miss Blake, look at Tom Pepp. Oh! Oh, if Mr. Cattacomb could but see him!"

Miss Blake, who never did things in a hurry, walked leisurely after the offending boy, intending to pounce upon him at St. Jerome's. In that self-same moment the Maze gate was thrown open, and Mrs. Grey, her golden hair disordered, herself in evident tribulation, came forth wringing her hands, and amazing Miss Jemima more considerably than even the whip had amazed the boys.

What she said, Jemima hardly caught. It was to the effect that her baby was in convulsions; that she wanted Mr. Moore on the instant, and had no one to send.

"I'll run for papa," cried the good-natured girl. "I will run at once; I am his daughter. But you should get it into a warm bath, instantly, you know. There's nothing else does for convulsions. I would come and help you if there were any one else to go for papa."

In answer to this kind suggestion, Mrs. Grey stepped inside again, and shut the gate in Miss Jemima's face. But she thanked her in a few heartfelt words, and begged her to get Mr. Moore there without delay: her servant was already preparing a bath for the baby.

Jemima ran at the top of her speed, and met her father and aunt walking to Foxwood Court. The doctor hastened to the Maze, leaving his sister to explain the cause of his absence to Sir Karl and Lady Andinnian.

Dinner was nearly over at the Court when the doctor at length got there. The baby was better, he said: but he was by no means sure that it would not have a second attack. If so, he thought it could not live: it was but weakly at the best.

As may readily be imagined, scarcely any other topic formed the conversation at the dinner-table. Not one of the guests seated round it had the slightest notion that it was, of all others, the most intensely unwelcome to their host and hostess: the one in his dread to hear the Maze alluded to at all; the other in her bitter pain and jealousy. The doctor enlarged upon the isolated position of Mrs. Grey, upon her sweetness and beauty, upon her warm love for her child, and her great distress. Sir Karl made an answering remark when obliged. Lucy sat in silence, bearing her cross. Every word seemed to be an outrage on her feelings. The guests talked on; but somehow each felt that the harmony of the meeting had left it.

Making his dinner of one dish, in spite of the remonstrances of Sir Karl and the attentions of Mr. Giles and his fellows, the doctor drank a cup of coffee, and rose to leave again. His sister, begging Lady Andinnian to excuse her, put on her hat and shawl, and left with him.

"Are you going over to the Maze, William?" she asked, when they got out.

"I am, Diana."

"Then I will go with you. That's why I came away. The poor young thing is alone, save for her servants, and I think it only a charity that some one should be with her."

The surgeon gave a grin of satisfaction in the darkness of the night. "Take care, Diana," said he, with assumed gravity. "You know the question the holy ones at St. Jerome's are raising—whether that lovely lady is any better than she should be."

"Bother to St. Jerome's," independently returned Miss Diana.

"If the holy ones, as you call them, would expend a little more time in cultivating St. Paul's enjoined charity, and a little less in praying with those two parsons of theirs, Heaven might be better served. Let the lady be what she will, she is to be pitied in her distress, and I am going to her. Brother William!"

"Well?"

"I cannot think what is the matter with Lady Andinnian. She looks just like one that's pining away."

The evening went on at the Court. Miss Blake came back, bringing the news that the Reverend Mr. Cattacomb's throat was easier, which was of course a priceless consolation. At ten o'clock Mr. and Mrs.

Sumnor took their departure, Sir Karl walking with
them as far as the lodge. Lost in thought, he had
gone out without his hat: in returning for it he saw
his wife at one of the flower beds.

"Lucy! Is it you, out in the damp? What do you
want?"

"I am getting one of the late roses for Margaret,"
was the answer. "She likes to have a flower to cheer
her when she lies awake at night. She says it makes
her think of heaven."

"I will get it for you," said Karl. And he chose
the best he could in the starlight, and cut it.

"Lucy, I am going over the way," he resumed in
a low tone, as they turned to the steps, "and I cannot tell when I shall be back. Hewitt will sit up for
me."

Of all audacious avowals, this sounded about the
coolest to its poor young listener. Her quickened
breath seemed to chafe her; her heart beat as though
it would burst its bounds.

"Why need you tell me of it?" she passionately
answered, all her strivings for patience giving way before the moment's angry pain.

Karl sighed. "It lies in my duty to do what I
can, Lucy: and as I should have thought you might
see and recognize. Should the child have a relapse
in the course of the night, I shall be there to fetch
Moore: there's no one else to go."

Lucy let fall the train of her dress, which she had
been holding, gathered round her, and swept across
the hall; vouchsafing back to him neither look nor word.

The chamber lay in semi-light: with that still hush

pervading it, common to rooms where death is being waited for, and is seen visibly approaching. Mr. Moore's fears had been verified. The infant at the Maze had had a second attack of convulsions, and was dying.

It lay folded in a blanket on its mother's lap. The peaceful little face was at rest now; the soft breathing, getting slower and slower, alone stirring it. Miss Diana, her hat thrown off, sat on her heels on the hearth-rug, speaking every now and then a word or two of homely comfort: the doctor stood near the fire looking on; Ann Hopley was noiselessly putting straight some things in a corner.

With her golden hair all pushed from her brow, and her pretty face so delicate and wan, bent downwards, she sat, the poor mother. Save for the piteous sorrow in the despairing eyes, and a deep sobbing sigh that would arise in the throat, no sign of emotion escaped her. She knew the fiat—that all hope was over. The doctor, who saw the end getting nearer and nearer, and was aware that such ends are sometimes painful to see, even in an infant—the little frame struggling with the fleeting breath, the helpless hands fighting for it—had been anxious that Mrs. Grey should resign her charge to some one else. Miss Diana made one more effort to bring it about.

"My dear, I know you *must* be tired. You'll get the cramp. Let me take it, if only for a minute's relief."

"Do, Mrs. Grey," said the doctor.

She looked up at them with beseeching entreaty; her hands tightening involuntarily over the little treasure.

"Please don't ask me," she piteously said. "I must have him to the last. He is going from me for ever."

"Not for ever, my dear," corrected Miss Diana. "You will go to him, though he will not return to you."

The door softly opened, and some one came gently in. Absorbed by the dying child though she was, and by the surroundings it brought, Mrs. Grey glanced quickly up and made a frantic movement to beckon the intruder back, her face changing to some dread apprehension, her lips parting with fear. She thought it might be one who must not dare to show himself if he valued life and liberty: but it was only Karl Andinnian.

"Oh Karl, he is dying!" she cried in the hasty impulse of the moment—and the dry eyes filled with tears. "My darling baby is dying."

"I have been so sorry to hear about it, Mrs. Grey," returned Karl, who had his wits about him if she had not, and who saw the surprise of the doctor and Miss Diana, at the familiarity of the address. "I came over to see if I could be of any use to you."

He fell to talking to Mr. Moore in an under-tone, giving her time to recover her mistake; and the hushed silence fell on the chamber again. Karl bent to look at the pale little face, soon to put on immortality; he laid his hand lightly on the damp forehead, keeping it there for a minute in solemn silence, as though breathing an inward prayer.

"He will be better off there than here," whispered he to the mother, in turning to leave the chamber. "The world is full of thorns and care, as some of us too well know: God is taking him from it."

Pacing a distant room like a caged lion, was Sir Adam Andinnian. He wheeled round on his heel when his brother entered.

"Was ever position like unto mine, Karl?" he broke out, anger, pain, impatience, and most deep emotion mingling together in his tone. "Here am I, condemned to hide myself within these four walls, and may not quit them even to see my child die! The blackest criminal on earth can call for his friends on his death-bed. When are that offensive doctor and his sister going?"

"They are staying out of compassion to Rose," spoke Karl, in his quiet voice. "Oh, Adam, I am so sorry for this! I feel it with my whole heart."

"Don't talk," said Adam, rather roughly. "No fate was ever like my fate. Heaven has mercy for others: none for me. Because my own bitter punishment was not enough, it must even take my son!"

"It does seem to you cruel, I am sure. But God's ways are not as our ways. He is no doubt taking him, in love, from the evil to come. When we get up above there ourselves, Adam, we shall see the reason of it."

Sir Adam did not answer. He sat down and covered his face with his hand, and remained in silence. Karl did not break it.

Sounds by and by. The doctor and his sister were departing, escorted by Ann Hopley—who must see them out at the gate and make it fast again. Adam was bursting from the room: but his brother put his arm across the entrance.

"Not yet, Adam. Not until Ann is in again, and

has the door fast.   Think of the consequences if you were seen!"

He recognised the good sense, the necessity for prudence, fierce as a caged lion though his mood indeed was.   The bolts and bars were shot at last, and Adam went forth.

In its own crib lay the baby then, straight and still.   The fluttering heart had ceased to beat; the sweet little peaceful face was at rest.   Rose knelt by her own bed, her head muffled in the counterpane.   Sir Adam strode up to his child and stood looking at it.

A minute's silence deep as that of the death that was before him, and then a dreadful burst of tears.   They are always dreadful when a man sheds them in his agony.

"It was all we had, Karl," he said between his sobs.   "And I did not even see him die!"

Karl took the strong but now passive hands in his.   His own eyes were wet as he strove to say a word of comfort to his brother.   But these first moments of grief are not best calculated for it.

"He is happier than he could ever have been here, Adam.   Try and realize it.   He is already one of God's bright angels."

And my young Lady Andinnian, over at Foxwood Court, did not choose to go to bed, but sat up to indulge her defiant humour.   Never had her spirit been so near open rebellion as it was that night.   Sir Karl did not come in: apparently he meant to take up his abode at the Maze until morning.

"*Of course* he must be there when his child is dying!" spoke she to herself, as she paced the carpet

with a step as impatient and a great deal more indignant than those other steps that had paced, that
night.   "Of course *she* must be comforted!   While
I——"

The words were choked by a flood of emotion.
Bitter reflections crowded on her, one upon another.
The more earnestly and patiently she strove to bear
and *for*bear, the more cruelly seemed to rise up her
afflictions.   And Lucy Andinnian threw herself down
in abandonment, wondering whether all pity had quite
gone out of heaven.

CHAPTER XVIII.

News for Mr. Tatton.

WHAT Mr. Detective Tatton's future proceedings
would have been, or to what untoward catastrophe, as
connected with this history, they might have led had
his stay at Foxwood been prolonged to an indefinite
period, cannot here be known.   He remained on.
Social matters had resumed their ordinary groove.
The Maze was left undisturbed; Mr. Cattacomb was
well again; St. Jerome's in full force.

It might be that Mr. Tatton was waiting—like a
certain noted character with whom we all have the
pleasure of an acquaintance—for "something to turn
up."   That he was contemplating some grand coup,
which would throw his prize into his hands, while to
the world and Mrs. Jinks he appeared only to be enjoying the salubrious Kentish air, and amusing himself
with public politics generally, we may rest pretty well
assured of.   But this agreeable existence was suddenly
cut short.

One morning when Mr. Tatton's hopes and plans were, like Cardinal Wolsey's greatness, all a-ripening, he received a communication from Mr. Superintendent Game at Scotland Yard, conveying the astounding intelligence that the real Philip Salter had not been in Foxwood at all, but had just died in Canada.

Mr. Tatton sat contemplating the letter. He could not have been much more astonished had a bombshell burst under him. Of the truth of the information there could be no question: its reliability was indisputable. One of the chief officers in the home police force who was in Canada on business, and had known Salter well, discovered him in the last stage of a wasting sickness, and saw him die.

"I've never had such a fool's game to play at as *this*," ejaculated Mr. Tatton when sufficiently recovered to speak; "and never wish to have such another. What the deuce, then, is the mystery connected with the Maze?"

Whatever it might be, it was now no business of his; though could he have afforded to waste more time and money, he would have liked very well to stay and track it out. Summoning the Widow Jinks to his presence, he informed her that he was called away suddenly on particular business; and then proceeded to pack up. Mrs. Jinks resented the departure as quite a personal injury, and wiped the soft tears from her eyes.

On his way to the station he chanced to meet Sir Karl Andinnian: and the latter's heart went up with a great bound. The black bag in Mr. Tatton's hand, and the portmanteau being wheeled along beside him, spoke a whole volume of hope.

"Good morning, Sir Karl. You have misled us finely as to the Maze."

"Why, what do you mean, Mr. Tatton?" asked Karl.

"Salter has turned up in Canada. Or, one might perhaps rather say, turned down; for he is dead, poor fellow."

"Indeed!"

"Indeed and in truth. One of our officers is over there, and was with him when he died. It was too bad of you to mislead us in this way, Sir Karl."

"Nay, you misled yourselves."

"A fine quantity of time I have wasted down here! weeks upon weeks; and all for nothing. I never was so vexed in my life."

"You have yourself to blame—or those who sent you here. Certainly not me. The very first time I had the honour of speaking to you, Mr. Tatton, I assured you on the word of a gentleman that Salter was not at Foxwood."

"Well, come, Sir Karl—what is the secret being enacted within the place over yonder?" pointing his finger in the direction of the Maze.

"I am not in the habit of enquiring into the private affairs of my tenants," was the rather haughty answer. "If there be any secret at the Maze—though I think no one has assumed it but yourself—you may rely upon it that it is not in any way connected with Salter. Are you taking your final departure?"

"It looks like it, Sir Karl"—nodding towards the luggage going onwards. "When the game's at the other end of the world, and dead besides, it is not of much use my staying to search after it in this. I hope the next I have to hunt will bring in more satisfaction."

They said farewell cordially. The detective in his natural sociability; Karl in his most abundant gratitude for the relief it would give his brother. And Mr. Detective Tatton, hastening on in the wake of the portmanteau, took the passing up-train, and was whirled away to London.

A minute or two afterwards Karl met his agent. He was beginning to impart to him the tidings about Salter, when Smith interrupted him.

"I have heard it, Sir Karl. I got a letter from a relative this morning, which told me all. The information has taken Tatton off the land here, I expect: I saw you speaking to him."

"You are right."

"As to poor Salter, the release is probably a happy one. He is better off than he ever could have been again in this world. But what on earth put Scotland Yard on the false scent that he was at Foxwood, will always be a problem to me. Tatton's gone for good, I suppose, sir?"

"He said so."

"And Sir Adam is, in one sense, free again. There will be less danger in his getting away from Foxwood now, if it be judged desirable that he should go."

Karl shook his head. There was another impediment now to his getting away—grievous sickness.

That Sir Adam Andinnian, the unfortunate fugitive, hiding in peril at the Maze, had some very grave disorder upon him could no longer be doubtful to himself or to those about him. It seemed to develop it-

self more surely day by day. Adam took it as calmly
as he did other evils; but Karl was nearly out of his
mind with distress at the complication it brought.
Most necessary was it for Adam to have a doctor; to
be attended by one; and yet they dare not put the
need in practice. The calling in of Dr. Cavendish
had entailed only too much danger and terror.

The little baby, Charles Andinnian, was lying at
rest in Foxwood church-yard, within the precincts con-
secrated to the Andinnian family. Ann Hopley chose
the grave, and had a fight over it with the clerk. That
functionary protested he would not allot it to any
baby in the world. She might choose any spot except
that, but that belonged to the Foxwood Court people
exclusively. Ann Hopley persisted the baby should have
that, and no other. It was under the weeping elm tree,
she urged, and the little grave would be shaded from
the summer's sun. Sir Karl Andinnian settled the
dispute. Appealed to by the clerk, he gave a ready and
courteous permission, and the child was laid there.
Ann Hopley then paid a visit to the stone-mason, and
ordered a little white marble stone, nothing to be in-
scribed on it but the initials "C. A," and the date of
the death. Poor Rose had only her sick husband to
attend to now.

He was not always sick. There were days when
he seemed to be as well, and to be almost as active,
as ever; and, upon that would supervene a season of
pain and dread, and danger.

One afternoon, when Karl was driving his wife by
in the pony-chaise, Ann Hopley had the gate open,
and was standing at it. It was the day following the
departure of Mr. Tatton. Something in the woman's

face—a kind of mute, appealing anguish—struck Karl forcibly as she looked at him. In the sensation of freedom and of safety brought by the detective's absence, Karl actually pulled up.

"Will you pardon me, Lucy, if I leave you for one moment? I think Ann Hopley wants to speak to me."

He leaped out of the little low chaise, leaving the reins to Lucy. Her face was turning scarlet. Of all the insults he had thrust upon her, this seemed the greatest. To pull up at that very gate when *she* was in the carriage! Mr. Smith and his churchwarden-pipe were enjoying themselves as usual at Clematis Cottage, looking out on the world in general, and no doubt (as Lucy indignantly felt) making his private comments.

"He is very ill again, sir," were the few whispered words of Ann Hopley. "Can you come in? I am not sure but it will be for death."

"Almost immediately," returned Karl; and he stepped back to the chaise just in time. Lucy was about to try her hand at driving, to make her escape from him and the miserable situation.

Since the night of the baby's death, Karl and his wife had lived a more estranged life than ever. Lucy avoided him continually. When he spoke to her, she would not answer beyond a monosyllable. As to any chance of explanation on any subject, there was none. It is true he did not attempt any; and if he had, she would have waived him away, and refused to listen to it. This day was the first for some time that she had consented to let him drive her out.

It had happened on their return. Lucy's eminently

ungracious manner as he took his seat again would
have stopped his speaking, even if he had had a mind
to speak; but he was deep in anxious thought. The
resentful way in which she had from the first taken
up the affair of his unfortunate brother, served to tie
his tongue always. He drove in, stood to help her
out—or would have helped, but that she swept by
without touching him—left the pony to the waiting
groom, and walked back to the Maze.

Adam was in one of his attacks of pain, nay, of
agony. It could be called nothing less. It was not,
however, for death; the sharpness of the paroxysm,
with its attendant signs, had misled Ann Hopley.
Rose looked scarcely less ill than her husband. Her
most grievous position was telling upon her. Her
little child dead, her husband apparently dying, danger
and dread of another sort on all sides. More like a
shadow was she now than a living woman.

"Do you know what I have been thinking, Rose?"
said Karl, when his brother had revived. "That we
might trust Moore. You hear, Adam. I think he
might be trusted."

"Trusted for what?" returned Adam; not in his
sometimes fierce voice, but in one very weak and
faint.

He was lying on the sofa. Rose sat at the end of
it, Karl in a chair at the side.

"To see you; to hear who you are. I cannot help
believing that he would be true as steel. Moore is
one of those men, as it seems to me, that we might
trust our lives with."

"It won't do to run risks, old fellow. I do not
want to be captured in my last hours."

Karl believed there would be no risk. Mr. Moore was a truly good man, sensible and benevolent. The more he dwelt on the idea, the surer grew his conviction that the surgeon might be trusted. Rose, who was almost passive in her distress, confessed she liked him. Both he and his sister gave her the impression of being, as Karl worded it, true as steel. Ann Hopley was in favour of it too. She put the case with much ingenuity.

"Sir, I should think there's not a doctor in the world—at least, one worthy the name—who would not keep such a secret, confided to him of necessity, even if he were a bad man. And Mr. Moore's a good one."

And the decision was made. Karl was to feel his way to the confidence. He would sound the surgeon first, and act accordingly.

"Not that it much signifies either way," cried Sir Adam, his careless manner reviving as his strength and spirits returned. "Die I soon must, I suppose, now; but I'd rather die in my bed here than on a pallet in a cell. So, Karlo, old friend, if you like to see what Moore's made of, do so."

"I wish it had occurred to me before," cried Karl. "But indeed, the outer dangers have been so imminent as to drive other fears away."

"It will never matter, bon frère. I don't suppose all the advice in the kingdom could have saved me. What is to be will be."

"Master," put in Ann Hopley, "where's the good of your taking up a gloomy view of it, all at once? *That's* not the way to get well."

"Gloomy! not a bit of it," cried Sir Adam, in a

voice as cheery as a lark's on a summer's morning. "Heaven is more to be desired than Portland Prison, Ann."

So Karl went forth, carrying his commission. In his heart he still trembled at it. The interests involved were so immense; the stake was so heavy for his unfortunate brother. In his extreme caution, he did not care to be seen going to the surgeon's house, but sent a note to ask him to call at the Court.

It was the dusk of evening when Mr. Moore arrived. He was shown in to Sir Karl in his own room. Giles was appearing with two wax-lights in massive silver candlesticks, but his master motioned them away.

"I can say what I have to say better by this light than in a glare," he observed to the doctor: perhaps as an opening preliminary, or intimation that the subject of the interview was not a pleasant one. And Giles shut them in alone. Karl sat sideways to the table, his elbow leaning on it; the doctor facing him with his back to the window.

"Mr. Moore," began Karl, after a pause of embarrassment, "did it ever occur to you to have a secret confided to your keeping involving life or death?"

Mr. Moore paused in his turn. The question no doubt caused him surprise. He took it—the "life or death"—to be put in a professional point of view. A suspicion came over him that he was about to be consulted for some malady connected with the (evident) fading away of Lady Andinnian.

"I do not suppose, Sir Karl, there is a single

disease that flesh is heir to, whether secret or open, but what I have been consulted upon in my time."

"Not disease," returned Karl hastily, finding he was misunderstood. "I meant a real, actual secret. A dangerous secret, involving life or death to the individual concerned, according as others should hold it sacred or betray it."

A longer pause yet. Mr. Moore staring at Karl through the room's twilight.

"You must speak more plainly, Sir Karl, if you wish me to understand." And Karl continued thoughtfully, weighing every word as he spoke it, that it might not harm his brother.

"The case is this, Mr. Moore. I hold in my keeping a dangerous secret. It concerns a—a friend: a gentleman who has managed to put himself in peril of the law. For the present he is evading the law; keeping himself, in fact, concealed alike from enemies and friends, with the exception of one or two who are —I may say—helping to screen him. If there were a necessity for my wishing to confide this secret to you, would you undertake to keep it sacred? Or should you consider it lay in your duty as a conscientious man to betray it?"

"Goodness bless me, no!" cried the doctor. "I'm not going to betray people: it's not in my line. My business is to heal their sickness. You need not fear me. It is a case of debt, I suppose, Sir Karl?"

Karl looked at him for a moment steadily. "And if it were not a case of debt, but of crime, Moore? What then?"

"Just the same. Betraying my fellowmen, whether smarting under the ban of perplexity or of sin, does not rest in my duty, I say. I am not a detective officer. By the way, perhaps that other detective—who turns out to be named Tatton, and to belong to Scotland Yard—may have been down here looking after the very man."

Mr. Moore spoke lightly. Not a suspicion rested upon him that the sad and worn gentleman before him held any solemn or personal interest in this. Karl resumed, his voice insensibly taking a lower tone.

"An individual is lying in concealment, as I have described. His offence was not against you or against me. Therefore, as you observe, and as I judge, it does not lie even in our duty to denounce him. I am helping to screen him. I want you to undertake to do the same when you shall know who he is."

"I'll undertake it with all my heart, Sir Karl. You have some motive for confiding the matter to me."

"The motive arises out of necessity. He is grievously ill; in urgent need of medical care. I fear his days are already numbered: and in that fact lies a greater obligation for us to obey the dictates of humanity."

"I see. You want me to visit him, and to do what I can for him. I am ready and willing."

"He is—mind, I shall shock you—a convicted felon."

"Well?—he has a body to be tended and a soul to be saved," replied the surgeon, curiously impressed with the hush of gravity that had stolen over the interview. "I will do my best for him, Sir Karl."

"And guard his secret?"

"I will. Here's my hand upon it. What would my

Maker say to my offences at the Last Day, I wonder, if I could usurp His functions and deliver up to vengeance my fellow-man?"

"I may trust you, then?"

"You may. I perceive you are over anxious, Sir Karl. What more assurance can I give you? You may trust me as you trust yourself. By no incautious word or action of mine shall his peril be increased, or harm come nigh him: nay, I will avert it from him if I can. And now—who is he? The sick man at the Maze—to whom Dr. Cavendish was called? Taking one thing with another, that Maze has been a bit of a puzzle in my mind lately."

"The same."

"Ay. Between ourselves, I was as sure as gold that some one was there. Is it Mr. Grey? The poor young lady's husband; the dead baby's father?"

"Just so. But he is not Mr. Grey."

"Who is he, then?"

Karl glanced around him, as though he feared the very walls might contain eaves-droppers. Mr. Moore saw his dread.

"It is a most dangerous secret," whispered Karl with agitation. "You will keep it with your whole heart and life?"

"Once more, I will, I will. You cannot doubt me. Who is it?"

"My brother. Sir Adam Andinnian."

The doctor leaped to his feet. Perhaps he had a doubt of Karl's sanity. He himself had assisted to lay Sir Adam in his grave.

"Hush!" said Karl. "No noise. It is indeed my most unfortunate brother."

"Did he come to life again?—Did Sir Adam come to life again?" reiterated the wondering surgeon in his perplexity.

"He did not die."

They went together to the Maze after dark, Karl letting the doctor in with his own key. The whole history had been revealed to him. Nothing was kept back, save a small matter or two connected with the means of Sir Adam's daily concealment: of those no living soul without the Maze was cognisant, save three: Karl, Hewitt, and Smith the agent. Mr. Moore was entrusted with it later, but not at first. During the lifetime of a medical man, it falls to his lot to hear some curious family secrets, as it had to Mr. Moore; but he had never met with one half so strange and romantic as this.

Sir Adam had dismissed the signs of his illness, and—it will hardly be credited—attired himself in evening dress. With the departure of Mr. Tatton, old habits resumed their sway, with all their surrounding incaution. Mr. Moore saw the same tall, fine man, with the white and even teeth, that he had caught the transient glimpse of in the uncertain twilight some weeks before. The same, but with a difference: for the face was shrunken now, little more than half the size it had been then. In the past week or two he had changed rapidly. He met them when they entered —it was in the upstairs sitting-room: standing at the door erect, his head thrown back. Mr. Moore put out his hand; but the other did not take it.

"Do you know all, sir?" he asked.

"All, Sir Adam."

"And you are not my enemy?"

"Your true friend, Sir Adam. Never a truer one shall be about you than I."

Their hands met then. "But I am not Sir Adam here, you know; I am Mr. Grey. Ah, doctor, what a life it has been!"

"A life that has done its best to kill him," thought the doctor, as he sat down. "Why did you not call me in before?" he asked.

"Well, we were afraid. You would be afraid of everybody if you were in my place and position. Besides, this disease, whatever it may turn out to be, has developed itself so rapidly that but little time seems to have been lost. I do not see how you will come in now, if it is to be a daily visit, without exciting the curiosity of the neighbourhood."

"Oh, nonsense," said the surgeon. "Mrs. Grey has a renewal of illness and I come in to see her. The curious neighbours will understand if they are exacting upon the point. Or old Hopley, your gardener—I'm sure his rheumatism must need a doctor sometimes."

Sir Adam laughed. "Hopley will do best," he said. "And then you know, doctor, if—if the worst comes to the worst; that is, the worst so far as sickness is concerned, I can be carried out as Hopley."

"What do you think of him, Mr. Moore?" enquired Karl gravely when the interview was over.

"I will tell you more about it when I have seen more of him," was the surgeon's answer. But his face and tone both assumed, or seemed to Karl to assume, an ominous shade as he gave it.

———

CHAPTER XIX.

Mrs. Cleeve at Fault.

Mrs. Cleeve was at Foxwood. She had been staying in London with her sister, Lady Southal, and took the opportunity to come down to see her daughter. Lucy's appearance startled her. As is well known, we are slow to discern any personal change either for the better or the worse in those with whom we live in daily intercourse: it requires an absence of days or weeks, as the case may be, to perceive it in all its naked reality. Mrs. Cleeve saw what none around Lucy had seen—at least, to the extent—and it shocked and alarmed her. The face was a sad, drawn face; dark rims encircled the sweet brown eyes; the whole air and bearing were utterly spiritless.

"What can be the matter with you, my dear?" questioned Mrs. Cleeve, seizing on the first opportunity that they were alone together.

"The matter with me, mamma!" returned Lucy, making believe not to understand why the question should be put: though her face flushed to hectic. "Nothing is the matter with me."

"There most certainly is, Lucy; with your health or with your mind. You could not be as you are, or look as you do unless there were."

"I suffered a great deal from the heat," said poor Lucy.

"My dear—you are suffering from something else;

and I think you should enlighten me as to its nature. After that fever even you did not look as you are looking now."

But not an iota of acknowledgment from her daughter could Mrs. Cleeve obtain. Lucy would not admit that aught was amiss in any way; at least, that she was conscious of it. Mrs. Cleeve next appealed to Miss Blake.

But that young lady, absorbed by her own pursuits and interests; by the Reverend Mr. Cattacomb and the duties at St. Jerome's, had really not been observant of Lucy's fading face. She could be regardful enough in a contemptuous sort of way of Sir Karl's delinquencies, and of what she looked upon as his wife's blind infatuation; she did not omit to note the signs of trouble and care too evidently apparent in him, and which she set down as the result of an uneasy conscience: but she had failed to note them in Lucy. One cause of this perhaps was, that in her presence Lucy invariably put on an air of lightness, not to say gaiety: and Miss Blake was rarely at home, except at meals; if she did get an hour there she was up to the ears in silks and church embroidery. What with Matins and Vespers, and the other daily engagements at St. Jerome's; what with looking after St. Jerome's pastors; what with keeping the young fry in order, including Tom Pepp, and seeing to the spiritual interests of their mothers, Miss Blake had so much on her hands that it was no wonder she was not very observant of Lucy.

"I do not think there is anything particular the matter with Lucy," was the answer she made to Mrs. Cleeve.

"You must see how ill she looks, Theresa."

"She is not ill. At least, that I know of. She eats her dinner, and dresses, and goes out, and has company at home. I really had not observed that she was looking ill."

"She talks of the heat," continued Mrs. Cleeve; "but that is all nonsense. Extreme heat may make a person thin, but it cannot make them sad and spiritless."

"Lucy is neither sad nor spiritless—that I have noticed."

"Perhaps you have not noticed, Theresa. You have so many out-of-door pursuits, you know. I suppose," continued Mrs. Cleeve, with some hesitation, and lowering her voice to a confidential tone as she put the question, "I suppose there is nothing wrong between her and her husband?"

"Wrong in what way, do you mean?" rejoined Miss Blake.

"Any misunderstanding or unpleasantness."

"I should say *not*," returned Miss Blake, with some acrimony. "It is rather the other way. Lucy is blindly, absurdly infatuated with Sir Karl. If he boxed her on the one ear, she would offer him the other."

"It cannot be that, then," sighed Mrs. Cleeve. "I only thought of it because there was nothing else I could think of. For I cannot help fancying, Theresa, that the malady is on her spirits, more than on her health. I—I wonder whether that ague-fever left unsuspected consequences behind it that are developing themselves now?"

Theresa, her attention given to the employment in her hand—a cross she was working in gold thread

to adorn some part or other of Mr. Cattacomb's canoni-
cals—a great deal more than it was given to the conversation, allowed the doubt to pass undiscussed.
Mrs. Cleeve had always been accustomed to worry
herself over Lucy: Theresa supposed it was the habit
of mothers to do so, who had only one daughter. So
the subject of Lucy's looks dropped for the time.

"What is that for?" resumed Mrs. Cleeve, directing
her attention to the small gold cords.

"This? Oh, a little ornament I am making. Please
don't touch it, Mrs. Cleeve, or you will entangle the
threads."

Thus rebuked, Mrs. Cleeve sat for some moments
in silence, inhaling the fresh air through the open
window, and the perfume of the late flowers. The
mignonette, in its large clusters, seemed as though it
intended to bloom on until winter.

"Theresa, how much longer do you intend to remain here?" she suddenly asked. "Your stay has
been a very long one."

Theresa was aware of that. She was slightly suspicious that Sir Karl and his wife had begun to think
the same thing, though in their courtesy they were not
likely to let it appear. In truth the matter was causing
her some little reflection: for she would willingly have
made the Court her permanent home. While Mr.
Cattacomb remained at St. Jerome's, *she* should remain.
It might have been somewhat of a mistake to institute
St. Jerome's, and to bring Mr. Cattacomb to it: Miss
Blake could recognise it now: but as that step had
been taken, she could only abide by it.

"I am not likely to leave at present," she replied.
"It would be very dull for Lucy to be here without

me. As the winter weather comes on, my out-door duties will be somewhat curtailed, and I shall be able to give her more of my time. Lucy would be lost by herself, Mrs. Cleeve. She was always rather given to moping."

Yes. There was no doubt Lucy did "mope." Mrs. Cleeve sighed deeply. A cloud lay on Foxwood Court, and she could not trace out its source.

The cloud, she thought, lay on Sir Karl as well as on Lucy. That is, his sadness, his weary face, and his evident preoccupation were quite as visible to Mrs. Cleeve as were her daughter's. But for Theresa's emphatic assurance to the contrary, she might still have doubted whether the cloud did not lie between *them.* She was a single-minded, kind-hearted, simple-natured lady, not given to think ill, or to look out for it: but in this case she did try to observe and notice. She could not help seeing how seldom Karl and his wife were together. Karl would drive Lucy out occasionally; but as a rule they saw but little of him. He was generally present at meals, and always sociable and kind, and he would come into the drawing-room when visitors called, if at home; spending his other time chiefly in his own room, and in walking out alone. Late in the evenings he would usually be absent: Mrs. Cleeve noticed that. She had seen him walk across the lawn in the gloom to one of the little gates; she had seen him come in again after an hour or two's interval; and she wondered where he went to.

The truth was, Karl was obliged to go to the Maze more frequently than he used to go, or than was at all prudent. Mr. Moore had not yet pronounced the fatal fiat on Sir Adam that Dr. Cavendish had—doubt-fully—imparted to Mr. Detective Tatton; but he concealed from none of them that the case was one of extreme gravity; ay, and of danger. That Sir Adam grew more attenuated might be seen almost daily; he himself assumed that he had but a short span left of life; and he would not allow Karl to be for one single evening absent. Sometimes in the day Karl also went there. The conviction that Adam would not be long among them lay on every heart more or less: and it will be readily understood that Karl should sacrifice somewhat of caution to be with him while he might.

"Karlo, brother mine, you'll come over to-morrow morning?" Sir Adam would say, when their hands met for the evening farewell—and he would keep the hand until the answer should be given.

"If I can, Adam."

"That won't do. You must. Promise."

"I will, then. I will, if I can do it with safety."

And of course he had to go. Under other and happier circumstances, he would never have quitted the invalid night or day.

The lack of what Karl considered "safety," as he spoke it in his answer, would have consisted in the highway before the Maze gates being peopled; in his being seen to enter. It was so very unfrequented a road that not a soul would pass up or down for a quarter of an hour together; nay, for half one; and, as a rule, Karl was safe. But he exercised his precaution always. He would saunter towards the gate, as though merely taking a stroll on the shady side path; and then, the coast being clear, ring—for by day-time he never used his own key. His ears and

eyes alike on the alert; he, if by mal-chance some
solitary passenger should appear, would saunter over
to Mr. Smith and talk to him: and then slip in when
the intruder should have passed, Ann Hopley having
the door by that time ready to open. Karl would use
the same precaution coming out: and hitherto had
escaped observation.

It was not always to be so.

The time passed on: Sir Adam fluctuating, some
days fearfully ill, some days feeling well and hearty;
and Mrs. Cleeve continuing at Foxwood, for she could
not bear to leave Lucy.

Karl went across one morning soon after breakfast. His brother had been very ill indeed the evening before: so ill that Karl had brought most unpleasant thoughts away with him. He was ringing at the
gate when it suddenly opened; Ann Hopley was letting out Mr. Moore.

So far as *his* visits went, there had been no trouble.
Foxwood had taken care to inform itself as to what
patient at the Maze it was that Mr. Moore was again
in regular attendance upon, and found it to be Hopley
the gardener. The old man had caught an attack of
rheumatic fever, or some other affection connected
with age and knee joints—said the Miss Moores to
the rest of the fair flock going to and from St. Jerome's.
There was neither interest nor romance attaching to
the poor old man; so the doctor was at liberty to pass
in and out at will without the slightest thought being
given to it. In the doctor's day-book the patient was
entered as "James Hopley, Mrs. Grey's servant." The
doctor's assistant, a fashionable young man from London, who wore an eye-glass stuck in his eye, could

have the pleasure of reading it ten times a day if he chose.

"How is he?" asked Karl of Mr. Moore.

"Oh, better this morning—as I expected he would be," was the surgeon's answer. "But I have ordered him to lie in bed for the day. This time I think he will obey me, for he feels uncommonly weak."

"Every fresh attack makes him weaker," observed Karl.

"Why of course it does: it must do so. I don't half like the responsibility that lies on me," continued the doctor. "We ought to have another opinion."

"How can it be had?" remonstrated Karl.

"There it is—how? I wish he could be in London under the constant care of one of its practised men."

"We wish this, and wish the other, Mr. Moore," said Karl, sadly, "and you know how impossible it is for us to do more than we are doing. Answer me truly—for I think you can answer. Would there be a fair chance of his recovery if we had other advice than yours? Would there be any better chance of it?"

"Honestly speaking I do not think there would. I believe I am doing for him all that can be done."

Ann Hopley drew the gate open again, and the doctor went out. Karl passed on through the labyrinth.

Sir Adam liked to use his own will in all respects, and it was the first time he had made even a semblance of obeying Mr. Moore's orders of taking rest by daytime. He looked very ill. The once handsome face seemed shrunk to nothing; the short hair was almost white; the grey-blue eyes, beautiful as Karl's, had a strangely wistful, patient look in them.

"I thought you would be here, Karlo. I have wanted you ever since daylight."

"Are you feeling better, Adam? Free from pain?"

"Much better. Quite free from it."

"Moore has been saying he wishes we could get you to London, that you might have more skilled advice."

"What nonsense!" cried Adam. "As if any advice could really avail me! He knows it would not. Did it avail my father, Karl?"

Karl remained silent. There was no answer he could make.

"Sit down, old fellow, and tell me all the news. Got a paper with you?"

"The papers have not come yet," replied Karl, as he drew a chair to the bedside.

"Slow coaches, people are in this world! I shall get up presently."

"No, Adam, not to-day. Moore says you must not."

"Good old man! he is slow too. But he won't keep me in bed, Karl, when I choose to quit it. Why should I not get up?" continued Sir Adam, his voice taking a tone of its old defiance. "I am the best judge of my own strength. If I lay here for a month of Sundays, Karl, it would not add a day to my life."

Perhaps that was true. At any rate, Adam was one whom it was of no use to urge one way or the other.

"What's the old adage, Karlo?—'a short life and

a merry one?' Mine has not been very merry of late, has it?"

"I wish we could get you well, Adam."

"Do you? We are told, you know, that all things as they fall, are for the best. The world would say, I expect, that this is. I wonder sometimes, though, how soon or how late the enemy would have shown itself, had my life continued smooth as yours is."

Smooth as yours is! The unconscious words brought a pang to Karl's heart; they sounded so like mockery. Heaven alone knew the distress and turbulence of his.

"I got Moore into a cosy chat the other day," resumed Sir Adam: "the wife was safe away, trimming the plants in the greenhouse—Rose is nearly as good a gardener as I am, Karl."

"I know she is fond of gardening."

"Ay, and has been amidst it for years, you see. Well—I led Moore on, saying this, and asking the other, and he opened his mind a bit. The disease was in me always, he thinks, Karl, and must have come out, sooner or later. It was only a question of time. I have said so myself of late. But I did not look to follow the little olive branch quite so quickly."

"We may keep you here a long while yet, Adam. It is still possible, I hope, we may keep you for good. Moore has not said to the contrary."

"You think he knows it, though?"

Karl was really not sure. His own opinion was this—that Adam had less chance of getting well where he was than he would have had under those of the London faculty, whose specialty embraced that class of disease.

"Shall you put on mourning for me, old fellow? It will be a risk, won't it? I shan't care to be held up to the world as Adam Andinnian, dead, any more than I do, alive. You'll not care to say, either, 'This black coat' is worn for that brother of mine: the mauvais sujet who set the world all agog with his scandal.'"

What kind of a mood was Sir Adam in this morning? Karl's grave eyes questioned it. One of real, light, careless mockery? — or was it an underlying current of sadness and regret making itself too uneasily felt in his heart?

"Don't, Adam. It jars on every chord and pulse. You and I have cause to be at least more sober than other men."

"What have I said?" cried Sir Adam, half laughing. "That you may have to put on mourning for me. It is in the nature of things that the elder should go before the younger. You look well in black, too, Karl; men with such faces as yours always do."

"I hope it will be a long while before I have to wear it," sighed Karl, perceiving how hopeless it was to change his brother's humour.

"I'd bet Foxwood with you that it will be before Christmas."

"Adam, is it right to speak in this way?"

"Is it particularly wrong?"

"Why do you do it?"

"Need of change, I suppose. I have had a solemn night of it, old fellow: and I hardly know yet whether I was asleep or awake. It was somewhat of both, I I expect: but I thought I was amidst the angels. I can see them now as they looked; a whole crowd of them gathered about my bed. And, Karlo, when a man begins to dream of angels, and not to be able to decide afterwards whether it be a dream or a shadowed reality, it is a pretty sure sign, I take it, that no great time will elapse before he is with them."

Before Karl left, Adam had talked himself into a doze. With his worn and haggard face turned to the wall, he slept as peacefully as a child. Karl stole away, and went into the greenhouse. Rose was there amid the plants; the sunlight shining on her beautiful hair turned it into threads of gold. She lifted her white face, with its sad expression.

"I knew you were with him, Karl, so I did not come in. Don't you think he looks very, very ill this morning."

"Yes, he certainly does. He is asleep now."

"Asleep! In the daytime!"

"He had a bad night, I fancy."

"Do you think there's hope, Karl?" she piteously asked—almost as if all hope had left herself.

"I don't know, Rose. Mr. Moore has not told me there is none."

"Perhaps it is that he will not say," she rejoined, resting her elbow on the green steps amid the plants, and her cheek on her hand. "I seem to see it, Karl; to see what is coming. Indeed, you might tell me the truth. I shall not feel it quite so much as I should had our circumstances been happier."

"I have told you as far as I know, Rose."

"There's my little baby gone: there's my husband going: all my treasures will be in the better world. I shall have nothing to do but live on for, and look forward to, the time when I may go to them. Six months ago, Karl, had I known Adam must die, I think the grief would have killed me. But the apprehension we have undergone the last few weeks—Adam's dread, and my awful fear for him—has gone a great way to reconcile me. I see—and I think he sees—that Death would not be the worst calamity. Better for him to be at rest than live on in that frightful peril night and day; each moment as it passes one of living agony, lest the next should bring the warders of Portland Island to retake him. No wonder it is wearing him out."

Karl went away echoing the last sentence; every word she had spoken leaving its echo of pain on his heart. No: it was no wonder that fatal illness had seized on Adam Andinnian before its time.

Well, on this day Karl was not to escape unnoticed so easily. Ann Hopley unlocked the gate, and then both of them stood listening according to custom. Not a sound broke the stillness, save the furious chirping somewhere of two quarrelsome sparrows: not a step could be heard awaking the echoes of the ground. Ann Hopley drew back the half of the gate, and Karl went forth.

Went forth to find himself, so to say, in the very arms of Mrs. Cleeve and Miss Blake. They were standing quite still (which fact accounted for their footsteps not being heard) gazing at these same two fighting birds in the hedge. What with Karl's naturally nervous organization, and what with the dread secret he had just left, every drop of blood went out of his face. But he did not lose his presence of mind.

"Looking on at a fight, Mrs. Cleeve!" he exclaimed in a light tone. "Birds have their hasty passions as well as men, you see. You wicked combatants! Let one another's heads alone. They'll not look any the better without feathers."

One of the noisy birds, as if in obedience, flew away to a distant tree; the other followed it. Karl stayed talking for a minute with the ladies; heard that they had come out for a little walk; and then he went on to his home. Mrs. Cleeve, as she continued her way, glanced inquisitively at the iron gate in passing.

"Do the same people live there still, Theresa? Let me see—a Mrs. Grey, was it not?"

"Oh yes, she lives there," slightingly returned Miss Blake. "She had a baby at the close of summer, but it died."

"A baby! Why, she was a young widow? Stay—no—what was it?—Oh, her husband was abroad. Yes, I remember now. Has he come home yet?"

"As much as he ever will come, I expect," observed Miss Blake. "The girl has just as much a husband as I have, Mrs. Cleeve."

"Why, what is it that you would imply?" cried Mrs. Cleeve, struck with the words and the tone.

"I once, quite accidentally, heard her sing, 'When lovely woman stoops to folly?' You know the song? It was, in one sense of the word, sung in character."

"Oh, dear!" cried Mrs. Cleeve! "But—but what does Sir Karl do there?"

"Sir Karl? Oh—he is her landlord."

The taunting kind of way in which Miss Blake

said it, turned Mrs. Cleeve's delicate cheeks to a rosy red. All kinds of unpleasant thoughts began crowding into her mind.

"Theresa, what do you mean?" she asked, her voice dropping with its own dread. "*Have* you any meaning?"

And the chances were—taking into consideration the love of gossip and of scandal so inherent in woman—that Theresa Blake would there and then have disclosed that she had a meaning, and what the meaning was: but in that self-same moment she happened to turn her eyes on Mr. Smith, the agent. He was leaning over his garden gate, playing with a bunch of late roses; and he gravely lifted his hat to Miss Blake as she looked at him.

There was something in the grave look, or in the sight of the man himself, or in the roses, telling of summer, that recalled most vividly to Miss Blake's mind the private conversation she had once held with Mr. Smith, and the caution he had given her. At any rate, Jane Shore and the lighted taper, and the white sheet, and all the other accessories, rose up before her mental vision as plainly as one can see into a mirror. The penance looked no more palatable to Miss Blake now than it had then. As well keep clear of such risks, great and small. She changed her tone.

"I really don't know anything about the young woman, Mrs. Cleeve. Pray do not take up a mistaken notion. She is Sir Karl's tenant; that is all."

"But if she is not—quite—quite circumspect in her conduct, it must be rather unpleasant to have her close to the Court," said Mrs. Cleeve.

"Oh, she lives a perfectly retired life."

"She is very pretty, I think?"

"Beautiful as an angel."

Nothing more passed. The two sparrows came flying to a proximate tree, and began fighting again. But an uneasy impression was left on Mrs. Cleeve's mind; for she could not forget the strangely-significant tone in which Miss Blake had spoken, and its too sudden change to cautious indifference.

Karl was pacing one of the broad paths that evening, in his grounds, when he found himself joined by Mrs. Cleeve. She had thrown a warm shawl over her grey silk evening dress. He gave her his arm. The shadows were deepening: the evening star was already twinkling in the clear sky.

"I want to tell you of a little plan I have formed, Sir Karl, and get your assent to it. It cannot have escaped your notice that Lucy is looking very ill."

"I have seen it for some time," he answered.

"And I should have spoken to you of it before," resumed Mrs. Cleeve, "only that Lucy herself seems so much annoyed when I allude to it, telling me that nothing is the matter with her, and begging me not to take up fancies. Are you aware of anything being wrong with her general health?"

"No, I am not: there is nothing wrong with it that I know of," returned Karl, unpleasantly conscious that he was not likely to know more about his wife's general health than any other of the Court's inmates.

"Well, what I wish to do is this: to take Lucy to town with me when I leave, and let some physician see her."

"But you are not leaving us yet?"

"Not just yet, perhaps; but when I do go. In fact, I really must take her. I could not be easy to go back home and leave Lucy looking as she is, without having some good medical opinion. Have you any objection to this?"

"Not the slightest. I do not fancy any physician could do much good to Lucy—she has certainly, as I believe, no specific disease—but I think change of air and scene may be of much benefit to her. I am glad that she should go."

"Well, now that I have your permission, Sir Karl, I shall know how to act. Lucy has been telling me that she does not need a physician, and will not see one; and that she does not care to go to London. But that we have never had consumption in our family, I should fear it for Lucy."

Karl was silent. That Lucy had taken the unfortunate secret to heart in a strange manner, and that it was telling upon her most unaccountably, he knew.

"It is rather ungrateful of her to say she does not care to go to London, considering that she has never stayed with her aunt since that time of illness at Winchester," resumed Mrs. Cleeve. "Though, indeed, Lucy seems to have no energy left, and her cheerfulness appears to me more sham than reality. Lady Southal is anxious for her to go up with me."

"Are you intending to stay again with Lady Southal yourself?"

"I shall now; as long as Lucy does. And, armed with your authority, I shall insist on Lucy's going up with me. I wish you would come too, Sir Karl: my sister would be so glad to see you."

With his unfortunate brother dying at the Maze, it was not possible for Karl to quit Foxwood. But he was exceedingly glad that Lucy should be absent for a time. It would leave him more at liberty. At least, in spirit. With Lucy's intense contempt and hatred for the Maze and its troubles, Karl never went there but he was conscious of feeling something like a school-boy, who is in mischief away from home.

"I cannot leave home just now," said Karl. "But you must tell Lady Southal that I shall be most happy to take a future opportunity of paying her a visit."

"Are you busy, that you cannot leave?"

"My Uncle Joseph's papers are not arranged yet; I am anxious to get on with them," he said, by way of excuse. And in truth that, so far, was so. In his mind's terrible distress the sorting of the papers had been much neglected.

"At least, you will come to town to fetch Lucy home."

"Of course I will."

The affair decided, they strolled the whole length of the walk in silence. Karl's thoughts were no doubt busy: Mrs. Cleeve was wishing to say something else, and did not quite know how to begin.

"What a nice evening it is!" cried Karl. "How fair the weather continues to be!"

"Yes. But the hedges are showing signs of winter. I noticed it particularly when I was out with Theresa this morning. That was the Maze, I think, that we saw you coming out of."

Karl assented. There was no help for it.

"Does the young lady live there alone still?"

"She has her servants with her."

"But not her husband."

"Mr. Grey, it is understood, spends a good deal of his time in travelling."

"Sir Karl, I think I must ask you plainly. I have been wanting to ask you," she said, taking courage. "Is there any reason for supposing that this lady is not—is not quite what she ought to be?"

"Why, what do you mean?" returned Karl, standing still in his surprise. "Are you speaking of Mrs. Grey?"

"It is almost impossible to avoid attaching some doubt to a young and lovely woman, when she lives so unaccountably secluded a life," returned Mrs. Cleeve, calling up the most plausible excuse she could for her suspicions.

"The very fact of her keeping herself so secluded ought to absolve Mrs. Grey from it," said Karl warmly. "She is a good and honourable lady."

"You feel sure of that?"

"I am sure of it. I know it. Believe me, dear Mrs. Cleeve, that Lucy herself is not more pure and innocent than that pure lady is," he added, taking Mrs. Cleeve's hands in his earnestness, in his anxiety to convince her. "She has had great trouble to try her; she may be said to live in trouble: but heaven knows how good she is, and how persistently she strives to be resigned, and endure."

Mrs. Cleeve kept the sensitive hands in hers; she saw how worthy of trust he was in his earnestness; and every doubt went out of her.

"I am very glad to hear it. I hope she and you will pardon my foolish thoughts. You go to see her sometimes, I believe?"

"When I think I can be of any use, I go. Her husband was once my dear friend: I go there for his sake."

"Why does he not live here with her?"

"He cannot always do just as he would. Just now he is in bad health."

"And she lost her baby, I hear."

"Yes. It was a great grief to both of them."

The sounding of the dinner-gong stopped the questioning. We may be assured Karl lost no time in conducting Mrs. Cleeve to the house.

CHAPTER XX.

At the Red Dawn.

FOXWOOD was going on quietly with the approach of winter. Mrs. Cleeve had gone to London with her daughter; leaving Miss Blake to keep house at the Court. Some ladies, fearing the world's chatter, might have objected to remain with so young and attractive a man as Sir Karl Andinnian; Miss Blake was a vast deal too strong-minded for any thought of the kind. She was busy as ever with St. Jerome's and its offices; but she nevertheless kept a tolerably keen look-out on the Maze and on Sir Karl's movements as connected with it. He went there more than he used to do: by day now as well as by night: and she wondered how long the simple neighbourhood would keep its eyes closed to facts and figures, that, to her, were so offensively plain.

There had been a sharpish frost in the night, but the glorious morning sun had chased its signs away. At midday it was shining hotly; and Karl was almost glad of the thin screen of leaves left in the labyrinth as he made his way through it. Some days had passed now since Adam had had any sharp amount of illness: he was wasting away rapidly, and that was the worst outward sign. But his will in these intervals of ease was indomitable, and it imparted to him a fictitious strength.

As Karl came in view of the lawn, he saw Rose standing by one of the distant beds, talking to Hopley. The old man was digging; and had bent himself nearly double over his work. Karl crossed over, a reprimand on his lips.

"Adam, you should not. You promised me you would not again take a spade or other gardening implement in your hand. Your strength is not equal to it, and it must do you harm."

"Just hark at him, Rose. It would not be Karlo if he did not find fault with me. What shall you do for somebody to croak at, brother mine, when I am gone?"

Was it Hopley who spoke?—or was it Sir Adam? The falling-in mouth and the speech, the crooked back, the tottering and swelling knees, the smock-frock and the red comforter and the broad straw hat, all were Hopley's. But the manner of speech and the eyes too, now you came to see them as he looked up at Karl, were Sir Adam's.

Yes. They were one and the same. Poor old Hopley the gardener was but Sir Adam in disguise. With the padded knees and the false hump he had managed to deceive the world, including Mr. Detective Tatton. He might not perhaps have so surely deceived Mr. Tatton had the latter been looking after Sir Adam Andinnian and been acquainted with his person. But the decrepid gardener bore no resemblance to Philip Salter: and, that fact ascertained, it was all that concerned Mr. Tatton.

It may be remembered that when Mrs. Andinnian was staying at Weymouth, she and her servant, Ann Hopley, were in secret communication with one of the warders of Portland Prison: in point of fact, they were negotiating with him the possibilities of Sir Adam's escape. This man was James Hopley; a warder—as Karl had taken him to be, and also Ann's husband. In the scuffle that took place the night of the escape, the man really killed was the other prisoner, Cole: and it was he who was taken to Foxwood and lay buried in its churchyard. Hopley was drowned.

At that period, and for some little time before it, Phil'p Smith was at Portland Prison. Not as a prisoner: the man had never in his life done aught to merit incarceration: but seeking employment there, through the interest of one of the chief warders who was a friend of his—a man named O'Brian. From the date of the frauds of Philip Salter, Philip Smith had been—as he considered it—a ruined man: at any rate he was unable to obtain employment. A ruined man must not be fastidious, and Smith was willing and was anxious to become a warder if they would make him one. It was while he was waiting and hoping for the post, and employed sometimes as an assistant, and thoroughly trusted, that the attempted escape of the prisoners occurred. Smith was one of those who put off in the boat after the fugitives: the other two being Hopley and O'Brian. In the scuffle on the Weymouth shore, Sir Adam was wounded and left for dead. O'Brian saw him lying there apparently dead, and supposed him to be so. O'Brian, however, afterwards received a blow that stunned him—for the night was dark, and friends and foes fought indiscriminately—and Smith contrived to get Adam away into a place of concealment. It is very probable that

Smith foresaw in that moment how valuable a prize
to him the living and escaped Sir Adam might become. O'Brian really believed him to be dead, and
so reported him to the authorities. A dead man is
worthless: and Sir Adam was allowed to be retained
by his friends for interment: the beaten and dis-
figured Cole, shot in the face, being looked upon as
Sir Adam.

After that, the path was easy. Sir Adam, very
badly injured, lay for many weeks hidden away. Smith
continued at Portland Prison keeping his own counsel,
and unsuspected, visiting Sir Adam cautiously at intervals. As soon as it was practicable for him to be
moved, the step was ventured on. He was got away
in safety to London, and lay in retirement there, in a
house that had been taken by Smith: his wife (formerly
Rose Turner) coming up to join him; and Ann Hopley,
faithful to Sir Adam's fortunes through all, waiting on
them. She had no one else left to be faithful to now,
poor woman. Smith managed everything. He had
withdrawn himself from Portland Island, under the
plea that he could no longer, in consequence of his
disabled arm, aspire to a wardership—for his arm had
been damaged that fatal night, and it was thought he
would never have the full use of it again. The plea
was unsuspiciously recognised by the prison authorities;
Smith retained his friendship with O'Brian, and occasionally corresponded with him, getting from him
scraps of useful information now and then. From
that time his services were devoted to Sir Adam. It
was he who communicated between Sir Adam and his
mother; for, letters they did not dare to transmit. It
was he who first disclosed to Mrs. Andinnian the fact

that Miss Rose Turner was her son's wife; it was he who made the arrangements for Sir Adam's taking up his abode at the Maze, and provided the disguise to arrive at Foxwood in, as the decrepid old husband of the servant, Ann Hopley. To do Mr. Smith justice, he had fought against the scheme of coming to the Maze; but Mrs. Andinnian and Adam were both bent upon it; and he yielded. Adam and his wife had stayed in London under the name of Mrs. Grey, and she retained it.

Amidst the injuries Sir Adam received was one to the mouth and jaw. It destroyed those beautiful front teeth of his. After his recovery he sought the services of a clever but not much known dentist named Rennet, went to the pain of having the rest of his teeth extracted, and an entire set of false ones made. Two sets, in fact. The journey Rose took to London, when Miss Blake espied her with Karl, was for the purpose of getting one of these sets of teeth repaired, Sir Adam having broken the spring the night before. The teeth had to be conveyed personally to Mr. Rennet and brought away; for they were too cautious to entrust him with their address.

And now it will be seen how Sir Adam had concealed himself at the Maze. In the daytime he was the toothless, hump-backed, infirm old Hopley, working at his garden with enlarged knees and tottering steps: as soon as dusk came on, his false padding was thrown of with his smock frock and coarse clothes, and he was the well-bred gentleman, Sir Adam Andinnian, in his evening attire and with his white and even teeth. His assumed role was maintained always during the day; his meals were taken in the kitchen to be safe in case of any possible surprise, Ann attending upon him with all respect. The delay in admitting Nurse Chaffen, kept waiting once on the wrong side of the kitchen door, was caused by "Hopley's" taking out his set of teeth and putting on his broadbrimmed hat: for it was convenient to assume the teeth during the short period devoted to dinner. The deafness was of course assumed as an additional precaution. Thus he had lived, in a state of semi-security, tending his flowers and occupied with the care of his garden generally, an employment that he loved so well. The day that General Lloyd's party went in, Karl was transfixed with apprehension and amazement to see Hopley showing himself. Adam enjoyed it: it was so like him to brave things; and he feared no danger from a pleasure party like that.

Well, I think that is all that is needed in the way of explanation; and we can go on. Karl was looking at the digging with regretful eyes.

"You ought to be glad to see me at work again, Karl, instead of groaning over it," cried Sir Adam.

"And so I should be, Adam, only that I fear you will feel its effects unpleasantly by and by."

"I asked him not to do it, but he only laughed at me," said Rose.

"Somebody must do it. I can't see the garden quite neglected. Besides, if I am well enough to work there's no reason why I should not. I am not sure, Karl, but I shall cheat you now."

"Cheat me?"

"By getting well. What should you say to that?"

"Thank heaven for it: and do my best to get you away to a place of safety."

"By George, old fellow, I don't know that I shan't. I am feeling as blithe as a bee. Rose, take yourself a trifle further off, out of the mould."

He was throwing about the spadefuls almost as well as he had ever thrown them in his strength. Rose was cheated into something like hope, and her face for the moment lost its sadness.

"I wish to goodness I had a draught of beer," cried Adam. "Where's Ann, I wonder."

Karl went to fetch it. Ann Hopley shook her head at the idea of hope, when Karl spoke of it as she gave him the beer.

"You never saw any person, who was to live on, have the look in his face that he has, sir."

"He looks fairly well to-day."

"And so he will at times to the last, as it strikes me. I have had a good deal of experience in illness, sir. As to his talking about getting well—why, sir, you know what he is: saying this and that without meaning it. There's no doubt he feels pretty sure himself how it will be."

Karl sighed as he went back with the beer. Yes, there was no real hope.

That same night—or rather on the following morning, for the dawn was more than glimmering—Karl in his bed began to dream that he was out in a shower of hail. It seemed to be falling with great violence: so much so that a sharper crash awoke him. Lying awake for a moment and questioning where he was, he found the noise to be reality. The hail was beating on the chamber windows.

Was it hail? Scarcely. It was crashing but on one window, and only came at intervals. It sounded more like gravel. Karl rose and opened the window. Smith the agent stood underneath. A prevision of evil shook Karl as he leaned out.

"He is very ill indeed, sir," said Smith in the lowest whisper possible to be heard, and extending his finger to indicate the Maze. "Mr. Moore's there and thinks it will be for death. I thought you would like to know it."

"How did you hear it?" asked Karl.

"Ann Hopley ran over and knocked me up, that I might go for the doctor."

"Thank you," replied Karl. "I'll be there directly."

Now it so happened that for some purposes of cleaning—for the Court was not exempt from those periodical visitations any more than the humble dwelling of Mrs. Chaffen—Miss Blake's chamber had been temporarily changed to the one next to that recently occupied by Lady Andinnian. Miss Blake was in the habit of sleeping with her window open; and, not being asleep at the time, she had heard Mr. Smith's footsteps and the crashes at Sir Karl's window. Of course she was curious as to what could cause the noise, and at first thought of housebreakers. Had Mr. Smith chanced to turn his head in the right direction during the colloquy with Sir Karl, he might have seen an elaborately night-capped head peeping forth cautiously.

"Why, it is Mr. Smith!" thought Miss Blake, as he walked away. "What an extraordinary thing! He must have been calling up Sir Karl."

Listening inside as well as out, Miss Blake heard the bell that was in Hewitt's chamber ring gently; and, after a minute or two, the latter proceeding to his master's room. Then they both went down together, and Hewitt let Sir Karl out at the hall door, and came upstairs again. Miss Blake, after a good deal of self-puzzling, arrived at the conclusion that the affair must be in some way connected with poachers —who had been busy on the land latterly—and returned to her bed.

With death on his face, and a look of resignation than which nothing could be more peaceful, lay Sir Adam for the last time. His weary life, with all its bitter turmoil, was nearly at an end; night *here* was closing, morning *there* was opening. Karl's grey eyes were wet as he bent over him.

"Don't grieve too much," said Adam with a smile, as he put his cold hand into Karl's clasp. "You know how much better off I shall be. Rose knows it."

"You were so full of hope yesterday, Adam."

"Was I? It cheated the wife into a few hours of pleasantness, and did its mission. I did not think I took *you* in. Why, Karlo, I have just been waiting from day to day for what has now come: moreover, I have seen how much best it all is *as* it is than anything else would be. I would not accept life if you'd give it to me, unless the whole time since that Midsummer Eve could be blotted out."

Karl swallowed a sob.

"You don't know what it has been, Karl. No one can know what it is to live under a hanging sword, as I have, unless they experience it. And few in this world can do that. It was all a mistake together. The shooting of Scott when I ought to have horse-whipped him; the escape from Portland; the taking up my abode here; everything: and these mistakes, Karl, have to be worked out. I have paid for mine with life."

Karl did not answer. He was only nervously pressing the wasted hand in his.

"It is all, I say, for the best. I see it now. It was best that the little lad should go; it is best that I should; it is best that you should be the true owner of Foxwood. It would have been too much of a complication otherwise. The boy could never have put forth a claim to it while I lived; and, after that, people might but have pointed their scornful finger at him as the son of a convict. I thank God for taking him."

"Should you talk so much, Adam?"

"I don't know. A man in my condition, about to leave the world behind, prefers to talk while he can. You will take care of my wife, Karl. There was no settlement, you know, and——"

"I will take care of her to the best of my power, Adam," came the earnest interruption. "She shall have a proper and suitable jointure as the widowed Lady Andinnian."

"No, Karl; not that. She and I have talked over the future at odd moments, and we do not wish it. Rose does not mean to acknowledge her marriage with me, or to live in any kind of state in accordance with it. She will be Mrs. Grey to the end. Unless, indeed, any occasion were to arise, such as a tarnishing breath of scandal brought against this past period of her life. Then, of course, the truth must be declared, and you, Karl would have to come forward and testify to it. I leave that in your hands."

"With every surety," assented Karl.

"A few hundreds a year, say four or five, are all that she will want from you, or take. Her late uncle's money must come to her sometime, and that of itself would be almost enough. She purposes to live a retired life with her aunt; and I think it will be the happiest for her. In my desk, Karl, you will find a paper in my handwriting, setting forth all these wishes of hers and mine; it will serve as a direction for you. —No," he went on, after a pause, "for her own peace, the world must never know her as Lady Andinnian. She dreads it too much. See you not the reason? She would have to stand before the public convicted of perjury. That past trial is rarely out of her mind, Karl—when she appeared falsely as Miss Rose Turner. The foolish things people do in their blindness! It was my fault. *Her* fault lay only in obeying me: but your charitable people would not accept that as an excuse. Be it as it may, Karl, Rose's life henceforth will be one of modest position and strict retirement. Ann Hopley goes with her."

Looking at the matter from all points of view, it might be, as Sir Adam said, for the best.

"And you will be Sir Karl in reality as well as in seeming, brother mine; and Foxwood will be your true home and your children's after you. That is only justice. When you arranged to marry Lucy Cleeve, you deemed yourself to be the inheritor, and she deemed it. My death will set all right. And now about Smith, Karl. The man did me a great service, for I should have been retaken but for him; and he has been faithful to me since. I should like you to allow him something in the shape of an annuity—a hundred and fifty pounds a year, or so. Not the cottage: he will not stay in this neighbourhood when I am gone. It was through me that his arm got injured: which, of course, partly incapacitates him for work; and I think I am bound to provide for him."

"It shall be done," said Karl. "Ungrudgingly."

"I have mentioned it in the paper, and the sum. He—he—he—"

Sir Adam's hesitation was caused by faintness. He broke down, and for the time said no more. Nor did he recur to the subject again.

The day went on, Adam partially sleeping through it. At other times he lay in a kind of stupor. Mr. Moore attended at intervals; but nothing further could be done. At dusk Hewitt came over for a last sight of his old master; for a last farewell: and he sobbed bitterly as he said it.

Karl did not go home—at which Miss Blake was in much private wonder. Discarding the poacher theory, she shrewdly suspected now that he must be at the Maze, taking the opportunity of his wife's absence to play the gay bachelor away from home. She asked Hewitt, she questioned Giles; Giles knew nothing, Hewitt fancied Sir Karl might be "detained at Basham" on some business.

And so, the night set in. When quite awake Adam had the full possession of his senses, and exchanged a few words, sometimes with his wife, sometimes with Karl. About three o'clock he fell into a calm sleep. Karl watched on; Rose, weak and sick and weary, dropped into a doze in a distant chair. Ann Hopley was in the kitchen below.

Save for the faint sighing of the wind as it swept round the house, stirring the branches of the trees, there was no sound to be heard. Stillness reigned unbroken in the dying chamber. How many of us have kept these watches! But who has kept them as this was being kept by Karl Andinnian!

With that bitter aching of the heart known but to few, and which when felt in its greatest intensity is the saddest pain the troubles of the world can give, Karl sat gazing on his brother. In his love for him, every pang endured by Adam in the past was a sting for him, every hazard run had reflected on him its dread apprehension. He sat thinking of what might have been; looking on what was: and an awful regret, than which nothing like unto it could be ever again experienced, tore at his heart-strings for the wasted life, cut short ere it had reached its prime. More than willingly in that moment would Karl have given his own remaining days to undo what his brother had done, and to restore to him freedom and honour. It might not be. Adam's course was run: and he was passing away in obscurity from the world in which he had virtually no longer a place. Never for a moment did the immunity from perplexity it would bring to himself or the release from the false position he had been compelled to assume, occur to Karl; or, if it did, it was not dwelt upon: all of self and self-interest was lost in the regret and grief for his brother. He saw Adam living at Foxwood Court with his wife; its master; held in repute by men; he saw himself settled near with Lucy; his fortunes advanced by his brother's aid to a position not unacceptable to Colonel Cleeve; he saw his mother alive still and happy: a united family, enjoying comfort the one with the other. This might have been. His mother dead of a broken heart; Adam, dying before his eyes, an escaped fugitive; his own life blighted with pain and sorrow unutterable for Adam's sake, his wife estranged from him —this was what was. Be you very sure that no earthly pang could be keener than that despairing heart-ache felt by Karl Andinnian.

How many a night at that still hour had Adam lain in his terror, listening to this moaning wind with supernaturally quick ear, lest it should be only covering other sounds—the approach of his deadly enemies! How many times in a night had he quitted his bed, his heart beating, and stolen a cautious peep beside the blind to see whether they might not be there, in battle array, waiting until the dawn should come and they might get in to take him! Ah, it was all at an end now; the fever, and the fear, and the wasting restlessness. Why! if the men were drawn up round his bed, they would not care to touch him. But the terror from force of habit stayed with him to the last.

He started up. How long he had slept, and how the night was going, Karl in his abstraction hardly knew. Adam's eyes looked somewhat wild in the shade of the night-light, and he put up his feeble hand.

"What is it?" asked Karl gently.

"I thought they were here, Karl; I saw them in the room,"—he whispered—and his eyes went round it. "They had muskets I think. Was it a dream?"

"Nothing but a dream, Adam. I am with you. Rose is asleep in the arm-chair."

"Ay. I have not dreamt of them for a week past. Stay by me, Karlo."

Karl would have risen to administer some cordial: but Adam was holding his hand in a tight grasp; had shut his eyes, and seemed to be dropping asleep again.

He slept about half-an-hour, and Karl's imprisoned arm went from a state of pins and needles into the cramp. When Adam awoke, there was a smile on his face and a peaceful rest in his eyes. He was quite collected.

"Karl, I dreamt of them again: but they had turned to angels. They were here, all about my bed. Oh Karl, I wish you could see them as I saw them! you'd never be afraid of anything more in this world. What's that?"

Karl turned round: for Adam's eyes were fixed on something or other behind him. He could see nothing save a streak of light, herald of the dawn, that came in at the side of the blind.

"Do you mean the light, Adam? It's the dawn breaking."

"Ay. *My* dawn. Draw up the blind. Karl."

Softly, not to awake Rose, Karl drew it up. Rose-coloured clouds, heralds of a beauteous sunrise, flooded the East. Adam lay and gazed at it, the smile on his face changing to a rapt look that seemed to speak of heaven, more than of earth.

"It will be better there than here, Karl. For me."

"Better for all of us."

"I am very happy, Karl. The world is fading from me: heaven opening. Forgive me all that I have cost you."

Karl's heart and eyes were alike full.

"Just as the men who had troubled me were changed into angels, so my fear has changed to rest. The angels are about the bed still, Karl; I know they are; waiting for me. The same lovely light shone on them that is shining yonder; and they told me without words that they were come to bear me up to God. I read it in their tender faces—so full of pitying love for me. It won't be so very long, Karl: you'll come later."

Karl's tears were falling on the up-turned face.

"I should like to have seen your wife, Karl; just once. Tell her so, with my love. Ask her to forgive me the worry I know I have caused her."

"I will, I will."

"Oh, Karl, it has been a dreadful life for me; you know it has. I began to think that God had forgotten me—how foolish I was! He was full of mercy all the while, and kept me here in safety, and has now changed it all into peace. Listen, Karl! there's a sound of sweet music."

Karl could hear nothing but the wind.

"It is the angels singing," whispered Adam, a smile of ineffable beauty on his face. "They sing on the journey, you know. Good-bye, Karl, good-bye!"

Karl bent his face, his tears streaming, his heart aching. These partings are too bitter to be told of. This was most essentially so.

"Where's Rose, Karl?"

She was already by Karl's side. He yielded his place to her, and went down to Ann; and there sobbed over the kitchen fire as a woman might have done.

But in the midst of it all, he could say as his brother had done, "Thank God." If ever a poor sinful weary man had need to rejoice that he was removed to that better world, it was Adam Andinnian.

Rose's bell called Karl up again. The last moment was at hand. Ann Hopley followed: and they all stood round the bed and saw him die. The red clouds had dispersed; the sun was just showing itself above the verge of the horizon.

CHAPTER XXI.

Laid to his Rest.

FOXWOOD heard the news. Mrs. Grey's shakey old gardener was dead, James Hopley. Mr. Moore, when applied to for particulars, went into a learned dissertation on chronic rheumatism, and said that he was not able to save him.

Ann Hopley astonished the undertaker. She gave orders for three coffins: and they must be of the best, she said, if it cost her a hundred pounds. Her poor husband and she had saved money, and she should like to spend it on him.

There was again a battle with the clerk. It had been bad enough when Ann Hopley chose the ground for Mrs. Grey's little child, within the precincts of that belonging to the Andinnian family; but to insist upon it that her own husband, a servant, should also lie there, was a piece of presumption the equal of which the clerk had never before heard of. However, Sir Karl, not waiting to be appealed to this time, called on the clerk, and said the woman might bury her husband there if she pleased; he did not think it right in people to assume exclusiveness after death, whatever they might do in life. The clerk lifted his hands when Sir Karl's back was turned: radical notions such as these would tend to demoralize the best conservative community.

It was while his brother was lying dead, that Sir Karl—truly Sir Karl now—heard from his wife. She was ready to come to Foxwood, as Mrs. Cleeve was about to return to Winchester, and she appointed the following day, Tuesday, for Sir Karl to fetch her. It happened to be the day fixed for the funeral, and Karl wrote back to say that he could not leave home that day, but would fetch her on the Wednesday instead. To this he received no reply; and he of course intended to abide by it.

Tuesday came. About twelve o'clock in the day the funeral turned out of the Maze gates; sundry curious ones amid the juveniles being assembled to witness the exit. A funeral was not an every-day event at Foxwood: and, besides, the Maze had been exciting interest of late. It was a simple funeral. The plumed hearse and one mourning coach; the undertaker and carriers walking. In the coach went Ann Hopley, smothered in a hood, with Hewitt to bear her company. Foxwood said it was very neighbourly and civil of the butler: but Miss Blake felt sure he had received private orders from Sir Karl, and she wondered what Sir Karl was coming to.

Now Lucy, Lady Andinnian, looking at things as she had been looking, poor wife, for some time past, was very resentful that Sir Karl would not fetch her on the day she named. She reasoned with herself that his refusal must arise from one of two causes: either he was neglectfully indifferent; or else he had some engagement with Mrs. Grey: for, of deterring occupation, she believed he possessed none. Proudly angry, she determined to take her own way, and return home without him.

Accordingly, on the Tuesday she started with her maid from London. But, like many a one who does things in off-hand inexperience, she made a mistake, and took the wrong train. That is, she took one that did not stop at Foxwood. Lucy discovered this after she was in the carriage, and found they must get out at Basham. Leaving Aglaé and the luggage to wait for the next train, which would not be up for two hours, Lucy took one of the waiting flies, and drove on.

Lucy was full of thoughts and anticipations. She wondered where her husband was, what she should find him doing, and what excuse he would make. It lasted her all the way: and they were close on Foxwood village before anything occurred to arouse her. She woke up to find the driver, who was a Foxwood man, had come very nearly to a standstill, and was staring at a funeral procession just then entering the churchyard.

The first object that caught Lucy's eye was Hewitt. Hewitt attired as a mourner, and following the coffin. For a moment Lucy's heart beat quicker, and her gaze was strained: who could it be that was inside? Gradually her eyes took in the whole of the scene: the spectators collected in the distance, watching; the person enveloped in a silk hood and cloak at Hewitt's side: Mr. Sumnor in his surplice.

All in a moment, as it seemed, just as the clergyman began to read, springing she could not tell from whence, there advanced Sir Karl Andinnian. He was in black attire, but wore neither crape band nor scarf; and it might have been thought he was only an ordinary spectator. Hewitt, however, drew a step back to give his master the place of precedence, as though out of proper respect, as did Ann Hopley: and Sir Karl took off his hat and stood there, close to the coffin, his head bent low.

"How very strange it is!" thought Lucy. "Who can be in the coffin?—and who is the woman in the black silk cloak and hood? There is Mr. Smith, the agent, too!—he is standing near with *his* hat off now."

"Lucy! Can it be you? We did not expect you until to-morrow."

The voice was Miss Blake's. St. Jerome's devotees were no more free from curiosity than their inferiors; and a few of them had chanced to be taking a walk past the churchyard just at the critical moment; of whom Miss Blake was one.

"I thought I would come to-day, and not give Sir Karl the trouble of fetching me," replied Lucy. "Aglaé is coming on from Basham by the next train with the luggage. How are you, Theresa? Will you come inside?"

Miss Blake's answer was to open the fly door, seat herself by Lady Andinnian, and turn her gaze on the churchyard. The scene bore a charm for her as well as for Lucy.

"Why, that's Sir Karl there!" she exclaimed in surprise, the spectators' heads having intercepted her view while on the ground.

"Yes," assented Lucy. "And there's Hewitt—and Sir Karl's agent—and a mourner with her face hidden. Who is it that is being buried, Theresa?"

"Why, it's only the old gardener at the Maze. As to Hewitt, I suppose he had to go to keep the woman in countenance. The old man was her husband, you know."

"But what should bring Sir Karl there?"

"And standing first, as though he were chief mourner!" commented Miss Blake, devouring the scene with her condemning eyes, and giving the reins to her thoughts. "*I* don't know why he is there, Lucy. There are several things that I have not attempted to understand for some time past."

"Is not that the part of the churchyard where the Andinnians lie?—where their vault is?"

"It is. But Hopley is being buried there, you see: and that infant, that you know of, was buried there. The clerk is in a fine way over it, people say: but Sir Karl ruled that it should be so."

Thoughts connected with Mrs. Grey, and the inexplicable manner in which Sir Karl seemed to yield to her humours, even to the honouring of her servants, flashed into Lucy's brain. It did not tend to appease her previous anger against him.

"Why could not Sir Karl come for me to-day, Theresa?"

"It is of no use to ask me, Lucy. Sir Karl does not explain his motives to me. This funeral perhaps kept him," added Miss Blake, sarcastically, unconscious how very near she was to the truth. "After you left he seemed almost to live at the Maze. Last week he was there, as I believe, for a whole day and a whole night. I *must* speak, Lucy. Out of regard to decency that girl ought to quit the Maze, or you quit Foxwood."

"Drive on," cried Lucy to the coachman, in a tone as though the world and all things in it were grating on her. And the man did not dare to disobey the sharp command.

But Miss Blake preferred to get out; and did so. She had said what she did say from good motives: and she took credit for not making worse of the account—as she might have done. Not a word would she say about his being called up in the night—and she knew now that it was to the Maze he was summoned. With her whole heart she pitied Lucy.

"May I be forgiven if my duty ought to lie in silence!" she muttered as she joined the Miss St. Henrys and others in the crowd. "Lucy seems to have no friend about her in the world but me."

The interment was over. The procession—what was left of it—went its way back again, Hewitt and Ann Hopley side by side in the coach. Sir Karl strolled away over the fields, and presently found himself joined by Mr. Smith.

"So your mission at Foxwood is over," he sadly cried to the latter. "I have no more need to make believe I want an agent now."

"Ay, it's over, Sir Karl. Better for him almost that he had fallen in the fray off Weymouth; that I had never saved him; than have lived to what his life has since been."

"Better for him had he never come to the Maze," rejoined Sir Karl.

"It was none of my doing. As you know, sir."

"No: but you opposed his leaving it."

"As he was here, I did. I had but his interest at heart, Sir Karl: although I know you have thought the contrary. The chances were that he could not have got away in safety. In his own person he dared not have risked it; and a decrepid figure like Old Hopley's must have attracted attention. But for that detective's pitching upon Foxwood to make a hunting place of, I believe Sir Adam would have been most secure here."

"Well, it is over, with all its risks and chances," sighed Karl. "He did not forget you when he was dying. His wish was that you should enjoy a moderate annuity during your life: which I have undertaken to pay."

The agent's thanks, and they appeared very heart-felt and genuine, were cut short by the approach of Mr. Moore. He joined them as they walked along; and the conversation fell on the illness of the deceased.

"There was no real hope from the beginning, once the disease had set fairly in," cried the surgeon. "There never is. In Sir Adam's case, the terrible anxiety he endured day and night brought it on, and caused it to develop with unusual rapidity: there was not a shadow of chance for him."

"You did not tell me that," said Karl.

"I was not quite sure of it myself at first: though I suspected it. I did not tell you, you say, Sir Karl: well, no, not in so many words: but your own eyes might have seen it as its progress went on. Sir Adam knew it himself, I fancy, as surely as I."

"Do you remember saying you wished he could have further advice?" asked Karl. "Did not that prove that you had hope?"

"I wished it chiefly for the satisfaction of those

connected with him. All the advice in the world could not—as I suspected then, and soon saw—have availed to save his life. We sometimes say of people, death has been a happy release for them. In his case, Sir Karl, it has been most unquestionably so: he is at rest."

CHAPTER XXII.

Repentance.

Down on her knees, in self-abasement, the tears
of contrition raining from her eyes, her face scarlet
in its agony of shame, cowered Lucy Andinnian at
her husband's feet. She would not let him raise her.
It seemed to her that a whole lifetime of repentance
could never wash out her sin.

The elucidation of the misunderstanding that had
kept them apart for months was taking place.

On the day after the funeral, Karl sought his wife
in the dressing-room to tell her of what had occurred.
She had scarcely spoken a word to him since her
return, or allowed him to speak one to her. Very
briefly, in half a dozen words, he informed her his
brother was dead, and delivered the message Adam
had left for her. For a few minutes Lucy's bewilder-
ment was utter; and, when she did at length grasp
somewhat of the truth, her confusion and distress
were pitiable.

"Oh, Karl, Karl, do you think you will ever be
able to forgive me? What can I do?—what can I do
to atone for it?"

"You must get up, Lucy, before I say whether I
forgive you or not."

"I cannot get up. It seems to me that I ought
never to get up again. Your *brother* at the Maze!—
your brother's wife! Oh, what must you have thought

of my conduct? Oh, Karl, why do you not strike me as I lie?"

Sir Karl put forth his arms and his strength, and raised her to the sofa. She bent her face down on its pillow, to weep out her tears of shame.

"Come, Lucy," he said, when he had waited a few minutes, sitting beside her. "We shall not arrive at the end in this way. Is it *possible* that you did not know my brother was alive?"

"How could I know it, Karl?" she asked, amid her streaming tears. "How was I likely to know it?"

"You told me you knew it. You said to me that you had discovered the secret at the Maze. I thought you were resenting the fact of his being alive. Or, rather, of my having married you, knowing that he was."

"Why should I resent it? How could you think so? Was *that* the secret you spoke of in Paris the night before our wedding?—that Adam was alive."

"That, and no other. But I did not know then that he was married—or suspect that he ever would marry. I learnt that fact only during my mother's last illness."

"Oh, Karl, this is dreadful," she sobbed. "What must you have thought of me all this time? I almost wish I could die!"

"You still care for me, then; a little?"

With a burst of anguish she turned and hid her face upon his breast. "I have only loved you the better all the while," she whispered.

"Lucy, my dear, I say we shall not get to the end in this way. Look up. If you were in ignorance of my brother's existence, and of all the complications for you and for me that it involved, what then was it that you were resenting?"

"Don't ask me, Karl," she said, her face growing scarlet again. "I could not tell you for the very shame."

He drew a little away, making a movement to put her from him. Never had his countenance been so stern to her as it was now; never could he be so little trifled with.

"If there is to be an explanation between us, Lucy, it must be full and complete. I insist upon its being so. If you refuse to give it now—why, I shall never ask you for it again. Do you not think you owe me one?"

Again she bent her face upon him. "I owe you everything, Karl; I owe you more reparation than I can ever pay. Never, as long as our lives shall last, will I have a secret from you again, heaven helping me. If I hesitate to tell you this, it is because I am ashamed for you to know how foolish I could be, and the wicked thoughts I could have."

"Not more foolish or wicked, I dare say, than I was for making you my wife. Speak out, Lucy. It must be so, you see, if there is to be a renewal of peace between us."

Keeping her head where it was, her face hidden from him, Lucy whispered her confession. Karl started from her in very astonishment.

"Lucy! You could think that! Of me!"

She put up her hands beseechingly. "Oh, forgive me, Karl; for the sake of the pain, forgive me! It has been killing me all the while. See how worn and thin I am."

He put his arm out and drew her to his side. "Go on, my dear. How did you pick up the notion?"

"It was Theresa." And now that the ice was broken, anxious to tell all and clear herself, Lucy described the past in full: the cruel anguish she had battled with, and her poor, ever-to-be renewed efforts to endure patiently, for his sake and for God's. Karl's arm involuntarily tightened around her.

"Why did you not speak to me of this at once, Lucy?" he asked, after a pause. "It would have cleared it up, you see."

"I did speak to you, Karl; and you seemed to understand me perfectly, and to accept it all as truth. You must remember your agitation, and how you begged me not to let it come to an exposure."

"But I thought you alluded to the trouble about my poor brother; that it was the fact of his being alive you had discovered and were resenting. *That* was the exposure I dreaded. And no wonder: for, if it had come, it would have sent him back to Portland Island."

Lucy wrung her hands. "What a miserable misapprehension it has been!—and how base and selfish and cruel I must have appeared to you! I wonder, Karl, you did not put me away from you for ever!"

"Will you go now?"

She knew it was asked in jest: she probably knew that neither would have parted from the other for the wealth of the world. And she nestled the least bit closer to him.

"Karl!"

"Well?"

"Why did you not tell me about your brother when you found I knew nothing, and was resenting it? If I had but known the real truth, we never should have been at issue for a day."

"Remember, Lucy, that I thought it was what you knew, and spoke of. I thought you knew he was alive and was at the Maze with his wife. When I would have given you the whole history from the first, you stopped me and refused to hear. I wished to give it; that you might see I was less to blame than you seemed to be supposing. It has been a wretched play at cross-purposes on both sides: and neither of us, that I see, is to blame for it."

"Poor Sir Adam!" she cried, the tears again falling. "Living in that dreadful fear day after day! And what must his poor wife have suffered! And her baby dying, and now her husband! And I, instead of giving sympathy, have thought everything that was ill of her, and hated her and despised her. And Karl— why, Karl—*she* must have been the real Lady Andinnian."

He nodded. "Until Adam's death, I was not Sir Karl, you see. The day you came with her from Basham, and they told her the fly waiting at the station was for Lady Andinnian, she was stricken with terror, believing they meant herself."

"Oh, if I had known all this time!" bewailed Lucy. "Stuck up here in my false pride and folly, instead of helping you to shield them and to lighten their burthen! I cannot hope that you will ever quite forgive me in your heart, Karl."

"Had it been as I supposed it was, I am not quite sure that I should. Not quite, Lucy, even to our old age. You took it up so harshly and selfishly, looking at it from my point of view, and resented it in so extraordinary a fashion, so bitter a spirit——"

"Oh don't, don't!" she pleaded, slipping down to his feet again in the depth of her remorse, the old sense of shame on her burning cheeks. "Won't you be merciful to me? I have suffered much."

"Why, my darling, you are mistaking me again," he cried tenderly, as he once more raised her. "I said, 'Looking at it from my point of view.' Looking at it from yours, Lucy, I am amazed at your gentle forbearance. Few young wives would have been as good and patient as you."

"Then do you really forgive me?" she asked, raising her eyes and her wet cheeks.

"Before I answer that, I think I must ask whether you forgive my having married you—now that you know all."

"Oh, Karl!"

She fell upon his shoulder, her arms round his neck. Karl caught her face to his. He might take what kisses he chose from it again.

"Karl, would you please let me go to see her?" she whispered.

"See whom?" asked Karl, in rather a hard tone, his mind pretty full just then of Miss Blake.

"Poor Lady Andinnian."

"Yes, if you will," he softly said. "I think she would like it. But, my dear, you must call her 'Mrs. Grey' remember. Not only for safety, but that she would prefer it."

They went over in the afternoon. Miss Blake,

quite accidentally this time, for she was returning home quietly from confession at St. Jerome's—and a wholesale catalogue of peccadilloes she must have been disclosing, one would say, by the length of the hearing —saw them enter. It puzzled her not a little. Sir Karl taking his wife *there!* What fresh ruse, what further deceit was he going to try? Oh but it was sinful! Worse than anything ever taken for Mr. Cattacomb's absolution at St. Jerome's.

Lucy behaved badly: without the slightest dignity whatever. The first thing she did was to burst out crying, and kiss Mrs. Grey's hand: as if—it really seemed so to Mrs. Grey—she did not dare to offer to kiss her cheek. Very sad and pretty she looked in her widow's mourning.

It was a sad interview: though in some respects a soothing and satisfactory one. Lucy explained, without entering into any details whatever, that she had not known who it was residing at the Maze, or she should have been over before, Karl and Sir Adam permitting her. Rose supposed that for safety's sake Karl had deemed it well to keep the secret intact. And there the matter ended.

"You will come and stay with me at the Court before you leave," pleaded Lucy.

Rose shook her head. "It is very kind of you to wish it, Lady Andinnian; very kind indeed under the circumstances; but it could not be. I shall not pass through these gates until I pass through them with Ann Hopley for good. That will be very soon."

"At least, you will come and stay with us sometime in the future."

"I think not. Unless I should get a fever upon

me to see the spot once more that contains my husband and child. In that case, I might trespass on you for a day or two if you would have me. Thank you very much, Lady Andinnian."

"You will let me come over again before you leave?"

"Oh, I should be pleased—if Sir Karl has no objection. Thank *you*, Karl," she added, holding out her hands to him, "thank you for all. You have been to us ever the most faithful friend and brother."

The church bell at Foxwood was ringing for the late afternoon service as they quitted the Maze—for Mr. Sumnor, in spite of his discouragement and non-attendance, kept on the daily service. The ting-tang was sounding from St. Jerome's, and several damsels, who had come round by the Court to call for Miss Blake, were trooping past. Lucy bowed; Karl lifted his hat: he had ceased to care who saw him going in and out of the Maze gate now.

"Karl," said Lucy, "I should like to go to prayers this evening. I shall take no harm: it is scarcely dusk yet."

He turned to take her. Mr. Sumnor and the clerk were in the church; hardly anybody else—just as it had been that other evening when Lucy had crept in. Even Miss Diana was off to St. Jerome's, in the wake of her flighty nieces. Lucy went on to her own pew this time.

Oh, what a contrast it was!—this evening and that. Now she was utterly still in her rapt thankfulness; then she had lain on the floor, her heart crying aloud to God in its agony. What could she do to show her gratitude to Him, who had turned the darkness into this radiant light? She could do nothing. Nothing, save strive to let her whole life be spent as a thank-offering. Karl noted her excessive stillness, her blinding tears; and he probably guessed her thoughts.

While he was talking with Mr. Sumnor after the service, Lucy went in to the vicarage. Margaret, lying in the dusk, for the room was only lighted by its bit of fire, could not see who had entered.

"Is it you, Martha?" she said, thinking it was her sister. "You are back early."

"It is I—Lucy," said Lady Andinnian. "Oh, Margaret, I was obliged to come to you just for a minute. Karl is outside, and we have been to church. I have something to tell."

Margaret Sumnor put out both her hands in token of welcome. Instead of taking them, Lucy knelt by the reclining board, and brought her face close to her friend's, and spoke in a hushed whisper.

"Margaret, I want to thank you, and I don't know how. I have been thinking how impossible it will be for me ever to thank God: and it seems to be nearly as impossible ever to thank you. Do you remember what you once said to me, Margaret, about bearing and waiting? Well, but for you, I don't think I *could* have borne or waited, even in the poor way I have; and—and—"

She broke down: sobs of emotion checked her utterance.

"Be calm, my dear," said Margaret. "You have come to tell me that the trouble is over."

"Yes: God has ended it. And, Margaret, I never need have had a shade of it: I was on a wrong track all the while. I—I was led to think ill of my husband; I treated him worse than any one will ever know or would believe: while he was good and loyal to the core in all ways, and in the most bitter trouble the world can inflict. Oh, Margaret, had I been vindictive instead of patient—I might have caused the most dire injury and tribulation, and what would have been my condition now, my dreadful remorse through life? When the thought comes over me, I shiver as I did in that old ague fever."

A fit of shivering took her actually. Miss Sumnor saw how the matter had laid hold upon her.

"Lucy, my dear, it seems to me that you may put away these thoughts now. God has been merciful and cleared it to you, you say; and you ought to be happy."

"Oh, so merciful!" she sobbed. "So happy! But it might have been otherwise, and I cannot forget, or forgive myself."

"Do you remember, Lucy, what I said? That some day when the cloud was removed your heart would go up with a bound of joyous thankfulness?"

"Yes. Because I did—and have done—as Margaret told me; and endured."

The affair had indeed laid no slight hold of Lucy. She could not forget what might have been the result, and quite an exaggerated remorse set in.

A few nights afterwards Karl was startled out of his sleep by her. She had awakened, it appeared, in a state of terror, and had turned to him with a nervous grasp as of one who is drowning. Shaking, sobbing, moaning, she frightened her husband. He would have risen for a light, but she clung to him too tightly.

"But what has alarmed you, Lucy?—what is it?" he reiterated.

"A dream, Karl; a dream," she sobbed, in her bitter distress. "I am always thinking of it by day, but this time I dreamt it; and I awoke believing it was true."

"Dreamt what?" he asked.

"I thought that cruel time was back again. I thought that I had not been quiet and patient, as Margaret enjoined, leaving vengeance to God, but had taken it into my own hands, and so had caused the Maze's secret to be discovered. You and Adam had both died through it; and I was left all alone to my dreadful repentance, on some barren place surrounded by turbid water."

"Lucy, you will assuredly make yourself ill."

"But, oh Karl, if it had been true! If God had not saved me from it!"

CHAPTER XXIII.

Only a Man like other Men.

THEY stood together in the north parlour: Sir Karl Andinnian and Miss Blake. In the least severe terms he knew how to employ, Sir Karl was telling her of her abuse of his hospitality—the setting his wife against him—and intimating that her visit to them had better for the present terminate.

It took Miss Blake by surprise. She had remarked a difference in their behaviour to one another, in the past day or two. Lucy scarcely left Sir Karl alone a minute: she was with him in his parlour; she clung to his arm in unmistakable fondness in the garden; her eyes were for ever seeking his with a look of pleading, deprecating love. "They could not have been two greater simpletons in their honeymoon," severely thought Miss Blake.

Something else had rather surprised her. Walking past the Maze on this same morning, she saw the gate propped open, and a notice, that the house was to let, erected on a board. The place was empty; the late tenants of it, the lady and her maid, had departed. Turning to ask Mr. Smith the meaning of this, she saw a similar board at his house: Mr. Smith was packing up, and Clematis Cottage was in the market.

"Good gracious! Are you going to leave us, Mr. Smith?" she asked, as that gentleman showed himself for a moment at the open window, with an armful of books and papers.

"Sorry to say that I am, madam. Business is calling me to London."

"I hear that Mrs. Grey has left, too. What can have taken her away?"

"Don't know," said Mr. Smith. "Does not care to stop in the house, perhaps, after a death has taken place in it. Servants must die as well as other people, though."

Without another word to her, he went to the back of the room with his load, and began stuffing it into a trunk with his one arm. Miss Blake summed up the conclusion in her mind.

"Sir Karl must have summarily dismissed him."

Little did she foresee that Sir Karl was about, so to say, summarily to dismiss herself. On this same day it was that he sought the interview. When the past was touched upon by Karl, and her part in it, Miss Blake, for once in her life, showed signs that she had a temper, and her face turned white.

"You might have done me incalculable mischief, Miss Blake: mischief that could never be repaired in this world," he said, standing to face her. "I do not allude to the estrangement that might have been caused between myself and my wife, but evil of a different nature. What could possibly have induced you to take up so outrageous a notion in regard to me?"

Miss Blake, in rather a shrill tone—for she was one of those unfortunate individuals whose voices grow harsh with annoyance—ventured upon a disparaging word of Mrs. Grey, but evaded the true question. Karl did not allow her to go on.

"That lady, madam," he said, raising his hand with a kind of solemnity, "was good and pure, and honourable as is my own wife; and my dear wife knows it now. She was sacred to me as a sister. Her husband was my dear and long-tried friend; and he was for some months in great trouble and distress. I wished to do what I could to alleviate it: my visits there were paid to *him*."

"But he was not living there," rejoined Miss Blake, partly in hardy contest, partly in surprise.

"Indeed he was living there. He had his reasons for not wishing to make any acquaintance in the place, and so kept himself in retirement; reasons in which I fully acquiesced. However, his troubles are at an end now; and—and the family have ceased to be my tenants."

Whether Miss Blake felt more angry or more vexed, she was not collected enough at the moment to know. It was a very annoying termination to her long and seemingly well-grounded suspicions. She always wished to do right, and had the grace to feel somewhat ashamed of the past.

"What I said to Lucy I believed I had perfectly good grounds for, Sir Karl. I had the interests of religion at heart when I spoke."

"Religion!" repeated Sir Karl, his lips involuntarily curling. "Religion is as religion does, Miss Blake."

"After all, she did not heed me; so, if it did no good, it did no harm. Lucy is so very weak-minded—"

"Weak-minded!" interposed Sir Karl. "If to act as she did—to bear patiently and make no stir under extreme provocation, trusting to the future to right the wrong—if this is to be weak-minded, why I thank God that she is so. Had she been strong-minded as you, Miss Blake, the result might have been terribly different."

Miss Blake was nettled. Her manner froze.

"I see what it is, Sir Karl; you and your wife are so displeased with me that I feel my presence in your house is no longer welcome. As soon as I can make arrangements I will quit it—thanking you both for your hospitality."

She paused. Sir Karl paused too. Perhaps she had a faint expectation that he would hasten to refute the decision, and request her to stay on. But he did nothing of the kind. On the contrary, he, in a word or two of politeness, acquiesced in the proposal of departure, as though it admitted of no question.

"I should not have trespassed on you so long—in fact, I should not have stayed at all after your first return here with Lady Andinnian, but for St. Jerome's," she rejoined, her temper getting up again, while there ran in her mind an undercurrent of thought, as to whether she could find suitable lodgings in Foxwood.

"You will not have to regret that, in leaving," he observed. "I am about to do away with St. Jerome's."

"To do away with St. Jerome's!"

"In a week's time from this it will be shut up, and all the nonsense within its walls cleared away."

"The nonsense!" shrieked Miss Blake.

"Why you cannot call it sense—or religion either. To tell you the truth, Miss Blake, the place has been an offence to me for some time. It has caused a scandal—"

"For shame, Sir Karl Andinnian! Scandal, indeed!"

"And this little bit of fresh scandal that has arisen now, people don't like at all," quietly persisted Sir Karl. "Neither do I. So, to prevent the bishop coming down upon us here, Miss Blake, I close the place."

Miss Blake compressed her lips. She could have struck him as he stood.

"What do you mean by a 'fresh' scandal, pray?"

"Well, the story runs that Mr. Cattacomb was seen to kiss one of the young ladies in the vestry."

Miss Blake started, Miss Blake shrieked, Miss Blake wondered that the very ceiling did not drop down upon the bold false tongue. To do her justice, she believed St. Jerome's pastor was by far too holy a man for any wickedness of the sort. Not to speak of restraining prudence.

"Sir Karl, may you be forgiven! Where do you expect to go to when you die?"

"To the heaven, I hope, that our merciful God has provided for us," he answered, meeting the query solemnly and with some emotion. "Some of those dearer to me than life have gone on thither to wait for me."

At which Miss Blake drew up her pious head, and intimated that she feared it might be another kind of place, unless he should mend his manners. And Sir Karl closed the interview, leaving her to understand that she had received her congé.

The circumstance to which he alluded was this. A day or two before, some prying boys, comrades of Tom Pepp's, were about St. Jerome's as usual. For,

ever since its establishment, the place had been quite
a point of attraction to these young reptiles; and keep
off they would not. On the morning in question,
hovering around the vestry window and the walls
generally, a slight inlet of view was discovered, in
consequence of the blinds being accidentally drawn
somewhat aside. Of course as many eyes were applied
to the chink as could find space; and they had the
pleasure of seeing the parson steal a kiss or two from
the blushing cheek of Miss Jemima Moore. Rare
nuts for the boys to crack! Before the day had closed,
it was being talked of in Foxwood, and reached the
ears of Miss Diana. She handed the case over to the
doctor.

Down he went to St. Jerome's on the following
morning, and caught Mr. Cattacomb alone in the
vestry, just getting into his sheep-skin. Mr. Moore
wasted no time in circumlocution or superfluous greet-
ing.

"You were seen to kiss my daughter, yesterday,
young man."

To be pounced upon in this unprepared manner
is enough to try the nerves of almost any hero; what
must it have been then for a modest young clergyman,
with a character for holiness, like Guy Cattacomb?
He stammered and stuttered, and blushed to the very
roots of his scanty hair. The tippet itself turned of
a rosy hue.

"No equivocation, sir. Do you acknowledge it, or
do you not?"

Gathering up his scared wits, and a modicum of
courage, in the best way he could, the Reverend Guy
virtually acknowledged it to be true. He added that

he and Miss Jemima were seriously attached to each
other; that he hoped sometime to win her for his wife;
and that a sense of his utter want of means had alone
prevented his speaking to the doctor.

"Now, look here," said the surgeon, after a pause
of consideration, perceiving from the young man's
earnest manner that this was the actual state of the
case, "I say *No* to you at present.   It lies with yourself whether I ever say yes.   If you and she care for
one another, I should be the last to stand in your way,
once you have proved yourself worthy of her.   Get
rid of all the rubbish that's filling up your foolish
brain;"—and he gave his hand a sweep around—"become a faithful, honest clergyman of the Church of
England, serving your Master to the best of your
power; and then you may ask for her.   A daughter
of mine shall never tie herself to a vain fop.   No;
though I had to banish her to the wilds of Kam-
schatka."

"I'll do my best, sir, to become what you will ap-
prove of," returned the parson humbly, "if you will
only give me hope of Miss Jemima."

"It is because I think you have some good in you,
that I do give you hope, Mr. Cattacomb.   The issue
lies with you."

Now, this was what Sir Karl alluded to.   When it
fell to Miss Blake's lot to find it was true and to hear
the particulars, she thought, in her mortification, that
the world must be drawing to an end: at least, it was
signally degenerating.   That adored saint to have turned
out to be only a man after all—with all a man's frail
nature!   All Miss Blake's esteemed admirers seemed
to be slipping from her one by one.

She and the congregation generally were alike incensed.   Mr. Cattacomb, lost to any future hopes, fell
in their estimation from fever-heat down to zero: and
they really did not much care, after this, whether St.
Jerome's was shut up or not.   So Sir Karl and Farmer
Truefit found their way was made plain before them.

"What a heap of silk we have wasted on cushions
and things for him!" cried Charlotte St. Henry, in a
passion.   "And all through that sly little cat, Jemima
Moore!"

CONCLUSION.

A SWEET calm day in early spring, Sir Karl and his wife stood on the steps of their house, hand in hand, ready to welcome Colonel and Mrs. Cleeve, who were driving up to pay a long visit. Lucy had recovered all her good looks; Karl's face had lost its sadness.

Things had been getting themselves straight after the dark time of trouble. Some pleasant neighbours were at the Maze now; Clematis Cottage was occupied by Margaret Sumnor. There was a new vicar of Foxwood. Mr. Sumnor, who had not been without his trials in life, had died in the winter. His widow and second family went to reside in London; Margaret, who had her own mother's fortune now—which was just enough to live upon quietly—removed to Clematis Cottage, to the extreme delight of Lady Andinnian. St. Jerome's had been converted into a schoolroom again: its former clergyman had retired into private life for a season, and no more omnibus-loads of young ladies came over from Basham. Sir Karl was earning popularity everywhere. Caring earnestly for those about him, actively promoting the welfare of all unceasingly and untiringly, generous in aiding, chary of fault-finding, Sir Karl Andinnian was esteemed and beloved even more than Sir Joseph had been. Nothing educates and softens the human heart like the sharp school of adversity.

"Lucy, you are a puzzle to me," said Mrs. Cleeve, when she had her daughter to herself up stairs. "In the autumn you were so ill and so sad; now you are looking so well and so radiantly happy."

"I am quite well, mamma, and happy."

"But what was the cause of your looking so ill then?"

Lucy did not answer, evading the question in the best way she could. That past time would be ever sacred between herself and her husband.

"Well, I cannot understand it," concluded Mrs. Cleeve. "I only hope you will continue as you are now. Sir Karl looks well, also; almost as he did when we first knew him at Winchester, before his brother brought that trouble on himself and all connected with him. To tell you the truth, Lucy, I thought when I was last here that you were both on the high road to consumption. Now you both look as though you were on the road to—to——"

"A fine old age," put in Lucy, as her mother broke down for want of a simile. "Well, mamma, I hope we are—if God shall so will it."

"And—why you have made this into a dressing-room again!" cried Mrs. Cleeve, as Lucy took down her hair, and rang for Aglaé.

"Yes; I wanted it as one when I went back to my own room."

"What do you do with the other room—the one you slept in?" questioned Mrs. Cleeve, throwing open the door as she spoke—for she had a great love of seeing into house arrangements. "You have had the bed taken away!"

"The room is not being used at present," replied Lucy. "Karl—Karl——"

"Karl—what?" asked Mrs. Cleeve, wondering at the sudden timidity, and looking round. Lucy's sweet face was blushing.

"Karl thinks I shall like to make it the day nursery."

"Oh, my dear! I am glad to hear *that*."

Lucy burst into tears of emotion. A very slight occurrence served still to bring back the past and its repentance.

"Mamma, you do not know, you can never know, how good God has been to me in all ways; and how little I deserved it."

And so we leave all things at peace. The dark storms had rolled away and given place to sunshine.

THE END.

PRINTING OFFICE OF THE PUBLISHER.

October 1872.

Tauchnitz Edition.

Each volume 1/2 Thaler = 2 Francs.

CONTENTS:

Sold by all the principal booksellers on the Continent.

Collection of British Authors.

Rev. W. Adams:
Sacred Allegories 1 v.

Miss Aguilar:
Home Influence 2 v. The Mother's Recompense 2 v.

Hamilton Aïdé:
Rita 1 v. Carr of Carrlyon 2 v. The Marstons 2 v. In that State of Life 1 v. Morals and Mysteries 1 v.

W. Harrison Ainsworth:
Windsor Castle 1 v. Saint James's 1 v. Jack Sheppard (w. portrait) 1 v. The Lancashire Witches 2 v. The Star-Chamber 2 v. The Flitch of Bacon 1 v. The Spendthrift 1 v. Mervyn Clitheroe 2 v. Ovingdean Grange 1 v. The Constable of the Tower 1 v. The Lord Mayor of London 2 v. Cardinal Pole 2 v. John Law 2 v. The Spanish Match 2 v. The Constable de Bourbon 2 v. Old Court 2 v. Myddleton Pomfret 2 v. The South-Sea Bubble 2 v. Hilary St. Ives 2 v. Talbot Harland 1 v. Tower Hill 1 v.

"All for Greed,"
Author of—
All for Greed 1 v. Love the Avenger 2 v.

Miss Austen:
Sense and Sensibility 1 v. Mansfield Park 1 v. Pride and Prejudice 1 v. Northanger Abbey, and Persuasion 1 v.

Nina Balatka 1 v.

Rev. R. H. Baynes:
Lyra Anglicana, Hymns and Sacred Songs 1 v.

Currer Bell:
Jane Eyre 2 v. Shirley 2 v. Villette 2 v. The Professor 1 v.

Ellis & Acton Bell:
Wuthering Heights, and Agnes Grey 2 v.

Isa Blagden:
The Woman I loved, and the Woman who loved me; A Tuscan Wedding 1 v.

William Black:
A Daughter of Heth 2 v. In Silk Attire 2 v.

Lady Blessington:
Meredith 1 v. Strathern 2 v. Memoirs of a Femme de Chambre 1 v. Marmaduke Herbert 2 v. Country Quarters (w. portrait) 2 v.

M. E. Braddon:
Lady Audley's Secret 2 v. Aurora Floyd 2 v. Eleanor's Victory 2 v. John Marchmont's Legacy 2 v. Henry Dunbar 2 v.

The price of each volume is ½ Thaler = 2 Francs.

The Doctor's Wife 2 v. Only a Clod 2 v. Sir Jasper's Tenant 2 v. The Lady's Mile 2 v. Rupert Godwin 2 v. Dead-Sea Fruit 2 v. Run to Earth 2 v. Fenton's Quest 2 v. The Lovels of Arden 2 v.

Shirley Brooks:
The Silver Cord 3 v. Sooner or Later 3 v.

John Brown:
Rab and his Friends, and other Tales 1 v.

Eliz. Barrett Browning:
A Selection from her Poetry (w. portr.) 1 v. Aurora Leigh 1 v.

Robert Browning:
The Poetical Works (w. portrait) 2 v.

Tom Brown's
School Days 1 v.

Bulwer (Lord Lytton):
Pelham (w. portrait) 1 v. Eugene Aram 1 v. Paul Clifford 1 v. Zanoni 1 v. The Last Days of Pompeii 1 v. The Disowned 1 v. Ernest Maltravers 1 v. Alice 1 v. Eva, and the Pilgrims of the Rhine 1 vol. Devereux 1 v. Godolphin, and Falkland 1 v. Rienzi 1 v. Night and Morning 1 v. The Last of the Barons 2 v. Athens 2 v. The Poems and Ballads of Schiller 1 v. Lucretia 2 v. Harold 2 v. King Arthur 2 v. The new Ti-

mon; St Stephen's 1 v. The Caxtons 2 v. My Novel 4 v. What will he do with it? 4 v. The Dramatic Works 2 v. A Strange Story 2 v. Caxtoniana 2 v. The Lost Tales of Miletus 1 v. Miscellaneous Prose Works ͝ ͝ The Odes and Epodes of H͘ 2 v.

Sir Henry Lytton Bul· (Lord Dalling):
Historical Characters 2 v. The Life of Henry John Temple, Viscount Palmerston 2 v.

John Bunyan:
The Pilgrim's Progress 1 v.

Buried Alone 1 v.

Miss Burney:
Evelina 1 v.

Robert Burns:
The Poetical Works (w. portrait) 1 v.

Lord Byron:
The Works (w. portrait) 5 v. (*Second Edition.*)

Thomas Carlyle:
The French Revolution 3 v. Frederick the Great 13 v. Oliver Cromwell's Letters and Speeches 4 v. The Life of Friedrich Schiller 1 v.

"Cavaliers,"
Author of—
The Last of the Cavaliers 2 v. The Gain of a Loss 2 v.

The price of each volume is ½ Thaler = 2 Francs.

"Chronicles of the Schön-berg-Cotta Family,"
Author of—
Chronicles of the Schönberg-Cotta Family 2 v. The Draytons and the Davenants 2 v. On Both Sides of the Sea 2 v. Winifred Bertram 1 v. Diary of Mrs. Kitty Trevylyan 1 v. The Victory of the Vanquished 1 v. The Cottage by the Cathedral 1 v.

S. Taylor Coleridge:
The Poems 1 v.

Wilkie Collins:
After Dark 1 v. Hide and Seek 2 v. A Plot in Private Life 1 v. The Woman in White 2 v. Basil 1 v. No Name 3 v. The Dead Secret 2 v. Antonina 2 v. Armadale 3 v. The Moonstone 2 v. Man and Wife 3 v. Poor Miss Finch 2 v. Miss or Mrs.? 1 v.

"Cometh up as a Flower,"
Author of—
Cometh up as a Flower 1 v. Not wisely, but too well 2 v. Red as a Rose is She 2 v.

Fenimore Cooper:
The Spy (w. portrait) 1 v. The two Admirals 1 v. The Jack O'Lantern 1 v.

The two Cosmos 1 v.

Miss Craik:
Lost and Won 1 v. Faith Unwin's Ordeal 1 v. Leslie Tyrrell 1 v. Winifred's Wooing, and other Tales 1 v. Mildred 1 v. Esther Hill's Secret 2 v. Hero

Trevelyan 1 v. Without Kith or Kin 2 v.

Miss Cummins:
The Lamplighter 1 v. Mabel Vaughan 1 v. El Fureidîs 1 v. Haunted Hearts 1 v.

De-Foe:
The Life and surprising Adventures of Robinson Crusoe 1 v.

Charles Dickens:
The Posthumous Papers of the Pickwick Club (w. portrait) 2 v. American Notes 1 v. Oliver Twist 1 v. The Life and Adventures of Nicholas Nickleby 2 v. Sketches 1 v. The Life and Adventures of Martin Chuzzlewit 2 v. A Christmas Carol; the Chimes; the Cricket on the Hearth 1 v. Master Humphrey's Clock (Old Curiosity Shop, Barnaby Rudge, and other Tales) 3 v. Pictures from Italy 1 v. The Battle of Life; the Haunted Man 1 v. Dombey and Son 3 v. David Copperfield 3 v. Bleak House 4 v. A Child's History of England (2 v. 8° 27 Ngr.) Hard Times 1 v. Little Dorrit 4 v. A Tale of two Cities 2 v. Hunted Down; The Uncommercial Traveller 1 v. Great Expectations 2 v. Christmas Stories 1 v. Our Mutual Friend 4 v. Somebody's Luggage; Mrs. Lirriper's Lodgings; Mrs. Lirriper's Legacy 1 v. Doctor Marigold's Prescriptions; Mugby Junction 1 v. No Thoroughfare 1 v. The Mystery of Edwin Drood 2 v.

The price of each volume is ½ Thaler = 2 Francs.

B. Disraeli:

Coningsby 1 v. Sybil 1 v. Contarini Fleming (w. portrait) 1 v. Alroy 1 v. Tancred 2 v. Venetia 2 v. Vivian Grey 2 v. Henrietta Temple 1 v. Lothair 2 v.

W. Hepworth Dixon:

Personal History of Lord Bacon 1 v. The Holy Land 2 v. New America 2 v. Spiritual Wives 2 v. Her Majesty's Tower 4 v.

Miss A. B. Edwards:

Barbara's History 2 v. Miss Carew 2 v. Hand and Glove 1 v. Half a Million of Money 2 v. Debenham's Vow 2 v.

M. Betham Edwards:

The Sylvestres 1 v.

Mrs. Edwardes:

Archie Lovell 2 v. Steven Lawrence, Yeoman 2 v. Ought we to Visit her? 2 v.

Frances Elliot:

Diary of an Idle Woman in Italy 2 v.

George Eliot:

Scenes of Clerical Life 2 v. Adam Bede 2 v. The Mill on the Floss 2 v. Silas Marner 1 v. Romola 2 v. Felix Holt 2 v.

Essays and Reviews 1 v.

Frank Fairlegh 2 v.

"Paul Ferroll,"
Author of—
Paul Ferroll 1 v. Year after Year 1 v. Why Paul Ferroll killed his Wife 1 v.

Fielding:

The History of Tom Jones 2 v.

Five Centuries
of the English Language and Literature 1 v.

A. Forbes:

My Experiences of the War between France and Germany 2 v.

John Forster:

The Life of Charles Dickens 2 v.

"Found Dead,"
Author of—
Found Dead 1 v. Gwendoline's Harvest 1 v. Like Father, like Son 2 v. Not Wooed, but Won 2 v. Cecil's Tryst 1 v. A Woman's Vengeance 2 v.

Edward A. Freeman:

The Growth of the English Constitution 1 v.

Lady G. Fullerton:

Ellen Middleton 1 v. Grantley Manor 2 v. Lady Bird 2 v. Too Strange not to be True 2 v. Constance Sherwood 2 v. A stormy Life 2 v. Mrs. Gerald's Niece 2 v.

Mrs. Gaskell:

Mary Barton 1 v. Ruth 2 v. North and South 1 v. Lizzie Leigh 1 v. The Life of Charlotte Brontë 2 v. Lois the Witch 1 v. Sylvia's Lovers 2 v. A Dark Night's Work 1 v. Wives and Daughters 3 v. Cranford 1 v. Cousin Phillis, and other Tales 1 v.

Oliver Goldsmith:
The Select Works: The Vicar of Wakefield; Poems; Dramas (w. portrait) 1 v.

Mrs. Gore:
Castles in the Air 1 v. The Dean's Daughter 2 v. Progress and Prejudice 2 v. Mammon 2 v. A Life's Lessons 2 v. The two Aristocracies 2 v. Heckington 2 v.

"John Halifax,"
Author of—
John Halifax, Gentleman 2 v. The Head of the Family 2 v. A Life for a Life 2 v. A Woman's Thoughts about Women 1 v. Agatha's Husband 1 v. Romantic Tales 1 v. Domestic Stories 1 v. Mistress and Maid 1 v. The Ogilvies 1 v. Lord Erlistoun 1 v. Christian's Mistake 1 v. Bread upon the Waters 1 v. A Noble Life 1 v. Olive 2 v. Two Marriages 1 v. Studies from Life 1 v. Poems 1 v. The Woman's Kingdom 2 v. The Unkind Word 2 v. A Brave Lady 2 v. Hannah 2 v. Fair France 1 v.

Mrs. Hall:
Can Wrong be Right? 1 v.

Bret Harte:
Prose and Poetry 2 v.

Sir H. Havelock,
by the Rev. W. Brock, 1 v.

Hawthorne:
The Scarlet Letter 1 v. Transformation 2 v. Passages from the English Note-Books 2 v.

Mrs. Hemans:
The Select Poetical Works 1 v.

Mrs. Cashel Hoey:
A Golden Sorrow 2 v.

Household Words
conducted by Ch. Dickens. 1851-56. 36 v. Novels and Tales reprinted from Households Words by Ch. Dickens. 1856-59. 11 v.

Washington Irving:
The Sketch Book (w. portrait) 1 v. The Life of Mahomet 1 v. Successors of Mahomet 1 v. Oliver Goldsmith 1 v. Chronicles of Wolfert's Roost 1 v. Life of George Washington 5 v.

G. P. R. James:
Morley Ernstein (w. portrait) 1 v. Forest Days 1 v. The False Heir 1 v. Arabella Stuart 1 v. Rose d'Albret 1 v. Arrah Neil 1 v. Agincourt 1 v. The Smuggler 1 v. The Step-Mother 2 v. Beauchamp 1 v. Heidelberg 1 v. The Gipsy 1 v. The Castle of Ehrenstein 1 v. Darnley 1 v. Russell 2 v. The Convict 2 v. Sir Theodore Broughton 2 v.

J. Cordy Jeaffreson:
A Book about Doctors 2 v. A Woman in Spite of herself 2 v.

Not Easily Jealous 2 v.

Mrs. Jenkin:
"Who Breaks—Pays" 1 v. Skirmishing 1 v. Once and Again 2 v. Two French Marriages 2 v. Within an Ace 1 v.

The price of each volume is ½ Thaler = 2 Francs.

Edward Jenkins:
Ginx's Baby; Lord Bantam 2 v.

Douglas Jerrold:
The History of St. Giles and St. James 2 v. Men of Character 2 v.

S. Johnson:
The Lives of the English Poets 2 v.

Miss Kavanagh:
Nathalie 2 v. Daisy Burns 2 v. Grace Lee 2 v. Rachel Gray 1 v. Adèle 3 v. A Summer and Winter in the Two Sicilies 2 v. Seven Years 2 v. French Women of Letters 1 v. English Women of Letters 1 v. Queen Mab 2 v. Beatrice 2 v. Sybil's Second Love 2 v. Dora 2 v. Silvia 2 v. Bessie 2 v.

R. B. Kimball:
Saint Leger 1 v. Romance of Student Life abroad 1 v. Undercurrents 1 v. Was he Successful? 1 v. To-Day in New-York 1 v.

Kinglake:
Eothen 1 v. The Invasion of the Crimea v. 1-8.

Charles Kingsley:
Yeast 1 v. Westward ho! 2 v. Two Years ago 2 v. Hypatia 2 v. Alton Locke 1 v. Hereward the Wake 2 v. At Last 2 v.

Henry Kingsley:
Ravenshoe 2 v. Austin Elliot 1 v. The Recollections of Geoffry Hamlyn 2 v. The Hillyars and the Burtons 2 v. Leighton Court 1 v.

My little Lady 2 v.

Charles Lamb:
The Essays of Elia and Eliana 1 v.

Mary Langdon:
Ida May 1 vol.

Holme Lee:
Basil Godfrey's Caprice 2 v. For Richer, for Poorer 2 v. The Beautiful Miss Barrington 2 v. Her Title of Honour 1 v. Echoes of a Famous Year 1 v.

Le Fanu:
Uncle Silas 2 v. Guy Deverell 2 v.

Mark Lemon:
Wait for the End 2 v. Loved at Last 2 v. Falkner Lyle 2 v. Leyton Hall 2 v. Golden Fetters 2 v.

Charles Lever:
The O'Donoghue 1 v. The Knight of Gwynne 3 v. Arthur O'Leary 2 v. The Confessions of Harry Lorrequer 2 v. Charles O'Malley 3 v. Tom Burke of "Ours" 3 v. Jack Hinton 2 v. The Daltons 4 v. The Dodd Family abroad 3 v. The Martins of Cro'Martin 3 v. The Fortunes of Glencore 2 v. Roland Cashel 3 v. Davenport Dunn 3 v. Con Cregan 2 v. One of Them 2 v. Maurice Tiernay 2 v. Sir Jasper Carew 2 v. Barrington 2 v. A Day's Ride: a Life's Romance 2 v. Luttrell of Arran 2 v. Tony Butler 2 v. Sir Brook Fossbrooke 2 v. The Bramleighs of Bishop's Folly 2 v. A Rent in a Cloud 1 v. That Boy of Norcott's 1 v. St. Patrick's Eve; Paul Gosslett's Confessions 1 v. Lord Kilgobbin 2 v.

The price of each volume is ½ Thaler = 2 Francs.

G. H. Lewes:

Ranthorpe 1 v. The Physiology of Common Life 2 v.

"Guy Livingstone,"
Author of—

Guy Livingstone 1 v. Sword and Gown 1 v. Barren Honour 1 v. Border and Bastille 1 v. Maurice Dering 1 v. Sans Merci 2 v. Breaking a Butterfly 2 v. Anteros 2 v.

H. W. Longfellow:

The Poetical Works (w. portrait) 3 v. The Divine Comedy of Dante Alighieri 3 v. The New-England Tragedies 1 v. The Divine Tragedy 1 v.

Lutfullah:

Autobiography of Lutfullah, by Eastwick 1 v.

Lord Macaulay:

History of England (w. portrait) 10 v. Critical and Historical Essays 5 v. Lays of Ancient Rome 1 v. Speeches 2 v. Biographical Essays 1 v. William Pitt, Atterbury 1 v.

Mac Donald:

Alec Forbes of Howglen 2 v. Annals of a Quiet Neighbourhood 2 v. David Elginbrod 2 v. The Vicar's Daughter 2 v.

Mrs. Mackarness:

Sunbeam Stories 1 v. A Peerless Wife 2 v.

Norman Macleod:

The old Lieutenant and his Son 1 v.

Katharine S. Macquoid:

Patty 2 v.

Lord Mahon: *vide* Stanhope.

Mansfield:

The Log of the Water Lily 1 v.

Capt. Marryat:

Jacob Faithful (w. portrait) 1 v. Percival Keene 1 v. Peter Simple 1 v. Japhet 1 v. Monsieur Violet 1 v. The Settlers 1 v. The Mission 1 v. The Privateer's-Man 1 v. The Children of the New-Forest 1 v. Valerie 1 v. Mr. Midshipman Easy 1 v. The King's Own 1 v.

Florence Marryat:

Love's Conflict 2 v. For Ever and Ever 2 v. The Confessions of Gerald Estcourt 2 v. Nelly Brooke 2 v. Véronique 2 v. Petronel 2 v. Her Lord and Master 2 v. The Prey of the Gods 1 v. Life of Captain Marryat 1 v.

Mrs. Marsh:

Ravenscliffe 2 v. Emilia Wyndham 2 v. Castle Avon 2 v. Aubrey 2 v. The Heiress of Haughton 2 v. Evelyn Marston 2 v. The Rose of Ashurst 2 v.

Whyte Melville:

Kate Coventry 1 v. Holmby House 2 v. Digby Grand 1 v. Good for Nothing 2 v. The Queen's Maries 2 v. The Gladiators 2 v. The Brookes of Bridlemere 2 v. Cerise 2 v. The Interpreter 2 v. The White Rose 2 v. M. or N. 1 v. Contraband; or A Losing Hazard 1 v. Sarchedon 2 v.

The price of each volume is ½ Thaler = 2 Francs.

Meredith (Hon. R. Lytton):
The Poems 2 v.

Milton:
The Poetical Works 1 v.

Miss Montgomery:
Misunderstood 1 v. Thrown Together 2 v.

Thomas Moore:
The Poetical Works (w. portrait)
5 v.

Lady Morgan's
Memoirs 3 v.

"Mademoiselle Mori,"
Author of—
Mademoiselle Mori 2 v. Denise
1 v. Madame Fontenoy 1 v. On
the Edge of the Storm 1 v.

Mrs. Newby:
Common Sense 2 v.

J. H. Newman:
Callista 1 v.

"No Church,"
Author of—
No Church 2 v. Owen:—a Waif
2 v.

Hon. Mrs. Norton:
Stuart of Dunleath 2 v. Lost
and Saved 2 v. Old Sir Douglas
2 v.

Mrs. Oliphant:
Passages in the Life of Mrs.
Margaret Maitland of Sunnyside
1 v. The Last of the Mortimers
2 v. Agnes 2 v. Madonna Mary
2 v. The Minister's Wife 2 v. The
Rector, and the Doctor's Family
1 v. Salem Chapel 2 v. The Perpetual Curate 2 v. Miss Marjori-
banks 2 v. Ombra 2 v.

Ossian:
The Poems 1 v.

Ouida:
Idalia 2 v. Tricotrin 2 v. Puck 2 v.
Chandos 2 v. Strathmore 2 v.
Under two Flags 2 v. Folle-
Farine 2 v., A Leaf in the Storm;
A Dog of Flanders & other Stories
1 v. Cecil Castlemaine's Gage
1 v. Madame la Marquise 1 v.

Mrs. Parr:
Dorothy Fox 1 v.

Fr. M. Peard:
One Year 2 v. The Rose-Garden
1 v. Unawares 1 v.

Thomas Percy:
Reliques of Ancient English
Poetry 3 v.

A. Pope:
The Select Poetical Works (w.
portrait) 1 v.

The Prince Consort's
Speeches and Addresses 1 v.

Charles Reade:
"It is never too late to mend"
2 v. "Love me little, love me
long" 1 v. The Cloister and the
Hearth 2 v. Hard Cash 3 v. Put
Yourself in his Place 2 v. A
Terrible Temptation 2 v. Peg
Woffington 1 v.

Recommended to Mercy:
Author of—
Recommended to Mercy 2 v.
Zoe's 'Brand' 2 v.

S. Richardson:
Clarissa Harlowe 4 v.

Rev. W. Robertson:
Sermons 4 v.

Charles H. Ross:
The Pretty Widow 1 v. A London Romance 2 v.

J. Ruffini:
Lavinia 2 v. Doctor Antonio 1 v. Lorenzo Benoni 1 v. Vincenzo 2 v. A Quiet Nook 1 v. The Paragreens on a Visit to Paris 1 v. Carlino and other Stories 1 v.

Estelle Russell 2 v.

G. A. Sala:
The Seven Sons of Mammon 2 v.

Walter Scott:
Waverley (w. portrait) 1 v. The Antiquary 1 v. Ivanhoe 1 v. Kenilworth 1 v. Quentin Durward 1 v. Old Mortality 1 v. Guy Mannering 1 v. Rob Roy 1 v. The Pirate 1 v. The Fortunes of Nigel 1 v. The Black Dwarf; A Legend of Montrose 1 v. The Bride of Lammermoor 1 v. The Heart of Mid-Lothian 2 v. The Monastery 1 v. The Abbot 1 v. Peveril of the Peak 2 v. The Poetical Works 2 v. Woodstock 1 v. The Fair Maid of Perth 1 v. Anne of Geierstein 1 v.

Miss Sewell:
Amy Herbert 2 v. Ursula 2 v. A Glimpse of the World 2 v. The Journal of a Home Life 2 v. After Life 2 v.

Shakespeare:
The Plays and Poems (w. portrait) compl. 7 v. *(Second Edition.)*
> Shakespeare's Plays may also be had in 37 numbers, at $^1/_{10}$ Thlr. each number.

Doubtful Plays 1 v.

Percy Bysshe Shelley:
A Selection from his Poems 1 v.

Nathan Sheppard:
Shut up in Paris 1 v.

R. Brinsley Sheridan:
The Dramatic Works 1 v.

T. Smollett:
The Adventures of Roderick Random 1 v. The Expedition of Humphry Clinker 1 v. The Adventures of Peregrine Pickle 2 v.

Earl Stanhope:
History of England 7 v. The Reign of Queen Anne 2 v.

L. Sterne:
The Life and Opinions of Tristram Shandy 1 v. A Sentimental Journey 1 v.

"Still Waters,"
Author of—
Still Waters 1 v. Dorothy 1 v. De Cressy 1 v. Uncle Ralph 1 v. Maiden Sisters 1 v. Martha Brown 1 v.

Mrs. H. Beecher Stowe:
Uncle Tom's Cabin (w. portrait) 2 v. A Key to Uncle Tom's Cabin 2 v. Dred 2 v. The Minister's Wooing 1 v. Oldtown Folks 2 v.

The price of each volume is ½ Thaler = 2 Francs.

J. Swift:
Gulliver's Travels 1 v.

Baroness Tautphoeus:
Cyrilla 2 v.   The Initials 2 v.
Quits 2 v.   At Odds 2 v.

Colonel Meadows Taylor:
Tara: a Mahratta Tale 3 v.

H. Templeton:
Diary and Notes 1 v.

A. Tennyson:
The Poetical Works 6 v.

The New Testament
[v. 1000.]

W. M. Thackeray:
Vanity Fair 3 v.   The History of Pendennis 3 v.   Miscellanies 8 v.
The History of Henry Esmond 2 v.   The English Humourists 1 v.
The Newcomes 4 v.   The Virginians 4 v.   The Four Georges;
Lovel the Widower 1 v.   The Adventures of Philip 2 v.   Denis Duval 1 v.   Roundabout Papers 2 v.   Catherine 1 v.   The Irish Sketch-Book 2 v.

Miss Thackeray:
The Story of Elizabeth 1 v.   The Village on the Cliff 1 v.

A. Thomas:
Denis Donne 2 v.   On Guard 2 v.
Walter Goring 2 v.   Played out 2 v.   Called to Account 2 v.
Only Herself 2 v.

J. Thomson:
The Poetical Works (w. portrait) 1 v.

F. G. Trafford:
(Mrs. Riddell):
George Geith of Fen Court 2 v.
Maxwell Drewitt 2 v.   The Race for Wealth 2 v.   Far above Rubies 2 v.

Trois-Etoiles:
The Member for Paris 2 v.

Anthony Trollope:
Doctor Thorne 2 v.   The Bertrams 2 v.   The Warden 1 v.   Barchester Towers 2 v.   Castle Richmond 2 v.
The West Indies 1 v.   Framley Parsonage 2 v.   North America 3 v.   Orley Farm 3 v.   Rachel Ray 2 v.   The Small House at Allington 3 v.   Can you forgive her? 3 v.   The Belton Estate 2 v.   The Last Chronicle of Barset 3 v.   The Claverings 2 v.   Phineas Finn 3 v.
He knew he was Right 3 v.   The Vicar of Bullhampton 2 v.   Sir Harry Hotspur of Humblethwaite 1 v.   Ralph the Heir 2 v.
The Golden Lion of Granpere 1 v.

T. Adolphus Trollope:
The Garstangs of Garstang Grange 2 v.   A Siren 2 v.

"Véra,"
Author of—
Véra 1 v.   The Hôtel du Petit St. Jean 1 v.

Eliot Warburton:
The Crescent and the Cross 2 v.
Darien 2 v.

The price of each volume is ½ Thaler = 2 Francs.

S. Warren:

Passages from the Diary of a late Physician 2 v.   Ten Thousand a-Year 3 v.   Now and Then 1 v. The Lily and the Bee 1 v.

Waterdale Neighbours 2 v.

E. Wetherell:

The wide, wide World 1 v. Queechy 2 v.   The Hills of the Shatemuc 2 v.   Say and Seal 2 v. The Old Helmet 2 v.

A Whim

and its Consequences 1 v.

Mrs. Henry Wood:

East Lynne 3 v.   The Channings 2 v.   Mrs. Halliburton's Troubles 2 v.   Verner's Pride 3 v.   The Shadow of Ashlydyat 3 v. Trevlyn Hold 2 v. Lord Oakburn's Daughters 2 v. Oswald Cray 2 v. Mildred Arkell 2 v.   St. Martin's Eve 2 v. Elster's Folly 2 v. Lady Adelaide's Oath 2 v. Orville College 1 v.   A Life's Secret 1 v.   The Red Court Farm 2 v.   Anne Hereford 2 v. Roland Yorke 2 v. George Canterbury's Will 2 v.   Bessy Rane 2 v.

Dene Hollow 2 v.   The Foggy Night at Offord etc. 1 v.   Within the Maze 2 v.

W. Wordsworth:

The Select Poetical Works 2 v.

Lascelles Wraxall:

Wild Oats 1 v.

Edm. Yates:

Land at Last 2 v.   Broken to Harness 2 v. The Forlorn Hope 2 v. Black Sheep 2 v. The Rock Ahead 2 v. Wrecked in Port 2 v. Dr. Wainwright's Patient 2 v. Nobody's Fortune 2 v. Castaway 2 v. A Waiting Race 2 v.

Miss Yonge:

The Heir of Redclyffe 2 v. Heartsease 2 v.   The Daisy Chain 2 v. Dynevor Terrace 2 v. Hopes and Fears 2 v.   The Young Step-Mother 2 v.   The Trial 2 v.   The Clever Woman of the Family 2 v. The Dove in the Eagle's Nest 2 v. The Danvers Papers; the Prince and the Page 1 v.   The Chaplet of Pearls 2 v.   The two Guardians 1 v.   The Caged Lion 2 v.

The price of each volume is ½ Thaler = 2 Francs.

Series for the Young.

Kenneth; or, the Rear-Guard of the Grand Army. By the Author of "the Heir of Redclyffe." With Frontispiece, 1 v.

Ruth and her Friends. A Story for Girls. With Frontispiece, 1 v.

Our Year: A Child's Book, in Prose and Verse. By the Author of "John Halifax, Gentleman." Illustrated by Clarence Dobell, 1 v.

Ministering Children. A Tale dedicated to Childhood. By *Maria Louisa Charlesworth.* With Frontispiece, 1 v.

The Little Duke. Ben Sylvester's Word. By the Author of "the Heir of Redclyffe." With a Frontispiece by B. Plockhorst, 1 v.

The Stokesley Secret. By the Author of "the Heir of Redclyffe." With a Frontispiece by B. Plockhorst, 1 v.

Tales from Shakspeare. By *Charles* and *Mary Lamb.* With the Portrait of Shakspeare 1 v.

Countess Kate. By the Author of "the Heir of Redclyffe." With Frontispiece, 1 v.

Three Tales for Boys. By the Author of "John Halifax, Gentleman." With a Frontispiece by B. Plockhorst, 1 v.

A Book of Golden Deeds. By the Author of "the Heir of Redclyffe." With Frontispiece by B. Plockhorst, 2 v.

Moral Tales. By *Maria Edgeworth.* With a Frontispiece by B. Plockhorst, 1 v.

Friarswood Post-Office. By the Author of "the Heir of Redclyffe." With Frontispiece, 1 v.

Cousin Trix and her welcome Tales. By *Miss Craik.* With a Frontispiece by B. Plockhorst, 1 v.

Three Tales for Girls. By the Author of "John Halifax, Gentleman." With a Frontispiece by B. Plockhorst, 1 v.

Henrietta's Wish; or, Domineering. A Tale. By the Author of "the Heir of Redclyffe." With a Frontispiece by B. Plockhorst, 1 v.

Kings of England: A History for the Young. By *Charlotte M. Yonge.* (Author of "the Heir of Redclyffe.") With Frontispiece, 1 v.

Popular Tales. By *Maria Edgeworth.* With a Frontispiece by B. Plockhorst, 2 v.

The Lances of Lynwood; the Pigeon Pie. By *Charlotte M. Yonge.* (Author of "the Heir of Redclyffe.") With Frontispiece, 1 v.

The price of each volume is ½ Thaler = 2 Francs.

Collection of German Authors.

On the Heights. By *B. Auerbach.* Translated by F. E. Bunnett. Second Authorized Edition, thoroughly revised. 3 v.

In the Year '13: By *Fritz Reuter.* Translated from the Platt-Deutsch by Charles Lee Lewes, 1 v.

Faust. By *Goethe.* From the German by John Anster, LL.D. 1 v.

Undine, Sintram and other Tales. By *Fouqué.* Translated by F. E. Bunnett, 1 v.

L'Arrabiata and other Tales. By *Paul Heyse.* From the German by M. Wilson, 1 v.

The Princess of Brunswick-Wolfenbüttel and other Tales. By *H. Zschokke.* From the German by M. A. Faber, 1 v.

Nathan the Wise and Emilia Galotti. By *G. E. Lessing.* The former translated by W. Taylor, the latter by Charles Lee Lewes, 1 v.

Behind the Counter [Handel und Wandel]. By *F. W. Hackländer.* From the German by Mary Howitt, 1 v.

Three Tales by *W. Hauff.* From the German by M. A. Faber, 1 v.

Joachim von Kamern and Diary of a poor young Lady. By *Maria Nathusius.* From the German by Miss Thompson, 1 v.

Poems from the German of Ferdinand Freiligrath. Edited by his Daughter. Second Copyright Edition, enlarged. 1 v.

Gabriel. A Story of the Jews in Prague. From the German by Arthur Milman, M.A., 1 v.

The Dead Lake and other Tales. By *Paul Heyse.* From the German by Mary Wilson. 1 v.

Through Night to Light. By *Karl Gutzkow.* From the German by M. A. Faber, 1 v.

An Egyptian Princess. By *Georg Ebers.* Translated by E. Grove, 2 v.

Flower, Fruit and Thorn Pieces: or the Married Life, Death, and Wedding of the Advocate of the Poor, Firmian Stanislaus Siebenkäs. By *Jean Paul Friederich Richter.* Translated from the German by E. H. Noel, 2 v.

Ekkehard. A Tale of the tenth Century. By *J. V. Scheffel.* Translated from the German by Sofie Delffs, 2 v.

The Princess of the Moor [das Haideprinzesschen]. By *E. Marlitt,* 2 v.

The price of each volume is ½ Thaler = 2 Francs.

Dictionaries.

Dictionary of the English and German languages for general use. Compiled with especial regard to the elucidation of modern literature, the Pronunciation and Accentuation after the principles of Walker and Heinsius. By *W. James*. Twenty-third Stereotype Edition, thoroughly revised and richly enlarged. 8vo sewed 1⅓ Thlr.

Dictionary of the English and French languages for general use with the Accentuation and a literal Pronunciation of every word in both languages. Compiled from the best and most approved English and French authorities. By *W. James* and *A. Molé*. Tenth Stereotype Edition. 8vo sewed 2 Thlr.

Dictionary of the English and Italian languages for general use with the Italian Pronunciation and the Accentuation of every word in both languages and the terms of Science and Art, of Mechanics, Railways, Marine &c. Compiled from the best and most recent English and Italian Dictionaries. By *W. James* and *Gius. Grassi*. Sixth Stereotype Edition. 8vo sewed 1¾ Thlr.

New Pocket Dictionary of the English and German languages. By *J. E. Wessely*. Fourth Stereotype Edition. 16mo sewed ½ Thlr. bound ¾ Thlr.

New Pocket Dictionary of the English and French languages. By *J. E. Wessely*. Fourth Stereotype Edition. 16mo sewed ½ Thlr. bound ¾ Thlr.

New Pocket Dictionary of the English and Italian languages. By *J. E. Wessely*. Second Stereotype Edition. 16mo sewed ½ Thlr. bound ¾ Thlr.

New Pocket Dictionary of the English and Spanish languages. By *J. E. Wessely* and *A. Gironés*. Stereotype Edition. 16mo sewed ½ Thlr. bound ¾ Thlr.

BERNHARD TAUCHNITZ, LEIPZIG;
AND SOLD BY ALL BOOKSELLERS.

October 1872.

Tauchnitz Edition.

Latest Volumes:

Miss or Mrs.? by Wilkie Collins, 1 vol.

Patty by Katharine Macquoid, 2 vols.

Carlino by John Ruffini, Author of "Doctor Antonio," 1 vol.

Unawares by F. M. Peard, Author of "The Rose-Garden," 1 vol.

Without Kith or Kin by Georgiana M. Craik, 2 vols.

Aurora Leigh by Elizabeth Barrett Browning, 1 vol.

The Vicar's Daughter by Mac Donald, 2 vols.

A Waiting Race by Edmund Yates, 2 vols.

In Silk Attire by William Black, 2 vols.

Not Easily Jealous, 2 vols.

The Woman I Loved by Isa Blagden, 1 vol.

Madame la Marquise and other Novelettes by Ouida, 1 vol.

A Golden Sorrow by Mrs. Cashel Hoey, 2 vols.

The Irish Sketch-Book by W. M. Thackeray, 2 vols.

Prose and Poetry by Bret Harte, 2 vols.

A Woman's Vengeance by the Author of "Found Dead," 2 v.

Bessie by Julia Kavanagh, 2 vols.

Within the Maze by Mrs. Henry Wood, 2 vols.

A complete Catalogue of the Tauchnitz Edition is attached to this work.

Bernhard Tauchnitz, Leipzig;
And sold by all booksellers.

Printed in Great Britain
by Amazon